Momma Durtt

Momma Durtt

——A Novel——

Michael Shea

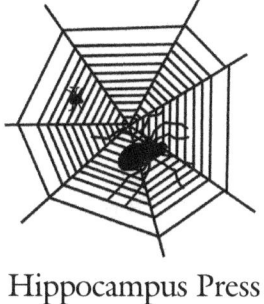

Hippocampus Press

New York

Published by Hippocampus Press
P.O. Box 641, New York, NY 10156.
www.hippocampuspress.com

Cover art © 2024 by Tom Brown
Cover design by Daniel V. Sauer, dansauerdesign.com
Hippocampus Press logo designed by Anastasia Damianakos.

First Edition
1 3 5 7 9 8 6 4 2

ISBN 978-1-61498-417-7 trade paper
ISBN 978-1-61498-429-0 ebook

CONTENTS

Foreword, *by Linda Shea* 7

Author's Preface..11

Momma Durtt 13

Momma Durtt [novelette version] 279

FOREWORD

My best recollection tells me that Michael began to write *Momma Durtt* sometime in 1988. We were living in a modest 1940s farmhouse in the middle of one hundred agricultural acres. I worked for local winery owners, in exchange for the sinecure. Their sort of "gal-Friday" I ironed baskets of fancy tuxedo shirts, errands, dog-sat, wrote correspondence, and served dinners. You name it. Most of the time I could keep our children with me while I worked.

The property had once produced an array of local produce-- Gravenstein apples, Santa Rosa plums, persimmons and figs. But just a few years prior, 90 percent of the older crops had been replaced by vines and they were just beginning to bear fruit. There were still little remnant orchards, patches of the older trees here and there and a long stately row of enormous walnut trees, but the almighty grape had taken over. The whole county was going in the same direction. There was just too much money to be made.

During this time Michael worked all the sorts of jobs that a strong, used-to-sweat guy could get, much like our hero in this book, Willy Yakima. His ad in our local paper featured an "Earth Mover"—just him, with a pick and shovel. During this same period, he also worked nights at an optical factory twenty miles south and taught ESL classes at the local junior college, something he was very good at, having done so much of it in the L.A. Basin during the 1970s.

Here's this guy who is fluent in at least four languages, can recite many literary tomes, but is getting his family by with an odd patchwork of jobs. Our finances were a day-to-day, stitched-together thing dependent on random story sales, odd commissions and good fortune at the mailbox. And of course, the reason for this was that his only "real" job was writing.

In 1989 Michael decided to get a Master of Arts degree from the University of San Francisco. Just sixty miles away, the university had a writing program that would accept an original novel as the master's thesis. The plan was that, with this degree, he could teach more regularly, and we would be more secure. It might be of interest to note here that when his first novel, *A Quest for Simbilis*, was published in 1974, he was only a few months away from completing a master's in Elizabethan Literature from UCLA. I didn't know him then, but from the offhand remarks he made to me I think he thought that since he had sold his first novel, he was on his way and did not need the master's. He let it go. Or maybe he took some job that made it impossible to finish. I don't know. Oh, the balance for money and the writer!

So there we were: not in his natal L.A., nor in the stomping grounds of the San Francisco/Cal Berkeley undergraduate years, but up in Sonoma County. He was learning to be a father, while working and juggling it all with his indomitable need to write. We were not poor, but like so many people, we had *just* enough. But day to day, the laughter and joy of raising the kids on those beautiful acres, within the still mainly old-style agricultural county, made us feel quite rich indeed.

There was a large creek that ran through the acres, a tributary of the Mayacama. It was thought to have been used as a fishing camp by the Native Pomo tribe, a sub-group of the Miwoks, for generations. Shell mound remnants were piled on the banks—ghosts, memories everywhere, and the creek itself teemed with life. Hundreds of little dime-sized spotted frogs covered the banks. Hawks, herons, falcons, foxes, deer, bobcats, coyotes, and the occasional rumor of a mountain lion, all coming to drink. So much of what now has proved to be so fragile. Life everywhere.

Della was about three and Jake was just a little—as Michael would call him—"pap-sucker" babe in arms. I remember Michael taking Della down the row of walnut trees with a paper bag and telling her that they were going hunting for "pure gold." Beautiful walnuts. She was his "little pal" and the inspiration for the novel's "Maxi," her middle name being Maxine.

In 1990, we purchased a small parcel with a log cabin, down the road from the vineyard. It too had a creek, although ephemeral, and creatures would come. Michael had a writing shed behind the house. One day he stepped out back and while looking at the hillside he turned his head to see that standing not too many feet from him was an enormous sow—a wild boar. When he told me, he said she might have been a five-hundred-pounder. She had full teats—meaning that she was nursing, and her brood could be nearby—something that could make her more protective and threatening to a human being. Maybe she sensed his wonder. Or maybe she had a message for him. He did not forget how close they stood, and the sow appears in this novel as Momma's earth spirit, avenging cohort.

Michael always transformed the people and creatures he encountered into material for his fiction. The book's grandmother Aurora and her family came from his years of enjoying his work with his primarily Hispanic students—the ones down in East L.A., and the ones up here working in settings perhaps a bit less agribusiness and more pastoral, but hard and grueling, nonetheless.

And personally, I can see his growing awareness of fatherhood, of family and community reflected in this novel—and, of course, of the interesting and rich hodgepodge of cultures that Sonoma County was at the time. There really was a biker bar on the River called the Pink Elephant, with heavy duty bikers, locals, the gay community, and everyone else having a beer mostly peaceably.

The novel reflects who and what really pulled the levers that controlled the destiny of this county, and of nature everywhere, of all the beautiful fragile life. The zoning departments, the developers. In the 1990s the population count of the then little town five miles down the road soared from 5,000 to 19,000. They, the power players, the Bev Carneys, had changed the destiny of this paradise. And now and for always, there are fewer animals and more sidewalks. I think that the novel attempts a bit to right that wrong.

Michael wrote a preface that he included with the submission of the novel to the Faculty Advisory Committee at USF. The work was in fact accepted as his master's thesis. Michael's wry humor and good will and appreciation of their acceptance of an unusual piece of work comes through in his preface. The novel remained in the can, as Michael was distracted by his various sequels to *Nifft the Lean* written in the 1990s, along with many short stories. But I mentioned to him the possibility of doing a novella of it for a magazine, and Michael did that, placing it in *Weird Tales* (Fall 2012). This version is printed at the back of this book.

—LINDA SHEA

Author's Preface

This story does its best to outrage your sense of reality. This can only be accomplished by using as much realism as possible, and as a result the work is full of unpleasant physical details and harsh language.

Someone once said that only laughter slays folly. (It was I, though the notion is far from original with me.) What is horrible in human proceedings must be laughed at, at least for starters. So another thing this book tries to do is make you laugh, because it has as its subject one of the more horrible human proceedings, the befouling of the earth.

Many readers—perfectly intelligent, blameless people in other respects—feel that unpleasant physical details and harsh language are a kind of pollution, a Befouling of the Page, if you will. To these, this work will seem worse than misguided—it will seem self-contradictory.

This objection is a reasonable one, and as such merits some response from the author, and so, in the spirit of the work as a whole, I offer mine: tough titty.

MICHAEL SHEA

August 6, 1992

MOMMA DURTT

One

It was Friday, so it was Kim's turn to drive the tanker. Alex, ever macho, made his usual bid to take the wheel on their return trip from Richmond, because Friday night traffic on the Bay Area freeways was so heavy.

"You've been driving truck how long?" Kim asked, pretending to calculate.

"Hey, screw me for just offerin to help."

She'd been a year ahead of Alex in high school, not so long ago, and had about that much more time than he did behind the wheels of big rigs. It was fun rubbing it in. He was exactly her height, and he had this Latino solemnity about his Man's Role. In the couple months they'd driven tanker together for KleenCo she'd never had any trouble handling Alex's bids for power—"respect" he called it. They actually got along pretty well. She thought his wispy Zapata moustache and solemn Latin profile were pretty cute.

"I'll let you drive up into the hills, Alex, how's that?" Meaning the low-gear climb to the Quicksilver Mine at the end of their run, the drudgery part, pulling twelve thousand gallons of still-bottoms and assorted toxic sludge up through the switchbacks.

This on the other hand was the fun part, cruising high in the cab, a big freighter in a stream of smaller freeway craft. The rig's bigness made her feel part of the colossal scenery here along the upper East Bay, powering past all the cracking towers and burn-off stacks needling the sky, the million-gallon tanks thick as toadstools on asphalt-capped hilltops, all linked by labyrinths of pipework, the mighty oil tankers riding off shore, the huge dock cranes like dinosaurs waiting for the container ships. The sheer scale of it all made Kim high.

"Thanks," Alex said, deadpan. "Thing is, like I said, we're runnin a little late. Chip made a very big deal about eleven P.M. sharp."

"Hey—they were a little late fillin us. I'm not gonna bust my butt about it. Chip nearly lives up there at the compound—what's the difference to him?"

Now Alex came up against one of the unspoken rules between the two of them, which was that they never acknowledged, in so many words, that KleenCo's operations might be breaking the law. They had Frankie's and Chip's official word that everything at KleenCo was "in compliance," and they never explicitly acknowledged otherwise between themselves, though they traded a certain amount of irony.

"Hey Kim? Frankie's Mr. Sunshine an all, a righteous guy, all that . . . but he's got associates we never met, am I right? Maybe some business goes on between him and his associates that we don't wanna conflict with. Maybe that's why Chip was uptight about the time."

Kim was pulling them out of the toll gate onto the Richmond San Rafael Bridge. She loved this bridge, a crazy, crooked cage of high-flung beams and girders, a vapor-lit zigzag of high-speed traffic flung across the black bay like a lightning bolt. She brought them up to speed, into the high, skewed trajectory over the wide-flung puzzle of nightlights: San Rafael ahead, Richmond behind, and just the very rim of star-spangled San Francisco away off down to their left—all hanging like galaxies under the tanker's unending leap. It was like being in a sci-fi movie, *Star Wars*.

"Stop nagging! We'll get there on time, but don't nag me about it."

He looked at her—loose ponytail, wide generous features. She had a country face, and her substantial tits showed even through her loose flannel work shirt. Alex's hormones gnawed at him even as she pissed him off. She constantly smartassed him, but he'd actually gotten used to that. He was angry now because it wasn't just their boss's possible criminal connections that were worrying him. His great-aunt Aurora had been after him about his job, and not about Frankie DaValli's possible mob backing. She had made Alex uneasy about things that he didn't know how to talk about.

But he had gotten Kim wondering about this 11:30 thing of Chip's. Was he just pushing them around for practice? Chip was a glum old fart, but that seemed unlike him. They made most of their pickups at night, part of a low-profile policy, but since Chip usually stayed overnight in the offices at the mine compound he'd never made a point of the exact time of deliveries. It began to worry her a little.

There was no reason to assume that Frankie DaValli was KleenCo's sole owner. Maybe it wasn't so far-fetched that he had East Coast backing, hoods in the waste racket. She and Alex had joked Chip about the rumor and he'd told them to watch their mouths, pissed enough that maybe they'd touched a nerve.

Feeling worried about it irritated her. She decided to pull off 101 and get a sixpack as they would normally have done. Alex threw a fit. She gave him a serene smile and ignored him.

He wouldn't come into the liquor store. She saw him out the window on the sidewalk, looking kind of ghastly under the neon light. His face was very *indio,* solemn and intent in profile, especially in his present anger, and his 49ers cap was funny when you thought of him as a face in some kind of Aztec picture. Mad though she made a point of making Alex, she was sure she could screw him whenever she wanted. She'd caught him looking at her tits a hundred times.

"What the hell are you doing?" he asked her, climbing back into the rig. "There's no way we'll make it now."

"I know. I just didn't feel like being pushed, And suppose they decide to fire us for being late? How would you really feel about that?"

Alex was too angry to answer for a while, but the question lay there between them, unexpected, full of angles, and made them both thoughtful. The twenty-an-hour that had made the job so exciting from the first, way out of scale for their youth, had the worrisome side now that maybe it was their inexperience Frankie *wanted:* that the money would be chump-change compared to what he'd have to pay someone who knew what was going on; that what they didn't know was going on could be a lot more extensive than they had yet considered; that losing this job might not be such a bad thing in the long run.

When they reached the Santa Marta plain, she gave Alex the wheel. The plain lay between hills to the east and west, the city of Santa Marta lying against the smaller, eastern range. He turned towards the western hills, taking River Highway. This highway followed the Ross River through the hills and out to the Pacific Ocean, but he branched off it as soon as they entered the range, and they started their climb towards the Quicksilver Mine.

They drank beer, Alex having to grab swallows between shifting the gears, fighting their way up the curves. The crazy-armed oaks and madrones danced and gestured in the sweep of their headlights. As the tanker climbed they got glimpses between the trees of the jewelled spread of Santa Marta down on the plain.

"If they fired us," Alex said, "I don't think I'd feel too bad. The shaft—it's been givin me the creeps lately." He shot her a quick, defiant little look—let her laugh if she wanted to. She nodded, somber, watching their headlights rake the trees.

"You know," she said, "we oughtta have a big, like Day-Glo skull and crossbones painted on the tank of this rig."

Alex visualized it. "Fluorescent white and silver on black," he emended. But she was exactly right. It would look unspeakably boss. And it was the truth about what they were doing. They traded a look, surprised at what they were feeling, pleased that they agreed.

When they pulled up to the compound gate, Chip stood just inside it, already switching it open, their headlights latticing him with the chain-link's shadows. He already had rubber boots and apron on, rubber gloves protruding from an apron pocket, a respirator hanging by its straps from his scrawny neck.

He stomped out, apron puckering flabbily in the headlights, mounted the step-up, and thrust his head in Alex's window.

"You sonofabitching kids think you signed on here for a day at the *beach?*" Chip's recessive hairline and back-sloped forehead suggested some browless animal—a rat or maybe a possum—especially with his big nose and loose front teeth thrust so furiously forward. "I cannot fuckin believe you come in a half hour late after what I told you. Now you swing your butt back up there, you fuckin squirt, and you fuckin *leave!*"

Kim scanned the compound as he spoke. Upslope to their right was the shaft-mouth, vomiting the white light of its arc lamps at the stars. To the left, behind the office, was a pyramid of disposal drums six tiers high, with the same field of stars behind it. There was just enough moonlight to sketch the rims and bulges of the shadowy drums.

The drums were there for appearances' sake—at least she had never been party to filling even one of them—and sometimes, for fun, she liked to "slip" and call them "disposal dummies."

But right now they didn't seem comic. The stack's stepped profile suggested one of those ancient ziggurats, and a dark grandeur haunted it, a sense of something immemorially evil.

They backed the tanker up to the mouth of the shaft, Chip hanging onto the door, then jumping down and hurrying inside, pulling his mask on. He staggered back out of the shaft in a moment, dragging the six-inch fill hose. He helped them hook it up to the tank's off-load spout and switched on the pump.

"When you're empty, just uncouple, drop the hose, an drive the fuck outa here—can you do that? Can you manage it?"

"Christ, he's pissed," Alex muttered to Kim, watching him stalk back down to the office.

Kim nodded. "I think because he's scared."

"You know what? I think it's time to quit."

"Yeah. I don't like the feel of this place. All of a sudden."

They were almost empty when, over the sound of their pump, they heard something out on the highway. Headlights swung through the gate. A dark blue van drove into the compound.

It stood idling down there, headlights-to-headlights with the tanker and about a hundred feet away. Chip hustled out of the office. He stood by the driver's side, a kind of cringe in his posture. He made a couple hesitant gestures towards the tanker as he talked, seeming to dismiss it.

The pump switched off. They uncoupled the hose and got up into the cab, both moving quickly while trying to seem casual, unconcerned. Before Alex had them in gear, the van rolled forward, easing up the slope right towards them.

For a moment they wondered if it was going to come bumper-to-bumper with them, but it swung right a few yards from them. Its driver's head was profiled in their headlights until he turned and faced directly into them.

It seemed deliberate, the man giving them his face as he passed. A big man, the face pale, a striking evenness in its features—and smiling? Yes, faintly smiling. Alex slipped into gear and they rolled down the slope and out the compound gate, light now, jouncing, the big rig feeling frisky.

"Would the guy let us see him like that?" Kim asked. "I mean if he was involved in something . . . illegal?"

"Shit, Kim—*we're* involved in something illegal. Why not face it?"

He was taking the curves showily, almost recklessly. Out beyond the trees the jeweled plain of Santa Marta spun below them. It was like flying again, the relief they felt leaving the shaft behind.

"Isn't it crazy?" she nodded. "How you can know something without really looking at it?" She was thinking of what they'd just done. Had done for months, knowing—never literally seeing it, of course, but knowing—that they were squirting this reeking black pus of chlorinated and fluorinated hydrocarbons directly into the earth. Until tonight her mind had never followed it down. It was going thousands of feet underground, and this notion, like a magic formula, made the lethal dregs seem to vanish. *Thousands of feet underground*—abracadabra, poof! it was gone. Who could it hurt, thousands of feet underground?

It hurt the earth—that was what she felt now, tonight for the first time. It gave her a gut-sick chill, sent a fear and a guilt through her that felt like a transmitted tremor of the wounded hill's nausea and pain.

"That guy's face?" Alex said. "I got a bad feeling from it."

"It was spooky, wasn't it?"

"You know what I think? I don't think we oughtta quit just like that. We get paid in a week, right? I think we should work right along, like everything's OK, nothin's botherin us. Then when we get our money I think we should call in sick and leave town. Give em our resignations over the phone, from somewhere else."

Kim cracked two beers, gave him one, thinking this over. "Chip's worried that we saw the guy, that's for sure," she said.

"Right. That's scary when you think about it. We don't wanna drop everything an run the same night we see him."

"I don't guess another week is gonna make what we've already done that much worse," Kim said, looking at him, thinking he did deserve some respect, thinking he was showing a better grip on their situation than she had. They could be in some actual danger, couldn't they?

"Something else we should consider," she told him. "Frankie and Chip know our addresses. Maybe we should find someplace else to stay they don't know about—maybe even together, watch each other's backs."

"Yeah. I got a friend would let us use his floor."

She chugged her beer and they flew downslope between the crooked dancing trees. She felt like there'd been an earthquake, shaking everything loose; what had almost been routine was shifting underfoot. It was scary, but also exciting. Nothing really major had happened, had it? They'd seen real fear in Chip's face, and then they'd seen another face, a strange one that had put the fear in Chip's, and now, suddenly, it was like waking up, realizing what they had been doing these last couple months.

But they would be OK. What they had done to the earth, she didn't feel so good about. But they'd gotten smart in time, they were going to come out of this OK. She was sure of it.

She looked over at Alex and smiled. Tonight she would see if she was right. Should she make a bet with herself? See if she could make him do it with his 49ers cap on, just for fun?

Two

Sol Lazarian parked the van a bit downslope of the shaft-mouth so that his two soldiers—Junior Wicke and Sonny Lee Beasley—would have the warm-up of carrying their burdens uphill before going down into the shaft with them—down into the bad light and tricky footing and hallucinatory air.

Sol shouldered the heaviest of the body bags and had made the climb himself before his men had even sorted out their loads. He stood up there looking calmly down at them—a big shape backlit by the lights in the shaft-mouth.

"That fucker went two-twenty at least," Sonny muttered to Junior Lee. He meant the body draped over Lazarian's shoulder.

"Fucker's strongern shit," muttered Junior. He meant Lazarian.

"Likes to show us, too." Sonny said this even more softly. "Likes to watch us scramble to catch up."

Sonny shouldered the other, lighter body-bag, and Junior Lee took up the two satchels of weights, and they climbed the slope. Their beer guts and biker boots made it hard work. Sonny managed to get a slight lead on the more massive Junior Lee, and snapped at him, showing off to Lazarian: "Come on, Junior—they ain't that heavy!"

Lazarian stood watching them climb up from the shadows, and when Sonny turned to snap at Junior Lee, Lazarian had one of his little visions.

There had been a time when these hallucinatory moments had frightened Lazarian, because they only happened with people he had determined to kill. The person would make some gesture, or some little turn of expression, and the gesture would seem to detach itself from the person, to expand and protract itself into a series of video replays behind Lazarian's eyes, He would experience this little gesture or utterance of the doomed person over and over in the space of a second or two—a second or two that had suddenly become an impossibly large space of time.

He was at home with them now—the visions were essences, little epitomes of the condemned person's character, a signature radiation they emitted at the brink of death, like particles being swallowed by a black hole. Like Sonny here. His rough red face in its frame of whiskers had two modes: it bullied or it toadied. That snarl at Junior and that sly look for approval at himself, these were the man in a nutshell.

The shaft-mouth was wide and high, vaulted with I-beams. It held a big donkey-engine for hauling carts up and down the track. There were a couple parallel tracks down the shaft, several ore-gondolas on spurs of siding—these supposedly now used to convey sealed drums of toxins down to the stopes and chambers where they were carefully stored in the mine's depths.

They laid down their burdens and Lazarian distributed the masks that hung on the wall—respirators with double filters that looked like the mouths of bugs. Standing in here, breathing the breath of the shaft, Sonny and Junior looked at each other, stupefied. Was this a smell they were inhaling, or was it a waft of pure uncanniness drifting through their mind-cells, like the first foretremors of a major acid high?

"You guys need some help with your masks?" Lazarian asked, smiling.

They began struggling with the complex straps. The madness of this atmosphere! A smell so potent it was . . . deafening. A pandemonium of stenches, an ethereal reek of exotic hydrocarbons that impacted the brain like a chorus of shrieking angels, a mob of divine sopranos gone mad. Sonny watched Lazarian don his own mask. The big man's beauty was always a little unbelievable whenever you looked right, at it. Pale, chiseled features, a small, almost rosebud mouth—a long, solemnly pretty face (except for something droll about that little mouth) whose eyes were black pools of luminous candor in deep sockets. It shocked Sonny a little when Lazarian had holstered the lower half of that face in the respirator. There was no sense of mismatch between those luminous eyes and what looked like the eating apparatus of a carnivorous insect. Lazarian's eyes were equally at home above either mouth.

"Man, this air is fucking me up, Sol," Sonny croaked, talking through the crude amplifier of his mask now, trying to get his ponytail untangled from the straps. Junior Lee, clumsier, shaggier, was having even more trouble.

"Relax, guys," Lazarian said. "Do some calm breathing through the filters." His voice seemed to come out almost unmangled by the amplifier, a mellow baritone with that little playful note in it somewhere. He re-shouldered his body-bag and took two electric lanterns from hooks on the wall, then just stood there giving them his calm eyes. They hustled, still woozy, to take up their loads again, and he gave Sonny one of the lanterns. "I want you to count your steps going down, guys. I'm checking the fill level. We think the guy that runs this place for us might be taking in deliveries on the side—ripping us off."

They would lose count, but it didn't matter. He was creating a pretext for leaving them down there while he came back up to get the body-bags and weights he was going to use on them.

They had descended just a few yards beyond the limit of the shaft-mouth's light when the tracks gave out. The steel rails had been salvaged at some earlier point of the abandoned cinnabar mine's history and never replaced. A black, six-inch hose ran down alongside the crude staircase of crossties—its topside end was what Chip had hooked to the tanker. The light of their lanterns made it seem to twitch and shift, a gigantic house-snake, the resident genius of the place.

They pushed their ragged bubble of light down through the blackness, and despite their labor it wasn't the three men who sweated down here; the air itself oozed a cold vapor astringent to the skin of their faces. With new awe Lazarian felt again the power of this dragon's-breath, this molecular blizzard of micro-razors, utterly hostile to human flesh. The brew that exhaled this breath was perhaps the perfect human solvent, concocted here offhandedly, accidentally by the superabundant genius of modern chemistry. Lazarian's smile bloomed within his mask, a secret flower.

He knew quite well, the shaft was overfilled, but still he was shocked, unready for the black pool when they reached it. As if this huge slug of earth-socketed poison had stealthily hastened up to meet them and had just now paused, pretending immobility, its flat, black eye dazzling their lights back at them, the cold exhalation of its breath licking the skin of their faces like a demon's tongue.

He had not been wrong to cross a continent with these corpses to sacrifice them here. Truly he felt it—this black pool was death's most absolute orifice, the threshold of a perfect annihilation. He watched Sonny and Junior Lee crouching awkwardly at the brink of this pool, getting out pliers and rolls of wire and weights from the satchels, and smiled within his mask.

"So what was your count, guys?" Their eyes, glaring white above the dark masks, shot him identical looks of guilty alarm. Lazarian had to laugh. Such simple organisms!

Nevertheless. Every life, however simple, in passing through death's impalpable membrane, forced open a seam between the spacetime of this world and the unknowable Outside. It created a brief aperture through which something might be seen. He pulled two packets of hundreds from his pocket and waggled them. "I know how neat and careful you're going to be," Lazarian told them, "so take your bonuses now."

They were so pleased! He would send them across, of course, with the money still on them. Like grave-goods in the ancient world, it was a ceremonial gesture. Death would reveal nothing to those who took it lightly.

"I want nice tight wiring now—you've got no need to hurry."

"You got it, Sol."

"Tighter than a tick's ass."

"Stretched over a rain barrel."

"OK. My count tells me they're overfilled—as I thought. I'm going to talk to their gate man. I should be back to give you a hand before you're done."

He took one of the lanterns, looking back as he climbed, seeing them crouched by the remaining lantern, working diligently beside the great black pool. He reckoned the pool to be a hundred yards higher than the last time he was down—rising on the flood-tide of Frankie DaValli's greed. He was supposed to be filling Lou's contracts and Lou's only. Judging by the fill rate he must have scammed up at least one of his own for every one of Lou's. If Lazarian had ever reported the fill level—even that of a month ago—Lou would have ordered him to kill DaValli, just like that.

Instead Lazarian had covertly killed and brought here two fairly important people from the Jersey waste disposal rackets. It was groundwork, in case Lazarian decided he wanted to possess the Quicksilver Mine for himself, which meant killing Lou, of course, along with a lot of Lou's key people.

Lazarian hadn't decided yet. First on his mind was whether anything would come of his sacrifices here. From the first time he'd entered it, as Lou's enforcer, checking up on Frankie, the shaft had stirred something in him, had spoken to him. Feed me more, it had seemed to say . . .

"You believe this fuckin stench?" Sonny asked. His voice was very careful—the tiniest bit of noise went echoing away up the shaft.

"Lift im a little higher." Junior Lee was looping wire around the ankles of the smaller of the two bodies. As he threaded the wire through a weight, his grip slipped, and the disk rolled, bounced off a lower tie and into the pool. They recoiled to either side from the tongue of black slop thrown back from the impact.

"You fuckin dipstick!"

"It slipped! Fuckin shoot me!"

"Don't slip!"

The volume of their own echoes subdued them—the noise took forever to die down. Sonny realized that they were just crouching there, frozen, listening. "So let's get to work," he growled.

And still they just crouched there, listening.

"Fuck's that?" Junior Lee asked softly.

It was a delicate noise: *slap*-suck, *slap*-suck, *slap*-suck. A shudder stirred the pool, and its edges now gently kissed its rocky rim. Some delayed aftershock of the weight's splash? They looked at each other. Sonny wondered if there was something about this air that was paralyzing him. It was Junior Lee who got them moving again. "Tilt im up again," he said.

They had crossed the country in a little under sixty hours, the corpses nice and stiff to start with, wired into the bed in Lazarian's customized van. But now that the rigor would have been useful, it was almost gone, and the slack shape was harder to manipulate. Sonny did the lifting, and Junior Lee wired the weights on in tight separate loops, so that the body bag began to look segmented, like a caterpillar. Sonny remembered a book about Houdini that he'd read in jail.

"Hey, Junior. You know, when you tie a guy in short lengths like this? Instead of tyin him in one long piece? Then it's harder for him to get out. You know, free himself." He pulled his filter down just a little to show Junior Lee he was smiling, making a joke.

Corrugations developed in Junior Lee's brow. The moron was concentrating and not getting it. With his face cut off by the mask, his seamed brow and glaring eyes looked eerie, like an expression of terror. "You fuckin idiot," Sonny snarled, resettling his mask.

They worked, falling silent, their least movements weaving fine webs of echoes around them, and themselves listening again as they worked.

They wired the last weight to the neck, and Sonny thumbed out the razor tip of a utility knife and cut the "window" Sol had prescribed—a foot-square flap cut out of the bag over the face to let the solvents in to work on the nude corpses while the bag's weighted husk kept buoyant fragments from detaching themselves and finding their way back up. He felt the blade encounter doughy resistance and, when he unveiled the face, found a deep unbleeding cut beside the nose.

"Sorry about that, wise guy."

"Who d'ya think he was?" Junior Lee asked.

"Some fuckin East-Coast greaseball hood, like the other one." The pair had gone to an Italian restaurant in Newark and staged a table-smashing fight, releasing a smoke bomb as they wrestled on the floor. When Lazarian picked them up at the rendezvous point, he already had the heavier of the corpses in the car—the guy still had a napkin tucked into the collar of his shirt. For this one they'd gone into the lobby of a plush high-rise and kicked up a drunken fuss, insisting on being given the number of Lulu's apartment, insisting this was the address the bitch had given them. The reception guy pushed a button and four really big guys in suits had come out of the elevator a moment later. Two of them had guns. Sonny and Junior Lee let themselves be thrown out without too much resistance. Lazarian had the second corpse in the car when he picked them up.

"Why'd he bring em all the way back here to get rid of em?" Junior Lee persisted.

"Hell, why'd he fly us out there to help him instead of usin local talent?" The pair hailed from River Nest, ten miles from here on the Ross River. "Who knows or cares? The guy's a goon."

"What's that?"

Slap-suck, *slap*-suck, *slap*-suck. The pool was quaking again, a little stronger, but still fairly gently. They were both long-term Californians, but they now found that cavalierness about earthquakes dwindled as the depth of your body under the earth increased.

"The stuff probably just keeps settling," Sonny said. "Down into cracks an holes down there."

"I don't see no bubbles."

The accuracy of the remark was irritating, coming from the moronic Junior Lee. "Let's just quit fuckin the dog, OK?"

"I *got* my end ready! Move your own ass!"

"One . . . two . . ."—they got a fair swing going—*"three!"*

The guy was launched. He lay face up on the air for an instant, his eyes and mouth pools of shadow in the lantern's oblique light. The shadow-face lived in that instant, grimaced as it fell.

They were late jumping back—feeling stupefied, foolish as they belatedly scrambled, the backwash drenching their boots. The lantern, resting on a low tie, was half darkened with slime. Cursing, Sonny wiped it off on his pants leg and set it higher up the shaft. They stood watching the pond settle, imagining the wise guy's journey, his long, slo-mo tumble down through the most perfect blackness there ever was.

Would the pond never settle? It seemed to be gentling now: *slap*-suck, *slap*-suck. Looking at each other, they realized they'd been standing paralyzed again, listening, waiting. They began to wire the other corpse.

It was far heavier to maneuver, yet they worked deftly, suddenly skillful—even Junior Lee. Both of them felt a new tension in the shaft. Having sent a man into it, they felt the depth of the pool now, felt it as something huge and homicidal crouching right beside them.

"Jesus!" Sonny yelped. He dropped a weight, and the pliers slid from Junior Lee's hand. A roiling sound, a silken fizz had drawn their eyes. The pool was bulging at its center—a dome of turbulence was rising there, as if lifted by some powerful under-pressure.

Had the masks melted from their faces? The air's icy poison seemed to fill their skulls, licking the brainmeat from the bone with tongues of cold fire.

The pressure-dome mushroomed to the ceiling and swept forward. They began to turn, to launch themselves up-shaft, and as they did so a voice in Sonny's skull was telling him, *A step too late, a heartbeat too late*—as they both stumbled over the second body and fell to scrambling on hands and feet up the notched earth. Hearing the black wave hiss just behind him, feeling on his nape the gust of air-pressure it shoved before it, Sonny had fought his way almost as high as the lantern, when a liquid fist punched his legs out from under him, and a cold, melting hand gripped his waist and dragged him back down.

He rammed a desperate knee against the earth, felt bone crack, felt fingernails splitting against the rock, but held, clinging fast against the terrible back-drag of caustics draining off of him.

He looked back and saw Junior Lee, half in the pool, his drenched arms scrabbling for the shaft floor, trying to drag himself out, and then there, just beyond Junior Lee, Sonny saw what *stood up* from the pool—what stood up and moved to strike up a second, greater wave from its surface.

Sonny was turning, scrambling again, one leg useless, the other bootsole squirting out from under, but his fingers, yes, getting purchase on the rock, fighting himself another tie higher, and then another, while that voice in his head was saying, dispassionately, *A step too late. A heartbeat too late.*

To his right he saw a thick black tongue of wastes rocket past him along the wall, climbing up past him, and then curving out across the path of his escape, and come sweeping back down at him like a gathering arm.

He had climbed almost as high as the lantern, which made a mirror of the liquid wall that rushed upon him. He saw his own face in the blackness, beside the mirrored lantern: a bug-mouthed being on its belly, eyes bulging at its oncoming death.

Then the satin mass wrapped him in blindness that scalded his eyes, flipped him on his back, and snatched him down, down, down, his legs kicking and the stepped earth under him beating him, braining him, blotting out his mind.

A perfect blackness was the aftermath, where echoes of screams and thundering waves collided again and again with the stone walls, subsiding only slowly to a liquid chuckle.

Three

Lazarian lingered near the shaft, giving his soldiers time to finish their work. He regarded the stars and a late rising moon, worn and waxy like an eroded chip of soap. Two satchels of weights, each containing a body-bag, were at his feet. He savored the night air, half dreamy, half excited. He was a man all but determined on a career change.

His retainer from Lou was a small fortune, and he had been Lou's chief enforcer for almost five years.

But Sol Lazarian was a freebooter in essence, not a career man. His eye was always on the main chance, the only score that mattered—spiritual advancement; true power.

And there was something here, something right under his feet. He felt it with a force little short of conviction. If death was a door he had spent his adult life knocking on, then here, in this little mountain he stood on, was a door that had something behind it.

Behind him, the shaft uttered a sound. A soft polysyllable of . . . music?

He hung the lantern from his belt and took his satchels up. He started down the shaft.

The hose-snake danced to the descending rhythm of his legs, the low-slung lantern weaving a puzzle of shadows on the floor. He moved silently, listening to the blackness that closed in behind and before him. He heard the claustrophobic hum of being deep in the earth, the blood itself growing loud in its silence and then, *again*. He heard it again, a pulse of music, coming from deeper down.

A voice? If so, a deep black gospel voice—so far, so faint, right on the frontier between hearing and imagining. Lazarian's downstepping legs slowed, eased themselves into the beat:

Ta-da dum
Ta-da
Ta-dum, *da.*

If real, it was beautiful, that sad, velvet-and-molasses gospel voice. It gave him a delicate attack of the creeps, an horripilation of the fine black lanugo which, unknown to any other living person, covered the back and shoulders of the pale giant.

Again it came—his descent was now a dance to it:

Ta-da dum
Ta-da
Ta-dum, *da.*

Fear, in Sol Lazarian, was a darker shade of joy—it was the same energy at a different frequency. When he broke a man's life in his arms, his prey's shock was his joy's fuel, its material.

And when any horror laid its hand on Lazarian he felt not crushed, but light, combustible, packed like dynamite with a savage sympathy for that larger joy, that joy more monstrous than his own, that might be about to detonate and consume him.

Already at thirty-eight—young for a real master—he had consumed half a dozen other first-rate killers. Real Samurai, not moronic buttons—of those he kept no count. And all these gifted men had learned that to endanger Lazarian was to inspire and ignite him. His startling face got eerily prettier, his manner even more serene. You had him distracted. You watched him fail to spot your trap. You sprang it on him, jumped him from behind. And suddenly, there was Sol Lazarian's forearm across your throat, and Sol Lazarian's mellow baritone crooning unspeakabilities into your ear, and there was your neck breaking.

Here now was the pool. Lazarian dropped his satchels and raised his lantern high, his eyes above the mask beholding the miracle with awed serenity: perfect emptiness.

Above the pool, there was a wide new zone of drenched shaft floor. And absolutely nothing else.

But the greater marvel he saw only after long moments of looking, when he lowered his eyes and found it, right at his feet.

The black fringe of the drenched zone was a smooth curve, except at its crest, where it jutted out into a sharply drawn silhouette—that of a wild-haired figure with two out-thrust arms.

The detail was breathtaking—all ten fingers individually shadowed in ten sharp little tongues of poison. Lazarian, in his greed for revelation, had found omens in the vaguest things, veiled oracles in the chance set of a corpse's expression, or in the accidental gesture of dead hands. This silhouette, so exquisitely executed, sent lightning down his spine.

This shadow seemed like one of the four lives swallowed down here that was still struggling to escape, return from Death's other side, distorting its black membrane with his desperate reaching for the light.

Lazarian's sacrifices were accepted. Acknowledged. Here was his turning. At last he had knocked on a door behind which Something lived.

Ta-da dum

ta-da

That faint, remote music, grave and sweet. "Teach me to serve you," he answered it. His voice was gentle, but the air seemed to boil with the echoes he made.

Silence followed the echoes, but not the silence of an absence. It was there, choosing not to answer, waiting to see what he would do next. To see if he had the nerve, the inspiration, to find his way closer to it.

He carried his satchels back up to the open air; these weights would be for other offerings, when he had determined who they should be.

Gazing at the stars, he considered what must be done to kill Lou and his core staff. Though he had laid some groundwork, it would take several days back in New Jersey, at least.

It had to be done. Lazarian himself must own the shaft. And Frankie DaValli was essential. The magic of DaValli's shameless greed had made this portal. His accidental inspiration must not be interfered with.

At this very moment he knew Frankie to be toying with a further scam, beyond his double-dealing of the shaft's storage space. A scam on a bolder scale. If DaValli had a totem animal, surely it must be the Weasel.

Lazarian must help him along, of course. Interfere as little as possible, but keep Frankie moving towards his goals. Help him keep conjuring.

The phone woke Frankie DaValli at 2 A.M. Sitting in bed, with a lamp on, talking to Chip on the phone, Frankie could see himself in the mirrors on the bat-wing closet doors. There he sat, a tight, lean guy, bare-chested, reclining against the headboard, looking completely in control as he talked on the phone. The image was reassuring because what Chip was telling him had the pins and needles going all up and down his spine.

"I'm not blaming you," Frankie said carefully. "And I know he's not the kind of guy you like to say no to. But really, Chip, how the *fuck* could you let him dump a homicide in our fucking shaft?"

He still looked pretty good in the closet doors, a dark-haired, hawk-faced guy, a little like Clint Eastwood but with more nose and hair—a guy finding out at 2 A.M. that he's just been made an accessory to murder, and still looking pretty calm about it.

"Hey, he didn't ask. You pay pretty good, Frankie, but not so's I'd die for you."

"Just a minute, Chip." Frankie sat listening. A faint sound from out on his condo's deck? Since he's leased the place, out in the hilly neighborhoods, he'd had to get used to the noises of possum and raccoon blundering around in the night—startling, big-animal noises to an L.A.-bred ear. "Go on," he told Chip.

"Well, he had these guys helpin him carry his loads, you know? Well, I kept an eye out the window, and I only saw *him* come out. Maybe I missed em. Maybe they were in the van when he came back down to talk to me again."

Was that a soft creak of the living room floor, just beyond his bedroom wall?

"Anyway," Chip was saying, "he said he was gonna stop by an see you, he didn't say when—"

"Gotta go, Chip," Frankie croaked, hanging up, as his door opened and Sol Lazarian stepped into the bedroom—the suddenly-small-seeming bedroom. His dark clothes breathed out a cold, unearthly odor, as if he had just stepped in from outer gulfs of space, with tatters of an alien atmosphere still clinging to him.

"No, please," Lazarian extended a gracious hand, "don't get up! Forgive my barging in, but we need to talk."

He sat on the foot of Frankie's bed. This was really happening—there they were in the mirrors too. Lazarian's breadth filling two of the glass panels so that his image seemed slightly folded.

"I'm always glad to see you of course, Sol, but really got to protest this kinda treatment of my privacy." He felt the bite of Lazarian's weight on the bedsprings, making a slope in the mattress like a gravitational field that tried to draw him towards the eerie goon's greater mass.

"I am sorry, Frankie. Only the most urgent business could bring me to do this. You've just been talking to Chip. Do you know *who* I put in your shaft tonight?"

Frankie looked at his reflection and saw a dazed man. He looked back at Lazarian and nodded, though in fact he did not want to know—no part of him did.

"One was Joe Sammartini, the favorite kid brother of Bones Sammartini, Lou's toughest competitor in northern New Jersey. The other was Bobby D'Angelo, Lou's key inside man in Sammartini's trucking company—the cornerstone of Lou's defenses."

As Frankie sat listening he remembered an anecdote about Lazarian that Randy had told him. Randy was Frankie's old friend from high school in L.A. They'd both romanticized the Mafia in those days, and Randy had actually gone on to become a lower-echelon attorney for "some New Jersey interests"—had been Frankie's connection to Lou, in fact. Randy, an L.A. groupie in his soul, still glorified mob lore, and quite possibly distorted the facts.

"So Lazarian's taking out this guy," Randy had recounted, "this restaurateur, has got the throat-lock on him. Lazarian's buttons are there watching, see? He's got the guy's neck and then he does his thing, talks to him in his ear, says like 'OK, Joe'—whatever the guy's name was—'OK, Joe, I'm sending you across,' etcetera etcetera, whatever weird shit he says. Then he breaks the guy's neck and drops him, and they see he's sprouted this big woodie in his pants."

Lazarian was sitting there, waiting for an answer. "I'm not sure," Frankie said carefully, "exactly what it is you're telling me."

"That Lou already has serious trouble on his hands. That he'll be calling me back soon to tighten his defenses. That his life is in my hands. I'm telling you that the Quicksilver Mine, if it belongs to anyone, belongs to me now."

The mirrors doubled Lazarian's bigness. This was a pure psychotic, Frankie understood with awe. The killer dog had slipped the leash. And whether or not Lazarian was sexually twisted, Frankie sensed something much more solemn and fundamental than sex at the heart of his madness. Something almost religious.

"I'm—" He had to clear his throat. "I'm a realistic businessman, Sol. If I can draw my fair salary for services rendered in good faith—"

"Let's not waste time, Frankie. Besides Lou's contracts, you've got a whole set of your own, and a pair of drivers to haul them. If things were still in Lou's hands here, and I reported your fill levels to him, he'd tell me to kill you." Lazarian chuckled. "And I wonder what he'd tell me to do to you if I told him about your other project. The one that involves sewage, of all things. The one financed by certain developers who are feeling the pinch of the building moratorium. Dave Shugg, Jake Beaker, and Beverly Carney." Naming these names, Lazarian coolly watched Frankie's eyes, openly curious about what kind of face Frankie would try to put on this, confronted with such inside knowledge of his doings.

Frankie had kept his face nicely blank, just his eyes getting a little bigger as Sol named the names. He glanced over at the mirror, saw his own eyes ask him *So what can you do?* Lazarian's bigness on his bed's foot was like . . . sorcery. Never had he been this completely invaded—his bedroom, his trickiest scams—all of a sudden this big, dark, brimstone-reeking Ice Man sat right in the middle of them all. Sol had him bare-ass naked and dead to rights. He shook his head wonderingly.

"Sol, in all honesty, I gotta ask you, what the hell are you talking about?"

Lazarian smiled. Christ, the guy's face was . . . beautiful, there was no other word for it! "If I meant to take it from you, would I be telling you all this? I want good money, of course. I'll take an even split on your toxic intake, Lou's and your contracts combined. On the larger project, I'm not going to dampen your entrepreneurial spirit by taking more than twenty or thirty percent. And at the same time, I'm ready to give you what help I can. With me facilitating things your chances of pulling it off at all are much improved."

Hearing these terms, Frankie had the urge to come clean, shake on it. Just the relief of knowing that his life was not here-and-now in danger, that this call was just business, loosened him up. But what exactly was "business" to this Ice Man? It would never be just money with Lazarian, and the dark side of the Ice Man's goals Frankie wanted no truck with. So he looked at Lazarian with a face of polite, uncomprehending attention. After a moment, Lazarian laughed. It was a fierce, tuneful laugh—you thought of a boys' choir in a mischievous mood.

"I'm not fishing, Brother Weasel! Think it over today. You and the principals are having some kind of meeting today, aren't you?—no need to answer that! Later, sometime in the afternoon, you and I will talk in detail. I just wanted you to have a chance to absorb it—that I'm the new owner. And I wanted you to know up front that a real partnership is possible here between us, to our mutual profit. Laying my cards down like this, I'm showing real faith in you, Frankie. Keep that in mind as you chew things over today."

When the Ice Man left Frankie listened but heard no sound of exit, and finally had to get up and look all through the condo to assure himself that the goon was gone.

He tried to sleep, because nothing else could be accomplished for the next few hours. Mostly he wrestled with all his new problems. When he did find sleep, briefly, he wrestled in his dream with some dark slippery thing—they were both either floating in the night sky or deep under dark water, and the slippery thing fought him with a terrible sinewy power.

In the gray dawn he had a blender of carrot juice in the kitchen, and still felt so ragged around the edges that he had some bourbon and water on rocks. It helped. He saw that however it went he might as well proceed with the lakeside part of the setup—there was plenty of room to back out. Resolved, he dozed in his armchair, and it was almost eight when he woke up.

He called the number of the contractor Kim had given him—her brother-in-law, Willy Yakima. Chip bitched about his using "yokel labor" like Kim and Alejandro. Compared to what he'd have had to pay some wised-up old farts, he'd saved twenty an hour each on those kids all these weeks, and they'd done just fine. You give people a plausible explanation of what they're doing for you, and they accept it. He expected to get very good value from this Willy Yakima.

Four

Willy caught the call from Frankie DaValli just before he stepped out of the trailer to drive Maxie to school. Kim's call for him came moments after he had fired up the truck, his seven-year-old daughter strapped to the seat beside him, and barreled up their dirt gravel road, slaloming around the worst of the potholes, late as usual to meet the schoolbus at the stop nearest their place,

"I make us one minute and thirty-seven seconds late!" he shouted over the big Dodge engine, consulting the digital watch his daughter had picked out at K-Mart for his last birthday.

"*Sure,* Daddy! *Sure,* it's exactly thirty-seven seconds!" Maxie had lately learned about tongue-in-cheek statements. She was discovering sarcasm in a big way.

"It's your fault, you miserable little sluggard," he told her. "Why do you take so long to brush your hair? Why don't you just smooth it down with some wood-glue at night—it'd be nice an dry an smooth by morning!"

"There it is, Daddy! That's no minute and thirty-seven seconds—we're right behind it!"

"You insolent little pup!" He poked a tickling finger into her ribs and got a quick pinch at her cheek, which in size and texture, he thought, marveling, was exactly like an apricot.

"The day's shot anyway," he said, checking the watch, and passing the bus when it came to its next stop. "I might as well take you all the way to school!"

"Yeah!"

They were late this way whenever possible so Maxie could

beat the bus to school and have first crack at the tetherballs.

"You just missed him," Barbara was telling Kim on the phone. "Did he take that job yet from DaValli? The guy I work for?"

"He just called. Willy's going up to Muscovy Lake to meet him as soon as he drops Maxie. Something up about it?"

There was a brief silence between the half-sisters. Barbara poured coffee in her cup, and a healthy jolt of milk—which made it just about the color of her skin. Kim, Alex snoring beside her in a sleeping bag, took up the 49ers cap and set it on his head, then changed the angle slightly.

"It's just I think I've decided to quit working for him pretty soon."

"Do you know how irritating it is when you do this?" Barbara asked. "Beat around the bush?" They had really needed the money from this job, and now, complications.

"It's not that he won't pay or anything. It's just, well, his business breaks a few laws I think. He's connected to some strange people."

"Jesus Christ, Kimberly! You're so careless about things!"

"I've just now been figuring it out! There's not necessarily anything wrong with Willy's job, I just thought I oughtta say something."

"Well, Willy'll make his own call on it—I'll have him call you. Are you coming with Lucky and me to that County Planners Meeting?" Lucky was their mom. "The one about the new dump? It's next Thursday."

"I'll try."

On her way to the workshed Willy had built just upslope of their house trailer, she detoured to pull an apple from one of the dozen trees they still maintained. Their seven acres were a corner of old apple orchard, most of it long sold to vineyards, which now surrounded their remnant, their arrow-straight rows stretching to the limit of vision beyond the Yakima fence line.

Barbara lingered under the tree, chewing apple, sipping coffee, looking with anxious love at their green and quiet property. That they'd paid the mortgage these last three years awed them both a little when they thought of it. Now after a full summer of the building moratorium—brought inexorably down by the illegal excess discharges of the sewage treatment plant into the Ross River—they were in real danger of missing their next month's payment. In another month, there would be the salvation of their harvest—a salvation that scared the shit out of her.

Was that a whiff of it? Since having Maxie, Barbara had found her sense of smell to be eerily acute. Was that a whiff of skunk on the morning air? A scent of their little dope-crop down in the grove?

She struggled to decide but couldn't—it was right on the border between sensation and imagination. She hated this crop of Willy's. The closer they got to harvest, the more excruciating the suspense became. They didn't smoke the stuff themselves—the only reason for the risk was profit. Unless you had a million dollars to invest in growing grapes, and five years' start time, dope was the only cash crop a person could get ahead with.

Looking at the sea of vineyard around them reminded Barbara of her father. You were supposed to hoe only the row they gave you, weren't you? This here six hundred acres of vine needs some pesticides—Sanchez, get crackin. She could still remember her father, a black-haired little figure on a tractor, going back and forth in the sea of grapes under a flawless blue northern California sky. She was just eight when he died, but she could still remember his belly's obscene enlargement with hepatic failure, a slight, gnarl-handed brown man with sweet black eyes, pregnant with the poisons he'd been hired to dispense.

She went to her workshed. She had an idea for a wild-boar

brooch she was eager to try out. These were hard times, and Willy had good instincts, usually. Barbara saw that in the economy ahead, they must secure this property—must own it outright. Maxie must have that core of security growing up. They would just have to play the next couple weeks as they came.

After dropping Maxie, Willy stopped by the Gravenstein Kwik-Stop, where skinny Bea with her red-rinsed hair and her constant Pall Malls let him fill his battered cooler from the drink-machine's ice dispenser.

"Those birds thirsty again?" she asked as she rang up his sixpack, referring to the Road-Runner decals, all scuffed and worn now, that Maxie had plastered to the cooler one summer afternoon.

"I'm startin to think these birds have a beer-addiction, Bea," he nodded.

Gravenstein was a town of twelve thousand lying amid vineyards at the northern edge of the Santa Marta plain. A right-angled route to the lake would have been fastest—straight south on 101 to Santa Marta, straight west on River Highway. Willy took a meandering diagonal southwest across the plain on slower winding two-lane country roads.

He pulled out a beer to help him enjoy the scenery. It gave him a little pang to think that Maxie had put those decals on his cooler when she was only five. Just yesterday she had seemed to fit entirely in the crook of one of his arms, and already her childhood was thing of layers and levels, a little history.

And these surroundings here were what he wanted her to know as she was growing up. That abandoned barn in that field, up to its windows in blackberry vines, shedding shingles so that you could see blue sky through the net of its roof-slats. Or little houses like that one there with its fieldstone porch pillars, its front yard umbrellaed by a big old oak, with three, four, five different vehicles in it, all sunk to their bumpers in golden foxtails, seeming to float wheelless, like boats.

Where the rise and fall of the two-lane permitted, you could see to the west—still small with the distance—the front ranks of all the new housing developments that would march across this plain in the next ten years and gobble up everything rural left in it. Willy couldn't even say Thank God for the Moratorium because he himself had been working on those developments—had been part of the problem and glad of the work! It shamed him to have been a framer on those candy-ass cookie-cutter projects. He was a bootleg country contractor (license? I don't got to show you no stinkin *license!*) and earth-mover who could jerry-rig anything, fix anything, build anything.

Thank God for this contact from Kim. He would give this DaValli an unbeatable bid. Then in another two weeks, they would have the harvest.

He cracked another beer. It was early—all right, he admitted it—early for a second beer, not even nine yet. When the stress and anxiety of this crop was behind him, he was going to have to really start looking at this drinking question. Barb never said much directly anymore, just looks now and then—but it was getting to be time, he admitted it.

There was a field of just-baled hay, all aligned by the baler, like butter cubes, each with an identical rhombus of shadow attached to it, and there beyond was River Highway.

Willy swung out onto the highway, judging he had clearance, but there coming up fast behind him was a new black Trans Am. It whipped out around him and whooshed past. A sweatered arm thrust out of the Trans waving thanks as it pulled back in front—as if Willy had slowed down to let him in.

DaValli, waving thanks, had the thought that this guy could easily be Willy Yakima headed out to meet him. The guy—you could see the whole type in a glance—was perfect. Squat and block-muscled, snarled hair pouring out from under a bill-cap, steering a battered old Dodge pickup with one thick-fingered hand on the wheel, a wrist like a fencepost with a bland-eyed, kind of flat-looking face, the kind of guy who would have six different cars in pieces at home, could tear down and rebuild anything—as long as he stayed with it—could nurse battered equipment along, lay a foundation, set a septic tank—you name it, and all at under-the-table prices.

Well, good—a bargain was what he wanted. Because, should he even be *doing* this? Making his scam . . . well, *real* like this? The idea of it, the bigness, the boldness, was what had fascinated him, that and the dance of persuasion, stringing these hard-headed developers along, selling them. He had never clearly seen how he could get away with doing what they wanted him to do, but since it would cost him nothing to back out, he'd gone ahead with it.

Just how much did Lazarian really know? Did he realize that if Frankie carried out his tentative plan, he would have to leave town—leave the country in short order? With a suitcase of cash of course, but still . . . On balance it was safest to go ahead, because Lazarian might know that this was the next step—though how he could know was beyond Frankie.

He branched off River Highway on the road that climbed into the hills alongside Muscovy Creek.

The creek carried down the lake's drainage to the Ross River. Here and there its thick braid of water was visible from the road, and Frankie imagined it running as black as ink. If it was all done at night . . . ? How the Christ could anyone get away with it?

When he climbed to the lake itself, the plan seemed even more insane—a crime as wide and blatant as the big blue pane of tree-fringed water itself. He imagined a giant squid of blackness squirming in the lake, filling it shore to shore. You thought of Muscovy Lake as a secluded place till you remembered all the homes hiding in the trees around most of its shore, and the two villages.

His lakeshore property, already leased through KleenCo since no money of his own was involved, was on the least inhabited side of the lake at least. The lot was on a promontory of the lake's rim, where the largest of the encircling hills pushed its flank out into the water. He took the narrow dirt road through the trees that screened the shore from the highway and parked in their shade just above the beach. The tip of the point was a bluff of naked rock, which was fringed by a narrow gravel beach.

In his $150 oxblood loafers Frankie crunched along the beach and stepped up to the bluff of eroded rock. He squatted and shifted the loose rock heaped against the bluff's base.

Behind this loose talus, flush with the native rock, was a plug of concrete—very old and sandy concrete.

He had learned of this poking through the old records of the Quicksilver Mine. A drainage outlet from the wild and woolly days when the leachates from a mercury mine were ejected into the nearest waterways without qualm. The thrill of actually finding it here had been enough to make him lease the spot at once.

Willy took the long way around the lake—the one that took him through both Muscovy Junction, right at the top of the Creek Highway, and Little Muscovy a couple miles south along the rim. The first one had the post office and the second one the sheriff's substation. Willy had lived here in his early teens and was glad to see little change. The little motels from the forties and fifties were now mostly rental courts, and the booze-bait-and-tackle stores, some of them, had become gentrified little bookstores or cafés, but the yuppies were still only just beginning to discover real estate up here.

He saw DaValli's little headland—hadn't there been a name for it?—when he was still a little ways off. There was a guy down there on the beach, dark sweater and slacks, that had to be DaValli.

He looked more incongruous the closer Willy got. Between the breeze-licked waters, the weathered rock, and the shaggy sweep of the great hill up into the sky behind him, DaValli looked dark and glossy, a plastic doll on a beach of weathered stone.

Willy rolled smartly onto the property, wanting to make an impression of alertness, energy—braked beside the Trans Am too smartly, his big tires puffing a light blanket of dust over its gloss. DaValli took no notice, stepped up and gave Willy a grin and a nice, sinewy handshake, A lean guy in great shape, full of the joy of life. "I passed you back on River and I *thought* you might be Willy Yakima. Kim says you're an ace."

"There's not much I haven't done in construction, Frankie."

"Here it is in a nutshell. I need a pump-shed. Cinderblock, nothing big, nothing fancy. I'm still waiting on my main financing, but I wanted to get things started in a small way."

"Well, walk me over it, Frankie, and I'll give you a bid."

After a little discussion, Willy knew the job was strange, no matter how you squinted at it. Sheet aluminum roof, cinderblock walls, but only three of them. He was to build it with its back up close to the bluff, with "no need for" a wall on the bluff-end of the structure. Its only real purpose, after all, was to conceal the unsightly pump apparatus that would one day be supplying a house on the lot.

An easy enough job, though. Willy could bid this one really cheap, pull a grand and a half out of it. . . . He stood there gazing consideringly at the site, looking as if he was visualizing the project—the way you did when you were cooking up a bid—and seeing the great gray sweep of the hill rising behind it.

"Cinnabar Point!" he said suddenly. "That was what they used to call this spot—I was trying to remember. You know, it suddenly hits me—that mine-shaft you run, it's right in this hill here, isn't it?"

For the fraction of a second, there was something uncomfortable in DaValli's eyes, and then he was grinning, nodding. "Right around on the east face of it! Can you believe it? I've been operating here for months, and I finally get around to taking a little hike to the other side of my hill, and bam, right down there, Muscovy Lake and one of the sweetest little building sites I ever saw!"

"Well," Willy said, feeling in that moment a magical little flare of intuition, and raising his bid then and there by two grand. "I can swing it for 7500 for you. I'd need about half up front to get rollin, and I could do it in less than a week. You could hold off on the advance until this evening, so you could see me make a start here . . ."

"Hey, Willy, take the check now! I'll stop by later just to say hi! I told you, you're an ace, an I know it!"

Willy stood there grinning, absently hefting a piece of the rock shed from the bluff. His intuition was right, something faintly fishy here, good money but the kind that made you nervous. "I don't see any problems with it. You might have a little trouble with this loose rock coming down into your shed, with no wall there, but other than that . . ."

Frankie had been writing the check. He ripped it off smartly and tendered it snappily between two fingers, smiling winningly at Willy. Four thousand dollars. "We're on, then," Frankie said.

"Great," said Willy. He tossed the rock onto the heap of others that lay against the bluff.

Five

The rock, which weighed less than two kilograms, struck the hill, which weighed half a billion. The impact sent the merest whisper of a tremor through the concrete plug. This opened a tiny fissure, a micro-pore through the old granite's grainy core.

Out of this microfissure there leapt an exotic chemical fragment—an exquisite little molecular net, which sank swiftly downward through the gravel of the beach.

It was an astoundingly elaborate hydrocarbon making its first appearance in nature—an elf-web of miraculous complexity.

The little net slipped down through the gravel—she might have been a starship cruising through the asteroid belt, so separate were the huge stones to her tininess.

Then she found the waterline. The diffusion gradient snatched her like a hurricane out, out, out into the open water of the lake.

Electrically quick, she moved through waters that seethed with micro-life, laddering her way like lightning through the Brownian jostle. . . .

Until suddenly she was seized by a colossal current. A tsunami of hydrodynamic power plucked her up towards . . .

A shape. A shape of planetary vastness.

It was one of the gill-slits of a fingerling trout (*Teleopennidae maculatus*)—a vast, membranous maw, ponderously flexing, with a rhythm like the slow-beating wings of the Cosmos-bearing Bird.

Into this hugeness, the exquisite little molecular net was swallowed. She entered the endothelial labyrinths of the fish.

Here, between cell wall and cell wall, she moved as swift as a reflection amidst a hall of mirrors. She moved like a rumor, like a revelation. In the twisted, tight-coiled innards of a million cells there was an uncoiling, a writhing of change, the minute stirrings of a new fertility.

Six

Madrona Manors was a fucking graveyard. It was a bunch of two-story skeletons. Dave Shugg himself, its owner/developer, was the brightest thing in it right now, standing by his truck on the freshly asphalted roadway between the gaunt frames of two-by-sixes.

Doug Fir has that nice orangey-yellowy color to it when it's fresh, but let it stand a month or two and it starts to look gray, senile. Shugg, standing by his glossy red Ram Charger, wearing his L. L. Bean boots, new whipcords, and green Pendleton, was the only spot of color here now.

It burned Dave Shugg's guts to look at this. It wasn't just the eight million or so he stood to realize over the next couple years, once he got these suckers built. Nor was it the fact that meanwhile his construction loans were eating him *alive*. It was the waste.

Shugg had started his career with a hammer in hand, pounding pitons like any young yahoo. Now, worth millions, he still drove a pickup with the best utility boxes on it and the best tools in those boxes. He still only felt really comfortable in work clothes, though he never got a smudge of dirt on them from dawn to dusk anymore.

Because building houses was a wonderful profession. Houses were Life itself. You took raw land. You took a weedy stretch of dirt. Emptiness, just trees and grass with cowflop in it and turkey vultures lazily circling it in the sky. . . . You took this nullity, you called in the big cats, and you munched it up, you brought in the truckloads of bright, fragrant lumber, all neatly strapped in black steel ribbon . . . and presto! Soon you had houses, with people in them. Soon there was life, where before there had been only weedy desolation.

Shugg let down his tailgate and took the brunch he'd brought out of his coolers, Mexican beers, José Cuervo Gold, rock salt and sliced limes in two little tubs, chips, dip. . . . Here came the wop's black Trans Am.

"Frank! Good to see you!"

"Hi, Davey!" Big smiles and a hearty handgrip. Early on, each had intuited the nickname that the other liked least.

Behind them, as they greeted one another, epoxied to the underside of the Trans Am's aerofoil, an exceedingly tiny gun-mike moved, just fractionally, in response to a microwave signal from its controller.

Lazarian, in his little headset, could actually hear the cordial dislike in the greeting. The sound quality was really remarkable. Bill Beiderbeck, one of Lazarian's West Coast technical contacts, was to be commended.

Lazarian's van was tucked away among the oaks, just off the road about a half-mile from Madrona Manors. He settled himself, as one who prepares to hear good music. What would the Weasel's gambit be? He might try to play for short-term cash from the developers. Might be deciding to cut and run.

"A shot for starters, Frank?"

"Fine, Davey! To keep you company. I can tell you're a hard drinker from the old school."

"Don't tell me you're one of that wine spritzer crowd. L.A. boy you said, didn't you?"

"An L.A. homeboy and proud of it, Davey! That's what qualifies me for our project! I didn't grow up near Hollywood for nothing. I know how to turn shit into gold!"

"Ha ha ha! Good one, Frank. Mmmm! Hits the spot, no?

Tecate chaser for that?"

"OK, but one of these lime wedges first I think, Davey."

"They do look good."

They stood munching lime wedges, sipping beer, as if they had nothing but relaxation on their minds. Frankie stole a look at Shugg—a big, florid guy of fifty-five, shoulders still powerful, carrying about thirty too much around the middle. A bully. Best to hit him with the pitch square between the eyes. But Shugg spoke up first, with an angry wave around them.

"They talk about murdering trees, look at all these corpses! Skeletons! If the CEPs had their way, people would start living in caves again! Totally natural!"—the last word was a bitter sneer.

"CEPs?"

"Clean Environment Pussies!"

"Davey. Truth be told, it's *everybody* downriver of Santa Marta wants the moratorium. It's not just extremists. I mean, you get shit in your water, you raise a stink about it!"

"Shit? It's effluent! Treated wastewater! It's ninety-seven percent clean!"

"You're talking hundreds of thousands of gallons of it! And what is that other three percent? It's liquefied turds! Liquefied toilet paper!"

"Just who the hell's side are you on, Frank?" Shugg asked it with a laugh that slipped towards a growl.

"I hear you minimizing the problem. Davey, it makes me think you minimize the service I'm planning to do for you. Which is pretty fucking major and very risky for me personally. So today I want to talk about the substantial up-front cash I'm going to need if we're going to proceed at all."

"You already know my feelings about up-front—"

"Excuse me. Some of my key people want front money, plus I'm gonna have to buy my way out of some existing contracts just to have room. I'm gonna have to have three-quarter mil cash before I can proceed to hook up."

"Frank, it's not trust, it's the principle—strictly c.o.d.—it's the way I operate, and—"

"Hey, is this a regular service I'm giving you? Am I the fucking garbage man in my *truck*? So you think I'm gonna hook up with the plant, literally *link* myself to this whole deal, without front money?"

"Well, you can ask them too." Shugg nodded towards Jake Beaker's black Mercedes now pulling up. "They're gonna say the same thing."

Shugg noted sourly that it was Bev Carney who got out the driver's side. She was impeccable, sharp-featured little dark-Irish face, slender but just tall enough to have physical authority. She wore a cream silk blouse with pirate sleeves, a short black skirt, and supple flats of some kind of reptile skin. And Christ, look at poor, puffy Jake Beaker slowly climbing out the passenger side.

Shugg and Beaker went back to piton-pounding days together. But Jake, as soon as he had his first half mil or so, never touched another sinker, and couldn't get out of work clothes quick enough. From then on it was clothes out of the *New Yorker* and glossy foreign cars. They still drank together. Poor wheezy Jake, with the bruised patches under his eyes, had always been a gourmand at the bar as well as the table, and the bottle, knife, and fork had almost killed him already.

Jake himself always insisted that Carney was a legitimate partner, fully invested. Yeah, but where had she gotten the money to invest? To Shugg she would always be the cool piece who had jerked Dave off and moved in on him. She was sharp and cool at the bargaining table at least—he would give her that much.

Greetings and amenities were traded, enthusiasms for the clear, sunny day. Beaker joined the other two men in another shot of Cuervo, and Bev accepted a beer. They all munched limes for chasers.

Frankie noticed Bev was wearing wine snob earrings—slender silver bottles with some varietal name in exquisitely fine engraving. She had a great sense of costume—wore her power gear lightly. Nice sharp humor in those black eyes of hers. He smiled at her and Jake.

"Davey says you'll absolutely refuse my demand for a three-quarter mil cash advance. So I can start by telling you that I won't do anything without it."

They all sparred for a while, being amiable but hard-nosed. Then the three developers excused themselves to stroll off down the asphalt a little way.

Bev Carney saw that they would have to put down some start money, though a smaller sum. Shugg fought the idea, kept harassing Jake for support, while Jake tried to get it across kindly that he was behind Bev on this. She could see just how Shugg saw her, the bitch fucking the boss. Long ago she had indeed yielded to Jake's pleas, and had soon learned to enjoy his greed for her. She still fondly remembered afternoons with him kneeling, his muzzle thrust into her tufted loins, gobbling her like a kid with a birthday cake all to himself.

But for years now it had been all business—good, sharp business, deep in the black. Soon Shugg capitulated. He'd been after Jake's allegiance more than anything—they'd all known they'd have to ante up something. The two men strolled on, Shugg pretending to show Jake the layout, leaving the bargaining to Bev.

"Another beer?" DaValli greeted her.

"A shot of Cuervo instead, I think."

He poured two. They drank and munched limes to quench the fire. She liked DaValli's moves, his lean body's fluid postures. All the body English he put into his talk was faintly suggestive of fucking. At the same time she caught an animal scent about him. He had the crouched intensity of a coyote, and a gust of its rankness too. She found it not un-erotic, this hint of animal dirt at his core. This was OK. When she was aroused, her wits got sharper if anything. She smiled at him.

"We can see our way to three hundred thousand. Once you're fully hooked up, another four-fifty. And your last seven-fifty upon completion."

DaValli smiled, and opened beers for them. There was no hurry to answer because it was now unlikely he would even go through with it at all. If they pitched three they might be talked up to four, but that would be tops.

"Lime with that?" he asked her, digging one out. Four hundred just wasn't enough to cut and run for—his fingers on the limes felt a shivery sensation. Something was squirming under his fingers. He looked down.

The lime slices were covered with a seething, glittery jam of maggots. Snatching back his hand, he saw their tiny, gem-cut perfection, saw them drip like little twisting, tapered pearls from his fingertips.

"Shit!" he roared. He smacked the tub from the tailgate, and they both jumped back from the spew of glittery white and green. Then in a fury he stomped the squirmy fruit fanned on the asphalt, his oxblood loafers flashing, leaving white cheesy smears of annihilation on the blacktop.

Shugg and Beaker had hurried over and now Jake Beaker, knees suddenly failing, knelt by the mess and vomited richly on it.

Bev tossed her own guts in a surprising, instantaneous reaction. It fairly leapt out of her, yet by instinctive reflex she leaned far over and avoided getting a single drop of it on her clothes.

While Shugg saw to Beaker, Frankie helped her aside and

gave her a beer to wash her mouth out with. Her recovery was quick and complete. She laughed. They both chided Shugg about his limes. Then she turned to Frankie.

"We're seeing Morris this afternoon." Morris Hacker was the plant manager of the Lago Puro Wastewater Treatment Plant. "I understand you'll be seeing Mary and Fletcher later today?" Mary Straff and Edwin Fletcher were subordinates of Morris Hacker's, were the chief engineer and chief of maintenance, respectively, of the Lago Puro Wastewater Treatment Plant. "So once you've discussed the specifics of hooking up with them we can meet this evening—say around seven?—for our preliminary transaction."

"Wonderful," Frankie said.

Willy could just manage, on his way back to Gravenstein to rent Reed's backhoe, to stop home and see Barbara. The odds for a little fooling around weren't great, but if you didn't try your luck, you didn't get anything.

He could hear her polishing wheel going in the shed when he got out of his truck. He pulled an apple from the nearest tree and started crunching it—it was a great breath freshener after a few beers. Barbara was at work on some jewelry, it was mid-morning, in just a few hours she would have Maxie and errands to deal with . . . a busy mom could be a harried, testy creature. There wasn't time for much maneuvering. He would have to be pretty direct, go for the first opening.

"Howdy, you sweet, golden-brown little filly, you!" he told her, stepping into the shed. She gave him a preoccupied smile. She was polishing a small animal shape of copper. "Is that a boar?"

"You can tell! Good!" Her black hair was ponytailed for work. There was that delicious, slightly pointed angle of her ear-crests. He decided to stay with the humorous yokel approach. "You look just as firm and shapely as a ripe country apple, Barb."

She nodded, smiling coolly, studying her boar. Its snout was twisted in a snarl. "And you," she said, "look like maybe this guy liked your bid, and maybe you've had a beer or three."

He smiled blandly. "I've brought you a present. I was thinking how too many husbands let day after day slip by and never remember those special little gestures that are so precious to their little women."

"You know what I think?" She was getting up, facing him. She raised her right hand and made a fist, smiling a little more now. "I think it's time for a beer-gut check."

For a man of the short, block-muscled type, Willy had a rare metabolism. He burned beer right up and, for all he guzzled, was nearly fatless. Barbara, firm and shapely, was also solid, and she was a serious hitter. Up came her shoulder, out came her elbow. She twisted at the waist to put her whole back into it. Tightening up, he watched her generous breasts lagging creamily behind the punch, mounding up to the right in her shirt as she landed it: *whump*.

Willy gasped and sank to his knees, not having to fake it much. He reached out and grabbed her hips. "Now you gotta take my present, OK? You'll like it, I promise!"

"So let's see it."

He grabbed her around the back, hooked her stomach up against his face, and blew a loud bugle-like noise against the bare skin of her stomach. She started to fight free, laughing a little but not enough yet. "Wait!" Willy cried. "Just a joke! I really do have something!" He was struggling to his feet, hoisting her in two arms, struggling to the couch and falling onto it with her.

She was chuckling a little, but still fighting pretty hard. "Just tell me, you goon! Let me *up* and tell me."

"I will! I will! But first, just one kiss, *one* quick little— *mmmmm!*" Not giving her time to react, he pulled aside the crotch of her shorts and darted his snout in between her legs, his tongue and lips briefly finding her. Now she was laughing hard enough, and he could feel her relaxing. "It's a *check*, Barb, a *check*—you want it?"

She was shifting her hips to a more comfortable position, unbuttoning her shorts. "Just how big is this check?"

He stood up grinning, unbuckling his belt in a hurry. "It's a nice *fat* one!"

He should hurry to pick up the backhoe, but before he left home again Will headed down to the edge of their seven acres farthest from the county road—went on foot as always, always varying his path, so that no obvious track would be worn to the copse.

The thicket of big old oaks and madrones was near his back fence, and beyond the barbed wire vineyard stretched away to the limit of vision.

Maxie was plausibly forbidden ever to come near the copse because it was so thickly overgrown with poison oak. The oily leaves, at their orange-yellow nastiest in the late summer, infil-trated the trees' foliage everywhere. Millennial vines, some as thick as a forearm, coiled around every trunk and branch.

Taking a stick from the grass at the copse's fringe, Willy lift-ed aside a strategic tendril of the poison oak. Just within the shadow of the canopy, discreet pruning had created a subtle zig-zag path through the vines. Even from here just inside the copse, it was hard to make out the shed at the thicket's core. He'd car-ried it inside in sections that bolted together. The door fit its frame snugly, and he thrust himself through and shut it quickly behind him. Letting the smell out, even in this relative rural emptiness, was like sending up little flares. It was rank as a tomcat this close to harvest.

And here he was under the grow lights, timer controlled, amid his darlings, twenty of the bushiest little green skunks you ever saw, their branches interpenetrating, neatly sharing eighty square feet, with their neat little generator, also on a timer, purring away inaudibly to the outer world.

So much careful preparation here, painstaking construction and husbandry! He felt a wonderful, titillating intimacy with this treasure, as if he was entirely inside a funky and beloved cunt. He felt a greed so delicious it was like lust. The *colas* on his she-skunks were fat—he'd get close to a pound off each! He was looking at four thousand dollars per, more or less.

A prayer went up from the heart of him before he left: two more weeks of no bad luck, then a quick bulk sale, probably to Gutley down on the river. Because after all, Dear Lord, if people could make nice legitimate fortunes off of distilleries, and in the process send half of male America out shitfaced onto the highways to maim and slay innocent women and children, then by Christ he and Barb, doomed to sink if they clung to the legitimate channels this economy offered people of their station, had the by-Christ right to earn a little independence, secure a little property, insure a little stability for their daughter, by selling a weed that, to Willy's knowledge, had never killed anyone, and of which he knew from personal experience, when as a young yahoo he had smoked it, that the worst thing it did to the user was waste his time—ruling out, of course, all the harm its illegality per se could do you.

He went to Reed's Rentals because he knew had a Micro-Mule., which had a little backhoe on one end and a little skip loader on the other.

"You'll wanna trailer for it too," Reed said.

"Well, I'm not gonna toss it up in the bed of the Dodge, am I, Reed? Hey, Raleigh!"

Raleigh had an auto wrecking yard right beside Reed's equipment lot. His black-bearded face had poked up from among the chassis piled beyond the chain-link fence, and his blunt, grease-black hand had waved.

"Let's say two hundred for both, all day?" Reed asked, cocking his head consideringly, his tall gauntness seeming to come to a point in the sparse red dab of his goatee.

"Two hundred till tomorrow night—today's half gone already."

"OK. Hey, tell Barb that me an Raleigh are comin to that meeting about the new dump."

"She'll be glad. She's afraid no one will show up to talk against it. Hell, if anyone can tell em about dumps, it's you guys."

The old Gravenstein Landfill was up on the hill right behind them. The two lots fronted Gravenstein Highway just north of the town, and Raleigh's Wrecking Yard was right on the corner formed by the turnoff up to the dump, which had just this year been filled and capped.

"I'll tell you what," Reed said. "It may just be a transfer station now an all, but that sucker's been stinkin worse lately than it ever did!"

It was just past noon when Willy finally got the hoe up to the site. It took almost another two hours to get his stakes and strings laid out. At last he was ready to take his first concrete bite out of the job. He started at one of the corners near the bluff, carefully extending the bucket on its jointed arm.

The little rig was well worn, and the hydraulics were a little jerky. The arm gave a jerk just as it reached down to take its bite, and then struck the bluff a smart little blow, bonging softly like a bell.

Seven

When the backhoe's bucket hit the bluff, a spiderweb of new micro-fissures branched through the old concrete plug.

Moments later, from the gravel just below the waterline, vanishingly fine filaments of blackness plumed up, like smoke-leaks from a buried inferno.

Instantly invisible, instantly diffusing to the body of the lake, they were, at the level where life is thickest, a cataclysm. In the world of the very small they were a disaster past the scale of the greatest earthquakes the larger world has known.

Through the dense galaxies of microscopic life the black, molecular titans moved, each more than a micron across. To many of the lives in that microbial starfield—to the bacteria, to some blue-green algae—the giant molecules were their equal in size, or nearly, and their assault was more that of predators. ravishers, than of disease.

The larger lives they overswarmed, in a fury of chemical energy, ransacking the ghostly fairy-slippers of paramecia, vandalizing the diatoms, shattering the stained glass windows of those micro-cathedrals . . .

And every cell assaulted yielded—unjacketed by lipo-solvents—yielded up its whiff of selfhood, the intricate wisp of its chromosomes.

This apocalypse of new fertility branched, swift and secret, everywhere—across the lake, down-creek and downriver, upriver, outwards through all the layered aquifers of the hills, out through the watercomb under the plains, under miles of dairy pastures, and yet farther out through the plain, even under the cities of that plain, it unstoppably, secretly spread.

Eight

Chip liked Fletcher's choice of a bar—the Rite Spot. It had been here when he first came to Santa Marta in the fifties, and this stretch of Sequoia Boulevard had still had pastures and small farms along it here and there. It was all liquor stores, motels, and car-lots now, but the Rite Spot had the same old tilted martini glass in white neon tubing and was, indeed, as Fletcher said, a perfect Old Farts' bar.

Chip also liked the idea of having a drink or three. He'd kept himself on a pretty good leash about drinking for the last ten years or so (though why the Christ had he waited till into his fifties to start getting a handle on it?) and knew how to really enjoy a few drinks when he took them now.

Chip didn't like Fletcher himself. Chip had worked at the treatment plant for most of the sixties and had found Fletcher to be an arrogant asshole from the very first. Chip had never gotten any higher than head of maintenance for the clarifiers, and it wasn't long after he'd had to start reporting to Fletcher, the new chief of maintenance, that he'd "moved on to greener pastures." They still saw each other sometimes, because when you hit your sixties, how many people could you find who had known the same world you had and had developed the same fundamental attitudes about it? But this evening it was going to be nice talking to Fletcher and secretly knowing that he, Chip, was the wise guy in the transaction for a change.

Ah, the ambience! The sparkly plastic waterfall advertising Hamm's Beer! The aged jukebox with Sinatra and Tony Bennett on it! And here and there at the bar, half a dozen genuine Old Farts! Chip nodded at them while the bartender poured his bourbon and water-back. If you were going to relax with a drink, this was the kind of a place to do it, quiet, dark, and no glittery bullshit.

There sat Fletcher in one of the battered wooden booths. Fletcher was naturally skinny like Chip himself, but with long, grasshoppery arms and legs, and a long bony face with a habitual sarcastic grin that sometimes seemed it would split the face in half.

"You look like death warmed over, Chip."

"So do you. But wait'll I get a drink in me, and I might improve some."

"Well, I hope you're ready to lay some flex hose."

"I'll bet we're at least as ready as you are to lay two miles of irrigation pipe."

To transfer sewage from the plant to the mineshaft, Chip would have to bring flex hose down the hillsides to the edge of the plain. From the plant, Fletcher and Marv Straff would have to convey it for two miles across the plain to the edge of the hills in dummy irrigation pipe.

Chip sat giving Fletcher his grin back, liking being on top in this face-off, but wishing he could let Fletcher *know* he was on top. For years Fletch had mocked him for leaving his cinch job at the plant, and when Chip looked at Fletcher's salary and bennies and security today, he agreed. He himself had moved on to pastures not-so-greener, to working here and there and drinking too much and getting old.

This time, though, he was really moving on, was going to be long gone with two hundred thousand cash once the smoke cleared. And if he knew Frankie, not a drop of sewage would actually get moved. Whether or not the conspirators at the plant would manage to hang onto their advance money from the developers, they would definitely be left there with their dicks hanging out—with their secret out-take from the sewage tanks, and their miles of dummy irrigation pipe. If they were lucky, they would be able to take everything apart again before anyone found out.

"Here's to us," he told Fletcher jauntily. "Throw that one down and I'll buy your next!"

"Done."

"So you've got Hacker moving?" Chip prompted. Morris Hacker, the sewage plant's manager and Fletch and Marv's boss, was proving to be the weak sister in the conspiracy.

"Fuck Hacker. Marv and I are goin ahead, over the weekend. He'll come to work Monday and it'll be a done thing—the out-take'll be in."

This meant some advance money would shortly flow from the developers. Chip nodded, smiling.

"Tell you somethin else I'm gonna do too," Fletcher said, "when I'm in there with that backhoe over the weekend. You remember the service roads to the sludge ponds?"

"Hey, I only worked there for a decade, Fletcher."

"They just got repaved so you don't notice a new patch of blacktop on em. I'm gonna cut a subtle little trough across that one the trucks use to haul off the sludge. You'll hardly be able to see it's there, but I'm gonna make the angle just right." Fletcher was an artist with a grader or a backhoe.

"I'm not following you."

"We got a couple new young hot-dogs drivin truck right now."

"I'm still not followin."

"Don't you remember what I told you happened"—he started cackling, had to fight it down—"what I told you happened to *Parsons?*"

Chip had to laugh too, then—Fletcher had made it so vivid—and Fletch himself, always sarcastic but rarely raucous, surrendered to a prolonged cackling.

Frankie DaValli and Marv Straff came in together, probably having met on the sidewalk. They too were laughing, Marv clapping Frankie on the shoulder, Frankie clapping back in self-defense. Marv was a hearty guy. Above the top button of his cowboy-style workshirt a vigorous tuft of chest hair poked out. He had a potato nose, a sunburned, gnarled forehead, and receding curly hair—a happy bear of a man.

They bought beers to take to the booth, and Marv punched up Dean Martin singing "That's Amore" on the jukebox.

"If you've told Chip," he said to Fletcher, sitting down, "then it's systems go—no more futzing around. We can start talking specs." Marv Straff was a glutton for a project, any project, loving nothing better than to tuck in to some specs, to get some machines rolling and start moving things around.

"I told him Hacker could fuck himself and we're settin the out-take this weekend."

"Actually I'm seeing Morris tomorrow for lunch," Straff told Frankie and Chip. "I might still get his go-ahead, but if he waffles, I'm just gonna present him on Monday with a fait accompli."

Chip said, "I'm ready to start stringing flex as soon as we have the advance, right, Frankie?"

"Absolutely. I'm seeing one of the principals tonight. Our side of the advance should be in hand by morning."

Straff's thoughts were already into strategies. "We can't just string a straight run, but I can start having sections of six-inch dropped in some of the pasture between us and the hills."

Frankie saw Chip shoot him a veiled glance and get into it with the other two, talking hardware and schedules. The poor old fart was thinking that he and Frankie together had the other two foxed, were going to grab themselves some easy money and run. There had seemed to be no point in sharing Lazarian's new role in this with Chip, nor the fact that Frankie no longer knew what the fuck they were really going to do, and that they were even considering actually *taking* half a billion gallons of sewage into a shaft with room for less than half of it. Because with Lazarian in the picture, you stepped through the Looking Glass, into a world where normal cause and effect didn't apply.

He hated what the Ice Man had done to him. Yesterday he was the mover and shaker, running a scam here, toying with a bigger one over there. Yesterday he had been totally what he lived to be—a persuader, an operator.

Now he felt like a balloon on a string, nodding and smiling at everyone, without a clue where anything was heading.

Anything, though, was better than having Sol Lazarian piqued with him. Better than having Sol Lazarian after him.

"Excuse me, guys—I'm gonna make a call."

From the phone in the corner by the restrooms, as he called Bev Carney's number, he watched the three men talking in the booth, their hands gesturing, illustrating sequences, shapes, sizes. Like three busy flies crawling over a huge invisible turd on the table between them. The image popped into his mind out of nowhere, and made him smile.

Chip outstayed them all at the Rite Spot. He fucked up, booze-wise, woke up alone in the booth, his dentures slipped out of alignment in his slack mouth, the clock above the Hamm's sign reading near eleven.

When the bottle snuck up on him like this his mouth never got away from him, he never really did anything either. Just started drinking with an ever grimmer determination till he passed out. He had to ask himself after all these years, why did he fucking bother. Other people at least got high times out of drinking, got into a little colorful trouble.

His head was thudding—not exactly pain yet, but getting there—his vision OK but his reflexes definitely slowed. Nonetheless he headed back to the mine. His flop in a rental court was just two miles away, but that seemed too goddamned bare-ass lonely for words. Up at the shaft, with no other people around him for miles, he felt less lonely. Just accepting the fact that he was too drunk to figure that one out, he started driving across the plain.

Climbing through the switchbacks up into the hills, he felt a little spooked by the forest flanking him. Big, misshapen things jerked and stirred behind the trees under his headlights. The farther he got from the city the more Chip felt that their smooth sewage con was full of holes. Just the crazy mix of people involved, any one of them a possible weak point, could get them into hard trouble, fast. Cash or no cash.

What a nest of vipers people could be, he thought self-pityingly. At the least, what a puzzle—just like that puzzle of lights that the city made down there on the plain.

To the north of that major puzzle which was Santa Marta the lights thinned away, and then, after a dark stretch, there hung the smaller galaxy of Gravenstein. A little way out into the black rural fringe of this, their house trailer leaking light sparingly, from only one little window, into the surrounding dark apple trees and vineyards. Barbara and Willy lay on their bed talking, not under the covers yet, the lamp on.

They heard a thud and a murmur from the tiny hallway outside their door.

Since she had been five or so Maxie, a couple hours after falling asleep, always got up to pee in a sleepwalking state. She had to be intercepted from trying to get into a kitchen cupboard, or groping her way into a closet, unlikely nooks disguised as bathrooms by her dreams.

He steered Maxie into the bathroom and got her seated. She faintly whimpered, ". . . the pig . . .," her gray eyes tranced above her flushed cheeks, and peed.

As Willy stood there waiting to carry her back and tuck her in, he suddenly had a powerful vision of how fragile was this softly lit nook of safety in which he sheltered his little girl.

For the very water that quenched, bathed, and flushed her, they depended on a well at the whim of the earth; depended even more immediately on an increasingly erratic one-third horsepower submersion pump wheezing underground. The money to replace it, like the endless money needed to secure the very ground beneath their trailer, depended just as precariously on his rattly one-ton flatbed and his gallant but battered pickup—depended beyond that on the whole web of the economy, a hodge-podge of precarious households like his own all clinging together to a vast electronic framework of information and a cultural faith in paper-thin symbols like Credit and Government.

This little bubble of light in this bathroom here, with a pink-cheeked girl in it, drowsing as she peed, was pinched between giant fingers of such chaotic circumstance!

So how the Christ could he have any misgivings at all about something that could net him seventy grand cash money for a fifteen-mile trip down the river with a twenty-pound load?

When he got back to bed Barbara had turned off the light and gotten under the covers.

"What it boils down to," she said to the ceiling, "is that I agree. In both cases we gotta take the risk. And the DaValli job—how illegal can a shed be? Even missing one wall? As far as the other . . . we're too close now to give up. I guess what bothers me is that you don't seem worried enough about it. Somehow it makes me worry even more!"

"But I am! Believe me, Barb, I worry about it!"

"Well, you don't *act* worried enough." She sat up suddenly and pounded her fist on his chest. "You're just such a *thick-necked oaf*"—she was punctuating the words with more blows—"with your *bump*kin expression, and you've *always* got a *beer-buzz* on!"

"Hey seriously, I'm really looking at cutting back on drinking."

"Then you must really know what it looks like by now. You've been looking at it for years!"

Above the main puzzle of Santa Marta's lights, the low eastern hills that backed the city were freckled with a fainter pox of residential lights, like the nimbus of stars above a galaxy's plane. Here Bev Carney kept a modest condo. (She would attend to the work of getting a serious dwelling once she had made her fortune a bit larger and more secure.)

In bed with her, Frankie DaValli, in that moment before ejaculation—that pause of inevitability—had the detached and wondering thought: *Christ! What a full day!*

And after the juicy fireworks of mutual release, the same thought came filtering down through his brain in fragments, all the deals made, the wheels started turning.

"I'm glad we did this immediately, aren't you?" Bev smiled down at him pausing, naked, on her way to the bathroom. "It clears the air. We see it in perspective and know it's not going to make any difference in the way we do business. I mean, for instance, were you intending to pitch a higher advance, along about now?"

"Not me. No way." He smiled, lying drowsy, head sunk in

the pillow. He watched her talk into the shower stall, the compact opulence of her little buttocks bunching with marvelous, easy muscularity.

Why bother to deal, after all? Was he captain of his ship? Mad Lazarian steered. Mad Lazarian said there "might be a way." Who was Frankie to tell mad Lazarian he was full of shit?

Before he even had time to marvel at his tiredness, he sank into sleep. He had hectic dreams full of loud, insistent: people. He was clutching a goblet or bowl to his chest, and all these urgent people wanted to pour him a drink, fill his bowl with something.

No! he kept protesting. The bowl was too small, no more would fit in it. Then he looked down into it and was stunned. It was *deep* in there. It had no bottom. It was just a hole full of distant stars.

Down in the light-puzzle's southeastern corner, Santa Marta's poorer fringe, Kim woke up, needing to pee. She struggled out of the doubled sleeping bags she was sharing with Alex on his friend Nelson Pogue's dirty living room rug. They shouldn't have had so much beer at Dad's office; she had checked her messages before meeting Alex there with her gear, and they knew Chip had work for them tomorrow.

She picked her way down the dark hall, bare feet cringing from the littered floor. She lifted the toilet lid and peed crouching above the bowl, knowing better than to risk contact in the bathroom of a house occupied by a young male slob. At least Earl was never here. They only expected to be here a few days, but she would probably do a little cleaning after work.

Cringing her way back across the millennial scuzz on the carpet, she stepped on something furry, bony, and alive, and missed a heartbeat before she realized it was Buster, Pogue's long-haired red cat, a brainlessly friendly animal who yelped, then instantly purred when she picked him up.

She got back in and laid him on top of the bag between her and the snoring Alex. It was nice to be lying down in a place where no one could find you. Not even Pogue knew yet—he hadn't been home since Alex had let them in with a key Pogue had given him long before.

Tomorrow's work would be outdoors, laying some kind of pipe. Daylit work, out in the hills . . . they more or less had to keep working for KleenCo till the next paycheck, both to finance their leaving town and not to seem alarmed, not to suggest by quick flight that they'd seen something dangerous for them to have seen.

When Kim considered that they really *hadn't* seen anything, that it was finally only their slow-to-wake fucking *consciences* kicking into gear, she felt pretty easy. They hadn't really made contact with the really bad side of whatever was happening at the shaft. Now, after a few days' sunny outdoor work, some cash in their pockets, she and Alex would be down south exploring L.A. together. Alex's personality needed some work, some guidance, but he was such a sweet guy at heart, one who could really laugh with you. It was going to be fun heading south with him. Things were turning out well, really, they were shaking off a bad, really negative involvement, getting out in the world . . .

It was only when she remembered that pale face in the window of the dark blue van that a sense of danger touched her again. Whoever that guy was, even though he'd been looking right into their rig's headlights, Kim felt his eyes had found her, had seen and known her, right down to the bone. Then she was glad of this harborage, however it stank. She stroked Buster's flat, bony head with her knuckles, and smiled to hear his ragged purr. Glad to have this place where she could lie unconscious while no one who meant her harm could find his way to her sleeping side.

The neighborhood of Pogue's house was poor and piece-meal, gapped with vacant lots. By one of these vacant lots, one street over from where Kim lay, Lazarian's blue van was parked. While he had sat looking from its window, he had enjoyed a clear view of Pogue's house across the lot between them, while the scant street lighting left the van in darkness to anyone look-ing out from the house. At present he lay on his bunk, eyes closed, headphones on—lay luxuriating in cool, high-ceilinged caverns of Gregorian plainsong.

He glided down sonorous corridors, soared up into shad-owy, echosome vaults. He rode the tide of somber male voices, sinuous tenor solos unspooling threads of liturgy, followed by basso unisons, phalanxed baritones surging like smooth surf through the caverns, then gentling down, then receding, drain-ing majestically away:

miser—e—re no-o-o-obis

Pure incantation, this music was! And what conviction in its simplicity. The Powers Beyond were *there* for the makers of this music. To them it was as plain as day that the Cosmos was a prop, was pillars and grained arches, ceilinged with false-painted infinities, and that overarching this Cosmos were vaster, realler ones, vault on vault of huger truths, and that a few gifted souls, strenuous souls burning with heartfelt desire, could break through, out into the grander Sky—could do this, in essence, by a kind of knotting of the soul into a single muscle that batters unceasingly at the hard, arched stone of the imprisoning world.

Lazarian's blows, all his ardent homicides, had at last broken a rift in the stone. And a Power had acknowledged him—reached through, and touched his senses!

But what was the protocol of reverence here? What precisely had he done that made the connection, and what must he do to deepen the bond? To win further revelation?

Man's first priests in their stone cases must have groped just as Lazarian was groping now to find the magical gesture, the idiom for conversation with the Powers.

Ah, for some text, some map of these deeps! But what Lazarian sensed here was a personality . . . the hellish slapstick of that wild-haired, outreaching silhouette! Wasn't there a cryptic mockery here?

Lazarian had intended all four men as sacrifices to the shaft, but before he could complete his sacrificial gesture with the second two, the Power had snatched their lives from his hands. Acknowledging him, yes, of course, but also taunting him, no?

His groping intuition told him meekness was not called for. Why not give it the life of one of its servants then? One of these two children who brought its poison substance to it? Would that boldness, that touch of defiance please it? He could not know. It was left to him to improvise.

Done then. When guessing, do it fluidly, without hesitation. These children would be working for the next few days, helping something else along that Lazarian sensed held far more magic than their little lives. The various elements, he saw, could all be scheduled quite handily.

Nine

Santa Marta got some of its hottest days at the summer's end. Willy had gotten to the site by six, and by nine, as he finished straightening his foundation ditches with a shovel, he had a sweat going. He was heading to the water when he saw DaValli's Trans Am come jouncing in on the rough road-cut through the trees. He threw a wave in its direction and knelt by the water; planting his hands in it, he bowed and thrust his head in.

To his left, unnoted by him, delicate black filaments were streaming up from the gravelly bottom. Barely visible, and only in the right angle of sunlight, the leakage looked like smoke from some buried combustion beneath the lake bottom.

"That musta been refreshing! Looks like you're going great guns here, Willy!"

"We'll have her whupped in no time, Frankie. Beer?" Willy thought DaValli might like some authentic blue-collar slang. The guy was so So-Cal, so Hollywood himself. He finger-combed his hair back to drip coolingly down his spine, and broke out two beers.

"Thanks," Frankie said. "You a fan of the Roadrunner?"

"My daughter is. Actually I always kinda root for the coyote. The underdog and all."

"Me too." And Frankie looked a little coyote-ish as he said it, Willy thought. "So what are we lookin at, schedule-wise?" Frankie asked.

"Well, depending on a couple of ifs——" and he proceeded to explain factors controlling his finish date. But once Frankie had gathered that it would be in about a week, his attention seemed to wander.

"Do you hear that?" he broke in after a moment. "That sound something like a radio?"

"You know . . . I do hear something."

"And *smell* something? Like garbage?"

"Yeah, as a matter of fact. Coming from downshore there, I think."

"It's funny, there's nothing down that shore for a good quarter-mile."

"That's right." Willy had fished almost everywhere off of the shoreline when he was a kid. "You wanna go take a look?"

They were already moving that way, Frankie not seeming quite aware that he was leading them down the beach, his eyes looking vaguely troubled. "Yeah," he said, "why not?"

Below Frankie's parcel the shoreline retreated into a deep cove that was densely crowded with trees and vegetation. A small creek entered the lake here; blackberry vines and poison oak webbed the oaks and bays and willows that jammed the cleft. As they rounded the shore's curve into the cove, Frankie said, "I don't remember a path here; I walked this parcel all over when I bought it."

"Looks pretty well established," Willy said. The path of bald packed earth cut through the grass along the bank and plunged into the cove's lush shadows, which whined with wide-awake mosquitos even in full day. Pausing before he led them down it, Frankie said,

"That's definitely a radio I hear."

Willy nodded, sniffing. "And that's definitely garbage . . . and smoke."

"There's no houses around here, no structures at all. I was offshore in a boat, studying the site."

Frankie was leading them into the cove now, the mosquitoes' whine stitching itself through the radio's noise, which seemed to be partly static and white noise, mixed with fragments of words, twinges of music—as if the radio were tuned between stations. The smell shifted, though there was no movement in the air. It seemed to come in gusts, from differing directions.

They neared a curve in the path, saw the vegetation opening out just ahead. Just as they stepped into the clearing, the roar of a beast exploded right beside them. It stunned them, a volcano of stench and noise opening right at their feet. A huge sow confronted them, huge and half-feral, her back crested with bristles, her lower canines beginning to thrust out in tusks.

Her forelegs were splayed and planted, her rage coming from her huge throat in waves, a guttural baying; a reddish snotlike mess drizzled from her muzzle, and her eyes glared blind yellow light. She stood there, volleying at them her deep porcine bark. She must have weighed four hundred pounds.

A large, gutted carcass, an animal too torn to identify at once—a calf? a large dog?—lay in front of her. They had interrupted her breakfast.

Beyond her spread a trash-heaped yard, and within this zone of trash, an old two-story house. Even as they took it in, edging slowly back from the sow, something huge erupted from the front door out onto the porch. This shape bellowed, in a voice that dwarfed and extinguished the beast's

"SHEBA! SHUT UP!"

It was a huge woman wearing an extravagantly besmirched and smudged mu-mu that, under the grime, had a blue-and-green floral print. The sow snorted, spraying red slime on the carcass, wheeled and trotted ponderously away into the trash, and disappeared into some burrow in the debris.

The woman boomed again, this time at the two men:

"Come on up!"

The trash lay in reeking dunes before the house, smoldering

here and there, and sending up black filaments of foul smoke. It couldn't be walked around—the vegetation meshed with its borders. One of the strange things to both men afterwards was that they went forward at all, but at that moment the unreality of the scene drew them to test it. They stepped into it as if it might disappear once their feet touched it.

It wasn't the relatively clean trash country houses accumulate—old furniture, vehicle parts, junk lumber. It was all these and all else, sticky virulent trash, smashed bottles and cans oozing ancient food, leaky buckets of crankcase drainage, thinner, and spoiled housepaint, ancient split-bellied, gut-spilling trashbags of immemorial rinds, grinds wipes, and leavings.

It rose in peaks and sank in hollows. They had to choose their footing carefully, move teetering across random planks and shards of lumber. The huge woman stood staring from her porch, radio squawking incomprehensibly on the rail beside her.

"Man," Willy whispered to Frankie as they teetered their way towards her. "The perfect neighbor."

Frankie could only gape with disbelief. Two weeks ago there had been nothing here. This big house's gables poked well above the trees, and he would have seen it from his rented boat. He had studied the shore with binoculars, for Christ's sake—believing back then that drainage into the lake was an exciting possibility, and not the blatant madness he had since come to see it was.

The house was of heavy redwood beams and siding, bleached with sun, stained with mold and lichen. All its windows were glassless, curtained with rags, and the whole structure crouched low to the earth with a centuried sag. Plainly, it had been here forever.

The woman stood on the porch, watching them approach, though it didn't seem exactly like watching—the stoniness of her black eyes made their aim uncertain. The stench here was shifty, coming in gusts, though there was no breeze, the flavor of its foulness changing with each gust. The noise of her radio was shifty too—it muttered almost-phrases, bursts of . . . warning? Mockery? Utterances that almost crossed the threshold of intelligibility, just failing to cohere, to be deciphered.

Now they stood below the porch, looking up at her, both of them feeling vaguely tranced, as if their tricky approach had been some kind of complex genuflection, and they now stood at the shrine of a huge, solemn idol, dizzied by its incense, awaiting its will.

Her hair hung in lank black snakes beside her pale face, with its stern and regular features of a handsome country woman gone abundantly to fat. A wen beside her nose, swollen and angry looking, seemed the token of some secret vulcanism in her quiescent mass.

Willy glanced at Frankie, but his tongue appeared to have frozen. "Excuse us, ma'am," Willy said. "We didn't know anyone lived in here."

She gave him her eyes, and he remembered being a boy in the DeYoung Museum and looking up into the black eyes of the Kodiak bear in its diorama. Impenetrable eyes, seeing icy spans of space and time far beyond his small self. "I'm Willy Yakima," he added, his voice cracking slightly, "and this is Frankie DaValli, your, ah, neighbor over on this side here."

The radio muttered in her answering silence. To both men it seemed Willy's words were still traveling to reach her across the vastnesses her eyes surveyed. Her voice, when it came, enveloped them in mellow resonance.

"Howdy, neighbors. I'm Mamie Durtt."

Frankie realized that his jaw was hanging. Standing in this smoking filth heap was like sniffing glue! Where had this incredible pig-woman come from? Why was she suddenly given to *him* to deal with? Wasn't his life strange enough? Up at the shaft, he had Sol Lazarian. Now, down here, this! He mastered himself with an effort.

"Hello, Mamie. We just, ah, heard your radio, came to pay our respects. And, well, I guess we'll get on back to work now."

Her stillness was perfect. It seemed unbelievable that she should ever have spoken.

They turned and began to pick their way back across the dunes, Frankie still marveling at the strangeness of his recent fortunes. And as he ginger-footed forward, a snatch of song crackled out of the radio behind them, a husky contralto singing a stately verse of blues:

> *Momma Durtt get you*
> *By de-grees,*
> *She jus take hold*
> *An' squeeze an squeeeeze . . .*

He almost lost his balance, windmilling his arms, looking sharply to Willy to see if he'd heard . . . but heard what, exactly? The words were already melting out of shape in his memory. A moment later, he couldn't recall what it was thought he'd heard.

They regained the path and plunged down it, and as the unbelievable place was swallowed up by the vegetation behind them, a great, enveloping bubble of hallucination seemed to burst. They looked at each other unbelievingly.

"Jesus!" said Willy. "That is one strange, humongous woman!"

"Did you hear, like, a verse of a song from the radio? As we were leaving?"

Willy's pale eyes clouded with an effort at recollection. "It's hard to be sure what I heard. I mean, I can't even quite believe I *saw* that place!"

"Yeah."

Ten

Boldness, Morris Hacker thought, brushing his hair. Granted it was not a major feature of his life. You didn't get to be the manager of a major municipal installation, like the Lago Puro Wastewater Treatment Plant, by being wild-natured. You did it by buckling down to those books and passing those exams at the top of the field every time.

But he had always felt himself to be a man of will and intensity. A man with boldness in him, who had just happened not to have used boldness as a life-strategy, but who could be bold at the hour of need. He was slender, small-featured, with gray-green eyes, and it was his little vanity to feel that, appearance-wise, he looked neat and fierce. He brushed his smoothly barbered hair this morning feeling just that—neat and fierce.

Most people saw in him a man who was undeniably neat—never without a tie, for instance—but cold and shy, rather than fierce. And while on social occasions he privately felt that most people would perceive a physical mismatch between himself and his wife Marjorie, most actually felt her gangly grace and beaky charm made her at least as attractive as her cold, shy husband.

This morning, since he was not going in to the plant till after his early lunch date with Marv Straff, he had rolled over and said to her, "Marjie, what say we knock off a nice juicy little piece?" Hacker felt entitled to speak plainly and firmly to his wife on a large number of subjects, but this formula was the only touch of poetry he used with her.

They'd done it doggie-style, she smelling sweetly of her skin cream and warm sheets, he driving her to her unmusical orgasmic bleat, which he loved to wring out of her. The whole thing had been perfect. Neat and fierce.

Now she was reading in bed. Marjorie tended to lie low mornings and evenings when Hacker was home, under the pretext of a mild hypochondriac routine they had worked out over years to their mutual satisfaction. This way she was spared all the instructions and detailed advice she would get doing any kind of task with Morris around; she kept her nightstand cluttered with tissues and antihistamines and read Elmore Leonard and John D. MacDonald until he was out of the house.

He brought her a cup of coffee and took his own out onto the patio. The beauty of his lawn and his flowers, which he always relished, was like an intoxicant this morning, foretelling him the splendor of his new and larger home, once he bought it. Half a million dollars, soon to be his. There was the real intoxicant!

And not just because it would be his, but because it showed him the sphere of power his co-conspirators had raised him to. People of city-making stature, whose hands shifted millions on the game-board of life. As Bev Carney had said to him at that charming dinner they had had with Jake and Dave, "When the system breaks down around us, Morris"—she was referring to the moratorium that had frozen all new construction in the city—"when the system breaks down, it's *always* that handful of bold individuals who aren't afraid to take inspired shortcuts—it's always that bold few who save the situation."

Intoxicating, yes, to enter the sphere of such people, to rise above the mire of politics, where special-interest groups could push everyone around by casting blame, like all the counterculture types down on the river, shouting pollution till the slavish state officials submissively wagged their tails and declared a moratorium. . . .

He realized that Duke had not yet come out to join him, which normally he would have done as soon as he'd heard his master open the patio door.

Duke was his big Doberman, a hundred and ten pounds of trim solid dogmeat, pruned of ears and tail, most definitely neat and fierce—though trained to the proper cringing Doberman affection towards Morris himself. At everyone, every*thing* else, Duke barked. A young, vigorous, powerfully vocal dog, and mean as hell. Morris loved Duke.

"Duke! Here, boy! Come on, Duke!"

He waited. The flap door in the side of the garage should have banged by now, and he should be hearing the hustle and pant of Duke's approach as the dog rounded the farther corner of the house. Instead, silence.

But with his senses focused in that direction, his nose caught a whiff of something. Dogshit? There, he caught it again, rank and definite. Morris began to suspect there was a reason for Duke's reticence this morning. He rose. Moving with an ominous poise, he followed the flagstone path to the garage-side of the house.

And as he stepped around into the side yard, which extended to the rear wall of his garage, outrage punched Morris Hacker right between the eyes. He beheld an unholy mess.

Closest to him was the mess he'd smelled: a fecal heap, shockingly large, which lay near a huge hole that had been broken through his honeysuckle-draped fence of redwood slats. But the dung and the hole weren't all. All the plantings along the house wall and the garage's rear wall—the marigolds, the tulips, the lupins—had been uprooted. They lay on the lawn, broken and tangled in a long columnar grave of exploded garden soil. Morris was speechless and, for several heartbeats, breathless. Then he stormed up to the hole in his fence. The shattered slats and torn vines were doubly stupefying: how could he have failed to hear this? As for the mess nearby, it was unlike Duke's usual product—a dog owner, after all, got to know these things. More than that, the sheer volume of it was appalling. An odd detail in the mess snagged his eye briefly, but the ruin of his flowers was already dragging him over that way, grinding his teeth at the sheer wanton thoroughness of the damage. Not one flower was left replantable—each individually savaged to pieces!

There was such a monstrous completeness about this little orgy of destruction. Fence-chewing, flower-mauling, and yard-crapping—the full complex of puppy crimes. As if some massive fit of regression had seized the intensively trained Duke in the night and sent him, crazed with the spirit of disobedience, out into the moonlight to pillage, maim, and befoul.

Duke *was* young, his puppyhood not far behind him. He tried hard, but he was a very high-strung dog. None of this thawed a spot of mercy in Morris's icy rage. He strode to the garage's rear door. Duke had good reason to be so quiet in there, to be huddled way in under the very center of one of the cars, where he undoubtedly was, taking vain shelter from retribution. Because Morris was going to beat the living crap out of that dog, if there could possibly be any left in him.

He thrust the door open and lunged inside, roaring: "Duke!" His heel squirted out from under him and he fell almost flat on his back to the floor, miraculously saving skull and spine from the concrete with a back-thrust arm.

He sat up, his stunned arm sticky, dripping. Had he gashed it? No. No, he'd soaked it in the puddle he had slipped on—the puddle he was *sitting* in right now. A wide, foul, red puddle that spanned this whole corner of the garage. And he wasn't the only thing sitting in it, either. No. There were parts of *Duke* in it too. There, for instance, was Duke's head, half-stripped to the skull.

This lay companionably near, but not connected to, a piece of Duke's spine. In fact, this puddle—Morris grasped it now—this puddle *was* Duke.

Morris Hacker did not spring howling to his feet. He did this mentally, so to speak, his mind struggling to tear itself free from this impossibility, but the utter strangeness of it so matched his outrage that the net effect was like a moment of musing calm.

Morris's second dressing of the morning was a dazed and uncertain affair. It felt like someone else's skin he scrubbed and shoved into clean clothes. Marjorie came dazedly in and out of the bathroom, bringing him materials for his reassembly, and her squawks of amazement helped him. Each time she cried, "I can't *believe* this! Who would *do* such a thing!?" Morris's anger got another degree stronger than his shock. Her dismay focused him.

"'*Who*'? Marge? '*Who*'? Are you serious? It was some kind of animal! Could you bring me *both* shoes, please? . . . Thank you. Just get a grip on yourself and look up the number for Animal Control—County Government listings, front of the book."

Fully suited, a second cup of coffee before him as he took up the phone, he felt himself again, but his talk with Animal Control, the succession of idiots he had to re-explain things to and who couldn't quite *grasp* the situation he described, left his head buzzing, by the time he hung up, with the fact that *he* still couldn't quite grasp it either. He left Marjorie with instructions to call the police and get an incident report taken—Duke was covered and the insurance company would want the report. He left looking calm and intrepid for her, but not feeling it, and went out by the back to have a last look at the mess that was to await the authorities' scrutiny untouched. There in the fecal heap was that detail he had glimpsed: a little cluster of three black-padded toes with long nails. A piece of one of Duke's paws.

In a hilly residential neighborhood resembling Morris Hacker's, but of more expensive homes built somewhat higher in the hills, Aurora Hurtado was washing the glass doors that opened onto the deck of the Sawyer residence.

The late morning sun was at her back, and with each stroke of her squeegee she cut a swath of her mirrored self from the blur of suds: a small, nut-brown woman with a seamed little monkey-face that supported big black horn-rimmed glasses. A red scarf, knotted under her chiseled little chin, cocooned her hair, which was like tarnished silver, with a lot of black still in it despite her more than seventy years (the exact year of her birth was unknown to her).

Also mirrored in the doors were the deck behind her, and the back yard's wide green lawn bordered with flowers.

And it was back there, somewhere in the yard behind her, that something was starting to bite at her.

It was quite definite now, the bite, *la picadura*. This had been her term for it all her life, this minute subliminal itch, like an ant nipping her deep in the brainstem.

She kept wiping the glass. When these solicitations came, these little manifestations of the Hidden, they were not to be pursued. Whether you had been seeking them, through the use of herbal magic or prayer, or they came unsought, like this one, you had to let them grow strong, reach for you. You must begin by ignoring them.

The phone shrilled. Aurora pulled aside the door and stepped into the kitchen. Extensions multiplied its noise throughout the sunny, white-carpeted interior of the three-quarter mil house.

It was *la duena* herself, Mrs. Sawyer, calling. Meagan, the Sawyers' obsequious golden retriever, came panting up to meet Aurora at the phone.

"Hi, Aurora!"

"Hello, Mrs. Sawyer."

"Put me down to Meagan, would you?"

Stoically, Aurora held the receiver to the dog's ear, while Mrs. Sawyer talked baby-talk to her. As it invariably did on these occasions, the dog's tail wagged.

"Did she wag her tail when she heard my voice?" Mrs. Sawyer asked. Aurora answered as she always did.

"No, Mrs. Sawyer. Perhaps the fault was mine, and I was holding the instrument insufficiently close to the animal's ear."

"Well, I'm just checking to see if Debra called." Debra Durkin was Mrs. Sawyer's slightly less rich, slightly less attractive sidekick.

"Yours is the first call I've taken today, Mrs. Sawyer."

"Well, if she calls, please remind her we're meeting Dave Shugg and his friends at the club this afternoon. And Nick says to bring her appetite, because he's getting the makings for a major barbecue back at the house." Nick was her husband, Nick Sawyer, one of the five county supervisors. "Did you see my note about the briquettes and fluid?"

"Yes, you have all the necessary materials in the shed, and the Webber is set up on the deck."

She spoke calmly, though now the *picadura* was gnawing her, plucking at her, giving her that delicate headache that marked its higher levels of intensity. When she stood out on the deck again she felt it giving her a distinct directional signal. Over in that corner of the yard. Was that some tiny turmoil in the lawn's fabric? She approached it.

A mole, half socketed in the soil, was writhing, digging blindly at the sky with the blunt little shovels of its forepaws. Its throat rippled, working at the unswallowable gulletful of death.

The gardener had poisons out for everything. But this was a Sending; she had unmistakably felt it reaching for her. Her spine felt as if cold flames were licking up and down it.

From one of the Velcro-sealed sleeve-pockets at her specially sewn workshirt she took her two-inch lock-back Buck knife. Holding the mole's silken, tapered little muzzle firm with her left hand, she slit its throat with one precisely sufficient stroke of the honed blade.

This was a small messenger from the earth, although its message was not yet intelligible to her. She must send it back, with her acknowledgment. Only if she made an answering gesture could the revelation proceed. Luckily the means were at hand.

She unlidded the great domed Webber and laid the mole on its grill. She went to her battered '65 Dodge Dart and got her knapsack, which contained, among much else, all the essential ceremonial herbs.

It was a pity to lose this job, to offend the Sawyers, who had never offered her any discourtesy. Two of Aurora's grand-nieces, Graciela and Lucina, owned the quite successful little domestic employment agency that had placed her with this county supervisor and could place her again within a day. The California rich loved to hire domestics who spoke flawless English with charming accents. Aurora only worked at all to be out and about among people. She had lodging and spending money thrust on her by five different households of her many energetic, prosperous kin in the Santa Marta area alone. Even more of her extended family vied for her tenancy of their homes down in San Francisco, though down there was too far from the hills for Aurora's taste.

She opened the knapsack—tough woven llama's wool dyed with a rainbow pattern bleached and smudged by years in the field—on the deck by the Webber. She pulled out a big leathern herb-wallet. She dressed the mole with the appropriate aromatics and astringents, speaking appropriate phrases; she wove it a tiny necklet of thyme to collar its gaping throat. She used kindling from the wood-box, drenching the split oak with starter fluid.

It smoked and sizzled in the flames. As it burned, no scent of cooked meat came from it. Instead it gave off a piercing chemical stench. Aurora recognized this stench. There could be no mistaking it for another.

She'd been at her niece Aida's house and Aida's grandson Alejandro had driven up, run over to give Aurora a kiss where she was gardening in the front yard, and run inside—probably to borrow something from his grandmother. A complex and deeply disturbing scent had faintly clung to the boy, and it also wafted delicately from his pickup truck. She'd gone over and poked her head in the truck. The boy's work gloves on the seat . . . they reeked of it.

She'd inquired into his work, had a talk with him a few days later. These materials you are handling, she told him, there is something worse than poisonous about them. Something evil.

She hadn't been wrong then. The mole was now a smoking rack of bones. The smoke rose in a greasy black braid till an upper breeze unraveled it and tugged it in fragments to the west, the hills where Alejandro was still working around that shaft.

This was an unmistakable warning, but she did not yet feel that inner sigh, that slackening of relief that comes when one's contact with the Hidden has ended. She stood waiting, heart and mind still open, but unwillingly so. This was something very big, and she was not done with learning of it yet, and she was afraid, and feeling suddenly that she was too old, too worn by years of strenuous life, to bear fear like this, to face something as big, and as evil, as this.

What was that sound she was hearing?

Very faint. A soft, muted buzzing? Yes. Inside the house, wasn't it?

The glass door rumbled softly aside. All the kitchen's polished white surfaces freckled, measeled with buzzing blacknesses. The room swarmed with flies.

In the middle sat Meagan. The dog was covered with flies, wearing a second fur of flies. Their shiny legions coruscated up and down her flanks, and yet the dog sat quite calmly. She noticed Aurora's attention and thumped the floor with a friendly tail, scattering black buzzing clouds, and her happy tongue slid out to pant, flies quickly clustering to it, blackening its pink.

Aurora came slowly into the room, fighting her almost overmastering urge to flee. She leaned close to the dog, flies striking her face and hands in a meaty little hailstorm, and studied the animal's coat.

Under its seethe of flies, working inside the reddish fur, was a busy, glittering whiteness. Maggots working in the dog's skin, maggots which Aurora saw swelling, darkening, metamorphosing without pupal interval into adult flies.

Meagan weakly thumped her tail, seeming cheerful, but tired. Aurora backed out of the kitchen and thrust the glass door shut.

She was sorry for the Sawyers—but in some way this touched them personally, or these sendings would not have come to her here. She was sorry for the Sawyers, but now she would have to look after her own.

Eleven

Driving through his neighborhood towards the freeway, Morris Hacker tried to imagine a bear ambling down its gently curving streets, past the handsomely landscaped yards.

What else could have devoured something as big and fierce as Duke, never mind asking how it could have done it so silently? But a bear was unimaginable here. There were brushy slopes above the neighborhood, you got raccoons, possums, sure, skunks, deer . . . but a *bear?*

Pulling up onto 101, his shiny new Civic felt more than usually light and frail. Big semis bellowed past, and gravel trucks with double trailers heaped with the takings from the Ross River's bed. Construction was frozen in Santa Marta, but everywhere else it was booming. The gravel trucks raged south and north to the concrete batch-plants, shedding inch-and-a-half blue shale, real windshield-crackers.

Hacker's steering felt skittish in the wind of their wakes, and his heart too ran skittishly. A primitive equation was forming in the back of his brain: Duke's half-stripped skull lying a-tilt in ponded blood, Duke Morris's bold and fanged protector, equaled *Morris's* skull a-tilt in ponded blood.

No rationalization could cover the horror of that backyard holocaust. That . . . bowel movement with part of Duke's paw in it was deeply unsettling—had Duke's devourer dallied in Morris Hacker's yard long enough for a fragment of its meal to go the length of its guts? Why hadn't he or Marjorie *heard* anything? What the hell had *done* this to him?

Coffee Joe's was crowded, the air dense with conversations, the music of silverware, and a heavy traffic of food aromas. Hacker's stomach shifted uneasily. From a table in the back, Marv Straff waved him over. His burly subordinate was just tucking away a last mouthful from a gravied plate. Hacker joined him.

"I got too hungry to wait, but don't worry, you won't be eating alone, Morris—I got another roast beef sandwich on its way."

"Fine—I'm not terribly hungry anyway." Hacker smiled thinly. Already he felt the tension of Straff's unvoiced question, about whether their "project" was to proceed this weekend. The question was there, just behind the genial wrinklings of Straff's sunburned brow. And in himself Hacker felt, not this morning's boldness, but hesitation. Doubt.

He discovered that somewhere between his fall in the garage and here, his answer for Straff at this meeting had metamorphosed from yes into no. DaValli, after all, *had* to be more thoroughly checked into. The weekend after this would be soon enough for Fletcher to put in the hidden out-take valve.

Straff would normally have come right to the question, but he must have sniffed his boss' latent opposition and was making small talk.

"So ya didn't bring an appetite?"

"Not much, actually."

"If you wanna go light, they got wonderful Danishes here." Straff lit a filterless Camel and inhaled with relish. The waitress brought his open-face sandwich, and he gobbled a few more drags of the cigarette before adding its butt to several others in the ashtray. Hacker ordered a Danish and watched Hacker chow down.

It dazed Hacker slightly, watching Straff's fork lift dribbly gobbets to his wide, robustly toothed mouth. The waitress set in front of him a sweet roll with a little eye of jam at its center.

Suddenly the horror Hacker had just suffered had to come out. He needed to have his outrage shared, and soothed.

"Marv"—Hacker heard, but did not care, the naked bleat pain in his own voice—"something ate my dog last night, Marv!"

For just a beat, Straff stared at him, frozen in mid-mastication. But there was no mistaking the sincerity of Hacker's words. A laugh exploded from Straff, hurling before it a brown bolus of macerated bread and gravy.

The missile adhered with a *splop* to the top of Hacker's sweet roll, just half an inch offsides of the red bullseye.

Straff manfully fought down his laughter, but it took a while. "I'm *sorry* . . . Christ, Morris . . . it's just the way you *sprang* that on me!"

"I'd love to be laughing with you," Hacker said bitterly, laying his napkin like a shroud over his polluted roll. "Now, as to what we're here to discuss——"

"Wait now, you gotta explain this. Something literally *ate* your dog? I mean, that's dreadful, what could possibly——"

Hacker waved dismissal. "It's a personal matter, I shouldn't even have mentioned it. As for this weekend's business, I think it'll just have to wait a week, for reasons we've been discussing."

Straff made a good-natured shrug of surrender and began to cut a new bite of his sandwich. Hacker felt off-balanced by the lack of resistance.

Straff sensed this. "You know my views," he said, chewing, "but it's your call. I'll pass it on to Fletch—I'll be outta town for the weekend, since it's not going ahead." It was worked out; he would leave a message, Fletcher would miss it, and the out-take would go in.

Watching Straff eat was still a little sickening. Hacker sipped some water. He sensed a subtle scorn in the ease of Straff's acceptance, and he itched to justify himself.

"We just *can't* take this DaValli at his word, without checking out——" Setting his glass down smartly, he hit the rim of the ashtray, which flipped and catapulted its contents. A blanket of ashes, studded with butts, settled across Straff's plate,

Hacker's laugh was a head-turning bray. Good-natured Straff managed to laugh too, shrouding his plate so now it matched Hacker's. "I can't believe the day I'm having. I get out of the car in the lot here? The wind blows a candy wrapper covered with melted chocolate right against my pant leg. I've got this big brown smear on my shin now."

They left a large tip to atone for the mess. Outside, crossing the parking lot, Straff said, "DaValli's site is the old Quicksilver Cinnabar Mine. Not to worry about storage space—whoa!" His heel skidded out from under him. He pinwheeled his arms and just barely stayed on his feet.

"God damn it!" he roared, looking down, last shreds of good nature gone. "Dogshit!"

"Boy, what a heap of it you stepped in!" said Hacker, with delight and awe. "You even got some in your laces!"

"Hey," said Straff, brightening, "you stepped in it too. It's all over your heel there!"

Aurora drove out of the hills, curving past lovely, wide-lawned homes. The road felt restive, sinewy, an earth-snake angry under her wheels. Steering required full concentration. She still had that delicate headache that came with the *picadura* when it was protracted—a hollow, brittle feeling, as if her skull was a light-bulb, ready to pop.

The nearest payphones were in the lot of the Safeway at the foot of the hills. She nosed her Dart, her trusty old mule of a car, into a slot among the more colorful, upscale cars of the neighborhood. She wanted very much to go into the store for some cold beer, which would be a perfect medicine for her nerves just now. No time must be lost in warning Alejandro, however, and the girl working with him—Kimberly, was it?

She called his grandmother Aida, who reported that when she had tried Alejandro's number this morning, an inarticulate young man with a hangover had told her Alex was staying somewhere else for a little white, he didn't know where.

Hanging up, Aurora consulted her memory, which contained the vast archives of the names and faces of her extended family. Wasn't Kimberly the daughter of Lucky Morales? An Anglo woman who had married the son-in-law of one of Aurora's nephews . . . Rodolfo was his name, a good man, hard worker until the pesticides got him. Kimberly's last name wasn't Morales, being by Lucky's second marriage . . . but yes, Lucky herself was still close friends with Lupe, the sister-in-law of Emma, one of Aurora's granddaughters!

Aurora called Lupe, remembering Lucky quite clearly a big friendly woman with a grating laugh, drinking beer at family barbecues. When she reached Emma, it turned out Lucky was there visiting.

"Hi, Abuelita!" Lucky foghorned in a voice haunted by cigarettes past. Abuelita was what all her kin called her whatever their precise relationship.

"Lucky, I must talk to your daughter Kimberly. Do you have her number?"

"You bet, hon." And she started to recite it, when Aurora interrupted. "Lucky, does Kimberly drive an old gray van?"

"That's right, an Econoline."

"I am calling from a payphone at a Safeway, and I think she just pulled into the lot. Would you like to speak with her, as long as we have this connection?" It was a courtesy instinctive among those who have been mothers.

"Matter of fact, I do, hon. I wanna be sure she's coming to the city planning meeting about the new dump."

"Then hold the line, dear, and I'll bring her to the phone."

She stepped away from the boothlet and called the girl.

Kim turned at her call—everyone in the lot did, people in bright clothes and Ray-Bans.

"Kimberly!"

Kim *knew* that old woman with the heavy black horn-rims— she got surer as she got closer.

"Lucky, your mother, is on the phone, dear. She would like to talk with you, and then, so would I."

Kim felt a dark little qualm of superstition. How had this woman done this?

"Mom?"

"Hi, sweetie!"

"Jesus Christ, Mom, how did you know where I *was?*"

Aurora suggested they do their shopping together. She would get some beer, and then they could sit down and drink it and talk.

Though the girl was friendly, Aurora sensed that she was uneasy at this sudden intimacy. But as she walked the aisles with her, she was unable to make conversation that would put the child at ease. Her headache had grown sharp and probing, and dizziness teased at her equilibrium. All the ferocious colors in a supermarket! And the smells—these especially assailed her, the faint background reek of disinfectant everywhere, the bitter/sour tang of cockroach poison billowing out on the underbelly of the bakery's aromas, and near the meat lockers, the spoiled, menstrual whiff beneath the smell of fresh carnage.

But over and above all these there was a king-stench—light but pervasive—that penetrated every other smell, and which she could not identify. Aurora was keeping a hand on the cart for steadiness now and was feeling very bad—all the sinews in her taut old body felt like hot wires, and her heart was drumming, drumming, drumming.

They had reached the produce section when Kim, noticing, stopped. She put a hand on her shoulder—bird light and monkey-tough, the little shoulder felt. "You're sweating. Are you all right?"

"Do you smell that? Do you hear that?" For now she was beginning to hear a buzzing noise—something distinct from the fluorescents, which sawed away distinctly in her sensitized ears. This other buzzing had a scraping whine in it, like dry fiddle-strings. Then she turned slightly and saw.

"Dios y Diablos!" It was torn from her. A little girl nearby shrilled:

"Momm-e-e-e! The cantaloupes! They're getting all slimy!"

The pyramid of melons was caving in at the apex. The fruit wasn't falling from the table—it was putrefying, blackening, and collapsing at astonishing speed. This collapsing crown of decay wept a stinking, pallid pus that streamed sizzling down like acid on the underlying fruit, which sizzled and smoked.

A circle of stunned, gaping shoppers surrounded it, eyes tearing at the stench. A man vomited loudly all over his cartful of groceries, which caused an instantaneous reflex-vomiting in the woman next to him.

Kim stood with her jaw hanging, and a slender hand gripped her arm like pincers. "Loves?" Aurora moaned. "Do you see it?"

"Jesus, yes!"

But Aurora realized that she did not see it—not the fly the size of a large dog that was perched on the collapsing pyramid.

Its bristled sponge of a tongue sopped the putrescence. The fluorescent lights smeared hellish rainbows of diffraction across its great red eye-globes. Everyone else here saw the decay, but this was for Aurora alone.

And the moment she understood this, the fly vanished.

And the putrefaction ceased, leaving the pyramid half destroyed. Aurora was sweating heavily now, but she knew it was over. Her headache was gone, her heart, already, was beginning to slow.

The other shoppers were looking at one another, trading their amazement. A woman raised the timid question: "Pesticides?"—and raised a storm of nervous laughter at the incongruity. Aproned help arrived with mops. The sick were gently parted from their carts and helped away.

They were a quarter of an hour getting through the checkstand, where stunned conversations raged. They went to Kim's van. Aurora rested on the back seat, her legs up, drinking her beer savoringly but steadily, and opening a second bottle before she said anything.

"I came here to find you by phone, and you showed up. And now we have witnessed this in the market together. It was a warning of danger. It was for everyone, and I think the danger is a very great one. But it was also a warning specifically to us."

Kim had turned the pivoting driver's seat to face her guest, and now with her toes she gently swiveled herself left, right, left. "When I was watching those melons rotting? You know, of course I thought my eyes were tricking me . . . but I thought I saw something, like, standing on the melons. This black shape, about this big"—she held her hands at a goodly spread—"that I couldn't quite make out."

Aurora looked at her for a moment, nodding gently. "My poor dear," she said. "There are so very many difficult lessons still ahead of you. Because I think you have been given a touch of the Gift. But whether or not you will pursue it, I think that you and I, in the immediate future, are meant to work together."

Twelve

At the club Nick Sawyer nagged Dave Shugg and Jake Beaker to give him a game of tennis. His afternoon partner had been called away when they'd barely started.

"One thing I hate, guys, it's *tennis interruptus*. Look—play me two on one, you only gotta cover a half-court each. Come on. You could use the exercise"—a slight pause here, letting it dangle but stopping short of comment on the shape the two older men were in—"work up some appetite for our barbecue."

Sawyer, in his shorts and tennis shirt, was tall, tan, robust, being jolly, giving it a lot of body language, showing them how in shape he was.

It really burned Shugg. For Jake—sallow, puffy, smiling listlessly as he sipped his Scotch, the challenge was a joke. Shugg himself didn't even know the rules of tennis. He'd love to thrash the ass off this smiling, booming yuppie goon, but his gut and his tired old legs didn't stand a chance.

Sawyer knew it and this was basically business, of course, part of the ego-sparring you did before sitting down to the dealing table, weaken the other guy's status any way that came handy— Shugg had done it plenty himself over the years. What galled him about this Nick Sawyer, Second District County Supervisor, was that when you stripped off all the bells and whistles, what he *was* was a realtor. That was how he'd made his little pile and bought his way into the political club. Realtors were necessary, of course, even essential, but they were still basically people who pimped the houses that the real *creators* like himself had built.

"Tell ya what," he told Sawyer. "I don't even know the rules, like I say. But I'll go get Bev. She at least *likes* the silly game."

Bev was over in the spa with Shawna Sawyer, Nick's wife, and Debra Durkin, Shawna's slightly less rich, slightly less attractive sidekick. Shugg sent a messenger into the women's Jacuzzi room. Bev came out in a robe.

"Sawyer wants to kick some butt on the tennis court. I told him you played a little."

She nodded and went back in. She came out in five minutes in court gear, including the racquet she kept in her locker. While in college, Bev Carney had weighed a pro career as a serious option, before deciding on the MBA.

"What's your call on it, Dave?" she asked, smiling slightly, already guessing what Shugg wanted. She got straight to the gist of business, Shugg thought—you had to give her that.

"I think you should saw his legs off."

"Total humiliation."

"Yeah. With a guy like this, I think, bottom line, it'll make him cheaper."

In response to their initial feelers, the developers had gotten indications of willingness from Sawyer with a half-million price tag. They had all felt he could be had for less.

Considering, Bev said, "I think you're right. I'll take the gloves off."

She aced him, shut him out, whatever the hell you called it. The scoring was incomprehensible to Shugg. All he knew was that whenever there was a trade of shots, it was brief and always ended with Sawyer lurching and scrambling and failing to reach the ball, which invariably struck inside his court before escaping.

At first, Sawyer put on a reasonably fair imitation of loud, good-natured amazement at her prowess. He ended sweaty and grim, legs trembling slightly, and you could see how hard he had to work to get a shaky grin on his face. It all went so fast that it was just ending when Shawna and Debra came out of the spa, which was probably just as well, ego-wise.

"I wondered why you guys sent a woman out as your stand-in, but I guess now I know," Nick told the two men, trying for the jolly jibe.

"Isn't she great?" Jake Beaker enthused, giving him back his fake heartiness. "You didn't score once!"

"You mean she *beat* you?" Shugg put in. "I mean, it *looked* like she just pure whipped the shit out of you, Nick, but I couldn't be sure, I don't even know the *rules* of tennis. I've always thought it was kind of a pussy game"—this last delivered conspiratorially, with a nudge to the ribs.

The group had assembled at the club by convergence, so its departure was in caravan: blonde Shawna in her dark blue BMW (with her tennis-visor on; she had the right profile for a BMW—the nose just a trifle too sharp, perhaps); Debra Durkin her little red Lexus (she was weak-chinned, and you felt the car's color tried too hard); Nick in his large, silver Mercedes, Jake in his black Mercedes, and Shugg himself in his new Ram Charger, bringing up the rear.

To him, the logistics of deploying personnel and materials were second nature, and it struck him as almost comically disproportionate, the total horsepower and cubic haulage being mobilized here to convey six people about two miles up into the hills.

The thought itself surprised him after a moment. It was precisely one of the themes of a Clean Environment Pussy.

Well, so what if it was a waste? They had made the money, and they could waste it! They'd earned it—at least he and Jake had—had put some of these fine homes up in these very hills, places where hard-working people could enjoy some perspective on life, could look out right now and see Santa Marta's lights coming on like a little sea of stars, could feel that by their honest labors they'd risen above the hustle and squalor of the general fate.

Sawyer's commodious drive held all six vehicles. The back way was handiest here. Bev and Jake made compliments about the beauty of the deck, the big, capacious redwood deck, and Nick Sawyer was polling his guests for drink preferences. They all paused by the Webber, standing center-deck, unlidded. In the growing dark the homely appliance had a faintly sinister look, like a little altar of unknown rites.

"What the hell is that?" Nick asked softly in the bemused silence. The circle peered closer at the charred little rack of bones on the grill.

"Is that a *gopher?*" asked Debra.

"No, look at the paws," said Shawna. "It's a *mole.*"

"Do you hear that?" asked Nick. "That kind of buzzing?"

"Yeah," Shugg said. "In the house."

Nick marched to the glass doors, the beginning-to-be-alarmed homeowner. "Unlocked!" he announced indignantly. With two practiced shoves, he swept first the door and then the inner drape aside. The doorway vomited a living wall, a buzzing black avalanche of flies that instantly engulfed Nick Sawyer from head to foot and swallowed the others in whining blizzard.

Uncannily, while the blizzard battered and blinded all six of them, it was only Sawyer they adhered to. He became a man-shaped crust of them, flailing, dancing, and clawing them from his face to get the breath to scream. Everyone fled the deck for the drive, Nick last, tumbling off the steps and roiling across the concrete, leaving a smear of black pulp behind.

"Look!" Bev shrilled. The column of flies pouring from the doorway tapered to an end. The insects swooped, in one cohesive storm cloud, out to the drive to condense around them. "Back into the house!" Bev trumpeted.

Shawna and Debra, with loathing, gripped Nick's arms and guided him. Stampeding back across the deck, they fell into the kitchen and heaved the door closed behind them. A hailstorm of flies pelted the glass outside. Though the kitchen swarmed with them, they had shut out the main body.

They put Nick on a stool and surrounded him and pelted him with rolled-up magazines and flyswatters, scraping the jam of crushed insects off him as he twitched and moaned and yelped his disgust. At length they reached a point where the flies that filled the air stopped landing on him as if he were a magnet. They got him into the shower.

Shawna Sawyer rose splendidly to this household emergency. In the utility room she found paper particle-masks for everyone (Jake Beaker had inhaled a fly or two and was still coughing), and then she made drinks. She gave each drink an ingenious little roof, using the miniature paper parasols stocked for the Mai-Tais for which Sawyer barbecues were so justly famous, and then found straws that her guests could edge under their masks at one end and the parasols at the other. They all finished their first drinks right away and had seconds immediately.

Shawna was superb with a telephone—resourceful and commanding. She found the number of a small fly-control service specializing in dairies and feed-lots, and mobilized them with the promise of a huge bonus. Within the half-hour two women in coveralls arrived with a pair of big, wide-mouthed vacuums and other equipment.

They were on their third drinks by then, grim but composed, making a little conversation now, except for Nick, who sat freshly clothed and masked, but pale and mute.

"It's an infestation," Shugg said. "I cut up a nice fresh bunch of limes yesterday—remember?—and an hour later they were fulla maggots."

"The county oughta do something," coughed Jake Beaker. His eyes were running and his color was bad. Second District County Supervisor Nick Sawyer glared at him.

"First, they'd have to do a feasibility study," Shugg said. He was wondering what the hell was going to happen to their deal now, with Sawyer in this state, but he couldn't help adding, "Then they'd want a new property surtax to pay for the study."

The two coveralled women from Flyz-Begone were now giving them respirator masks, not unlike those used in the Quicksilver Mineshaft. The flies their vacuums had not sucked from the air and walls were now subjected to a potent spray that soon had everyone's eyes turning red. Out on the deck the pair had set up a killing-light, a little cross-shaped device which drew a coating of flies to itself and then fried them with a blue flash of electricity.

The conspirators sat in their bugmouthed masks, watched it crackle and flare, watched a black snow of crisped flies fall. Shawna and Debra were guiding the women into farther rooms. Bev Carney looked at the three men in turn, Sawyer last.

"Are we going to do business or not?" she asked. After a beat, it made her and Shugg and even Jake laugh, seeing themselves in the masks, "doing business." Sawyer's eyes looked wild, outraged. Bev turned on him.

"I'm starting to wonder, Nick, if you're going to be up to this. I'm personally ready to overlook this little domestic hygiene crisis of yours, but are you going to pull yourself together? Should we look elsewhere for what we need?"

Sawyer blinked—you could see him struggling to get a grip on himself. "So let's talk specifics," he offered.

To Dave Shugg's mind, the effectiveness of Bev's threat didn't say much for the moral fiber of the other four county supervisors. They began to talk price, and right away Shugg knew they could get what they wanted from Sawyer for well under half a mil.

"My God!" came Shawna Sawyer's wail from a distant room. "Meggie!" She had found what remained of Meagan.

Thirteen

When Lazarian reached him on his car phone, Frankie was just pulling onto 101 southbound. One of his customers in Richmond had a friend he wanted Frankie to meet. Why not? If the shaft was already far too full for the sewage, what was another fifty-K gallons of toxics?

It was dusk, the sky orange above the red river of taillights, a magic hour. When he answered the phone and recognized Sol's voice, it sounded ghostly, as if Lazarian were contacting him from a different sphere.

"Forget about small change, Frankie." Just like that—*I know everything you do.* "Come up to the shaft. Meet my friend. I'll expect you in twenty minutes."

Being known like this, having the Ice Man's surveillance catching him at every turn, was unnerving. Driving up into the hills he felt spooked, had to fight a persistent sense of unfamiliarity. Each well-known turn seemed subtly different. How had he failed to notice before the grotesqueness of these trees in his headlights?

Sol's van was up near the shaft-mouth, and Frankie pulled up beside it. The stranger lounging by the van with Lazarian looked slight beside him, a skinny guy in tight black slacks and sport coat. His expression was unnerving, a fierce, flickery grin that blanked to deadpan, then flashed on again. Beside him loomed Lazarian, his idol's face like ivory in the black cowl of his hair, and behind them both the shaft spat white light up at the stars.

The shaft was frightening. It had never struck Frankie this

way before, a huge thing that owned *him,* and could swallow him at will.

"Brer Devil! I'm Brer Beiderbeck—Bill Beiderbeck." His hand was bony and dry and cool, and lizard-strong. "We gonna go down an look at yo' Tar Baby. Drink?" Frankie had met other white weirdo hustlers who talked black to be funny. This Beiderbeck's eye, though, glinted with the true coin of craziness.

He opened a big battered leather case on the ground— almost a suitcase. Frankie glimpsed stainless steel canisters, coils, tubing, bright instruments—but what Beiderbeck took out was a bottle and two shot glasses. He used the case for a bar, asking casually as he poured, "Why is it you don't drink, Sol?"

"Why waste time?" the Ice Man asked with a dreamy smile. He was thinking, *You are on the brink of passing all doubt.* He was feeling just what he'd imagined he would feel stepping out of an airplane for a skydive.

Frankie was glad of the whisky. "You've got . . . some kind of a plan for us?"

"I got diddly till I know what*choo* got. I've got some ideas though already, I'll admit it." He picked up and dropped the black rap at whim. His eyes seemed, right at the cores, molten. His case snapped open, swallowed the crockery, and shut again.

They turned to the shaft-mouth. Its cold reek seemed to Frankie to ripple, visible against the stars. Masking up, he couldn't believe his fear, the turmoil in his guts. He owned this fucking hole, and anything here he'd *put* here himself! What was wrong with him?

Lazarian let the others precede him down. The fine hair stirred across his back with his first following step, for this was the stepping-off, with this one move entering pure reality, the cloud-studded atmosphere, the wide world all blistered with hills and veined with highways under him, and all the wide sky clamoring with the voice of a hurricane at his descent.

The chemist walked point, and Frankie felt glad of him there, lantern high, his bug-mask matched by his long, grasshoppery limbs. This Beiderbeck with all his scientific ju-ju was the right guide here, making Frankie think of those underworld guides from the classics, old Virgil or Dante or whoever they were, showing the chump the ropes in hell. His crazy-leg shadow danced along the wall on top of the fill hose like a cartoon spider. He boogied a little as he went and exulted over the air quality.

"*Mmmm*. Dis *am* some fine shit! Whachoo be cookin down heah, Frankie, is some righteous poison! Whadda bookay!"

"What's that?" Frankie asked. "Is that a fuckin *hand?*"

For here was the pool, and Lazarian, hanging back, waiting for these others' shock, their confirmation, felt the sane earth fall from under him again, felt wings unfolding from his heart in answer. The hieroglyph on the shaft floor had changed. Now it was no desperate drowner's upper half that thrust out its silhouette—it was the shadow of a single splayed hand.

"You know," Beiderbeck answered Frankie, "that's exactly what it's shaped like. Man! It's so exact!"

And as they stood there finding nothing to say for a moment, a moment from Lazarian's youth returned to him. He had just brought a corpse to a dump along the Jersey shore. The man, a plump restaurateur, was folded, wrists wired to ankles. Lazarian wasn't really trying to hide him, just to set him in his rightful niche, wedging him into the flank of a hill of trash.

Then on impulse he adjusted the restaurateur's head (how limber the snapped stalk of its neck!) so the dead face could survey the surrounding scene. The sun was down and the afterglow was candy-red on a ceiling of clouds above an indigo sea. The bloody light lay on the waste around them, the broken bones and failed organs of a profuse civilization. There on a distant shore the light-show of Manhattan was just coming on, you could just make out the twin Trade Towers.

"Chief Hambone!" Lazarian had suddenly cried, saluting the corpse like a noble savage he was entombing—"I set you amidst your grave-goods. Behold your wealth, O soup-stirring chieftain! And behold the wonder of our world, the little galaxy that spawned us!"—sweeping his arm here at the lights of New York.

And just in that moment of brash comedy, Lazarian's younger, vainer self was touched, electrified by the cosmos he stood in. It was all domed under a bubble of blood—these wastes, the steel-hard sea, the starry coast—it all lay under this blister of red sky that, if but ruptured, *squeezed,* would squirt them all tumbling out into the more colossal hell they drifted through.

That would be the ultimate drain, that hole in the ruptured sky. To pass through it alive into what lay beyond, to graduate from this vast dump below . . .

Clear though the hand's outline was, its orientation was ambiguous. Did it reach for him, or demand *from* him?

"It could still be settling," Beiderbeck said, "and forcing up bubbles. But . . . muy weird, no?"

Lazarian studied their eyes, Beiderbeck's intrigued, but already setting it aside. Frankie's . . . ?

Frankie was thinking that since Beiderbeck saw it too, the hand wasn't a hallucination, but beyond question he was powerfully stoned. This crazy fear. And this air! These fumes were downright *toxic,* full sense of the word. Could the hand be a joke of Sol's, who was watching him even now? But what for?

Beiderbeck opened his case and became all business. He hooked a canister to a slender steel cable that paid off a spool. He gave a windup and tossed. Cable shrilling, the canister bulleted through the black surface. Both Frankie and Lazarian felt a shock, a delicate shiver, at the impact.

"Whoooo-ee!" Beiderbeck gave a little dance-and-shimmy. "Dat feel so *silky* goin *in!*" The canister caps had remote triggers, and he filled three flasks at different depths. He rinsed them with a little flask of benzene, wiped them dry with chamois and laid them in velveted sockets in his case.

Frankie watched fascinated. At some point in the operation, fear had left him, and the cold, powerful atmosphere had become almost sensual—like cold satin dragged through his naked pharyngeal chambers. There were, in fact, just the most tenuous wisps of music coming to him, weren't there? Something slow, seductive. And was this a tingling in his balls? What was happening to him down here?

"Is somebody humming?" Beiderbeck asked, hands pausing in his case.

"I hear it too!" said Frankie. "Reeel faint—"

And then the humming was real. It was Lazarian there behind them, his dark choirboy's eyes smiling above his mask:

"*Mmm*-mmm . . . *mm*-mmm . . . *mmm*-mmm . . . *mm* . . ."

Where had Frankie just heard that tune?

Lazarian led the way back up, legs reluctant. His soul lagged, caressed the shaft's walls, their stone fragile, just a membrane with looming reality outside it. The sky they climbed to was just a bigger ceiling. He stripped his mask off and breathed the taintless air regretfully, this atmosphere devoid of magic.

So he would take a plane and fly through this lesser sky, to New Jersey, Great Babylon in the world of waste. He must make this shaft, this gate, his uncontested own. It would need some days doing, Lou "The Dumpster" Bonifaccio having a big life, one that could not be had without taking many other lives with it.

"Listen, guys," he said. Beiderbeck had poured two more shots. They looked at him, whisky balanced in their fingers. "The idea you mentioned, Bill, the colloid one. Explain it to

Frankie. Remember, there's very large money in making it work. Can you drive him back to the City, Frankie? I've got an errand to run." After a few days Frankie might guess he was back East. Frankie would be alert to chances to cut and run, but greed would be the glue that held him.

Beiderbeck sniffed, shook, and sniffed again from a little silver pocket-rocket, which he shook and passed to Frankie as the blue van rolled out the compound gates below them. Frankie figured it was better to stay on even ground with this guy till he had him figured out, so he took the sniff.

"Jesus! That's fire! Isn't that coke?"

"Shit no! I don't honk no powdered white yuppie-boogers! That's *crank!* Shot for the road?"

"Christ! OK, I might as well."

Frankie drove fast down the hill, the Trans Am roaring with downshifts, trying at least to scare this high-handed asshole a little. The chemist took another snort from his rocket and settled in comfortably.

"Now an ignorant layman like you, DaValli, is not gonna really understand what I'm describing. Just do your best, OK? I think that the shit in your shaft just me be colloidalized. If there is enough potential homogeneity in it, the introduction of a sufficiently complex catalyst could *organize* that stew of hydrocarbons. Create a colloid that would *cohere,* and would, given the right specific gravity, float just below the surface of the water. You could put a valve on that old drain plug and let out your colloid in pulses. Unperceived, it could cross the lake, take the creek to the river to the sea . . . I don't know what seawater would do to it, nor marine thermal currents, but even if it surfaces off shore, who could pin down its origins? Right away, I mean. You should have ample time to suck in your poop, scoop in your chips, and run."

Frankie drove in rapture for a while, taking in this new vision—his toxins, a great black worm, stealing off past miles of unguessing folks, sneaking itself cannily, cleanly out to sea, leaving the shaft free to guzzle one point five mil dollars' worth of raw sewage.

They were shooting south on 101, near the southern county line, and Beiderbeck burst out, "Here! Take this turnoff!"

Frankie's jacked-up reflexes obeyed before his mind caught up. "Just ten minutes," soothed Beiderbeck. "A short detour." They were rolling past grassy slopes crowned with big, crooked oak trees. Frankie knew this as the turnoff for an X-rated drive-in located exactly on the county line. "Take that dirt branch-off left there!"

The chemist's hot-centered eyes flicked covetously over the scenery as the Trans Am rocked and bobbed up the dirt track climbing the hills' crestline. "I *love* this place!" Beiderbeck hissed, his face twisted with joy. "I mean, we're into pollution? We have to come see pollution at its source, genuflect at the shrine."

Up here the big oaks were islanded here and there on the slope, with deep pools of moonshadow under each one. In the little valley at the foot of the slope, a man and woman sixty-nined soundlessly on a twenty-by-fifty-foot screen, playing to a small lot with about a dozen cars at its soundposts. Up here amid the trees were at least as many more vehicles, here and there the glint of muscle trucks in which, faintly silhouetted by the light from the screen below, you could see the bizarrely haired, scarfed, and hatted heads of teenagers.

They parked in the shadow of a tree. "You see it," Beiderbeck almost crooned. "The *core* act of pollution! Human procreation! Look there!"

From a pickup under the next tree over came a belch, and a little flurry of trash erupted from its window—Styrofoam burger-shells, cardboard quivers sodden with the grease of fries. "By

Christ, it's too perfect to stand!" moaned the chemist. Frankie watched him with plain unease now. Beiderbeck had actual tears now oozing from his eyes—he grinned with a hate so exquisite it knotted his face in masochistic joy. He had to struggle to find his voice. Frankie waited tense, the beginnings of an awkward smile on his face. "It's wonderful," the chemist said hoarsely. "These . . . human pigs come here, spontaneously devout! They salute the icon of their Pig-God! Grunt and guzzle! Get yours! Squirt, dump, and run!" His voice grew steadier—still impassioned, but in rapture now, smiling almost gently. He touched Frankie's arm, earnest, loving even.

"And the cosmos is yours! It belongs entirely, lock stock and barrel, to ignoramuses just like you and all the other Pig-people! It's so awful it's sublime. None of you *guess* what you fuck with! The world is a cathedral of vast complexity, a temple of stained glass, of electromagnetic rainbow fabrics tented high above and far beneath us! What we vandalize together is past even my conception, light-years past yours and your fellow swines'!"

His free hand, the one not on Frankie's arm, had snapped open the case and taken out—a huge beefy nickel-plated gun! A .44? Who knew? One of those cannons from cop movies. Throwing open his door, the chemist told him coaxingly:

"Bear with me a minute—I've just gotta do this." And he launched himself across the grass towards the trash-spewing truck. His skinny frame half floated, like a leggy bird landing. As he entered the shadow of the other tree his pale, mad-monk face looked faintly luminous to Frankie where he sat.

As Beiderbeck reached the truck's side his pistol came up gracefully, with an almost balletic movement of his whole right arm. He brought the butt of the pistol down—

whack!

—against the windshield. Then Frankie heard him quite distinctly hissing, a crazed grin on his face:

"You're littering."

That deadly whisper, it was from the movies—Clint East-wood! That "Make my day" hiss. The chemist was holding the gun muzzle up, displaying but not aiming it. "You promise never to do it again," he said, "and this time we won't arrest you"—all in the same Clint Eastwood voice.

The kid sitting nearest the window was Rod Blair, who, until this astonishing confrontation, had been having belching contests with Sean and Eric, all on their fourth beer or so after eating Whoppers with cheese, their boards and wetsuits in the rack in the bed of the truck, just sitting there not bothering anyone. Rod Blair, nineteen, his hair shaved into a little straight-sided blond wheat-patch up on the center of his scalp, looked out of the crack-webbed windshield in front of him, then looked at the gaunt psycho in the tight little Frankenstein suit holding up the big shiny gun, and said,

"We promise! Sure. Right, guys?"

"Yeah!"

"Yeah, right! We promise!"

"This time I'll *trust* you," hissed Beiderbeck. He strode back, tall and stately, to the Trans Am, which Frankie already had fired up.

They rode, rocking, back down the crest of the ridge. Down on the screen, gobby cum-gouts of epic proportions littered a close-up of some not quite anatomically identifiable tract of skin. Frankie said, carefully, "Ya know, Bill, if you *are* on my side, I'm not so sure I *want* you on my side. I mean, you need to call me a pig, Sol needs to call me a weasel, hey, go ahead! What I do is business, not philosophy, not ethics, just business. But considering how you feel about me, I mean, are you really gonna be doin me any *good?*"

"Yes! Absolutely!" He sniffed and took a nip straight from the bottle. Frankie refused the sniff and accepted the bottle. "It's just point of view," the chemist explained delightedly. "To you, it's good. To me, it's death. That way, we're both happy!"

Fourteen

Two days later, on Monday afternoon, Morris Hacker stood on the catwalk above the clarifiers, an acre of concrete tanks where submerged propellers purred, dragging air and light into tainted water. Hosts of bacteria perished here to drift out like fine dark snow in the filtration systems beyond this sector.

Hacker often brought problems here. Hearing the bubbly *shush* reassured him that difficulties could be resolved and flushed away. He really felt like the captain of his ship here—the city a mile or so behind him, the pastured plains ahead. He would steer the city past these shoals where growth had gone aground, this moratorium.

The thing was that Hacker liked solid structures and tight systems. He liked things like this catwalk with its non-slip grid and the sturdy stanchions supporting it, loved the concrete contours of these tanks, the iron elbows of those intake lines, and the bright steel curvatures of couplings thickly gasketed and firm at a thousand p.s.i.

While on the other hand this whole conspiracy was just the kind of rickety, jerry-rigged system he hated. A conspiracy for the city's good of course, to redeem it from the shame of one accidental incontinence, when its lustily growing bowel had slipped and over-tainted the river with its discharge—but still an illegal, dangerous conspiracy. And there were so many people in it!

Not just DaValli. Once they brought pond-levels down by discharging into his shaft, they had to get someone from the state water-control level to review the pond levels, and recommend at least a temporary lifting of the moratorium. This not to mention the county supervisor. Men who might not know any specifics, but could definitely be aware some hanky-panky had gone on.

Thank God he'd put on the brakes when he had. Another week to weigh things, work out some ramifications, maybe look over DaValli's shaft. It was just plain too soon to let things proceed to the stage of actual physical set-up, and he was glad that he had the . . . *boldness* to call a temporary time-out when everyone was pressuring him to go ahead.

As he gazed philosophically westward, his eyes were aimed precisely—if he could only have seen them through the canopy of trees—aimed at Kim and Alex, who were unrolling a bulky coil of flex hose along the ground, with Chip just downslope of them choosing its route.

And in fact Hacker's line of sight was such that if extended *through* the hill, it was very nearly aimed at Willy Yakima, who had the walls of the lakeside shed four courses high now.

Behind Hacker, things were developing just as busily. Dave Shugg was on the phone with one of his suppliers, setting up a materials-delivery date for some ten days thence. Eighty miles farther east, in Sacramento, Bev Carney and Nick Sawyer were having a late lunch with Dwight Urbach, regional director of the Water Quality Control Board, and a man from whom a temporary lifting of the moratorium could be won, pending a special review of wastewater levels in the Lago Puro Wastewater Treatment Plant.

But the activity that would have perturbed him most was already accomplished, by Fletcher, the gaunt, sardonic, white-haired chief of maintenance. Over the weekend he had set the hidden out-take valve. Mega-gallons of raw sewage could now be shunted aside before even entering the plant. Pond levels could be brought down dramatically in a couple weeks this way and attributed to public responsiveness to a community call for voluntary wastewater abatement.

At the moment, Fletcher was leaning back in his chair with the latest issue of *High Society* on his lap. He was giving one of the full-page photos his careful attention: a bare-breasted young woman tickling a pair of transparent black panties (she was wearing them) while slouched back in a posture resembling Fletcher's own. This one was a distinct possibility. The peter-meter reading was favorable. He pinched a tiny dog-ear at the upper corner. All the best ones were now marked for later at home. He tossed the magazine on the desk that also propped his heels, and looked out the window of the barge's cabin, out across the burnished waters of Sludge Lagoon Two.

This was a pretty hour. The water sealed in the bouquet of the sludge pretty well, especially when this afternoon breeze came up, and the water was ripply gold in the oblique sun. His dredge-pump sucked sludge up into his huge tank with a peaceful, bovine *thrumm*-mm, *thrummm*-mm. On shore the three dump trucks, their drivers clustered around the first truck, waited for Fletcher to taxi the barge ashore, swing out his boom, and fill the trucks with their last loads for the day.

He considered these three drivers. Paul and Carter were sitting comfortably on the step-up of the truck, and even at this distance Fletcher could make out that they were discreetly sharing a beer. Fred, hired just this year, was junior dog, had to hover on their fringe and vie to get a word in here and there. All Fletcher's instincts, his years of observing blue-collar psychology, told him that it would be Fred who triggered his little booby trap.

The compressor in the dredge squeezed most of the water out of the sludge, and the resultant material was a densely viscous black pudding. For all Fletcher's years at the plant, the comic potential of this sludge had only been revealed to him last year, by Jimmy Parsons.

Parsons was a fat old fart, just a week from retiring at the time, who routinely sneaked a good skinful of vodka into himself in the course of a Friday afternoon, and was being freer than usual in his last few weeks.

The trucks were pulling out with their loads and Parsons was tailgating the guy ahead, Carter, blowing his horn, and when Carter had trouble shifting up Jimmy was slow to see it and had to jam his brakes on hard, and he did this just as wheels hit an irregularity in the road. His rear wheels lifted and his truck gave a shimmy like an elephant frisking, and most of Parsons's load heaved itself out of his bed and avalanched onto the cab, cascading off it and hitting the road with a blubbery *flop* he could hear all the way out to the raft, and that could still set him off just remembering it.

Fletcher had almost wet himself, he'd laughed so hard. Neither of Jimmy's doors offered him a clean escape, so he pushed open the left and dived desperately out and, sure enough, pulled down a great rubbery slab onto his head, which made him slip and sprawl flat on his back in the mess on the road. Now Fletcher had to lie down on deck of the barge and wave his skinny legs in the air to get all the laughter out of him—a white-haired, sharp-chinned gnome who looked as if he might crack his head in two with glee. Parsons wouldn't drink with him at the Rite Spot for months afterward.

Fletcher was a genius with a backhoe. Over the weekend, after setting the valve, he had cunningly and subtly deepened one of the dips in the uneven road bed, increasing its diagonal so that it would, at the right speed, make a truck wallow going through it—so much so that a flustered driver might jam his brakes on too hard in reaction. He'd patched it with the little mobile hot-box of asphalt, and it just looked like a minor repair.

Fred was the youngest and dumbest of the three, and tended to hot-dog his truck more in a bid to gain status with others.

Fletcher decided to make a bet with himself and put actual money on it that Fred would be the one. He took a five-dollar bill and slid it halfway under his magazine to weigh it down. If it wasn't Fred that spilled his load, assuming the trap worked at all, then Fletcher would subtract this five from his entertainment budget tonight and get a pint of Ten High instead of Jack Daniel's on his way home.

The barge gave a lurch.

Not a violent lurch, but sharp and distinct. He saw, in the water, fleeing the barge, the little shudder of ripples it had made.

The pump's gauges were just by the desk, and there wasn't a tremor, so he hadn't seized up on some clot in the sludge. The barge was moving, of course, as it dredged, but imperceptibly, only inches per minute.

Some moments passed, in which Fletcher had time to wonder why so slight a sensation was making him so . . . curious.

He got up and took a stroll on the barge, keeping the cabin and the machinery between himself and the three men on shore. He found absolutely nothing out of order, of course, and what did he expect?—until he reached the railing at the fore-end of the deck. On the middle member of the rail, there were two black smears of sludge.

Like that little lurch itself, this was a detail almost meaninglessly slight, yet naggingly odd. Most of the barge was generally quite clean. You found some spatters at the farther end under the offload boom, but here? And just on the rail?

Irritated, he shook off this, well, antsy feeling it gave him. For Christ's sake, here he floated in the midst of seventy million gallons of concentrated sludge and was he wondering where two little smears the size of his hands (or actually somewhat bigger) *came* from?

Back in the cabin the gauges told him he was still ten minutes from full. He felt a little restless now, but he made himself sit back down and prop his feet on the desk again. Considering his bet with himself, he decided it would not be cheating to blow the barge's great air horn suddenly, just as Fred drove into the trap, to help startle him. First, he could delay offloading, and then bark at them to get a move-on. That ought to get their speed up to the right levels.

Static exploded from the dusty old radio on one corner of the desk. This radio, its cord wrapped around it, hadn't worked or been plugged in for years—was unplugged now, and the burst of noise so startled Fletcher that his legs gave a spasmodic thrust and he slammed himself and his chair backwards onto the floor.

He lay stunned there on the floor, flares and stars blinding him, listening to an unbelievable burst of song, a gospel-momma voice like velvet thunder, like the world serpent smoothly uncoiling in the depths of the earth:

> *Momma Durtt get you*
> *By de-grees*
> *She jus take hol'*
> *An' squeeze an squeeze.*

What clarity! What honeyed power! And it ended just like that. Fletcher labored up to his feet, staring dizzily at the radio's dusty silence.

The barge lurched again.

More powerfully, this time, an emphatic tug that tilted it more sharply in the same direction as before.

And as Fletcher stood there feeling it resettle, there came something new.

A sound. A dripping, drizzling noise, a copious spattering on the deck. Not far from the cabin's door. Just a few yards down along the deck, a few yards out of sight.

And then steps. Wet, sticky steps, moving towards the cabin door, with a weight to them that he could feel in the planking under his feet.

Fletcher stood rooted, tongue frozen in his mouth, staring with all his soul at the doorframe.

The first thing that came through it was a smell. A reek of putrescent feculence washed in on him, wave on wave, bathed and embraced him, wrung tears from his eyes.

And then. Then a huge black hand gripped the doorframe, and a huge, muck-dripping face poked coyly into view, and coyly grinned at him.

Fifteen

As it turned out, Fred had been the last person to glimpse Fletcher in the barge's cabin window, and they could set his last appearance at a little after three-thirty, not long before he should have filled his tank and taxied to shore.

Fred said that the only reason he particularly remembered was because just as he looked that way Fletcher, who was standing with his back to the window, made a kind of sudden move away from the window and disappeared in almost the same instant Fred saw him. In the discussions that followed when Straff was called and he and Hacker came out, Fred admitted that you could say there was something strange about that move of Fletcher's—its suddenness.

Hacker sent the three drivers out to the raft in the motor skiff used for maintenance tours in the lagoon. "If he's had an attack or something, lay him in and one of you stay on the barge to make room for him."

As the boat pulled away Carter, the oldest—a guy with sad poached eyes and a beer-gut—said, "Right. Lay him in, an all of us stay on the barge. Set this full throttle and aim this sumbitch at the shore—*bam!*"

They laughed. Still, this was weird. Fletcher was a tough, wiry bastard. There wasn't a sick bone in him.

No Fletcher. Anywhere. There was one long stinking mess of sludge along the deck near the cabin. There was another pool of sludge on the floor of the cabin. There was the chair lying on its back. On the table was a skin mag with a five-dollar bill tucked halfway under it.

The plant was outside the city limits but some Santa Marta police came out to help the Sheriff's deputies, and they went so far as to drag a segment of the lagoon—wearing rubber gloves and disgusted expressions—out to a radius of about a hundred feet from the barge. Near dark they gave up.

The three drivers stayed there for hours answering questions. Finally Carter, exasperated by the useless repetition, burst out laughing at the mess. It brought all eyes around to him.

"Well, add it up," he said defensively, still chuckling a little. "Fletch decides to end it all. He's such an asshole he can't even stand himself any more. So he jumps overboard.

"Then he changes his mind. He climbs back out, makes a mess on the deck. But he's still not sure.

"He goes in the cabin and stands there thinking it over and making a mess in *there*. Then he changes his mind *again*. He leaves five bucks under his stiffener—I dunno, like maybe a to-ken of his appreciation to the company, his co-workers. Then he goes back out an jumps in again"

No one said anything. Then one of the deputies, a big red-neck who didn't even crack a smile, shook his head.

"There's a fatal flaw in that theory, boy. That five was clean."

A lot of people laughed. Morris Hacker and Marv Straff weren't among them.

Next morning, plant business had to proceed. The deputies marked off with little flagged buoys the area they had already dragged and continued the search from several skiffs while the barge was allowed to pull in to shore and offload into the trucks.

All three drivers had come to work hung-over—Fred the worst, because Paul and Carter had invited him along to Father's office, and Fred had outdone himself in the beer department to make a good showing for this special occasion. Fred's eyeballs felt like bearings fouled with sand when he moved them. He had a juicy, thumping headache.

Straff manned the barge—good old cheery Marv Straff, it was like Jekyll and Hyde! He was barking and snapping at everything in sight. When Fred had taken on his load he was a little slow gearing up, Straff barked at him again, and he saw red. The asshole said hurry up, so yes *sir!* Fred slammed into gear and stood on the gas.

The road heaved under him—it seemed to buck the whole truck off its back. His wheels spun on air for a stomach-floating moment, and tap-danced onto the asphalt as he jammed on the brakes. A slithering black landslide drowned his cab, blinding all the windows at once.

Fred sat stunned while, it seemed, a giant mollusk sucked his rig. He heard it smack and flop as it slid off to the road, then sat—still stunned—watching it thin from his windshield, letting some filtered daylight through the glass.

And then he saw an inverted face slowly smear itself down the glass, making rubbery mouths of horror at him as it slid across the windshield.

A face, a head, with no body following. A face much mangled, a pulpy head no longer spheroid—but Fletcher's face and head, unmistakably.

The rest of Fletcher was elsewhere in the load, as it turned out, all its parts much altered by their passage up the ten-inch bore of the suck-pump.

Fred was never to know that he had just won Fletcher's bet for him.

Fred drove like hell going home, his old pickup rattling and humming and his nerves doing the same. What a story to tell

Cheryl! What a story to tell Batch and Floyd. He picked up a sixer and stopped by their house, deciding he might as well cop a gram of speed while he was there.

Floyd took his money and then borrowed his truck to go make the cop. Fred said sure, just put a little gas in because I'm low and the gauge is broken. Sure, Floyd said. He was a cool, hard dude. He wore Raybans and a butch punk cut and a black leather vest and he gave a good jaw and sideburn.

Fred hung out with Batch at their house. It was a manly house, obviously one where just dudes lived. Fred felt envious. Dismantled motor parts on newspapers here and there on the rugless floor, trashbags and ashtrays everywhere.

Fred told Batch about these last two incredible days at the plant. Batch sat there and nodded and ground his teeth and grunted, and worked his fingers deep in the dense red beard engulfing his lower face, the fingers working into the whiskers like rooting piglets.

After a while Fred went back to piss off the back deck because the toilet was stopped up, and saw something strange. He was sprinkling the mountain of old trash bags that filled the back yard right up to the level of the deck, when an obese old rat waddled out from under the deck and started to cross the heap.

The rat was so fat and awkward it was funny, fascinating to watch him floundering his way towards the crest of the heap.

There was something he liked the smell of in one of the bags there. He crawled all over it, sniffing. The bag toppled from the crown of the heap. As it tumbled it flung the rat outwards, and he vanished into the overgrown creekbed that bordered the yard. This creekbed was a leafy maw of dense vines. The rat hung over it an instant, clawing the air, and then plunged in.

The noise of crunching vegetation. *More* noise of breaking, slashing, and a high unearthly rat's wail, followed by a hideous little noise of rupture. Then an arc of bright red spray fanned in the air above the vines.

After a while he thought perhaps he hadn't really seen it. There was no way to get through all the trash, then all the thorns, to check it out.

Floyd used Fred's truck to pick up his girlfriend from her job at Scully's Canoe Rental some miles upriver. When, grudgingly, he helped her load a few last canoes on their racks, he stepped unknowingly into some unusually thick and adhesive riverscum that dripped from the canoes' bottoms.

He took his girlfriend out to dinner as soon as they took her check to the check cashing place. Then he took her over to P. J. Smyles's place to score, and they snorted about half of the gram, and got back to Floyd's place about 10 P.M. with the rest.

Fred was already in deep shit at home—had had a fight on the phone with Cheryl about how late he was staying out. But he was understanding when Floyd told him the guy was selling really light grams, but what could you do? He was desperate just to get his truck back and go. He asked Floyd if he'd gassed the truck and Floyd said sure.

Ralph Huddles at the River Nest Mobil Station took a call. After he hung up he told his sister Henny, "Remember that dipstick Fred Bozman, ran off the road drunk last month?"

Henny looked up from her book, thickish, like herself, which dealt with the magic doings of sword-wielding women of King Arthur's court. "MasterCard refused that charge," she reminded her brother.

He was putting on his jacket. "Yeah, but then they accepted it. Clown's got a City job. He ran outta gas four miles outta town."

Fred ran out of gas on a fast curve of the highway without any shoulder. Drunken fools routinely took this stretch too fast, as Fred knew first hand. Before going to the farmhouse where he made his call, he wedged his truck as far over as he dared into the blackberry bushes without dropping it into the river.

But when Ralph arrived with the truck and a can of gas, they found that somehow some blackberry vines—very tough and cruelly thorny ones—had worked themselves under the hood, under the air filter, and had even jammed themselves into the carburetor. A routine gas call had become a tow the rest of the way home. Ralph got himself badly scratched up freeing the truck of those incredibly invasive vines. He didn't say a word the whole way. Fred sat speechless too, awed by the extravagant strangeness of his recent bad luck.

Early the next morning, after a major fight with Cheryl and a night spent half wired, half drunk, and dozing in front of the TV, Fred tottered bleared and shaken out to the back porch with a cup of coffee.

Too tired to feel his misery, he sat vacantly watching the familiar sight of their cat, Turtle, jumping up into the cab of his truck.

Once on the seat, the animal could be seen to look intently downwards. It jumped down to where the pedals were.

A few seconds later the cat came exploding out the window. It writhed and danced and yowled about the yard and then vanished with the most amazing leaps and bounds up into the weeds.

There was nothing in the cab of his truck. Just a little scum or mud around the pedals.

Later, when he and Cheryl were ready to leave in her car, he came out to look for Turtle again—and found her in the weeds.

Or rather, found an astonishing mop of fur on skin, like parchment. Though distorted by shrinkage, it was clearly Turtle's coat.

The next day, Wednesday, Ralph Huddles went to see Dr. Gummersbach. The lacerations he'd gotten from the blackberry vines itched unbearably.

The doctor cleaned and inspected these lacerations. There, quite distinct within the weepy tissues, tiny green shoots were growing from Huddles's flesh.

Fletcher's death, meanwhile, had changed things forever between Morris Hacker and Marv Straff. Straff astonished his boss.

"The goddamn valve's in place, and we're *proceeding*, Morris! No more hand-wringing, be a man for Christ's sake! If you refuse to do your share, I'll take your share of the money as well as my own. If you go to the law I'll drag you straight to jail with me. This thing can be done and that small fortune can be had, Morris, and we're going to do it, and have it."

When Morris saw he would have to go along, Straff tried to revert to their old boss-employee amiability. Morris wasn't having any. He lived through days of mute, unremitting horror. Now, with the police investigating Fletcher's accident in force, every fiber of Morris Hacker's body recoiled from the thought of proceeding with the hook up under their noses.

Marv laughed. "There's nothing *showing*, Morris! And most people only see what they're told to see—don't you know that?"

By Wednesday Straff had dropped sections of irrigation pipe in the pastures along the out-take route, and Chip and his helpers had just finished bringing the uptake line of flex-hose down from the hills to the edge of the plain. "Nothing showing"? It didn't jump right out at you—olive drab flex hose, sneaking through culverts under the highway's switchbacks, snaking under roots and bushes—but once you saw it you could damn sure follow it all the way up the Quicksilver Mine!

Hacker had lost all wish to look more closely into DaValli,

once it was settled they would be partnered in the crime. Let it be honestly swearable that he hardly knew the man.

On Friday there would be dinner at Nick Sawyer's, with the developers and Dwight Urbach of the Water Quality Control Board. And if the outcome was favorable, they were irretrievably, inescapably launched. The transfer of actual sewage would follow within days.

And, indeed, a substantial cash payment would be rendered on the initiation of transfer.

Even the prospect of the money scared him as much as it excited him. Morris Hacker moped at home after work, feeling vaguely but unshakably doomed. Marjorie started going on evening shopping jaunts to the malls, or out for moonlight jogs, to avoid his mood. He sat home, hearing the silence in his yard, feeling the absence of Duke. He realized he was still mourning his neat, fierce friend. Who would defend him now?

No sooner had Frankie DaValli paid Kim and Alex for finishing the flex hose than they called in sick—Wednesday, the very next morning. Frankie actually drove the tanker on a couple of pickups himself.

He loved it. For one thing, if Beiderbeck's idea worked, every truckload was pure gravy, five to ten grand a crack! And he was saving twenty bucks per hour each on his drivers. The sheer profitability was intoxicating.

More than that, it was physically intoxicating, a little. The smell of the tanker, of the shaft—since that bad night down there with Sol, he found them almost tasty. He got a crazy body-high off it. No doubt it was like a milder form of sniffing glue. He would only drive another day or so in any case, so screw it—part of the point of life was not just to get rich, but also to have fun, right?

Thinking of which, he recalled that when Bev had declined another date after the first, she'd said, "I think it would be just too confusing, don't you, until some business is out of the way and we *know* we have a working relationship? Until your uptake line is finished, say?"

That was OK with Frankie—games with tricky rules could be the most fun. He would call her soon, but maybe he would do another night pickup or two first, have the fun while it was happening.

He stopped by the lake-site on Wednesday though his own urge was to stay away from the place. His end was topside in the shaft and down at the drain end he felt uneasy. He didn't want to be there without Beiderbeck and Sol Lazarian for allies.

Willy said he would be done by Friday, though, and would like an inspection and some more money.

When Frankie saw how far along the shed was he wrote Willy a check for his balance plus a thousand dollar bonus. Just standing here on the little gravel beach was unpleasant. The lake seemed a big, wet, breathing animal, a giant victim that wordlessly accused him.

"God love ya, Frankie," Willy said, seeing the bonus. "It's good to know there's still people who can appreciate quick, quality work."

"Seen, ah, anything of our neighbor?"

Willy noticed that Frankie seemed less at ease here than he had at their earlier meetings—in fact, he was edging towards his car already. "I get a whiff now and then. Sometimes I think I'm hearing her radio," he answered, scratching his scalp.

And having said that, when Frankie was gone, Willy thought he heard it again. Just the faintest, faintest snatches of some old blues or gospel song. Willy scratched some more. His scalp had been itching him like crazy lately.

Sixteen

The County Planners' meeting was held on Thursday afternoon at 2:00 P.M., true to the County Government's policy of scheduling all public hearings so that as few working people as possible could attend them.

Barbara's mom, Lucky, came by for her in her big shabby black boat of a '72 Buick. Barbara was finishing the polish on a brooch—a rampant boar was how she thought of it, in heraldic terms. This was the second big piece she'd done in the last week or so.

"It's pretty!" Lucky foghorned, "but it looks mean as hell!"

"I keep doing pigs for some reason. She is mean, isn't she?"

They picked Maxie up from school and then drove out the north end of Gravenstein, and honked cruising up to Reed's rental yard. Raleigh was already in Reed's pickup in front of the lot. They waved and fell in behind, heading down to the meeting.

"This should be an all-family affair," Lucky said, speaking for Maxie's benefit, "but your Auntie Kim isn't here, she's with Grammie Aurora—you remember her, sweetie?"

"Yeah," Maxie said. "She was at that barbecue where you challenged that guy to a beer-drinking contest!"

Lucky nodded serenely, "—and Auntie Kim's helping Grammie Aurora collect some herbs in the hills. But she would be here if she could because this meeting that we're going to is Democracy, sweetie, it's people speaking up to the government about what they think it ought to be doing, and I'm glad we can be here as a whole family to practice Democracy together."

"That's right," Barbara chimed in, looking down at her little brown-haired, gray-eyed daughter there between them. Brushing her own black hair before leaving, Barbara, looking at her Mexican coloring and her coffee-colored eyes, realized that it was only at times like this that she remembered she was a Person of Color—when she had to go face a bunch of white-bread Suits in their seats of power.

But her mom was absolutely right. Maxie wasn't going to see her afraid. Barbara was going to speak up—she had to show her little girl how it was done.

And not ten minutes into the meeting, she was at the podium. The microphone made her voice too big for the room—the county planners at their curved table were hardly twelve feet away. The most vocal had been a bald guy with a fat blue tie and gray suit—Carson Brill—and a woman with aggressive shoulder pads, gold beads, and spiky feisty blond hair—Jan Devereux—so Barbara pitched her oversized voice at them particularly.

The smallness of the audience behind her was an embarrassment she had to struggle to master.

"I say," Barbara boomed, "that if all this new development the County has OK'd *demands* a new dump, then let the *developers* pay enough of a per-unit fee to build a transfer station, or build a recycling center *within* the new development, instead of trucking all the new population's *crap* out to the neighborhoods of people who've been here all along and who bought homes where they did partly because there were no *dumps* in them!"

"Hear hear," brayed Lucky, and Barbara saw her mother with stabbing strangeness—a big, cigarette-voiced woman in bright floral Hawaiian shirt and slacks—bright fingernails and lipstick. Beside her Maxie's intense, tanned little face looked pleased to hear her Mom's and Grandmom's voices boom so big.

Brill made a wry smile and let a beat pass. "Would you re-phrase that as a question?"

Several of the other Suits on the Board laughed—Devereux, a guy with a professorial beard and leather elbow pads, another guy with wire-rims and a benevolent librarian's face that Barbara had secretly imagined was on her side—and there were one or two traitorous snorts from among the audience too. Lupe, Lucky's beefy friend, a granddaughter of Aurora Hurtado, glared at the offenders. "Where do you live!" she called from her seat. "Aren't there some good dumpsites up in those fancy neighbor-hoods of yours?"

But then Barbara had found her voice again. "Yes!" she shouted. "Yes. I can rephrase that as a question!" She stepped aside from the mike and raised her naked voice against them. It was much more satisfying, more intimate, like a slap in the face. "When are you people administering the County gonna stop grabbing your ankles for the developers, and start making the developers pay for the facilities that their profitable houses make necessary?"

It felt wonderful, getting it out like that, and behind her Joe Reed and Hank Raleigh cried "Right!" and "Hear hear!"

A ripple of unity swept through the Suits at the curved table. Reed and Raleigh with their unruly black hair and grease-black fingernails carried the scent of proletarian revolt. Where was se-curity? You could see the Planners' faces start asking. Devereux squared her shoulder pads:

"You're not welcome here, Mrs. Yakeema——"

"Yakima. My name is Barbara Yakima."

"You're not welcome here if you're going to be abusive."

"Then don't abuse my criticisms. Don't laugh at them—*answer* them."

Ah, it felt wonderful! Maxie hugged her when she sat down.

"This meeting," said the guy with the leather elbow patches, "is strictly to hear public input on the proposed approval of a specific new dumpsite. Past county policy is not at question here."

Others spoke. But Barbara could already feel how it was going. Reed delivered a rambling complaint about how the dump behind his property had been run during past years. Lucky told these Suits—as if they gave a shit!—how sick it made her to think of that valley where her kids had hiked and picked blackberries being filled with garbage. The audience unwound, its individuals discharging their energies in the unfamiliar stress of public speaking.

Then the Planners polled themselves and found, after due consideration of public input, that they still agreed unanimously on the approval of the new dump. Grading of the site could begin tomorrow morning.

At his fine house and grounds near Toms River, New Jersey, Lou "The Dumpster" Bonifaccio, owner, among much else, of the Quicksilver Mine, sits down in his game room, among the guests who will shortly be joining him for dinner.

All but two will be joining him. These two lie in unzipped body bags on the plastic-sheeted billiards table. And Lou smokes his pipe solemnly, decorously, as he watches his doctor remove the right hand of one of them.

The doctor uses a scalpel, and then a battery powered bonesaw with a little wheel-shaped blade.

Ernie and Rick, Lou's bodyguards, lounge—neither fully seated—behind Lou and to either side of him, Tom Sheehy, Lou's lawyer, is in a morocco-leather armchair, a rawboned man with slicked-back red hair, and Sol Lazarian sits on the couch, ankle resting comfortably on knee—Lou's Chief Enforcer. He is just now affably declining the drink offered him by suave, portly Mazie (Massimo Baldassini), a *capo* of Lou's status, and Lou's major ally. In deference to the close bond between him and Lou, Mazie has brought only one of his own bodyguards on this visit, the huge Carlo, a mute with a deformed jaw.

The right hands of the two guests who will not be joining Lou for dinner are to be mailed to key associates of the deceased. Lazarian, later tonight, is to take the rest of the bodies out for proper disposal. It was Lazarian who brought them here, from origins in Long Island and Newark, just this morning.

The phone near Lou rings—a call that has been screened upstairs to have reached him here. He answers, and listens alertly.

"Sol," Lou says. "It's for you. If you gotta go, don't be long."

Lazarian has prearranged this call. He plays his part and hangs up. He tells Lou the business will have to be looked into. "Just don't be late for dinner," Lou says with an indulgent smile.

"You must rest easy knowin Sol's on the job for you," Mazie says—a compliment Sol is meant to hear before the door is quite closed behind him. And then, a moment later, "He doesn't even drink! That's what I call self-discipline!" And Mazie makes a little face, at which everyone else chuckles, except Sheehy.

"You let him work alone too much, Lou," the lawyer said, nodding thanks for the drink Marie handed him.

"Hey. I don't wanna be noodged tonight, Tommy."

"He's a man of ideas, Lou. I try to get it across to you. He's an intellectual. He reads books. You don't leave a guy like that without a partner, to keep an eye on what he's doing! Not a guy that's got ideas."

Lou and Sheehy get into it on this familiar issue. Lou's bodyguards are trading anecdotes about Lazarian. Mazie freshens drinks, including his own. As the doctor, who has removed the second corpse's right hand, is laying the stump of the wrist across the midriff, his knuckles brush a scratchiness under the corpse's shirt.

He opens the shirt. In the abdomen he finds a vertical incision, groin to sternum, that has been sutured. The sutures were the scratchiness he felt. "Lou?" he says.

Lazarian takes a last admiring look at the house and grounds. He is down in the woods that border the three-acre lawn, and his rented van sits idling under the trees near the drive. He thumbs a button on the remote control he holds.

Fifty pounds of plastique, a twenty-five-pound sphere per deceased, are converted into ferociously expanding spheres of hot gas. These overlapping spheres, their respective centers about two feet apart on top of the billiards table, move everything and everybody in the game room—in approximately one ten-thousandth of a second—outward, upward, and downward to the surrounding walls, ceiling, and floor, which in turn flee, to merge with walls and ceilings and floors throughout the house, which blooms in one great expanding bubble of pulped humans and walls and ceilings and floors, swelling out over the wide lawn, and high in the sky with a crack of thunder.

That same evening, Thursday, as his flight surged up from the runway of Newark Airport, Lazarian sat savoring it all, imagining details to flesh it out. He looked down and saw the Jersey coast falling away below, the poison toadstools of the Amboys far to the south. As if in a vision, his eyes filling in what didn't show, he saw the whole sweep of landfills and dumps and reeking factories he knew along this shore.

He remembered his moment with the restaurateur, also in the glory of the dusk, when this trashed world had seemed so easily escapable.

He mused on the question, What is trash? Clearly, trash is anything in the world that encounters a greater force which desires its destruction.

At the Chicago stopover he phoned DaValli. He caught him at the mine, just about to go out for a pickup in the tanker.

"Did your drivers quit?" Sol asked pleasantly.

"Called in sick. Hey—I don't mind saving the money. Driving the rig is kinda fun. It's all money in the bank for us, Sol."

"I might give you a hand. Get in the spirit of owning the place."

A slight pause. "Oh," said Frankie. "Well, my condolences for your loss of Lou."

"Thank you. I worked for him for six eventful years. He was an almost-great man—a moral dwarf, an appetite with a brain. We'll all miss him."

"So when'll we see you?"

"Well, I've got some collecting to do Friday. Why don't I take the tanker out Saturday morning. I want to make a special little offering to—what shall we call it?—the spirit of the shaft."

"You can call it whatever you want, Sol."

After the Planners meeting they all went up to Lupe's for dinner (Barbara knowing that Willy would be working late so he could finish the job tomorrow), and Reed and Raleigh didn't leave until near dark.

A few years ago hanging out together, doubling in each other's truck, would have been unthinkable for them. When Reed first bought his lot he hated the country western Raleigh had on his radio, all those overrated Texas Assholes—Willy Nelson always excepted. Reed's own preference fell strongly on the Hag and George Jones.

Reed was spare, with a red ponytail, and a wispy orange tuft that was all he could get to grow on his chin. Raleigh had a big slack gut and meaty arms with black curls on them and his hair jutted in curly tufts from under his watch cap. They disliked each other *bodily,* as repellent physical types.

After a while, though, Reed came to realize that this Raleigh was pretty much a loner like himself, and basically customers were the only people he saw on his lot. He began to mellow out to Raleigh's music.

One morning he went next door to Raleigh's office with a new four-barrel carburetor, and asked for a small loan, with the carb for collateral. The loan was less than the worth of the carb. Raleigh poked it with a meaty finger, and said, "OK."

Reed hadn't needed the loan—he paid it back that night with the same bills Raleigh had given him. After the loan, they knew they shared the same values in life, and became friends.

Reed dropped Raleigh in his lot and swung back into his own. The stars were just coming out, with a band of red still lying above the lumberyard across the highway. A little too soon to fall out. Reed would change the oil in his flatbed.

He drove the flatbed into his maintenance shed and over the concrete pit he used instead of a lift. This was when he discovered the crack in the pit's wall, and the black goop oozing from it and onto the pit's floor.

This was four-inch reinforced concrete. Willy Yakima had dug and poured it for him six years ago and Willy made it, as he made everything, tighter than a tick's ass.

Where could this black glop be coming from? Well . . . where *else?* He stepped out of his shed and looked up at the hill behind him. On that hill, recently filled and capped, lay the Gravenstein Dump, now the Gravenstein Transfer Station. Then he heard Raleigh, over in his lot, make the strangest noise-yelp of outrage that turned into an *ahhh* of awe.

"Raleigh!" he called. He scanned the chain-link fence that separated their lots. In Raleigh's yard the jumbled silhouettes of dead cars looked like the aftermath of an Armageddon. "Reed!" Raleigh shouted. "C'mere! Bring your twelve-volt!"

Reed grabbed his flashlight from the shed and ran to where his stepladder leaned against the divider fence—Raleigh had leaned a matching one against the other side.

He found Raleigh in the darkest corner of his lot, his flash-beam poking at the corpse of an old pickup. Sixty-four Dodge half-ton.

"First, look there!" Raleigh hissed. "It's got all four wheels and tires on it. I yanked all the wheels the day I brought it in, almost three years ago! Think I don't remember that? OK, now. Shine your light in on the steering wheel."

Hooked over the top of the wheel were the fingers of a skele-ton hand, with the two bones of the forearm dangling from it. The bones were perfectly bare, hanging together by dry carti-lage.

When they had stood there a while taking it in, they headed over to Reed's so Raleigh could see his pit. "You gonna call the cops?" Reed asked.

"You fuckin crazy?"

When they looked down into the pit the crack seemed a little bigger to Reed, and the ooze more abundant.

"Look there in the crack where it's comin out," said Raleigh. "Isn't that a swollen-up part of a trash-bag there?"

It was. Now it was past question. They stood taking it in. "So who are *you* gonna call?" Raleigh asked. "The County?"

"That's almost funny."

Seventeen

Reed woke to Raleigh's shout—it came from out on Sequoia Highway. He stumbled into his boots and came blinking out into the early morning.

"Look at that fuckin bulge!" Raleigh cried. The asphalt was domed up maybe half a foot across both lanes of the highway. You could drive over it because the swelling was so broad and gradual, but it was pretty startling. "Now look over into Glue-Lam's lumber stacks there."

In the lumberyard across the highway from them Reed could see where two stacks among the neat majority were tilted, planks spilling off, revealing a groundswell that ran between them.

"It lines up," concluded Raleigh, "with this bulge in the highway, and your workshed."

"Jesus Christ," Reed said slowly. "I am gonna call the fuckin county!"

Scat Collins, heavy equipment operator for the County, sniffed the morning air in the little valley in the foothills west of Santa Marta where the new West Regional Municipal Landfill was about to be born.

Scat Collins liked to move things. The blade on his 'dozer was almost a story high; its rear wheels were ten feet in diameter. Scat was a big man to match the machine, with his big face and neck of bare-shaved, healthy beef, and his hair a little blond stubble you could see his scalp through, He liked to move things *precisely,* move them from point A to point B along the path of least distance and least time.

He'd had his morning coffee, and he'd just stepped out of the porta-potty feeling fine. He mounted his rig, idling in wait for him. The shovels in their hardhats and county-issue orange shirts had set out the stakes for his morning's first pass at the hillside.

Scat called most of the guys on the groundcrews "shovels." One of his favorite jokes was, "Hey! Ya know the Japanese are gonna put the county crews outta business? Yeah. They just invented a shovel that stands up by itself."

Scat waved to the shovels that he was starting up, and slipped in the clutch of his well beloved pet yellow dinosaur. He settled himself into the big, butt-hugging seat of power. He sat easy and proud, jouncing softly with his brute's slow, mammoth gait.

The westward, more gently sloped flank of this valley was sited for the actual dumping ground. They would carve away the foot of this hillside, lay a layer of trash, compact it under the tractors' tracks, lay the carved-out earth back over it, then gouge a new terrace from the hillside just above the old, and so on up the hill.

To Scat's mind, the years-long process was visualized as a series of unbroken gestures, a graceful blanketing of trash with hillside executed in wide balletic sweeps of dozers and crawlers.

He edged gently up to his startpoint, where the skirt of the slope leveled out on the valley floor. He set the lower right corner of his blade about: a foot deep into the meat of the hill. At this setting he would have a blade-full in about a hundred feet. He geared down and spurred the monster to its work.

The snap of torn rock was muffled in the dark soil that rose in a thickening wave and spilled outwards in a wall that danced before the blade. It cut like butter.

He liked working the lay of the land like this—better than the brute scalping of construction work, say. His blade was nearly full now, twenty tons of dirt dancing in front of him . . . there

144 ·

was one of the shovels, Valdez, waving his arms at him and shouting—pointing behind Scat. Scat looked behind him.

The ninety-foot earth scar behind him looked like the first long incision made to gut an animal—because guts were blooming from the slice, dark, slick bulges that were growing even as he looked at them. At the start of the cut they were swelling up big, already as high as a man.

Then the stench hit him.

He swung his rig away from the seam and backed off about fifty yards. He did it instinctively, protecting his equipment in the face of the unheard-of.

He and the shovels—they were actually carrying shovels now, in some impulse to be armed against the earth—the three at them approached the ooze. At some places it bubbled and ballooned, at others it flopped and flowed. The stink was incredible. It was coming fast, presenting them with an advancing front that was ten feet high at the start of the cut, and growing along the rest of it. While they were still a ways off, Valdez shouted what was already obvious:

"It's shit from a dump! An *old* dump! Phew!"

Scat had to fight down his gag reaction. "Yeah! Those are old trashbags! And look there!" (Scat had three kids.) "Huggies!"

"An' there's some Coke an Pepsi cans—you can still read the labels!"

"Wait'll I get to my fuckin phone," raged Scat, turning now, breaking into a ponderous jog towards his County pickup. "Those fuckin engineers are gonna get their butts out here!"

Late that morning Willy bolted the last of the corrugated sheets onto the roofbeam of the shed. His scalp was itching furiously. It had been itching for days, and a lot of hair had been coming out in his comb, but it had never itched like this before.

He got down from his ladder and stood back from the little structure. This moment of completion, which at the end of any job he liked to savor with a beer or three while he contemplated the finished work, was ruined for him now by this infernal itching.

He fought to ignore it. He went to his cooler for a brew, clenching his teeth.

Suddenly he couldn't stand it any longer, and flung off his cap and started scratching his scalp furiously with both hands.

And felt huge clumps of his hair coming loose! Getting caught between his fingers and coming away in clumps, roots and all! He ran to his truck and turned out his sideview mirror.

"Jesus Christ," he said, awed. His forehead went all the way back past his crown. He tugged a lock just above his temple. It came right out. He shook his head furiously against the continued itching, and more came out, falling on his shoulders.

In an unbelieving fury, he began grabbing at his hair then, snatching it out, gaping as he got balder and balder. In a moment there was only a ragged fringe on the back of his neck and below his ears.

He stood staring at this strange-looking egg-head wearing his face. "There's no fucking baldness in my family!" he whined to his reflection. His reflection stared back at him, bald. Baldness made him look kind of . . . popeyed. And had his ears really been *that* big all along?

He was awed. But he was not—it began to come to him now as he stared in the mirror—he was not mystified. Because how often had he rinsed off his head in the lake there. The lake which had been teasing him with a smell as elusive as the faint, distant static of Mamie Durtt's radio down in the cove—a smell which yes, delicately weaving, he could detect right now.

Moving abstractedly, he got a beer from his cooler, and went down to the water's edge.

The sun was still high and, leaning close, he could see the bottom clearly. There! Jesus Christ! Fine, tiny tendrils of blackness, like smoke, wisping and twisting up from the gravel and dispersing into the water. And the smell—ethereal, unearthly, unmistakably there.

Something else was here. Something big was suddenly very close to him. Right behind him. The very earth under him seemed to give and shift with its presence. Then the voice boomed.

"Have a drink with me, partner."

Willy nearly fell into the lake. The voice felt as big as the sky, and at the same time as intimate as a whisper in his ear. Scrambling back, lurching to his feet, he confronted Mamie Durtt, vast in her filthy mu-mu, holding out a fifth of whisky that looked small as a beer bottle in her hand.

Lord God, she was huge. She was smiling. Her teeth were ragged brown stumps, and the glee in the black glass of her eyes was an ancient, reptilian glee. Willy's hand reached obediently for the bottle. No particle of him wanted what was in it, but a kind of gravity-field seemed to radiate from her hugeness, an aura of unrefusability that his hand obeyed like a will-less thing. He recognized, with quiet, total terror, that the cold glass neck he gripped was his fate. Was this a test? A punishment? It didn't matter, he had to take it. It was as if she stood not just in front of him, but behind him, above him—there was no way . . . *out* of her.

"Thanks," he croaked. Far away in the center of mind a voice he remembered as his own cried: *What the fuck is happening here?*—and he drank.

It was whisky, yes, but as it went down his throat the noise of a torrent drowned his ears, and astonishing images flickered in his brain. Animals he had never seen before devoured one another; clouds bled smoking black rain. He handed back the bottle.

"You looked better with hair," Mamie Durtt boomed, and took a swig. As if his own mind felt what she swallowed, another pulse of hallucination went through Willy. The trees shuddered and twisted in the windless air. The earth rippled sickeningly under his bootsoles. She handed him back the bottle—it seemed as full as before.

"The rest is for you, partner," she said. "Drink it up. All of it. Don't make Mamie mad."

"All this?" His own voice seemed to Willy the squeak of a trapped animal. "But see, I gotta drive home . . ."

She leaned a little nearer. Her black eyes were deep now, were chasms where something bright was falling, falling, infinitely far within. "If you drink it all, Willy Yakima, and you can move, then you can leave here alive."

Willy drank without hesitation, though he was melting already with what he had swallowed before. The blue-gold, cloudless sky was melting into the lake, and the earth under him was melting up into his feet and legs, and he himself, the felt hulk of his consciousness, was melting, as strange pictures lived in his mind. Trees like oiled dinosaurs muscularly embraced and crushed houses. A beached whale bled a blackness from its pores that turned the sands to glass. A shrieking man danced in his pajamas all furred with a white fungus thick as grass sprouting from his face and hands.

Willy drank, and now he was sitting on the ground, wasn't he? Yes. Looking up at her eyes, like black moons in a daytime sky.

"Here you sit in my lap," she boomed, "you insolent vermin! Here you claw at my teats and spit in my face and shit on my body! Drink up!"

Willy drank. Her eyes weren't moons now, the holes full of star-hung space. Willy drank, and saw kittens with webbed paws devouring their scaly, taloned dam. Human infants' faces blackening, shriveled like spider-prey. Mamie Durtt's voice lifted and dropped his mind like great hands made of thunder.

"I'm bucking you out of my lap, and you better hit the ground running, you odious little filth. Drink up! Momma says it's good for you!"

Willy drank. That is to say, his remote, melting right arm hoisted, his remote, melting mouth opened, and the liquor raged through the fleshy pipe in his neck. He saw fields of writhing rodents spewing blood in the grip of carnivorous grass. Saw a man breathe deeply till his cancered lungs erupted, all knobbed with tumors from his ribs.

Willy's head impacted with the gravel. An empty bottle chinked to the gravel directly in front of his eyes, loosely held by a hand. His own hand. He must be lying down then. Above him, under and all around him, Mamie Durtt's voice said:

"This is the one and only time I let you go. See to your wife and your daughter! Now move, you wretched little tick!"

Eighteen

Willy moved. His life depended on it, and he moved. For the longest time, though, the sun seemed to be moving faster than he was. The angle of the shadows changed, the air grew warmer and warmer, and still he had not reached his truck.

Not for an instant did he stop crawling, though. Hands, knees—he moved and moved them in endlessly changing sequences, some of which advanced his progress, and some of which dumped him on his face. Again and again he fell. Again and again, he struggled back up on all fours and kept crawling.

At last, he reached his truck. He gripped the door handle and dragged himself to his feet. In the sideview mirror, an astonished-looking bald man, the back of his neck crazily tufted with hair, woozed in and out of focus.

He must get out of here. But maybe he'd better see if he could walk around his truck once or twice before he tried driving it.

With the truck to lean on all the way around, he made the circuit in pretty fair time—well under a century. He decided he ought to be able to walk around it a little more skillfully before getting behind the wheel.

He walked around it many times, immediately losing count how many, and the last few times needing only one hand for support. But now he must go. Must save his family, their possessions.

He dumped himself inside and pulled the door shut at first try on his foot, which luckily felt almost nothing. Luckily too, the keys were already in the ignition.

Lurching and jouncing, frisking into the air and slamming back down, the truck took the dirt road a little too fast, but Willy was getting the hang of it, easing off the gas, getting down to under fifty when he threw his turn onto the highway.

Rubber howled. The trees across the highway rushed straight for him. He fishtailed back out of his slide. Now he had the highway under his wheels—first the left side of it, then the right side, then the left side again.

The right side—here it was again. Now he must stay as much as possible *on* this side. He remembered to ease his foot some more off the gas, and found dropping below sixty helped him.

A pterodactyl smacked against his windshield, rupturing, its entrails darting out of it to both sides, snaking round through the cab's windows, acid dripping from their slick, questing tips, while the beast gave out dinosaurian groans like an airhorn.

It was an airhorn: the highway returned, and he was on the left side of it almost nose to nose with an oncoming cement-truck. Luckily, he only gave the steering wheel a twitch, because he was up past seventy again.

His brain seemed like an ill-shored mineshaft—chunks of nightmare kept caving in on him, swallowing his senses. His windshield became a boat's glass wall, and an oil-slicked dolphin writhed drowning against the glass, clawing with flippers that were turning into distorted hands as Willy watched. He wrenched his head from side to side to throw off the vision. Here was the road again, and just ahead, the junction with the highway that followed the creek down the river, speed limit as you entered the little town of Junction, and Willy was at—*whoops!*—seventy again. Other traffic was edging out for the right of way, at the stop sign that there was no way Willy could obey. He jammed on his horn and rocketed through the turn in a gale of other horns and screeching brakes. Now the hood of his truck was an open pit where a huge spitted boar was roasting, alive, dripping a bright sweat of maggots that sizzled on the coals. . . .

Willy staggered into the Rusty Nail, a downriver bar with a lot of bikes out front. Merle Haggard was blaring from the jukebox. People he knew at the bar and tables looked at him with frank amazement. He clenched his mind. Why was he here? Oh yes. Was . . . ? Yes, there was Gutley at a corner table. Willy steered himself over there and dumped himself, with fair aim, into one of the chairs. Gutley stared at him.

"Jesus Christ, Willy! You're fuckin bald! That hair on your neck looks like it's fallin out right now!"

Willy was stung. He'd forgotten what he looked like now. "*You're* bald, asshole, so what about it?"

"Yeah, but I've *been* bald for years, asshole! With you, it's like, so *sudden!*" Gutley had long hair starting on the back of his head and a full beard. He had hairy bear's arms and a major pot. His look of amazed pity was extremely irritating to Willy.

"You wanna beer?" Gutley asked.

"Christ no," Willy shuddered. "I wanna 'range some biz. Twenty El-Bees of prime skunkweed, seventy-five K, no less."

Gutley didn't even bother pretending it wasn't a good deal. "I can do that. I'd need two or three days."

"S'OK, I gotta cut an bag it yet."

"So where do you wanna . . ." His ear cocked. Willy heard it too, outside, getting louder, getting very loud.

"Sounds like the biggest fuckin hog I ever heard," Gutley said reverently, and then the blatting, rumbling, flatulent din drowned out speech. The engine revved deafeningly and dropped to a menacing idle. The door of the Rusty Nail slammed open.

A huge woman in black leather and studs, her chrome-silver

butch like the bristles of an angry razorback, strode—no, leapt, with the immense, inhuman vitality of some colossal toad—leapt into the tavern and stood center-floor. Her voice was huge, enveloping:

"I can out-shout, out-drink, out-fuck, and out-fight all of you candy-ass face-fucks put *together!*"

There was a beat of silence. The jukebox had gone dead—there was only the rumble of the hog outside.

Not that several of the patrons did not intend to rise to the challenge, but they were still just taking in the sight of her, the sheer fact of her.

She turned to the bar, an old oak bar three inches thick. She smote the bar with her fist. The bar broke and buckled under the blow. Drinks from the two farther ends of it were catapulted in arcs towards each other—airborne bottles trailing little flags of foam to cross in flight above the stupefied head of the barkeep, a huge, walrus-mustached oaf named Wrench.

"Beer!" she roared. Wrench took up the beer spigot on its little length of hose and she snatched it from him, jetting beer directly into her gaping mouth, her throat working, her neck rivering with spilt foam.

Just before she had struck the bar, P. J. Smyles had risen to meet her challenge, and his table mates, younger hangers-on named Batch and Floyd, who were sucking up to him to sell them some more crank, had felt called upon to jump up too.

But when she had demolished the bar, all three of these men froze perfectly still, as if they were all suddenly trying to turn into furniture. But now the woman noticed them. Out darted her huge hand, and she snatched Smyles to her by the neck, making the two-hundred pounder look like a rag doll.

She locked his head in the crook of one elbow and jammed the nozzle into his mouth. When she released him, the spigot had him like a snake, one tight around his neck, both hands too weak to tear it loose, his belly swelling and overflow spewing from his jaws.

Batch and Floyd bolted for the door. The door banged shut in front of them. All the shutters on all the windows banged shut too—all by themselves. The woman jumped straight up onto the bar—scarcely seemed to flex her knees to do it, and the bar's two broken halves settled with a groan beneath her weight.

"All right!" she boomed. "You face-fucks wanna get in a pissing contest with me, you're gonna die! You're gonna drown! You're gonna *burn!*"

There was a huge chrome zipper down the front of her leather pants, which were swollen with her planetary girth. She ripped the zipper down, and her densely tufted sex thrust out—her livid oyster extruded, and a torrent of piss raged down.

Wrench dove to one end of the bar and vaulted out. As her water struck the floorboards the wood *whuffed* into flames, and flames were instantly raging, hot as an oil blaze, and black smoke geysering up.

Disdainfully, she zipped up. She leapt down and strode through the unopened door, which exploded before her. Before anyone dared move towards the door, there came the banshee wail of her acceleration, and then her thunder diminishing away.

Half an hour later, Willy and Gutley stood by Willy's truck in the parking lot, watching the firetrucks unhooking, and the crowd waving their arms and shouting while two sheriff's deputies scribbled on clipboards. The Rusty Nail's roof was already engulfed in the flames.

They agreed to make their transaction at the Sylvan Lodge, a downriver place declined from a fifties resort spot to a multi-unit rental for welfare and counter-culture people. Willy liked it because it was in the coastal hills, and not far from Highway One.

When the details were settled Willy urged Gutley: "You gotta take this seriously, Gut. You, everybody's gotta clear outta this whole area. Something's gonna happen here. I can't explain how I know, because you'd think I was crazy or blind drunk. But you gotta believe me."

"Believe you?" Gutley looked half dazed and half enraged. "You think I'm gonna have trouble believin *anything* after this? How far you think we gotta run?"

"I dunno. Out of the River area for sure, and—I'm not sure how I know this, but I wouldn't head into town, either."

Willy staggered a little turning to his truck. "You look like shit, Willy," Gutley said. "You OK to drive?"

It almost made Willy laugh. "Christ! You shoulda seen me gettin here!"

He got home near sunset. A note on the kitchen-nook counter told him Barbara and Maxie were at the mall with Lucky, who wanted Maxie to have new school gear while the fall sales were still on. Good. He could go right down and start harvesting the dope.

He drove his truck down to the copse—no need to fear a visible trail now. Within a day he would have the crop bagged and stashed and the entire shed dismantled.

He jumped out and took up the dead branch he used to move the poison oak vines aside. As he touched it to a vine, the vine coiled itself, darted out, and whipped him across the top of the head, then seized his nude scalp like a muscled tentacle and yanked him off his feet. As he scuttled out of range on all fours another vine whipped him stingingly across the back, slashing through his shirt down to bare skin.

He got his legs under him and faced the enemy. The whole copse was alive—wherever the omnipresent poison oak appeared it writhed and twisted, jutting from the angle of its natural hang, reaching, from everywhere, in Willy's direction, the whole grove acting like a single, multibrachiate giant that wanted his blood, all its oily red leaves bright, as fire in the blaze of the setting sun.

Willy stood feeling blood ooze from scalp and back. Already his skin was abundantly inoculated with the infernal poison that covered the vines right down to the least leaf and twig. Highly reactive to poison oak, Willy foresaw the misery that lay in the weeks ahead for him. He ground his teeth, and two tears of utter rage winked like diamonds into the corners of his eyes.

"That's my fucking dope in there" (he almost moaned it) "and NOTHING'S gonna take it from me! NOTHING!"

He whipped his truck around, and divots of sod flew from his tires as he rocketed back to his toolshed. He returned with chainsaw, axe, machete, pole-saw, his eyes fixed and glaring—a bald, squat, block-muscled psychotic with bright red lacerations on his scalp, and leapt like a Berserker to the struggle.

In the west, the sky was indigo and stars were coming out when Lucky drove in with Barbara and Maxie. Willy lay in the arm-chair of the trailer's family room, giving them a friendly smile as they came in, but too tired to move any other part of his body. He saw amazement in three different ages of the female face.

"Daddy!" Maxie cried, ever the exact reporter of observed fact—"you're *bald!* Your clothes are all torn up and your head is bleeding!"

"I know, little pal. I've been trimming some brush."

"Trimming some *brush?*" asked Barbara. "What happened to your hair?"

"What can I say, sweetie pie? It all fell out. Lucky? Any ob-servations on my appearance?"

"Jesus, Willy," his mother-in-law foghorned. "You look like

someone snipped you in pieces and glued you back together funny." They all went into the bathroom to clean Willy up. They filled the tiny space, all of them multiplied in mirrors, and Willy saw that indeed all his lacerations were amazingly colorful. "You look so different, Daddy," Maxie told him, sounding solemn, a little scared. "Your ears so big!"

"I know," he said, "but don't worry, I am your Daddy, sweetheart. See my ears have always looked like this, it's they had hair to hide in."

He returned to the armchair, where Maxie got into his lap and promptly fell asleep. *Willy Yakima,* he thought, *human sofa*—and fell asleep himself. When Maxie had been bedded, Barbara woke him up.

"Reed just called," she told him. "He's had some strange things happen over there and wants you to call him. You've got some strange things to tell me too, don't you?"

"Christ, Barb, we got big-time trouble. I mean this whole fuckin city does! You're not gonna believe what I'm gonna tell you, Barb. Is Lucky tucking Maxie?"

"Yes. She'll be right here."

"She should hear this too, except for the dope part."

"You think I haven't told her about that? Let her run a risk she doesn't know about when she visits here?"

"Oh. Well, fine. You're gonna have a hard time believing what's happened to me today, honey."

She had to laugh a little. "Looking the way you do, it may be a little easier for me than you think."

Nineteen

Scat Collins was still in the little valley, even though it was near to dark. Now, though, he was high up on the slope of its eastern flank, on the opposite side from where he'd made his cut this morning. People had indeed expected that trash would fill this valley—in fifteen years' time. But *eleven hours?*

The growing dark made the wide battle-scene infernal. Arc lamps and the headlights of the grunting earth movers swept the rising flood of filth, which burbled like a titanic, nightmare pudding.

Unstoppably, it rose, a millennial reek streaming up from it, bringing tears to the eyes. Scat's eyes still flowed, though his brain had for hours been numb to it. The ooze had a flexible, bony sub-structure of broken wood, metal, and plastic so that, as it rose against the wide earthen dike that all the desperate machines were rooting up in its path, it tended to pile up in sludgy domes and crests—pile up higher and higher, thirty, forty feet, and then suddenly topple over—instant burial alive.

One of the other big dozers had been lost this way, swallowed right on the crest of the dike. The vile blackness hit it like a fist, the driver's back surely broken in the instant of impact. You could hear its smothered wheels spinning impotently in there. It made Scat's skin crawl to see a good rig die like that.

All the biggest machines idled near the crest for backup while the more maneuverable ones worked on the dike. They worked like maddened dinosaurs, slaking their parched and roaring throats with diesel straight from the chrome tit of a tanker brought up to keep them supplied. They grunted and roared and heaped chewed earth and the air was thick with the black farts of their labor, and still they worked in constant retreat, backing inexorably up to the crest.

By the latest measure, it was rising at a foot a minute.

And got clearer by the second to Scat, watching from the rearguard on the crest, that his and the other big rigs were going to be ordered to fall back—to the next ridge eastwards, to start a containment dike out there.

Incredible.

He could still recall, so clearly, just how this valley had been this morning: the silence, the grass growing everywhere, the tang of dew in the air just beginning to be warmed by the sun. . . . And now this! An impossibility, of huge proportions!

And there were no news helicopters. It had been hours since they had started being conspicuous by their absence. That was par for the course, the basic self-protective instinct of the incompetent numb-nuts County brass.

But if they did fall back to the next rise . . . It was much lower ground—a ridge half this height. And the plain opened out just beyond. It was a nice straight shot east from there, and you'd be able to *see* it from Santa Marta's higher spots.

No, they wouldn't have a lid on it much longer, not if there was very much more of this shit down there still to come out.

And why shouldn't there be? Since this was impossible in the first place, why shouldn't it be limitless too?

"The pieces we've run in the *Press Republican* on wastewater abatement have really seemed to turn the tide," Nick Sawyer said to Dwight Urbach, regional director of the North Coast Water Quality Control Board. He was fixing Dwight a vodka and tonic with a twist of lime. Sawyer had indeed managed to get two features printed in the last few days, thanks to a City Desk guy who owed him for some Board of Supe scoops.

"And we've seen remarkable results already," Marv Straff said from the couch, smacking his lips over his own drink. Morris Hacker, definitely the most nervous person in the room, had to brace himself inwardly to do his part. "We're already a hundred million gallons below normal intake volumes." The lie seemed to echo, brazenly.

Urbach was a bald man of Straff's bearish build, but softer and paunchier. He nodded them a sketchy little smile of interest. His gaze was drawn to the kitchen, where Shawna Sawyer and Bev Carney were putting the last touches on dinner.

Dave Shugg, his drink already drained, said from the couch that faced Straff's, "But how does it work? I mean how can people, well, *eliminate* less?" He instantly felt that it came out too sneeringly. True, he was supposed to be the honest businessman here, unaware until just a few days ago that there were unlooked-for developments out at the treatment plant that might—what's this?—give grounds for a temporary lifting of the Building Moratorium. But he was coming on too strong. The fact was, since the moment he'd got here, he had been struggling with a sharp irritation at his fellow-conspirators.

"People *flush* less often," Straff was answering, genially, as if to a loved and puzzled child. "They stop washing their cars! They shower quicker! In a city of almost two hundred thousand, that's talking millions of gallons a day!"

"Quite right!" said Urbach, who still didn't seem very involved in the conversation, and who now moved towards the kitchen, smiling. "My, that smells *heavenly,* ladies!"

Bev beamed at him. There was a sleek sheen to the man—his pate seemed lightly oiled. She tried to strike the right note, sweet and ironic, like Beaver Cleaver's Mom:

"Just wait till you taste it, Dwight—Shawna has really put on the dog for us here."

Shawna, by the Osterizer, stiffened slightly. Bev brought out the raw veggies and dip tray to the huge, polished redwood burl-slab table between the couches.

Dave Shugg, who never touched such yuppie squirrel food, took a slice of raw cauliflower and munched it with sour yoghurt dip and pondered Urbach's words: *Quite right.* So it was in the bag then.

Sawyer hadn't disclosed his means of dealing with Urbach, and hadn't wanted to know the conspirators' precise means of operation on their side. Talk about slick! Shugg glared at the raw carrot stick he suddenly discovered he was eating. He just barely restrained himself from flinging it at the floor.

What did he care that these people were sly, greedy assholes? He was going to clear at least seven million when the dust cleared, in a year or so.

This doubleness in his feelings—it could almost scare you. He'd stopped in on Jake, corning over. There was a home-care nurse, Jake was in bed, looking awful. His cough had turned deep, and productive—he'd inhaled some goddam flies last week, it seemed.

And Shugg had stood there thinking how loathsome the poor guy was! He still felt it when he pictured Jake—a pasty-faced glutton rotting from inside who casually pays to have half a billion gallons of raw sewage pumped into a fucking mineshaft barely four miles out of town!

He didn't dare open his mouth to speak—he didn't know which half of his mind would take the opportunity to express itself.

"The point is, Dave," Marv Straff said, "that it's *weekly* flow that ultimately controls pond levels of the treated effluent. If this kind of public response continues even a few more days, we're looking at entering the rainy season with optimum minimums in our effluent ponds, which was the whole crux of our problem."

"Optimum minimums," Morris Hacker seconded, looking vaguely uncertain about the phrase.

"The real shame," Nick Sawyer said, "is that projects *already* well begun should have to come to a standstill, losing hundreds of jobs in the county, if the pond levels have already come down within operational limits!" He answered the phone. It was for Bev.

When she knew it was Jake she took it in another room. "Christ, Bev, I feel awful." His voice made her nape stir. The crackly husk of a voice, clogged with congestion. She had a date with DaValli later tonight. It seemed cold to cut her old partner entirely out of the evening just because he was repulsively ill.

"I'll come by for a while. I can't stay the night, but I'll stay over tomorrow night."

She made her apologies to the Sawyers. "So wonderful to meet you, Dwight," she said. Urbach's handshake told her that the special review of pond levels was in the bag.

When they all sat down to table, there was a curious, shared moment of hesitation. The spread was beautiful—an orange crab aspic in an oval mold (it made Shugg think, for no good reason, of a toilet seat), Arab cracker-bread and butter in little sculpted dabs (the dabs reminded Hacker of animal droppings), a marvelous bitter-lettuce salad sprinkled with nuts and raisins (the raisins put Nick Sawyer irrepressibly in mind of flies)—the spread could have been a plate in a magazine, but for just a moment there, it seemed to touch the party with a qualm of dread.

Except for Dwight Urbach, who rubbed his palms and genuinely beamed. Shawna smiled her gratitude. To save the mood she decided to bring the pièce de resistance on at once, a big tureen of *ragout du mistral*.

Its aroma perked everyone up.

"Mmm, that's fish, right?" Straff asked.

"That *does* smell good," said Shugg, "but more like chicken to me."

Susan gave an arch smile, pleased by the mystery, ladling out the warm yellow cream sauce studded with a pale meat that had melted into toothsome fibers.

Morris Hacker took in his first mouthful like a revelation, a sunburst of complex flavor. "It's pork," he said, swallowing. "It's wonderful!"

"Salmon," pronounced Straff conclusively, "and it's heavenly!"

"I'm sorry, gentlemen," said Urbach, almost rapturously. "It is lamb, beyond question—and delicious beyond description!"

Shawna smiled like the Sphinx. Things were going fine now, all the other dishes getting sucked into the generally awakened hunger. Silverware tingled, eyes glowed. Her chance discovery in an arcane old cookbook, the ragout was pork, but, she told them, "Final bets will be taken at the end of the meal, gentlemen, and we'll see who has the smartest taste buds."

The banter was lively and ran to culinary topics. Just as the silverware was beginning to slow and the first rush of greed tapering off, Nick Sawyer set his fork down abruptly, making it ring against his plate. He looked remarkably pale. "Excuse me," he said.

He got up and headed across the living room, moving quickly but in a curiously taut posture. Just as he vanished into the hallway he emitted a sharp, blatting flatulence, like a snapping banner that he briefly trailed from his stern.

It might have been a thunderbolt in the silence at the table. They avoided one another's eyes, and then their eyes began to look inward, growing worriedly aware of changes in themselves.

Now Urbach's fork struck the table.

"Where's the bathroom?" he barked bluntly, springing up, sweat like dew on his brow.

But Susan was rising too, back stiff. "I'll show you," she said tightly. They strode across the living room, seeming almost to race.

The Sawyers' lovely home featured two and a half bathrooms, one upstairs. Within two minutes, Straff, Shugg, and Hacker had found and stood calling vain entreaties outside the doors of these bathrooms.

Then they found their desperate ways outside. This was, for all three, a bodily necessity of the highest order, and no social protocols could prevail against it.

In the rosebushes Hacker squatted and groaned, light from the house windows making foliated half-moons of the blossoms, and a larger, bi-valved moon of his buttocks. Out back, Shugg crouched in the shadow of the deck, while Straff he could hear across the yard, beyond the gardener's shed. Even now Shugg confronted that bizarre division in his mind. *Serves them right, the greedy assholes!* he was thinking. And at the same time he was thinking, *Dear Jesus, this could kill us! Is it ever going to stop?*

Twenty

A deeper band of purple lay on the west, the stars were coming out, and Alex was driving up to the Quicksilver Mine.

As far as KleenCo was concerned, he and Kim had disappeared three days ago after finishing the flex hose and drawing their last check, and that was how they wanted it, but it wasn't right to slink out of town without even one look back—a secret look, just to see where things stood. It felt too chickenshit not to do it—like just one look at this goon in the blue van sent them running, not even daring to come back to the shaft where they'd worked every night for months.

Abuelita Aurora had tried to make him feel like a slacker because he wouldn't go into the hills with her and Kim, to cut herbs and do *brujeria,* that embarrassing granny-witch stuff. Aurora could think what she wanted about demons or Powers, but Alex's reason for leaving was pure and simple, that there might be things going on around DaValli's operation that he and Kim didn't want to be involved in.

Ever since he and Kim became lovers, he'd been ashamed of how he'd let Aurora spook him about the mountain.

Now he must be clear-headed. He had a woman to take care of, he had to deal with realities. The danger at KleenCo was getting hurt by goons like that guy in the van, or ending up in prison.

He saw some unusual lights in the skirts of the hills to the south as he began to climb towards the mine. Could they be working on that new dump at night? What was the rush?

He would've liked to be a little surer how much Kim was

buying into Aurora's witchcraft. She said she was keeping an open mind, and he told her she was humoring Aurora, who was a wonderful old lady, and that was fine with him because he loved her too! But a power in the mountain? Like a god or a devil? And hanging out there so it can *communicate* with you? Come on!

But she held something back, told him to drop it. Alex wasn't easy with it. He would feel a lot better if she out and out agreed it was all just bullshit.

Climbing the switchbacks, he was trying to remember just how far down the mountain you started to hear an approaching motor when you were up at the shaft. He parked at a turnout almost a half mile down slope to be safe.

This was definitely scary—and he'd come up here so casually, just a week ago! But something irrevocable had passed between them, when the guy in the van had looked into their lights. *I know you know,* the look said, and it was true, even though he and Kim didn't know what it *was* they knew. They knew he was death, and saw him knowing that they knew it. Just like that.

Walking these switchbacks, he imagined his truck on them, logoed with the huge skull, the way he'd pictured it, in Aztec style, black and red and silver, moving like a monster with fire-eyes in the night. They were right the way they drew things, those Aztec and Mayan guys, their dragons and giant gods growing out of the corn, elaborate and beautiful and terrible. That was how the world would look to you—Alex saw it clearly now, walking up the asphalt in the dark—that was how the world would look if you didn't have any vehicles or modern things, were just bare-ass naked on a mountain in the jungle.

He heard the offload motor before he reached the compound's fence. He approached it where the brush grew close to the perimeter.

The company's tanker was at the shaft-mouth. The truck, the shaft, the stars above the pyramid of disposal drums—Alex had been part of this scene a hundred times. There were two figures crouched by the offload valves—bigger shapes than his and Kim's would have looked from here. They stood up and were half backlit by the shaft-mouth.

It was the goon and DaValli. DaValli was pointing at the out-take valves, then at the shaft. The goon nodded. DaValli was showing him the ropes on the tanker. Was the guy just going to drive pickups? Was he just ordinary hired labor? The goon's head made a slight, heart-freezing turn. Now his shadowed eyes seemed to be aimed straight at Alex.

He couldn't be seeing anything. Did enough light reach here from the shaft? Alex didn't dare move his face even so much as to look at the leaves beside him, see if some faint light lay on them. He dared not even blink. Those eyes, two pits of dark, drank him in. Then the goon looked idly up at the stars.

Alex backed with endless caution into the trees. He didn't start running, afraid of making the least noise, till he was a quarter-mile down. He heard a car coming from above and dove into the trees—DaValli's Trans Am.

Alex went for a few beers at Father's Office. The picture he'd seen said there was nothing to fear. Whatever that flex hose had been about, KleenCo looked pretty much business as usual.

For the last two days Alex had been making some added money for their trip at Cristobal's Auto Paint shop—Cristobal was one of Aurora's nephews. There didn't seem to be any reason he shouldn't make a few more days' pay to stake them in L.A., especially since Kim was saying she didn't want to leave just yet because it would be running out on Aurora—that was how she put it.

But he didn't *want* to stay in Santa Marta. Not another

night—not really. And it had to do with that goon. Alex didn't want to be in the same city with him—pure and simple. Didn't want that guy to know even approximately where Alex and Kim could be found.

Kim would be late—it was amazing the hours that old woman could walk the hills, they never came out till long after dark. He headed for home after less than an hour.

The porchlight of Pogue's house was out. Maybe they shouldn't have been leaving it on round the clock. On the porch, fumbling for his keys in the dark, he stepped on something soft. He reached inside and turned on the feeble living room light, and saw it was a cat's tail. Red. Buster's? He picked it up unbelievingly. The bony tube of meat inside the fur was . . . faintly warm?

He wanted to leave it outside, but if it was Buster's, he owed it to Pogue to bring it in. He dropped it on the coffee table.

In the kitchen, filthy dishes and food containers covered every horizontal surface. He went to the fridge, his soles snapping and popping on the immemorial stickinesses of the linoleum. In the fridge, among its reeking mummies, he'd laid in a quart of beer, but found it half drunk with the cap replaced sloppily so the remainder was flat. Pogue must have stopped in some time today. Alex took the bottle back to the living room.

Sipping flat beer, he prodded the tail on the coffee table with his finger. It was Buster's all right. He knew the tail pattern from waking up in the mornings with Buster's butt in his face purring away. Buster was a smart old-timer who knew his turf. What the hell happened to him?

Unless. Unless this was one of those weird mob threats, like the fish and the horses' heads in *The Godfather*? Like that goon up there *did* see him tonight, had had him pegged here for days?

From the dark of the hallway to the bedrooms stepped a

man. The goon. Not ten feet away now, and Alex had sensed nothing, heard not a whisper, a creak . . .

"Hello, Alex. I'm Sol Lazarian."

Christ, the guy was huge! His voice low and polished and mellow, like one of those big wooden flutes. He was huge, yet so light, coming forward a couple more easy steps into the living room.

"What are you doing here?" Alex's voice cracked on "doing"—he couldn't help it.

Lazarian noticed the thing on the coffee table, and his brows cocked. "What's that? May I?"

And there he was on the other side of the table, his hand out. Strangely, Alex felt a shade easier, as if the man's calm was an aura you shared when he neared you. "It's the cat's tail. I found it on the porch." He handed Lazarian Buster's tail.

The goon held and felt of it, his sinewed hands gentle and precise. "The housecat here? Mmm. Not quite warm, still limber though . . ." The goon faintly, angelically smiled.

"Omens attend you, Alejandro Cruz."

The goon had done the cat, Alex thought. This was a kind of taunting, a rubbing it in, making the point.

"Marvelous forces are converging in your destiny," Lazarian went on, his eyes affectionately eager to explain, to get something tricky across to Alex. "To some of us it is given, by blind luck, perhaps, to pierce the veil. To penetrate the tarnished bubble of this world, to pass *knowingly* into the grander universe!" He swept his hand at the ceiling—Alex thought of the gestures of mad scientists in old black-and-white horror movies, those crazed theatrical sweeps of hand at heaven. There was only this coffee table between them, and the guy could obviously snap this table with his hands.

"What are you doing here?" Alex asked a second time.

"I've come for your life, Alex. I'm giving you to the god that is emerging in the Quicksilver Mine."

There passed a frozen instant. There sat the goon, courteously waiting, as if a decent interval must be allowed for Alex to decide on his response.

Then Alex's legs launched him, and his hand was taking the bottle by its neck, bringing it up clubwise—all this so rubbery and slow, it seemed, his nerves blurry with an evening's beer.

He was spun, given a hammer blow to the back of the head, then plucked from the floor, seized and folded. The goon's left arm crushed his back to the goon's chest and locked his arms. The goon's right was wrapped around Alex's head, locking Alex's chin in the crook of its elbow. He spoke softly, urgently in Alex's ear.

"Tell it I, Sol Lazarian, send you as a gift. Tell it I reverence it! Tell it I pray to be shown, to be lifted."

In a strangled voice blurred with spittle, Alex choked out, "Fuck you, asshole."

Lazarian broke his neck.

Alex's body twitched and spasmed. When it was still, Lazarian laid it on the couch and stood looking at it.

Lazarian held perfectly preserved in memory, like a photographic gallery, the face of every person he had killed. Wherever circumstances had allowed, he had closely studied his newly dead, believing their faces still resonated with the lives they had held; might convey his questions to their evicted souls; and might, through some fractional change of expression, convey back answers about what lay Outside.

The boy's sealed eyelids seemed only slightly troubled. A kind of thoughtful anger tugged down his mouth-corners. There was substance here, Lazarian felt. Here was a spirit that had grown larger with the revelation of its crossing-over. He looked like an Aztec sacrifice, lying at sunrise atop the pyramid, his face catching the rising sun while below, the worshippers who offered him up still stood in shadow.

Lazarian drank in his image. He stood savoring the room too, the delicious sense of vacuum left in any room whose occupant has just died, the special emptiness alive with his absence. . . .

Lazarian rubbed the spilled beer with a filthy dish towel from the kitchen, till its stain blurred into the other in the carpet. He trashed the bottle. He paused before taking up his sacrifice to touch, once more, the cat's tail on the coffee table.

What was so disturbing about this strange omen? It came from the Power he was courting—he didn't doubt this. It had that unmistakable quality of being a piece of a dream dropped into reality.

But wasn't there . . . ? The feeling kept gnawing at him: wasn't there a touch of something like mockery in this sign?

He couldn't lay this thought to rest. The tail of a devoured cat. There was a touch of . . . slapstick to it.

Looking around him, cocking his head, Lazarian suddenly felt a delicious shiver pass through him. Because suddenly he knew that this sacrifice was not waiting till tomorrow—that it was being accepted, acknowledged, here and now. Suddenly he felt that he wasn't alone in this house.

Never had he felt more alive than this moment, when he draped the slight body across his shoulder and began to carry it to the back door he had entered by. Every nerve of him was a silver flame, the plucked string of a harpsichord. Longing and joy sang in his heart a trio with that most potent music, terror.

The kitchen's sticky linoleum crackled softly under his soles. In every fetid shadow, half-seen shapes stirred at the verge of vision. Soundlessly he opened the back door and scanned the yard.

The yard was full of old lumberpiles, tall weeds, and scattered junk, ragged terrain of obstacles faintly glazed with the light from the curtained windows of the upper units of the shabby stucco six-plex next door.

The lot to the other side of the yard was vacant. He could hear the murmurs of TVs from the apartment windows, and the buzz of the sodium vapor lamp far down the shadowy black—nothing else. Through the yard's trash his eye picked out the path he had blazed coming in, from his van parked in the alley beyond the rear fence.

He stepped off the back porch, his soles crackling softly in the weeds. A freight train collided with his left side.

Lazarian was in the air, Alex's body freefalling away from him. Lazarian was tumbling through the weeds, the earth and the hard-cornered trash giving hammerblows to his head his shoulders, his back, his ribs. Then his hands and feet found purchase on the earth, and Lazarian was rising, turning.

A huge swine straddled Alex's corpse in the grass. The sagging black cheekflaps that hung from the huge brute's muzzle drizzled clots of phosphorescent mucus, foxfire-snot that plopped from its wet, tusked snout. The sagging purse of its throat gulped and shuddered with its growling. Its little poached eyes glowed hot red, meeting his, locking his, telling him: *Behold*.

The beast lowered its snout to Alex, bit deep, and shook him like a doll. There was a rending and a snapping noise, and the swine hoisted one of his arms in its jaws, turning as it did so, wheeling its mass ponderously around. And as it turned—as if it had tucked itself through a secret seam in the night air—it vanished utterly.

Lazarian stumbled to the corpse. Though impossibility had touched it, it was the same dead flesh it had been, minus one arm.

This was acceptance beyond all expectation. Lazarian's soul was ravished. For so long the Impossible had seduced and eluded him, and now the brutal power of its frank and open touch! His heart galloped. He had to grin his disbelieving joy.

"This is mockery, isn't it, Great One?" he whispered. "You smite me with your potent Slapstick, and I fall! Are you asking me for my anger? Are you asking me if I dare to show it?"

He was speaking to air, just where the secret seam had been that swallowed the beast—whispering through that crack in the world. "Accept my double offering tomorrow, Great One! Show me your will!"

Lazarian again took up the boy and darted through the shadows of the yard. He eased Alex over the back fence and lightly vaulted it himself. The van's engine came alive. Its noise diminished, away. Pogue's house stood empty.

Twenty-one

For the third night running Aurora and Kim rolled late out of the hills, dusty and thirsty, Aurora stolidly steering her old Dodge Dart and looking small at the wheel, looking too short to be driving it as precisely as she did.

"The seat's sagging," Kim had told her the first day. "You should have a foam pad for a booster."

Aurora shook her head, explaining, "As the seat has subsided over the years, *hija,* I have adapted incrementally, and am quite comfortable now."

"It makes your passengers nervous, though, *abuelita,* to see you straining to see over the top of the steering wheel."

Aurora smiled understandingly. "Young people have a great number of unnecessary or misguided feelings about things. It is part of your charm, dear."

Kim had learned at once that Aurora paid no attention to suggestions about how she should do things. For example, they took precisely two botas of drink when they went into the hills each morning—one of water, and one of watered wine. Though they spent hours at a time at a given spot, "listening," they covered a lot of terrain in a day. Two one-quart botas were not *enough* to drink for one day, and they always came parched out of the hills.

And always stopped here, at the first convenience store on the way into town, for a four-pack of cold Dos Equis. And Kim had to admit that after the day's ritual thirst these two bottles, sipped cold, were a supreme pleasure, at least as good as sex.

They always drank the first one parked out in the store's lot, to sip the others at leisure while they drove. "Abuelita," Kim said, "I don't know if I can keep going with you. Alex and I want to go, I mean for its own sake. We want to check out a new place, find new work . . . It's kind of exciting to us, L.A. and all . . ."

Aurora shot her a dark-framed look at the word "exciting."

"You are trying faithfully, I know, Kimberly, to listen with me in the hills. You are trying to open your spirit to *la picadura,* to feel the touch of the world. You have, I think, some gift, and maybe more than some. But you are headstrong. You have not mastered that yearling colt in your heart. I tell you this, though. If you are concerned with what is exciting, you are best off to stay and work with me. In what I feel coming will be more excitement, I think, than you yet know how to imagine."

Something had touched Kim's senses in that Safeway produce section, and she had felt this old woman beside her, seeing even more of this thing than she, and seeing it without surprise. Abuelita Aurora knew things . . .

But making fires with herbs? Sitting crosslegged under oak trees, silent for hours? There was no way this was *doing* anything.

The porchlight was out at Pogue's house, and there was no light inside, either, though there was Alex's truck.

"Alex always falls asleep with the light on," Kim said as they pulled to the curb.

After a beat of silence Aurora said, "I'll come in if I may. Just for a moment." Kim found herself glad of it—found herself a little afraid of going in alone.

She stumbled in the overgrown grass crossing the lawn. Mounting the shadowy porch, she saw a pale strip of jamb outlining the door. It wasn't closed all the way. She was reaching hesitantly to push the door inwards when Aurora seized her arm, and her heart leapt as if a snake had bitten her.

"Don't you *smell* it?" the old woman hissed in her ear. "Don't you *feel* it, just on the other side of the door?"

Lithe, surprising, the old woman stretched out one foot and jabbed the door with her toes. The two recoiled to the edge of the porch as it slowly swung open and Kim smelled it then, a powerful smell of . . . the shaft, that cold whiff of toxic hell, though now laced with something else. Bitter smoke.

Just inside the door stood a huge shape, molded of blood-red embers and night-black soot. The embers breathed, brightened, and dimmed the outlines of the creature's bristling, muscled haunches, its huge, spike-crested back. It leaked fumes that stung tears from Kim's eyes. The fine silky hair on her forearms felt like a million tiny live wires.

Clamped in the tusked snout, which drooled embers, was a pale object. The glow of the beast's hot substance faintly lit it: a human arm.

The monster dropped the arm, and at the instant of its impact with the floor the beast was gone, its stench was gone—the darkness was empty of them both.

Aurora found the living room light switch.

As terrible as the torn meat at the shoulder-joint was the arm's smallness. It seemed a child's, though Kim had felt that hand move covetously on her breasts. Her knees gave and she spewed her beers off the side of the porch.

Aurora made her rest on the couch and brought her water. From her knapsack she got an old shawl of a faded rainbow pattern, like the knapsack itself, and in this she wrapped the arm. When she came to Kim again she had it cradled in one arm like a casually held child.

"Kimberly. Look at me, dear. Yes. Open your mind. Calm

yourself. Alejandro's life may not be lost. This part of him I hold is a summons. It came more horribly than we looked for, but our questionings have been answered. We must go back to the hills."

"Do you think he's alive?"

"If he is not, he may be again. We are being told to come and see. We are being told this is a life-and-death matter, for all of us. We won't have to search any more—only to be near. I will enter the trance, and we will be shown."

It felt strange turning the tanker over to Lazarian. Frankie had really gotten into driving it these last couple days. As he ran through the drill during the offload, his fingers lingered on the stainless-steel couplings, his eyes lingered on the smooth female curves of the tank's sides.

Was it something in Lazarian's luminous eyes—was it the goon's feeling for the rig that Frankie was catching? Or was Frankie himself feeling it, this erotic quality to the moment? He felt a jealous reluctance to turn over the keys. There was in the smell of the shaft—and to a lesser degree the simpler smell of the tanker herself—something sly and intoxicating. Wasn't there? Something that woke a faint commotion in his loins.

Lazarian smiled, seeming to detect that he gave the keys grudgingly. "You can trust me with the job, Brer Weasel. I place the highest importance on it, feeding the shaft."

"Great. Each trip's pure profit, after all. Has, ah, Bill called you? I can't seem to reach him."

"I never try to reach Beiderbeck, Frankie. I'd relax—he'll call you."

"Right. I guess it would be, well, downright miraculous if he could actually pull it off, eh?"

Another faint smile from the goon here, privately enjoying

something about Frankie. "Bill Beiderbeck," said Sol, "is a miraculous kind of guy."

Frankie drove down to his gym in Santa Marta for some bodily purification before his late date with Bev Carney, toiled on the Climber till his sweat was streaming, and then he saunaed and let it stream some more.

Was this a whiff of the shaft coming out with his sweat? He glanced guiltily at the men baking with him in the dim light.

He went to the Jacuzzi, and there it was again, that dizzying scent of the caustic, satiny darkness . . . Ever so faintly it teased him. At last he realized it had to be an imprint of the smell in his own nostrils. Small wonder, after all, given its strength.

He stretched out in the jetting bubbles. "Relax," said Sol Lazarian.

The funny thing was, Frankie did feel like relaxing. This whole setup he had pieced together was by far the most complex, the most lucrative scam he'd ever pulled off. It made those porno films with the fake snuff footage look like a piker's gambit, and Frankie had been quite proud of that one not too many months ago. But now, having put this whole thing in motion, he seemed to feel now that it could roll on by itself, sink or swim, for all he cared.

He was never like this! The whole joy of a scam was the cooking, pulling the levers, promoting it, stroking the principal parties—the whole dog-and-pony show. It remotely alarmed him to find himself so slack and passive—except that this strange, lazy delight he was feeling made none of it seem to matter much.

Normally he got impatient in a Jacuzzi pretty quick, but tonight he lay there an hour and actually dozed off. He dreamed he was floating through dark, cool air, down, down towards the clustered, whispering crowns of trees. An erection sprouted from him and, like a single wing, it oared him through the scented gloom. Confused shapes filled the silky dark he sank through. From under the heavy-beamed grotto of a porch, a huge and murky shape edged out to receive him, a rubbery giant of the deep from which the rich bewitching aromas foamed and bubbled up to him, engulfing his senses.

He woke sharply and sat embarrassed for some minutes before it was decent for him to emerge. He had to dress fast, running late now for cocktails at Bev's condo.

"You say he inhaled some *flies?*"

"So it seems," said Bev, handing him his freshened drink, seeing the story couldn't be avoided. She was as concise as possible. She'd spent an hour at Jake's bedside hearing him wheeze, smelling that unpleasant faint odor he gave off. She left him with his night nurse, and stepping out of his house had been a wonderful relief.

"Incredible," Frankie told her. "Remember Davey Shugg's limes?"

"Do I remember? Are you serious?"

"You look ravishing tonight, Bev."

"I think that's a very strange train of thought," she smiled.

And it was, but suddenly he felt a sharp appetite for her.

Yet a strange thing happened a few minutes later, as they knelt naked, embracing on the bed. As Bev's clean flavors invaded his senses, they struck Frankie as a kind of shock, and his desire recoiled, baffled, from the taste and smell of her. The fire died from his nerves, and his sex slackened against the warmth of her thighs. He put her gently at arm's length and looked at her, puzzled.

"What's the matter, dear?" she asked, eyes still dreamy-bright.

"I don't know. It's the strangest thing. Suddenly . . . I'm not in the mood."

Bev looked at him a moment, still smiling, but the smile changing key now. "Well, great, asshole. What was all this come-on about?"

"I *was* in the mood. It's just that, when I started smelling you . . ."

"Are you after a kick in the nuts?" She wasn't smiling at all now.

"I don't mean that." He was starting to feel cornered, defensive. "I mean, it's like, you're so squeaky-*clean*."

She blinked. "Well, I shouldn't be surprised you want a little dirt, I guess."

"Meaning?"

"Meaning someone who—how shall I put this?—who sucks up shit for an illegal dollar—"

"Well, hey! You're sucking from the same tit I am, Miz Carney!"

"On the contrary." She snared herself in her black lace bra. "I'm making my money from the legitimate sale of quality homes. I'm *resorting* to you. You are making your money for—let's put it nicely, for acting as a kind of septic tank."

Watching her lithe movements dressing, Frankie was already feeling a pang of regret somewhere in the unfamiliar weave of his sensations. "Well, hell," he laughed, "it's a dirty job, but somebody's got to do it." He dressed. Tomorrow, after she saw the completed hookup of shaft with plant, she was scheduled to make the next major cash payment. Just as well to have sex out of the picture for the sharp dealing ahead. If Beiderbeck could actually pull it off, Frankie intended to pull about half the sewage and then sweat them for more money. It was best to stay as friendly as possible.

"No hard feelings?" he asked. "It's the materials I'm handling up at my site—I'm actually getting some kind of toxic reaction that's making my body weird. Come on, lemme take you out for a fancy dessert somewhere."

Bev smiled. He saw that she too had thought of the dealing ahead. "Come on," she said. "We'll have some good brandy and ice cream right here."

Twenty-two

Gently, Aurora laid Alejandro's arm under a manzanita bush. She ran her fingers lightly over it—here the torn stump still weeping blood through the fabric, and there his hand, still half-clenched, not yet letting go of its young life.

"Touch him," she said to Kim. The girl's face, after tears, had a cold, determined look, the will to be strong, but under the determination you could see the child in her mouth, which was bewildered, wounded. She touched the bundle, shuddered, then touched it again more lingeringly.

"Do you see," Aurora asked, "that it is still bleeding?"

"Should it . . . not be?"

"Not so long, no. Get me deadwood, Kimberly, small and dry."

Kim knew the drill from their daytime vigils up here. Leaving the Dart in one of the off-highway coverts the old woman used, they had made doubletime straight into the hills—dark, uncertain work that had calmed Kim's terror. She was not sure just where they were—maybe one or two hills south of the Quicksilver.

Aurora made a small, hot fire. Filling her big, battered trail-cup from her bota, she began to brew a mixture of the herbs she had taken from her pouches.

"Open the bedroll, *hija*," she said. "Take a nap if you can. Tonight may be very demanding."

Kim woke sharply. The moon was straight up, tangled in the branches of the oak. The fire was low red coals and the old woman sat there, back straight, legs crossed, her hands asleep on her thighs. Her slitted eyes, behind the dark-framed glasses, were locked in inward vision.

Kim lay back. Beneath the bedroll the earth seemed elastic, a drumskin. She could feel in its taut fabric the little weight of Alex's torn arm, the remnant of his life, lying a few feet away from her. Tears came for a while. Then she turned her face away and was asleep.

When she woke at dawn, Kim sat bolt upright. Aurora lay dead: sprawled back on the earth, glasses crooked on her frozen face, her gnarled hands, palms up and empty, on the grass . . .

"Abuelita!"

The old woman started violently, her glasses coming the rest of the way off. Kim retrieved them and helped her sit up, kneeling with an arm around her shoulders.

"Thank you, *hija*. I fell asleep! We are not yet to be answered."

They unrolled the second bedroll. Kim thought she would lie by the old woman till she slept and then take a look around, but within moments both were softly snoring again.

"Get ready, honey," Willy told Barbara. "This is real."

They moved softly through the grass. In the silver light half an hour before sunrise, the whole copse stirred at their approach, and terror went through Barbara. That had to be a breeze, and yet the air was still. And there! The red vines nosing outward, nudging the air in their direction, like blind creatures catching their scent.

"Watch," Willy said. He took up a dead branch and poked it at the nearest vine. The vine snatched it like a snake and broke it into three pieces with one python's flexing of its length.

Why on *our* property? she found herself numbly thinking. It seemed her mind would never take in the ugly miracle itself, the blind vegetation probing the air as if seeking them, mocking them.

They stood close together, his arm around her shoulders, hers around his waist. "Everything I told you last night?" Willy said. "It's as real as this, honey. This thing is big, and it's everywhere around here."

She knew what he was getting back to and bitter tears jumped into her eyes, surprising her. "No! I'm not leaving our land! No way!"

He stroked her hair. "It kills me too. But you know I'm right—you feel it yourself. Don't you." It wasn't a question. "It's in the ground, right under our feet . . . right now." His voice got quieter at the last and, yes, Barbara could feel it stirring in the earth under her: terror.

"Listen, Barb. Our property? It's in there, in that shed. If I make that harvest, then, whatever happens, we can buy a place. You know what we have to do."

"Cut and run." Her eyes were dead. After a moment he said, "Both trucks should be serviced. We'll need our full camping kit—I have to get propane, sterno . . . backup water jugs and extra gas, batteries for all the flashlights. We've got to get all our cash out. We should have some lightweight trail-food too. Mom'll need some gear too, but I think she should ride with us, her car's too low-slung if we have to go offroad." Now her eyes were busy with the generalship of motherhood. It didn't quite erase the pain around her eyes. Willy touched a fingertip to the grief lines there.

"It's close, hon—I really feel it." He nodded at the chunks of tattered vine that littered the grass from last night's battle. "I haven't even got in yet. It's gonna take a while, even if I can get Reed and Raleigh to help. I'm gonna pay 'em a couple grand each, OK?"

Unexpectedly, Barbara gave his ribs a short, sharp punch—not her full shot, but mad, with hurt in it. "You get us the price of some land in our pocket. You get us that, and you don't get your ass *arrested*, and *then* it'll be OK. Got that, asshole?"

Barbara and Lucky, who had stayed over on the folding bed they kept for her, drove off with Maxie at seven, driving in caravan the Yakimas' two pickups: the "good" ten-year-old Dodge and Willy's fifteen-year-old work truck, both to be serviced in the course of the day's errands.

As Willy reached for the phone to call Reed, Reed called him. Reed told Willy the night's developments in detail. When Willy told him he wasn't the least bit surprised at this news, it derailed Reed for a moment. "What?" he said.

"I can show you stranger shit than any of that right here on my property, Reed. In fact I need your help. Yours and Raleigh's. Top pay."

"Top pay?"

"Two thousand apiece for no more than two days' work."

"*What?*" Reed said again.

It was warm by mid-morning. Willy, Raleigh, and Reed sprawled in the shade of an oak, streaming sweat and catching their breath. Reed lifted the water-cooler above his head and thumbed out a stream of water directly onto the torn, bloody bandana that sheathed his head. The water spilled over and ran down his scratched, welted face. Then he tilted his head and let the water run into his mouth. Then he gave Raleigh the cooler and blew spray from his wispy 'stache.

"Just what exactly is supposed to *happen* that you keep talkin about, Willy? You say we should pull up stakes, but you aren't very clear about it."

"Hey. Reed. Numb-nuts." Willy's face looked midway between laughing and crying. He waved at the trampled grass around the copse. "What kinda specifics you *want?*"

Dozens of mangled fragments of poison oak still thrashed and twitched in the trampled grass, violent like spine-broke snakes on a highway. They dribbled sap and oil that turned the grass yellow where it fell.

What had been Willy's discreet aperture into the grove was now raggedly framed by a zone of lopped vines which, even as they bled, still stretched and strained to bar passage. They had to be cut much farther back before a man dared enter.

Willy struggled to a sitting posture. "Listen. I don't *know* specifics, guys, but as soon as I've got harvest I'm striking for the coast. I'll give you two grand apiece to get me in there, help me break down my shed, and bag my crop. An' then my whole family's pulling out. And we're not takin the freeway. Don't ask me why, I've just got this gut urge to get to the coast, and that's where we're going, and you two should pack all you can, and get some cash, and come with us, an that's my heartfelt advice to you both, take it or leave it and I hope you take it."

When Aurora awoke it was near mid-day, and she saw the girl a little way up the slope of the hill, looking around.

"Do you know where we are, Kimberly?"

"Cinnabar Hill is two ridges over that way." Kim felt a reluctance to say the name of the Quicksilver.

Aurora rubbed her eyes and slipped her black hornrims onto her tight little monkey face. "Are you willing to go there, *hija?* To reconnoiter?"

"Should I?"

Aurora took little bags of dry figs and shelled peanuts from her knapsack. She beckoned Kim to breakfast. "I must save my strength for tonight, dear," she said, passing Kim the bota of watered wine. "Something may be happening there that we should know."

Kim sensed motives not stated. "What will you be doing, Abuelita?"

"For one thing, I will be learning if you can be sent to do a tricky thing alone and return unhurt. For another, I will be free to concentrate. The power wishes to feel my readiness before it speaks."

Kim nodded humbly. "I'm weak on patience, I know. Should I talk to anyone there?"

"No! See what is to be seen. Stay wholly unseen yourself. Can you do it?"

"I'm not a child."

"Remember as you do this—remember that." She pointed to the bundled shawl. A wide stain spread under it, the bloody end still bright, wet red. "It is still bleeding. The question of Alejandro's life has not been fully settled."

Kim had done it scores of times herself, the procedure she was watching now: the tanker offloading into the shaft-mouth.

But seen at noon, from these trees surrounding the compound, seen with wide sweeps of gold grass and oak-studded slopes framing it, the procedure was discordant, a huge act of defecation, the metal brute humming and shuddering and emptying into the heart of the tawny hill.

She didn't need the blue van down by the offices to tell her that the man doing this job was the one who had looked into their headlights that night, the one who, without ever having spoken a word to them, had made them fear the work they were doing here. The face at this distance wasn't as clear as that night, but there was that calm in his movements. A calm with something deeper in it: rapture.

The man went to the passenger door of the tanker's cab and lifted something out. It was a corpse in jeans and T-shirt, a folded corpse with its single arm wired at the wrist to its ankles. Alex's corpse.

Hot tears stabbed Kim's eyes, and she felt a kind of stripping of her skin, as if everywhere Alex had touched her, those remembered touches flared again, as they were taken from her.

The big man hooked the corpse over one shoulder—Alex's body seemed so small! He approached the shaft. She could see him take down a mask, and then the shaft-mouth swallowed him.

Lazarian carried Alex down. The boy was light—he seemed rather to buoy than weigh down Lazarian's steps. The fill-hose thrummed softly by his feet—he'd set offload at slow so his offering of still-bottoms should nearly as possible coincide with the offering of the boy. Inventing protocol for the divine—what a joy, but also a bafflement it was to improvise dialogue with a god. How had the earliest shamans felt? Groping with sacrifice and ceremony towards the unstated will of a cosmic presence?

It awed and humbled him to be granted this dream—to pierce the Bubble with a gesture and a shouted word.

But what word?—for he had reached the pool. Whatever came. He hoisted and held the boy above his head. The very earth was a waiting echoey ear around him.

"I offer you these," he said, "this food, and this life, in adoration! Show me your will! Show me your place with you!"

He launched Alex outwards. The boy, a knot of shadows underlight by the lantern on the floor, rotated once and fell into the black explosion of the pool, and was gone.

The pool smacked its rim, gave the stone foamy black kisses. In the deep stone ear of the earth Lazarian stood harkening, focused like a single ear himself.

And heard something, faint and far above. (Chip was out with Frankie and the Carney woman, and there was no one but himself in the compound.) He heard the light *clink* . . . of steel couplings? And the growl . . . of an engine revving?

Kim had to climb to the crest of the hill to reach a place she could climb over unseen from the compound. She crossed the crest, getting down and bellying through the grass. As she advanced, her spirit felt simplified by terror. She felt like a lizard, moving without conscious goal.

Now directly under her she could see the front end of the tanker. Down by the offices was nothing but the van. She was powerless to help Alex, but she must witness all she could.

She inched downslope, sending no tumbling pebbles ahead to announce her.

She edged with endless caution round the shaft-mouth—one mask still missing from its peg. Should she go down and try to glimpse the monster at his work?

The clink of metal made her whirl.

The pump had shut off and the offload fitting had decoupled and fallen to the ground. But there was no one standing behind her.

She edged her way around the idling tanker and jumped again when—*ka-chunk*—it slipped into gear, even as she stared into the window of the empty cab. The driverless rig rolled forward, and she sprang back and crouched, trembling. Light and jouncy after offload, the rig swept downslope through a grand circle, geared down and came back up with a cough and a grunt. Its headlights came on as it slid, nose first, into the shaft-mouth.

It was shocking, hair-raising, to see the whole rig slide into the shaft and smoothly disappear, like a sword-swallowing feat performed by the hill.

Kim straightened slowly. She knew that all the branches off the main shaft had been submerged weeks ago. There was just the one shaft for both the truck (which filled it like a piston) and Alex's killer.

Might not Alex's life not be still at issue? Not be lost? After all, hadn't the world gone mad last night? And stayed that way?

Those first faint echoes grew fainter and farther for Lazarian. Still he stood, his whole self one collected core of attention, a radio astronomer's antenna, harkening to a dim and distant galaxy . . .

And then the growl again, far and faint, and then the growl; growing, definitely, the tanker's growl surely . . .

And then the growl grim and focused and powerful, the noise of something *inside* the shaft, its echoes streaming and tumbling down on him.

Lazarian asked no questions of his terror. He let it take him up, and wear him like a glove. He bent and seized the lantern. Now the growl was a roar, an avalanche of hammer-blows. He ran upshaft towards it—twenty, thirty yards—he must be higher than the awful backwash if he survived the truck—and then forty, fifty, an extra twenty yards to set: the lantern down midshaft, and then retreat again.

Now when the machine came he would see its pitch and angle just before it reached him and he would be able to dodge its wheels.

But he saw the tanker sooner than it reached the lantern, for it had, instead of its cab, a giant head of flaming embers, a grinning boar's head like the one that had mocked him last night. Its jaws gaped as it rushed down on him. Lazarian hit the earth, and hugged it.

For a deafening moment the huge stinking underbelly of the tanker roofed him, the tires hammering the earth like Thor to either side, and just as it overpassed him, its axle tagged him, one little kiss of contact that cracked two of his ribs.

And then in the perfect blackness Lazarian was up and running, running, hearing the roar of impact behind him, the hiss of backwash at his heels.

It almost caught him, gripped his feet and tangled his ankles in cold silken scarves, and he kicked and danced madly as he ran, till he was free, and running, slipping, running . . .

Outside he stripped off his mask and took the sun on his face, closing his eyes.

Clearly, he was chosen—but he was chosen to be *tested*.

And yes, this Power mocked him, unmistakably. This Power challenged his defiance.

The signs one was given! So grand, but so utterly ambiguous! What did his feelings tell him?

The Power had denied him his position as driver, as bringer of its food.

To defy it, he must keep feeding it, as the clearest way he could see of saying "Fuck you." That was how his feelings called it.

"You want my anger," he said to the air with a little, bitter smile, his eyes still closed. "You want my anger, and you *have* it. Yes. Laugh at me, slap me around—but now *I am in your face*. You will acknowledge me. You will open the door for me. Because I alone have *earned* it."

Lazarian took his van down to Santa Marta, where he leased another tanker. He had a pickup scheduled for late tonight, and he was going to make it.

Twenty-three

Rolling north across the Golden Gate Bridge in the late morning, Bev was exhilarated. One of the nice things about being worth several million was that you could see your money people in a pleasant, Saturday-morning kind of way. She had met her banker for coffee. She'd had brunch with the woman who managed her securities, and the cash, now in her trunk, had been ready for her.

Lovely San Francisco, falling away behind her with its sleek highrises spiked right into the bay's glittery flank—here in the city money was the kind of thing it should be, a pure, numerical intoxicant. You enjoyed its fine points with other connoisseurs, debated its nuances, weighed its possibilities.

She headed north with growing reluctance. Up in Santa Marta lay the tricky, dirty business of making new money. Usually she jumped into the work of making money with the feeling she'd had on the tennis court as a kid.

But in this deal it was as if the court was treacherous—soft clay instead of trustworthy asphalt. Your feet thrust for traction, and things gave. You thought DaValli was a nice, healthy greedball, then you got in close and he turned kinky. You arranged a simple barbecue to do some business, it turned into a blizzard of flies, and a week later Jake lies seriously sick from it.

(She remembered helping him cough last night, remembered disposing of the tissue that felt so disgustingly laden, thinking she actually felt something *squirm* within the tissue . . .)

You couldn't even trust simple things like having your calls returned. Dave, Straff, the Sawyers—none in when she called. She left messages, but still her car phone was silent.

She was crossing the high arching overpass of the Petaluma River and fiddling with the radio when she learned of the "refuse eruption" from the site of the new dump southeast of Santa Marta.

It seemed the story had just broken. It was everywhere she turned the dial, with the same phrase, refuse eruption, and the same sketchy set of data. By the time she'd gathered everything there was, she was passing the site. A couple miles out there to the left of the freeway, you couldn't see much—one of the low hills at the edge of the plain had a dark, glittery color to it, and you could see helicopters above it.

She met Frankie at his condo. She locked her car in his garage and they took his Trans Am out towards the mine.

"This town hasn't been all that big for very long," she told him. "If they cut into some old dump how did it get so much crap in it? How come no one remembers it was there?"

"You're asking the wrong guy, Bev, I'm from L.A."

They met Chip at a pullout from the highway near where the flex hose—along a dry creekbed—came down onto the plain. Out on the nearest pasture you could see the irrigation line—light six-inch pipe running like an axle through the big spoked wheels. She would check that line to the plant with Straff tomorrow.

She and Frankie transferred to Chip's Jeep and the old man took them up the road to the mine, using the pull-outs and taking Bev into the brush to show her the line at several places on the way. Driving into the compound Chip said, sounding surprised, "The tanker's gone an so's his van, Frankie."

"Whose?" Bev asked.

"Our driver's," Frankie said. They drove up to the shaft-mouth. He showed her where the flex went into the shaft.

"Wanna go down and look?" he asked, because seeing her standing there looking down into the dark, half stoned on the air already without knowing it, he knew that going down there was the last thing she wanted to do. She actually shuddered.

"Not necessary."

Back at his place Frankie invited her up for a drink, but she shook her head. She opened her trunk and gave him the satchel. Having stood at the threshold of the hole he was king of, she looked at him with a new uneasy awareness. His smile now made her a little afraid.

She had to do right by Jake, stay there tonight, visit with him a little, but it would be stuffy and depressing there, so she stopped by her office on the way to relax. She made a weak Scotch and water, sank into her chair, and turned on the TV. When she first saw the footage of the "refuse eruption" it brought her back up to her feet.

The earth movers had piled the dyke forty feet higher than the natural hillcrest already. It was the last thing you could call a hill before the plain opened out, and it wasn't that high for starters.

Scat Collins sweated with the rest, charging up with his load, getting a glimpse of the black clotted stew still rising, rising, scarcely fifteen feet below the lip—then rolling back down, setting his blade for another run. Fifty big machines, scrounged from everywhere in three counties, doing just the same thing—at least it kept the media vans well back from the action for fear of being crushed by those monster wheels. The helicopters tended to dip close for dramatic footage, battering the operators with their prop draft, till the operators started giving them the finger to spoil their closeups. They were staying a little higher now, but Scat hoped that the parasites were still getting a noseful, at least, of this nightmare mess.

Fury was growing in Scat's heart. Not at the media pimps, not at the pencilnecks and supes running this show, because this nightmare wasn't just happening. This nightmare was purposeful, was making a point. The Earth was making the point.

He had moved earth all his life. Earth, with its deep bones of a thousand kinds of rock, was tough, it was stubborn, you had to plan and go step by step if you were going to do much with it.

But once it had been moved, it lay there!—assuming you piled it at the angle of repose—it stayed there if you handled it right. It didn't fight back.

But in the last delirious thirty-two hours of non-stop, breakneck toil, that had changed.

Now this mess, everything in it was human made, of course! But the Earth was the one doing this. This human accumulation wasn't coming out under the laws of its own mechanics! Where could the pressure be coming from? And the volume!

No. The truth was that the Earth was spitefully doing this. You could feel it. Couldn't all these others working around him feel it, if they dared slow down and talk about it? The power that was squeezing this vast wad out of nowhere was Momma Earth like some sullen bitch saying *I won't take any more of this shit!* Just the way bitches got sometimes when they were on the rag or just went crazy.

When Janice did it, by God, he could just smack her a nice juicy one upside the head and bam! She snapped right out of it, But this was the fucking Earth on the rag, and even with a goddam thirty-ton dozer you couldn't do shit, it was a drop in the ocean!

Jaw clenched, he sank his blade deep and gunned into the climb. He was going to jam the biggest fucking bladeful yet down the hitch's throat. His rig shuddered and grunted and bucked up the slope. He rammed it full throttle and charged for the crest, soil flying back like spray from prow-cloven waves.

Now, just short of the crest, throttle back . . . throttle *back!* But his elbow wouldn't bend, his arm wouldn't pull the throttle back!

Bev couldn't believe the sheer extent of the mess the helicopter footage showed: two sizeable lakes of filth, the higher overflowing, the lower already brimming. Where was it all coming from?

She tried to decide its meaning for her own project—was it good? A public distraction from their own proceedings? Bad? Would it be taken by the public as a new warning against overconstruction?—but the struggle to believe it was actually happening blocked her thinking. Everything around her suddenly seemed unreal. All the files in those cabinets and in her computer there, all the deals and the whole apparatus of documents, seemed to melt into a rubbery network of gibberish surrounding her. She suddenly felt unbelievably tired . . .

Dear Christ! What was this guy doing? On the screen, a big dozer had just shoved its load of dirt to the dike-crest and was still going, up, up, over!

The footage zoomed closer as the huge rig and the man astride it plunged into that vast septic stew. And the man, just at the last as you got close enough to see him well, just before the sudden blackout of the footage that occurred when two eagerly swooping helicopters collided, raining debris and corpses on the place where the dozer had been swallowed (a higher copter catching this collision, which was run later on in the broadcast on a special on "The Refuse Eruption Casualties")—just before the transmission cut out you could see the guy, gesturing with one free hand, the other gripping his throttle . . . shaking his fist? Yes, and you could just see that the cords were standing out in his neck, that he was bellowing something. . . .

It was dusk when she got to Jake's. She paused on the porch a minute, steeling herself to the stuffiness and faint odor inside. Jake's inactive glutton's life gave him poor circulation. His home was overheated in the best of times. And that undercurrent of aroma . . . it was faint, but it was like carrion, wasn't it?

Then she stepped in, to be pleasantly surprised by the scent of room freshener. The day-nurse was new, Miss Wingate, a supple young woman with dark hair flanking her face and lingering, ironic eyes behind big-framed glasses. She had opened some windows as well as sprayed.

Bev was pleasant. Ms. Wingate demurely declined a drink though near her shift's end, and took orange juice. She asked admiring questions about Bev's and Jake's construction business. Bev felt in her eyes a teasing question about her relation to Jake, he the older, wealthier partner, Bev the, ahem, beautiful junior partner. Bev gave her back a cool smile, chatted courteously.

"I'm glad you freshened up," Bev told her. "The air needed it."

"Yes, but you can still just smell it underneath, can't you? Is there a basement? Maybe something died . . . ?"

"No basement. Well, I'm for freshening up myself—I'll just peek in on him first. Take whatever you want from the kitchen."

Jake was sleeping, his breathing wheezy, eyes slitted to empty strips of rheumy white, skin slack and cheesy. He looked so bad it made the skin crawl on her nape. The close air and dim light were disorienting; she could almost imagine that his skin here and there was dimpling slightly, incessantly, as if random nerve currents were firing, and his fine muscles faintly squirming. It made her remember him at a thousand moments in their past, the frankness of his greed for food, drink, sex, property. She saw him in snapshots of eager consumption that her mind had taken of him over the years. She had always assumed this hunger was good—honest, direct, wholesome.

She looked now with loathing at this blob, this impotent, paralyzed vessel of excrement and disease. She closed the door behind her with endless caution, afraid he would wake, and bleat, and need her ministering.

A shower, long and hot. It felt almost sexually delicious, needling softly against her nakedness. She should call Shugg, Straff, see how things had gone last night . . . but the water caressing her breasts, her back insisted that she stand there mindlessly and lose herself in it.

She shampooed her hair twice, then lathered in conditioner. She took the soft brush to her fingernails. She used the luffa on her back, blissfully grating off the delicate, greasy veneer of dead skin cells and sebum between her shoulder blades. She gave herself the works and only stopped, reluctantly, when the hot water began to give out. She turbaned a towel round her head and slipped on a fresh terrycloth robe.

She was someone else now, not the Bev Carney who had stepped into the bathroom a half hour ago. She went into the kitchen and mixed a drink. She took a sip. To hell with phone calls. She would go into the bedroom she used here, and get into that biography of Nastasie she'd picked up. Let everything wait till tomorrow.

She cocked an ear.

"Ms. Wingate?"

No answer. Stepping out into the living room, she found it empty. Ms. Wingate's book lay face down by her armchair, and the sound that had caught Bev's ear was a little more noticeable: a low burring noise, maybe the alarm of an electric clock.

"Ms. Wingate?"

She must be in Jake's room—that seemed to be the source of the sound, too. What was she doing in there?

Pausing outside Jake's door, she felt a sudden, powerful urge to turn and run—a reflex shortcutting conscious thought, such as she might respond to in mid-volley on the court. She shook it off and opened the door.

The air in the room was a blizzard of flies, and on the bed two human shapes made of flies struggled feebly together, their limbs and torsos seeming to melt into one another, sharing at each point of contact the fabric of busy flies that enveloped them. The topmost figure, by intent or chance, turned a face of flies towards Bev, big glasses framing two seething pockets of flies and resting on a fulcrum of bare nose-bone above two nose-holes all aboil with flies.

Bev turned to run—seeing as she did so the insects rising in a buzzing blanket, disrobing the tattered, scarlet shapes of gnawed meat in lax embrace on the bed. She turned and sprinted from the room, leapt across the hall, and was midway through the living room when they hit her in mid-stride, an airborne avalanche that toppled her, closed like a fist on her flopping form, and went straight to work on her.

Twenty-four

It was just dark when Reed and Raleigh drove hack from Willy's to pick up a few things from home before going back to Willy's the night. They weren't buying into Willy's panic, as they agreed it was between themselves. They were staying over because they could get to work earlier down at the grove that way. And they were just gassing up their rides and getting a little cash and extra gear because they figured there was no harm in taking some normal precautions, especially since they had just spent the day chopping brush that was chopping them back.

Bea at the Circle K in Gravenstein where they bought a few six-packs irritated them by letting her jaw drop two inches when they walked in. Bea was a cheery, skinny lady of sixty who had nothing against a little lipstick and powder.

"You poor dears!" she squawked. "What have you been *doing?*"

"Cuttin brush," Raleigh said curtly.

Bea cashed a fifty-dollar check for each of them. Rex over at the Texaco station did them the same favor, but the price was that Rex got to enjoy their colorful condition.

"Hoooo-*ee!* You look like something big, King Kong maybe, mistook you for a coupla bananas, an tried to *peel* you! Hooo-*ee!*"

In the new Safeway, where they got stuff for Willy's breakfast table tomorrow, the staff were schooled to suburban courtesy. The little blond checker shyly prompted: "Rough day?"

"No," said Reed thoughtfully, as if he found the notion surprising. "Easier'n usual, as a matter of fact. Why do you ask?"

They could see from a distance that the bulge in the highway in front of Raleigh's wrecking yard had gotten bigger. A couple trestles with yellow flashers had been stationed on the shoulder to either side of the dome, which was now a good two feet higher than the roadbed, the asphalt over it puzzled with cracks. If it hadn't been so broadly domed you couldn't have driven over it even slowly.

"The fuckin *County!*" Raleigh raged. "Assholes throw down a couple sawhorses an that's it—they go back to jerkin off!"

"It's a fuckin crime," Reed raged. "A guy could come zoomin down here half drunk thinkin he's OK and *whoom,* he's in the fuckin sky! I mean, I come down this stretch like that all the time!"

"Jesus Christ, look at the freeway there."

Beyond the lumberyard 101 crossed the railroad tracks on a low overpass. One of the freeway sodium vapor lamps was right near this low bridge, which had a little concrete balustrade. The light obliquely lit a large crack in the balustrade.

"Jesus, it goes right through the curbing of the roadbed too, see? And look—" Reed thrust a bony finger towards the lumberyard. "It's right in line with those crooked stacks an this fuckin bulge!"

Raleigh drove into Reed's lot behind him to help him load his stuff. They checked the maintenance pit—it was half full of ooze now.

"That's where all the county guys are right now," Reed said grimly. "Down at that new dumpsite. I mean, what if this shit here was the beginning of the same thing?"

Reed loaded more than he'd first intended—tool kit, fishing gear, his battered tent.

"Sssssst!" said Raleigh as they finished the load. They listened. There it was, coming from over in Raleigh's yard, a complex noise of metal things disturbed. Reed got out the Smith & Wesson he had just put in his glove-box.

They drove over, Reed's truck falling in behind Raleigh's.

Raleigh's entry was around the corner of his lot and a few yards up the branch road to the old dump. Raleigh made the turn and Reed came around right behind him—and had to jam on his brakes, because Raleigh had done the same just short of his gate. Out of his gate roared a battered black Caddy convertible.

Its side was caved in, its rear bumper trailing on end on the pavement and spitting sparks, its axles blazing with sparks too, its wheels crooked and tires flapping—the whole car by every appearance incapable of movement, but coming out like a rocket, hooking a sharp left round Raleigh's front end, roaring past the paralyzed and gaping Reed and hooking another shrieking left onto Sequoia Highway.

Almost instantly at speed, the Caddy hit the bulge in the pavement and was launched, hung in the air, and slammed belly down on a flat spray of sparks like a speedboat wake and went rocketing, racketing south into Gravenstein.

Reed and Raleigh got out of their trucks and came towards each other, walking like zombies.

"You see the guy driving?" asked Raleigh softly. "I saw him point blank in my headlights."

"I saw him. He wasn't two feet away when he passed me."

They stood waiting for each other to say it first. At last Reed said, his voice almost a whisper: "His face was a skull, right? No eyes?"

"No eyes." Raleigh's hoarse voice quavered slightly. "A little skin, like rags."

"And his skull was stove in, right?"

"Yeah. His skull was stove in. Like in a bad accident."

A long silence passed between them as they stared down Sequoia Highway. "An' you know what?" Raleigh burst out, something like rage, or tears, or both in his voice. "That Caddy? I got it three years ago August. An' I pulled the fuckin *engine* out of it the same week I got it!"

When he packed, Raleigh took the emergency roll of $500 from the toe of one of his old boots. Half an hour ago he'd meant to leave it here. He packed all his truck could hold. They went back to Reed's and packed some more of his things too.

Officer Richland of the twenty-man Gravenstein Police Department was conferring with Captain Danby, his superior, and the CHP guy, Rice, who had arrived at the scene just after they had. They were having some disagreement about how they were going to write their reports of the accident. To Rice it was obvious that the Caddy had had a driver who fled the scene.

"The problem is," Richland told Rice, "the guy in the gas station saw it, an he says no one ran from the scene. I mean Christ, how *could* they?"

The black Caddy had hit a tow truck broadside while running a red light at a hundred miles an hour. Even the stout frame of the truck's boom was bent in half.

Rice shook his head. "I still say we can report a strong *likelihood* that the driver of the Caddy fled the scene."

"Rice," said Danby, "those two vehicles are one vehicle now. They still haven't even got all of the truck driver out."

"There's nothing in that Caddy, my friend," said Rice, his voice near the edge of control, "but the corpse of a guy who's been dead for *months*."

The three of them had to stand in silence a moment to give this truth its due. Then Danby said carefully, "Did you take a close look at the Caddy's front end? I mean, around where the engine should be?"

Frankie bathed and re-dressed, and had the pork chop special at Sonoma Joe's on his way out of town—it was going to be a long night with Beiderbeck. He was southbound on 101 by a little after dark, and called Chip at the mine on his cellular to see if Lazarian had reappeared.

"No word," said Chip. "Maybe he hired someone else to drive the rig and went off on something."

"Well, there's no second-guessing him. You be up there tonight?"

"Nah, I've gotta walk the line with Straff tomorrow. He just called—said he was sick an he sounded it, but he's gonna meet me anyway. So I'm goin into town for a drink an hit the sack early."

"Well, I'll probably be sleeping up there. I can't believe this guy, this so-called genius, doesn't even drive."

Frankie would have to drive Beiderbeck's tank truck, filled with his expensive catalyst, up from the city, then take it back to the city and get his car.

His mood wasn't bad, though. He could actually smell the cash, thirty grand, that he'd tucked in his sports coat pockets for Beiderbeck. Smooth, used money with its skinlike feel! Its faint fetid smell kept tickling his nostrils, with some sharper spice mixed with it—a whiff of the shaft, wasn't it? Maybe it was imagination, but it made him want to cackle, made him feel high. Shit into gold.

He met Beiderbeck behind an abandoned-looking warehouse in the Potrero Hill district, the chemist's face all shadows and bone-white skin. Beiderbeck stood grinning at him.

"Something funny, Billy?"

"I think of the finesse, the endless cerebral subtlety, that concocted that"—Beiderbeck tabbed a thumb at the little 3-K gallon tanker behind him—"and I look at you, the new owner of this miracle I've made, you, slick as snot, with not one significant insight in your whole brain—all because there's a wad of cash in your pocket. There is a wad of cash in your pocket, isn't there?"

"Right here—all yours. And hey, what can I say? Isn't it

wonderful living in a free economy?"

Driving north, they didn't talk. Beiderbeck drank and snorted and Frankie declined both drugs. The thought of draining the shaft—actually doing it!—held him more and more enchanted. The bold and magical act of release kept running in his imagination. The sinuous black Dragon sneaking from the mountain's bowel, silken and secret, blackness emerging, the first tendril of a whole new ocean, a night ocean wide as the earth.

And the cold brimstone smell of it, more sublimely savage than whisky-and-methedrine to the brain cells, the nightmare intimacy of that smell. Frankie was getting a hard-on.

It was weird of him, he conceded that, but he enjoyed the hard-on anyway. When you pulled off something like this, you could be as weird as you wanted. Shit into gold. Mucho shit into mucho mucho gold.

Just south of Novato they unknowingly passed Sol Lazarian heading south in the rig he had leased late that afternoon, hauling a pair of 5-K tanks, scheduled for three different pickups, collecting abundant defiance to bring back and fling in the lap of the Power in the shaft.

Beiderbeck hooked up to the fill-hose and started the offload. "Let's go down for a look while she runs," he said cheerily.

Frankie was delighted to. The Dragon's breath buoyed their steps. It felt like walking downwards through stiff cream, his body's movement felt so smooth and cushioned.

"Hooo-*ee!*" the chemist crowed through his mask. "We been movin an shakin down here, Blood!"

A thirty-yard wet zone lay between them and the pool. Beiderbeck edged his way cautiously through it till he was in range, and then tossed one of his tethered canisters in, filled it, and hauled it out.

Topside, down in the office, he had Frankie hunt up a wide

flat pan; in the utility room Frankie found a pan for draining crankcases. They filled this with water in the bathroom and ran four inches of water in the old stained bathtub too.

Beiderbeck poured his canister of toxins into the oil pan. Its blackness bunched and billowed like smoke under the water as it entered, but not one wisp strayed from its bunched mass. It formed a solid cloud whose skin rippled and melted in a thousand shapes, but cohered absolutely and hung a precise inch beneath the water's surface.

Now Beiderbeck emptied the pan into the tub. A silver tongue of water hung from the pan-rim down to the tub water, and within that tongue a flattened black filament also hung, centered in the falling water, never emerging to its surface. And in the tub water, just below the surface, that muscular, supple cloud of blackness re-cohered.

"It's working fine," said Beiderbeck. He was quiet. Frankie was awed, but also full of glee.

"Whatsa matter, Billy? Surprise yourself?"

Beiderbeck gave him a long look, and bitter humor slowly rekindled in his eyes. "By tomorrow night," he went on, and then glanced at his watch. "By tonight, I should say, it'll all be catalyzed. I'll have the outlet valve installed and we can start"— now he was really grinning again—"start to *ease* dat slime, *evuh* so discreetly, out to de ri-buh, an out to de deep bloooo sea."

Once again just south of Petaluma they crossed Lazarian's path, directions reversed and the Ice Man's tanks now full, and this time the rigs, both in their respective left lanes, crossed under an island of light shed by a major truckstop, and Beiderbeck shouted:

"Small world—see Lazarian?"

"Yeah! Where'd he get that tanker? Where's ours?"

"Who knows? Who was that in the cab with him?"

"I dunno. Looked like someone even bigger than he is."

Twenty-five

Lazarian had seen Frankie, too, his casual slouch at the wheel, pretending the ugly little tanker was a zippy Beemer. A man up to his neck in magic and too cool to feel it.

No, he had to feel something. There was a dreaminess about Frankie these last few days. But the Weasel thought it was wealth, was Beating the Game that he was high on. He did not guess the greatness of the thing that held him in its hands and stroked him like a pet, and while this great and still faceless god used him for its own ends, Frankie preened in his soul over having balls and smarts and hitting the easy money. Frankie DaValli was pure L.A.

So naturally this was all easy for Frankie—to his blindness, the path was clear. Envy was therefore senseless and yet Lazarian could not wholly snuff out a spark of irritation that for himself, who adored, who believed, the path was made such a punishment, such an arduous puzzling nightmare.

The first tanker had been flung back at him. If this was contempt for a paltry offering, he brought a larger now; if it was meant to forbid further offering, why, still he brought a larger, because he felt in his bones that the Power dared his courage, taunted his docility. His cracked ribs ached, pierced him at certain movements. The pain was the god's laughter. Well, the god would find him tough. If only the god would show him its will!

And that was when he realized that something, something huge, was sitting at his side.

He was just entering the high-arcing freeway overpass of the

Petaluma river, the waters winking below, Petaluma starring the flats beyond, when he turned and found sitting at his side a huge woman in a filthy tent-like garment, her eyes bright black under wild black hair. The smell that came off her was glacial, a cold front that numbed the brain.

"Pleased to meecha!" she boomed. Her voice was echoing vacuum, the noise that far, colliding planets would make if they made noise. "I'm Mamie Durtt! I wancha to come up an see me, if you can."

And she seized the steering wheel and wrenched it hard right. At seventy miles an hour the tanker plowed through the concrete balustrade and launched itself over the water sixty feet below.

Lazarian thrust his door open. The lake of streetlamps that was Petaluma, just beyond the river, made him feel like an astronaut out of his craft for some External Vehicular Activity. As he leapt the thrust of his own small mass seemed to rock the little planet of the tanker's bulk ever so slightly, and then Lazarian was fighting, swimming himself outwards, scrambling away through the empty air from the steel giant falling with him, hanging for heart-floating moments in the nakedness of air, and then exploding against the water, colliding in a storm of bubbles with the silty, buttery bottom of the river.

The old woman had been brewing herbs since dark, silent, listening as she worked. Some she sipped and gave Kim also to drink. A different brew she poured into one of the leather botas.

Kim watched her for hours, trying to sit straight as she did so but at last reclining on the bedroll. Bleakly she asked herself where in her heart she would ever find the strength to endure all those lines she saw graven in Aurora's face, Surely she would die long before she had endured half so much as was written there.

At length, when Aurora had long been a crosslegged statue

of meditation, Kim saw the empty cup slip from her fingers and roll across the red-lit grass by the embers of the fire. Then Kim too was asleep.

To be roused, the moon perhaps an hour higher, by a brisk and trail-ready Aurora. She stood with her great-nephew's bundled arm held loosely in the crook of her own, waiting for Kim to collect herself and follow.

"What are we going to do, Abuelita?"

"I can't say—you must be unprepared. It will be terrible, but you must obey me without question."

They crossed the same two ridges Kim had crossed in the afternoon, but they were now on night's alien planet. The cool waxen touch of the leaves was startling, the dust underfoot seemed more silken, fine as talcum or ashes. She heard more things astir as well, quick paws in grass, distant hooves in the shadows.

Aurora led them across the shoulder of Cinnabar Hill, downslope of the compound. They could see its fence up there and Kim felt naked, crossing moonlit grass now, the oak trees sparse. They came around to the western face of the hill. There below was the lake, its bigness startling under the moonlight.

The slope swept, furred with silver grass, breathtakingly down to its shore. Descending, Kim imagined they might slip and be swept down to the waters as down a glacier.

At length they crossed the lakeshore highway—dark and empty—and passed between trees down a graded dirt road to a little gravel beach. A cinderblock shed stood backed against the bluff.

"My brother-in-law—" Kim began. Aurora held up her hand. Out on the lake, a sudden, oily movement. A slick shape—heart-stoppingly big—erupted from the water and poured itself back into it. She looked to Aurora, but the old woman had already turned, faced down shore.

"There, *hija*. Do you see it? Focus yourself."

She did see: in the black air above a tree-choked cove, a bruise of color, a faint meld of rose and orange—a glow.

The old woman led them to a path at the brink of the cove. She drew a length of twine from one of her many pockets. She tied one end to her own belt, the other to Kim's.

"From here on, Kimberly, you must move wholly with me. Drink this." The tea in the bota had a green, bitter taste.

"Am I going to . . . start hallucinating now, Abuelita?"

"No, child. What you see will be no hallucination. You must grip in your mind, as a hand grips its staff, two essentials: be empty, and do not hesitate."

They followed the path among the trees into an alien, poisonous atmosphere, a stench of burning garbage. The trees, dense hairy things like the legs of spiders, leaked a stronger and stronger glow as the stench grew denser, the air hot and oily.

Now Kim was feeling the heat. Now she was hearing the mutter and crack of things shrinking and snapping in fire. And now they were standing at the edge of the clearing that was Mamie Durtt's front yard.

It was an acre of embers and flames. It was a jagged, broken landscape of fire, under a Venusian atmosphere of red and purple light and tendrilling black fumes. Amidst lagoons of embers everywhere jutted skeletal trash aflame—the way shocked wheat stands on a stubble field as amber as itself.

And across this reach of fire, the house with its big hooded porch was a cave of waiting shadow. A shape stood on that porch, a big dark watching form. Somehow the glow from the fire failed to reveal it, as if the light recoiled and cringed from its contact. It was watching them, though, Kim knew.

"Take off your shoes and socks," Aurora told her.

Kim did not hesitate. Her fingers plucked her laces, shucked her socks. The bite of cold soil on her soles astonished her with the realization of what they were going to do, yet still her spirit was bowed and ready, an obedient question mark.

The old woman peeled her shawl and dropped it from Alex's arm. "We are carrying a soul here, child. Its power lifts us just enough that our feet will not quite touch the fire they feel. You are carrying this soul in your hands, as I am carrying it in mine. Be empty now, daughter, and do not hesitate."

Aurora turned and stepped into the field of fire. At the tug of the umbilicus of twine, Kim moved after her, weightless as a towed balloon. She trod the coals.

They crushed like dry clods beneath her naked heels. Their heat submerged her flesh, a fluid that somehow she wore, like boots, which wholly embraced but did not penetrate her skin. The heat embraced all of her. Her thoughts seemed a kind of radiation from the melting of her brain.

The two women moved like deer across open ground at dusk, not running, but with a fluid stride, bent on reaching cover. Under her feet Kim saw crumbling faces in the coals, smoking snouts of beasts, limbs and paws and hands all black and fissured that crumbled under her weight.

The juts and crags of larger refuse were skeletal, the blazing spines of huge creatures, fragile fascia of slender, inhuman limb bones, broken ribracks like crushed coffers, and from these bone-racks plastic garbage bags sagged, flaming paunches full of sizzling spaghetti-loads of intestinal tubing . . . the whole field of them grave-mates after some holocaust, fuming in the crucible of galactic cookery. And through them the two women walked, the very skin of this hot hell kissing but not consuming their naked footsoles.

And the nearer they got to the porch, beginning now to see who awaited them, the less their soles felt the fire, an unregarded medium they moved through now as they saw the goddess above them.

She was a huge woman, colossally nude, wetly black like melting tar all over—but from her shoulders glared the head of the tusked and bloody-eyed feral sow, surreally huge even on that mammoth-bosomed, mammoth-buttocked frame.

The women stepped from the coals and stood beneath the porch, looking up at her. Aurora lifted the naked arm above her head, displaying it to the goddess.

And Alex's hand moved. It clenched and unclenched in the firelit air, seeking a grip on its life, the effort cording the slender muscles of its forearm as its fingers struggled for a hold on treetops, on the sky and its stars. Kim's heart cracked in her. Her eyes bled for Alex.

"We humbly pray you," Aurora said—her voice above the mutter of the flames a bright frail thing—"we humbly pray you to give us back this boy's life. We wait to know your will."

The goddess leaned forward, firelight raddling her bristled snout with blood, drool hanging like a shredded fabric from her tusks. Her black hand, big and quick as a shovel blade taking a bite from a grave, thrust down and snatched up the arm. The goddess brandished it like a weapon. Her voice was cavern-lunged, and burbled with black phlegm.

"I give you *your* lives if you hurry. Begone! This one is mine!"

She flung the arm out into the field of fire. Falling, it twisted, wrestling the lurid air for purchase. It struck the coals and flexed and flopped, clawing the air as it seared and sizzled to bubbling black.

A sob split Kim's heart. Aurora bowed her head. Giving them no instant to recoil, the goddess leapt from the porch, high over them and out to the coals, and as it crashed down it became

wholly swine, black and big as a steer, a smoking engine of muscled rage that barged through the embers, cleaving them like a
prow, throwing out bow-waves of coals that splashed and coruscated to both sides. And as it reached the farther edge of the
field, leaving behind a path of bare cool earth through the embers, the beast melted into blazing coals itself and fell away to
either side. Now nothing but black smoke, in rippling strata,
overhung the pathway out into the trees.

Twenty-six

Willy, Reed, and Raleigh had penetrated to the shed by mid-morning. Willy set the others to unbolting the walls and roof of the shed even as he clipped and bagged, clipped and bagged. When the colos were gently packed into a duffel bag, he took the bag up and wired it to the under frame of his truck.

Reed and Raleigh broke down the generator, separated the tubs from the stumps and rootballs, and Willy got on the phone to firm up his date with Gutley.

The women had already taken Maxie and gone on a second round of errands, including warning friends and family. Willy stuck his bald and bleeding head under the shower for a few minutes, and then wrapped a towel around his neck and sat down to the phone.

The Rusty Nail had burned to the ground. (The firetrucks were there fast, but the place just went like a torch all the way.) That being the case, Gutley at this hour on a Sunday would be in River Nest, at either the Sawmill Tavern or the Pink Elephant.

Tim, the bartender of the Pink Elephant, didn't hear the phone for the first couple rings. The place was packed. Not only did he have all the biker overflow from the Rusty Nail, but all his regulars were here in force, along with a lot of his occasionals and people who had never been in before, though he knew them from around town.

And the talk! It jumped from table to table, chairs got turned outwards. Four-person talks became ten-person talks with someone shouting over from the bar to put in two cents. Arms waved, heads nodded, and people shouted, "That's not the half of it!"

Tim was a gaunt guy who'd been dry for ten years—since his fiftieth birthday. His apartment was upstairs and he seldom left this building. Outside he was gnawed by the craving to pour a drink. In here, pouring for others, he felt safe. And so he'd had no idea until today how much had been going on out there, up and down the river.

For instance, Phil Scully here at the bar got up to find both his racks of canoes overgrown by blackberry vines, overnight, and when he took the clippers to them they attacked him, grabbed his clippers, and pulled them to pieces. Phil *was* a solitary drinker (Tim knew the signs), but he did have a lot of scratches on him.

And then Frank Bozman, a young guy but still hitting the bottle far too hard (Tim knew the signs), chimed from a table that blackberry vines had torn his carburetor apart, and also swore that some kind of muck or slime had devoured his cat from the inside out and left nothing but a cat-shaped patch of fur when it was done.

This brought Duke and Cleary around at their table, two hairy guys in leather that a lot of people said were gay and liked mud-wrestling in their engine-littered bare-dirt dump of a back yard—brought them around to chime in that three of their big dogs had disappeared last night after barking like crazy for an hour outside, and then later this morning they had found the skeleton of the Rottweiler, which they knew by the uneaten skull and the license tag.

Earl and Minnie Pyle, who owned the Bide-a-Dog Kennel on Neely Road in the little neighborhoods among the redwoods across the river, said the kennel had been attacked by rats last night.

"Thank God we'd put that heavy screen on all the windows!" Minnie said.

"We lost one dog anyway," said Earl. "Schnauzer—had a heart attack. I swear to Christ these rats were biggern' cats! Dozens of 'em! Crazy—hungry an just tearin at that wire! I started slammen 'em with double-ought, an they blew up! Nothin left but big old spatters of green slime!"

"What about your roads over there?" asked fat Bill Barnstable, on City Maintenance. "Lotta bucklin an root damage over there?"

"Howja guess?"

"It was like that everywhere this morning." There were choruses of assent. "It's like fifty years of root growth happened overnight," said Barnstable.

Charlie Haas told them how he had to take the chainsaw to the lowest bough of his old oak because it was pushing into the wall of his house. Until sometime while Charlie was at work yesterday, this bough had—for the last century at least—pointed *away* from the house. He took a chainsaw to it and was willing to swear the bough twitched. In any case, it seized and broke the bar of the saw. This morning the wall was cracked all the way through.

"Your phone's ringing, Tim," Vince said.

"Oh. Hello? Hi, Willy!" (Willy Yakima was one of those guys who now and then talked about quitting drinking but never really would; he was too well adjusted to booze—Tim knew the signs.) "Yeah, he's in the corner. Hey, Gutley!"

Gutley told Willy he would call him back from the payphone in the back. He hadn't stayed in business twenty years without a fall by ignoring the details of discretion.

He had just made his connection when Tim got another call at the bar. A thoughtful dispatcher at the local CHP substation kept an open channel with the local taverns.

"Folks!" Tim called. "Listen up! There's a redwood tree down across the highway five miles west! Don't drive down. You'll just get turned back. It's likely to be there all day."

As the story developed, Gutley relayed it to Willy, who said what the whole bar had said: "A fucking redwood tree down?" Redwood trees never fell down. Though all second growth after the lumber bonanza of the turn of the century, the sequoias here grew a hundred feet high and eight feet thick.

"Hey," said Gutley, "did you or did you not see a giant punk dyke piss gasoline and burn down the Rusty Nail?"

"OK. A redwood is down. Having any other trouble with the roads clown there?"

"Mmm," said Willy. "That tree'll still be there tomorrow too—every hand in the county is out on that eruption." There was a pause. "I think," said Willy, "that we're gonna come by water."

Rod Blair sat on his board out past the break, letting the swells lift and drop him. He was just below the Ross River Estuary, where the wide jade river met the bluer sea. Pelicans wheeled in the cloudless noon air and sat in flotillas on the waters of the river's mouth. Seals sunned themselves on the spur of beach.

Farther down the beach Sean's truck (with a new windshield) was parked nose to nose with a couple others right on the sand, and Rod's friends were drinking and boogying. The law was no problemo, dude! There wasn't a ranger to spare today—everyone was at that crazy eruption. Rod could almost hear the speakers above the vast, easy breathing of the sea.

Man! Nature!

Rod had had four—five?—beers, and a couple doobs of Maui Wowie, and right now he was experiencing a moment of revelation. Nature! Nature in all its glory, wide sea, windy sky, and wheeling gulls—it was all theirs to stomp around in. Theirs! That old saying, *The whole world lies before you,* was true! He felt blessed and full of power. The surf's pulse underneath him, it seemed something he himself dispensed in his majestic repose; he pumped the surf tirelessly forth to crash against the sand.

Rod Blair ached to express his joy, to fire up Sean's 4 by 4, for instance, rip out onto the sand, whip some donuts and some eights and kick up some humongous bitchin waves of sand in celebration, like a salute to Nature.

A pale blur broke the water just left of him and was gone again.

A seal? Shy for a seal—usually they popped up and looked at you a moment, making you laugh, once you got past that slight shock of having something surface near you from the ocean.

Paler than a seal too, hadn't it been? Paler even than their silvery bellies that flashed when they threw a backwards dive?

But see? Case in point! More Nature! Nature everywhere, his for the taking. And there—one of those flotillas of pelicans was taking to the air now. Tubular! Big sword-billed birds that made you think of those flying dinosaurs, when their wings unfolded they looked as if they were coming apart in big, jagged sections as their heads came back to make Z-shaped profiles on their long necks. One by one, heavily, they oared themselves into the air. Their long wings labored awkwardly up into flight, like orangutans clambering up into trees.

What was that? From the corner of his eye he'd seen something big swoop down at the group of his friends. Yes, they were still ducked down, scattered, and there it was, pulling up from its dive and wheeling back towards them. A fucking pelican! You never saw pelicans getting near people! Gulls, yes, but——

A clattering, hammering racket descended on Rod's head. He cringed so violently beneath the avalanche of noise that he almost toppled from the board. Violent gusts of air battered him and something stung his shoulders.

There it was, climbing, wheeling for another dive—another fucking pelican! Christ but the fuckers were big up close, five-foot wingspans . . . and then, as it climbed higher and turned again in his direction, Rod saw its eyes.

From each socket writhed a cluster of stalks, eyes like greedy worms tipped with wet agates, fingering the air for the sight of him, while something yellow, that smoked, dripped from the cruelly serrated rims of its open bill.

Rod began paddling like mad, in a frenzy to catch the next swell, and that was when he felt something meaty and slick touch his feet under water, felt something surge up under the nose of his board and tip him backwards, aiming him skywards just before the bird struck him.

Two red lightning bolts of infinite pain demolished Rod's eyes and sank endlessly deep in his brain.

Now Rod lacked sight to see a further revelation, though for a few moments he still had nerves to feel it, the swollen beast, its skin a diseased white, that tore Rod, muscle from bone, with crimson-eyed-craving.

Twenty-seven

It had been years since Kim had seen so many of the Mexican side of her family, all the relations and close friends of Lucky's first husband, Barbara's father. All morning Sunday they tore from one house to another in Aurora's indomitable '65 Dodge Dart.

What the old woman was demanding—swift preparation and departure from the city this very day—was not to be accomplished by phone. It needed eye-contact. It needed Aurora gripping their shoulders and telling them, *Por el amor de Dios, hijo, hija—andale!*

And once persuaded, they needed help in packing, needed errands run. Kim and Aurora were at it for hours. Persuading Rigoberto and Amalia, Aurora's first cousin and his wife; persuading Lupe and Felicidad and Juliana over in South Santa Marta, the middle-aged children of Aurora's dead younger brother; persuading Raoul and Rogelio, the brothers-in-law of her elder sister Esperanza's daughter, Esperanza still living back in Jalisco, but her daughter, Aurora's niece Sylvia, deceased; persuading Cristobal, one of her nephews who had a body shop in East Santa Marta, and motivating him to go and persuade Colon, another nephew who lived south of him. Then Aurora herself and Kim went down the block to persuade Maly and Blanca, two of her spinster cousins at their little corner store, motivating them to go forth and persuade Hermelindo and Rigoberto, two further cousins, at their used car dealership while Aurora and Kim went on to visit other houses and shops to persuade and motivate other relations, enjoining them to go in turn to others and say to them *Andale!* Get what cash you can muster and pack your moveable valuables and get yourselves south of here, down to Novato, or Marin, or San Francisco, where further children, grandchildren, cousins, and other connections of Aurora dwelt and could be contacted for a place to stay until the horror that was coming—coming *soon*—was passed. Here was a list of their addresses and numbers that this sweet child Kimberly had Xeroxed this morning, and now for the love of God, move it! *Por el amor de Dios, Andale!*

At Rachel's, the sister-in-law of one of Aurora's nephews, they met Lucky (who had been Rachel's bingo-crony for years) and Barbara and Maxie on the same errand as themselves.

Mutual updates raged, and after a few minutes Aurora said she would take a nap. She gave Rachel and Lucky the names of some further people to warn and persuade, and went in to Rachel's bed. Kim came in to see her settled.

The wrinkles on her face looked deep. In her smiling eyes was a weariness past telling. Kim bent to kiss her. Aurora stroked her cheek lightly with her gnarled knuckles. "Hard things lie ahead, *hija*. I am near my limits, and I must lean on you as I grow tired. You must try to empty your heart of fear. You must prepare."

Rachel and Lucky occupied Maxie with lunch while Barbara and Kim caught each other up in detail.

"Kim? I'm sorry about Alex, sweetheart." Barbara helped her cry a little more about it. She hadn't held her sister for years, it seemed. It felt sweet, and right.

"We've gotta go together, Kim. Aurora too."

"She said we would join you—but there's a lot of other people we have to warn."

"Just get to our place before dark. there was . . . something strange on the roads last night."

The phone rang, and Rachel called Barbara to it—it was Willy. He'd been working his way through their book of family numbers.

"Listen, Barb, I'm glad I got you—I want you to buy a canoe."

Sol Lazarian, in running shorts, air-cushion Nikes, and baggy tank-top with a surfer's logo on the back, thudded along Petaluma Valley Highway. To passing cars he returned the occasional wave; he wore the vacant half-smile of the aerobically absorbed as convincingly as he wore the gear. His cracked ribs beat the drum of pain in him as his muscled legs patiently ate the miles. He was still, at midday, twenty miles south of Santa Marta.

Last night he'd dragged himself out of the water well upriver from the bridge. The radios and flashers and spotlights of rescue vehicles seemed sparse for the scale of the accident. After some hours a semi brought a big crawler-tractor on a flatbed. The machine pulled Sol's tanker from the river. Lazarian, hidden deep in the riverbank weeds, was asleep by then on a mattress of cardboard litter.

In the hour before sunrise he stripped and carefully brushed his clothing smooth and clean. It was plain now what the goddess wanted from him. His rage. His attack.

Well, his rage was ready. Standing half naked, his readiness felt almost sensual, a bodily ache.

All the great religious texts reported the gods going hand-to-hand with those they had chosen to test. He felt he was coming to that moment, that all-deciding confrontation, and if she met him in any form that permitted it, he meant to blow her methodically to shreds with double-ought and thirty-ought from his sawed-off riot gun.

As he was on the threshold of a great physical trial, he must eat. As soon as he heard the traffic grow lively in the streets, he walked into Petaluma and found a coffee shop.

The morning paper showed him marvels. The refuse eruption had overcome its dykes. A home care nurse had discovered three skeletons in the residence of developer Jake Beaker. County Supervisor Nick Sawyer, his wife, and several dinner guests were hospitalized in critical condition due to severe food poisoning. In Gravenstein, a fatal traffic accident involved an engineless car and a corpse that appeared to be at least six months dead.

It was wondrous. She was coming, stepping into mankind's midst and these were the reverberations of her approach. Lazarian's instinct was amply confirmed, and the meeting she called him to tonight would answer all.

He felt tired. Weakness made a cowardly protest in him against the danger of what lay ahead. His flesh, it seemed, was slack. He'd spent too long, these last weeks, in airplanes and behind the wheels of vehicles. His body needed purification, a ritual ordeal to purge it of its weakness.

It was just past one as he thudded down the county two-lane, reconnecting with the energy of the ground, oiled with sweat. He had started at a brisker pace, but relentless physics had forced him to throttle down. He was all muscle, but that muscle's weight punished his legs. Now he saw that he could complete the thirty miles to Santa Marta after dark. Stores would still be open—there would be things to buy.

Gravity drubbed weariness into his bones, Earth's stupendous mass counterpunching his padded heels, and his cracked ribs drummed pain, pain, pain. But his soul, his rage, grew readier with each stride. His lungs gorged joyfully on the open air, and his nerves sang like fiddlestrings.

Chip had a hundred thousand dollars in his safe deposit box right this very minute, because he had at last, in his old age, had the sense and the balls to kick the habit of wage-slaving flunk-eydom and to play *outside* the court that the wise guys and corrupt politicians drew in the dirt for all the fuckees of the world to stay in.

So now he could come to work with a half-pint of bourbon in his pocket and fuck anyone who said otherwise.

Straff and he should meet soon. They had been proceeding towards each other from their respective ends of the dummy irrigation line for well over an hour, checking for leaks. They might not meet exactly at the middle, because the going had been a little tricky for Chip. The late afternoon light made the pastures seem smooth, lush green carpets, but it was amazing how easy it was to trip in the god-damned grass, all the gopher holes and dips you didn't expect. And since more than half the pint was out of the bottle and in Chip himself, that probably had a hand in it too.

If Straff didn't like it, too bad. The irrigation line was his show, really. The valve at the foot of the flex was still closed, but this line had been pumped full of sewage so they could check its seams for tightness. Acceptance up at the shaft wouldn't start till tomorrow, once Frankie and Beiderbeck had drained the shaft a little to make room.

Chip was keeping a hand on the pipe to steady himself, and he thought the pipe was unusually cold to the touch, but all the joints were dry and clean so far.

He took another drink and progressed a bit farther. Now he found himself leaning heavily on the pipe for support. It was amazing how completely you could lose the knack of drinking on the job in just ten short years! It used to be easy.

Chip was definitely woozy. He was pulling himself along the pipe with both hands now, and at moments it seemed as if he was climbing it—that the pastures were a vertical green wall, and he was going up it hand over hand. He heard a faint song somewhere in the distance, as he hauled himself along the pipe.

. . . get there . . . by degrees . . . just take hold . . . squeeze an squeeze . . .

Was he hearing it, exactly, or . . . imagining it? He rested against the pipe for a moment. The world levelled back out. That was better. And here came Straff! Fine. Let him cover the rest of the distance, it was his fuckin pipe.

For a long time Chip watched him coming. It got clearer and clearer that the engineer was in terrible shape. Straff had a hand on the pipe for support too, but not from drinking. His body looked gaunt and shrunken. His cheeks were startlingly hollow, and his eyes full of rage or fever.

"Havin . . . a nice rest?" Straff sneered as he came up, Chip was stunned by how he looked close up. It took a moment for the sarcasm to register. He pulled out his bottle.

"Yeah! Havin a nice drink too!" Chip suited the action to the word. Amazingly, he found only a tiny swallow left in the bottle. "Ya see," Chip said, smacking his lips and tossing the empty over the pipe they leaned on, "I'm an independent contractor now, Marv. I do what the fuck I want an if you don't like it you can fire me."

Straff's gaunt, fevered face crumpled in some kind of seizure. "Hey," said Chip, suddenly worried. Would the guy need an ambulance? Did he have something catching? "Hey, what's wrong with you anyway, Marv?"

"Goddamned yuppie-ass gourmet cooks!" The words came out strangled with pain.

"I think you oughta be in the hospital, Marv," Chip said. It was almost sobering, how bad off the guy seemed. Chip began to realize that the guy was only on his feet at all through an act of pure will.

"Those candy-asses lying in the hospital!" Straff gasped. "We got a job to finish, you goddamned alkie!" His knees buckled with the effort of getting this out, but he hooked his arms around the pipe at his back and held himself upright.

"I don't have to answer to you," raged Chip. "I don't have to——"

And Straff screamed. It was ear-splitting. Chip's own legs went to water and he too grabbed the pipe for support in his shock. The scream seemed to cleave Straff's face in half. You could see every one of his teeth, every cusp and crown and filling, in the golden slanting sunlight as he screamed, his eyes squeezed shut to give his mouth more room to let this huge unending scream rise free.

Then the scream stopped short when Marv Straff's ribs collapsed and his chest caved in. His legs, plucked up like a puppet's, rose towards this collapse of his middle—his shoulders were caving into it too . . . he was being pulled into a hole in the pipe! Chip's own arm was wrapped around this same pipe! He must——

A small black hole, the size of his palm, opened against his side and started sucking him through, his bones collapsing like spaghetti . . .

Josh Ridley, eight, playing with his friend Bud Jessup in a creekbed on his family's dairy ranch, heard screaming. At first Josh thought it was his mom out on the three-wheeler to get them in for dinner. Then they realized it was real screaming, something awful.

It stopped before they had climbed out of the creekbed, but both boys swore they saw the same thing, and they stuck to their story under repeated questions: The irrigation the city had paid Mr. Ridley to let them string across his pasture had a pair of legs sticking out of it. Two legs stuck out of that pipe and kicked in the air and then got shorter and shorter and disappeared, with a crackling noise they could just hear at that distance. Then there was nothing.

When they dared to approach the pipe, they found no trace of what they'd seen—except a man's work-boot, the left one. Josh dropped it as soon as he picked it up. It was warm inside.

Twenty-eight

Five adults, none of them small, and a child did a pretty good job of filling the living room and kitchen nook of Willy and Barbara's trailer. It had just gone dark outside and their reflections in the windows added to the sense of numbers.

The last traces of the dope shed and cultivating equipment were erased, and all the major packing was done. The women had returned with their supplies, and an aluminum canoe. The men were waiting until Kim called to go to Reed's for his canoe. She had promised to call if she and Aurora hadn't arrived by now.

Barbara had poured one of her infrequent glasses of wine, and all the other adults, except Willy, had just cracked beers.

"How come you don't have a beer, Daddy?" Maxie asked. Everyone else looked curious too.

Willy was going to tell her that he just wasn't thirsty, but then it struck him that it went deeper than that. "Because I'm a changed man," he told her solemnly. He happened to catch his own reflection in the window as he said this, and once again he was startled in spite of himself by his total baldness. The others saw his little double-take, and burst out laughing.

"You got *that* right!"

"Naw, you *always* had ugly ears."

"You should tattoo a big *thumbprint* on the back there, Willy!"

"No! A Happy Face on the top!"

The phone rang. It was Kim. She had found a place they could pick up a canoe on the way back, but she and Aurora couldn't start yet. Raleigh got on the line to her. He had an older-brother attitude about Kim that Willy recognized as part of a longstanding (and scrupulously unspoken) crush on Barbara.

"You two get on over here," he told her. "There's things out on the road you don't wanna *meet*."

But there was no hurrying Aurora, who had some errands to run to help family members get out of town. Kim hung up with the promise to arrive with the second canoe soon as possible.

The men rolled out in two trucks—Willy in his with Reed, and Raleigh following—out of a vague sense that if there was trouble, they might lose one vehicle, but not both.

Gravenstein's streets were almost deserted, and it was only seven. It was eerie. "It's like the signals ought to be set on blink," Willy said.

"It's that corpse-car from last night," Reed added, shuddering at the memory. "Wouldn't *you* stay off the streets?"

"Let's stop in at John an Zeke's an ask Carl."

The little bar off the square, usually well attended, had exactly three patrons, all staring at the big color TV.

"That's where everybody is," Carl told them, nodding at the screen. Reed and Raleigh ordered beers out of courtesy, and they watched for a while.

A blow-dry with a microphone was talking, his background a crowd of people and vehicles spread out in an open field. Beyond the crowd could be seen glimpses of big graders working under arc-lights, climbing the slope of a great dyke with loads of earth.

Containment, in the words of the blow-dry, had at last been achieved. The flow had stopped. The dykes were now twenty feet higher than the refuse level, which had abruptly stopped climbing some two hours before, emboldening thousands of onlookers to flock to a scene that was increasingly taking on the aspects of a mass celebration.

In the lightwash of the camera crews people could be seen waving sixpacks, having tailgate parties around their RVs. The blow-dry interviewed several people who said yes, they'd been getting scared, with the trash-flux barely two miles from Santa Marta, and they'd definitely had thoughts of leaving town, and thank God it was finally under control. The camera cut to another blow-dry who had a county supervisor in tow. The supe assured people that all cause for alarm was now past. Investigations into the source of the bizarre eruption were already under way. He indulgently acknowledged that there was a lot of celebrating going on in the city, and asked people to observe moderation and caution on the highways.

The three men drove through Gravenstein's emptiness, none of them feeling any the less uneasy for the news they'd heard. They found activity in the lumberyard, half its tall vapor lamps lit, three people on forklifts shifting stacks of planks. The bulge in Sequoia Highway was a good foot higher than before, and the long, tentacular groundswell running from Reed's lot had grown, upsetting more bundles of two-by-sixes.

Willy crossed the highway to the fence of the lumberyard, leaving Reed and Raleigh to load the canoe. "Hey! Marta!" he called. "That you? It's Willy Yakima!"

She backed her forklift to the fence and jumped off—a lean chain-smoker with an electric bush of ponytailed black hair. Marta had been a friend of Barbara's since high school.

"Jesus, Willy, what happened to your *hair?*"

"I lost it. Listen. Some really weird things are going down here. That wreck last night? It came outta Raleigh's lot. You guys should get outta here."

She stopped him with a raised palm and pointed behind her. The crack in the freeway overpass was far wider than before.

"You don't have to tell me about weird," she said. "These

two guys don't have green cards"—she nodded at the other two forklift drivers—"and they'll do what I tell em. We're all outta here in another hour, max."

They loaded the canoe, drove around, and chained and padlocked the gate to Raleigh's lot. "Ya know it just occurs to me," Raleigh said. "Mine ain't the only wreckin yard around here by a long shot."

On their way back to Willy's, Reed stopped at the Circle K. Bea drove north out of town to go home, and Raleigh told her she ought to get herself out of town early tonight. "And till you get past my lot," he told her gravely, "keep your eyes open and drive carefully."

Frankie DaValli awoke with an erection, out of a dream that instantly slithered off his conscious mind, like a shed garment of heavy black silk. His eyes were gummy, and the room—the back room of the mine office—was almost dark. Jesus Christ! He'd overslept in a big way.

He limped into the bathroom, his erection taking forever to go down, and making his movements awkward. He washed his face at the little rust-stained sink and remembered Beiderbeck's coherent, muscular snake of blackness just under the surface of the lake. The man was a fucking genius.

He'd left Frankie a note on the desk in the front office. "Hiked Down. Ready when you are."

Last night, in San Francisco, after returning the tanker, they'd loaded two large satchels in Frankie's trunk: the components of the drain valve they were to set tonight. The satchels hadn't felt very heavy, and Beiderbeck had insisted on carrying them himself. It must have been difficult walking all the way down the hillside with them. Let the weirdo suit himself. Frankie would take the car down as planned, pick up the skiff he'd rented in Moscow Junction, and maybe he'd have a drink from the office bottle before going anywhere.

Coming back north in the small hours, they'd hit a detour—the fucking overpass was out. Then they'd had to stop at Frankie's condo because Beiderbeck insisted he wanted his balance in cash the moment he set and opened the drain—fifty thousand. Now.

They'd gotten back up here just before dawn, and he passed out the minute his back touched the cot. He'd slept the whole day, and he still felt like he'd just put in a hard day's work. That was how the drink felt too, not a raw jolt to just-wakened nerves, but mellow and soothing. It was disorienting. His skin was prickly, and resurgent lust coruscated across his genitals.

A second drink felt even better. A second drink felt just right. It brought back whisperings and rustlings from his dream, a sensation of silken smoothness, a smell . . . of the shaft? And why not? Because the dream had been, partly, about wealth, hadn't it? Yes. Frankie pulled Beiderbeck's fifty thousand from his pocket, handled the packets of hundreds. The naked, hefty potency of cash! He tingled all over. Time was wasting.

At the boat rental the skiff was waiting on a trailer. Driving along the lake's rim, he had to keep easing his foot off the gas, his eagerness rebuked by the trailer's unaccustomed drag. The boat was for checking the colloid's behavior in the lake, but what were they going to be able to see in the dark?

There was the skinny chemist in his little black Frankenstein suit—the headlights caught him standing at the shore, gazing out over the starlit water, kind of a romantic figure.

He was all business, though, and snappy. "Back it around, Frankie, get the lead out—it's been dark for an hour. . . . Left, left! Now straight back!"

Before Frankie could get out to help him, Beiderbeck had

hauled the boat off the trailer with a bang.

"Hey, I got a deposit on that—"

"Will you get *in?* You're not my only job, Frankie—I wanna get done, get paid, an get gone."

"Aren't you gonna show me the drain valve, how it works? And aren't we gonna turn it on first?"

Frankie was in the boat and Beiderbeck was shoving it the rest of the way into the water. He paused and pulled a little remote box from his coat. "We turn it on offshore. Let's get some drainage first, see how the stuff behaves in the water. Then I'll show you the valve, how to regulate it, the whole schmeer."

"I don't see any drain hose coming out of the shed."

"Maybe that's because I buried it in the gravel, dingus! Are we gonna do this or aren't we?"

Frankie rowed. "Isn't this far enough?"

"Another hundred feet or so—bear left there a little."

"How are we gonna see *what* it does in the water at night?"

Beiderbeck patted a coat pocket. "Infra-red binoc's. . . . OK, this is just about right. Ship the oars. Pull em aboard. Good. Now. You got the rest of my cash?"

"Right here."

"Fine." Beiderbeck reached into the pocket he had patted and pulled out his big, silver Clint Eastwood pistol. He pointed it straight at Frankie and thumbed back the hammer. "Gimme."

Frankie handed over the money. "Sol Lazarian's gonna kill you, you know."

"Why? You think I'm not delivering? *Au contraire.* You're just going a little more public than you thought you were. Will he kill me anyway? I don't know, and it doesn't matter enough. This is all too perfect to resist, you see, it has to be this way. Ah, you shit-sucking greedball, this is going to be such fun! I mean, why hide what you're doing? It has the beauty of perfect mindlessness! Are you ready now, Frankie? Here's how fortunes are made—with the push of a button."

And Beiderbeck pushed a button on the little remote box.

The flare of white light from the shore for a moment completely blotted the sight from Frankie's eyes, in just the same way that, a moment later, the flat roar of the explosion erased his hearing. The flare dimmed instantly and became a red and black mushroom of smoke and large debris. Pulverized concrete smacked and sizzled on the waters around them. A ragged corner of cinderblock crashed down astern and spat them with spray.

"Row us in, Frankie, row us in!" crowed Beiderbeck.

In a trance, Frankie began to row again. Over his shoulder he saw that there was absolutely nothing left of his new shed but a pillar of slowly dispersing smoke.

"Closer," snapped Beiderbeck. He sounded vexed now, his eyes straining at the beach. The smoke was gone, and there was a black, ragged hole in the bluff, a glittery wound of torn stone. The moonlight put a sheen on it, it seemed lacquered with an ebony gloss, but nothing came out of it.

"What the fuck . . ." began Beiderbeck softly, unbelievingly.

And just then they heard a soft, cracking noise, the report of wet earth-flesh splitting. A sudden black bubble domed out from the black wound. With a vast wet noise of skin-rippling friction a slug of blackness, eight feet thick, surged in a graceful arc up and out from the flank of the mountain. It hit the water with a sound of ice-crystals avalanching on satin, a salacious hiss of unholy pleasure. Every hair on Frankie's neck was standing erect.

Twenty-nine

Bea nosed her old Chrysler out of the Circle K's lot and north on Sequoia Highway, out of town. Big solemn Raleigh, his face all scratched, had carried conviction.

She nosed cautiously through the curves out of town, ready to execute his advice: "You see anything strange comin towards you, pull right off the road!"

The lights in the lumberyard were reassuring, a note of normality, people out and working. The lights showed up that bulge in the road a lot better than those useless little flashers they'd put out. The bulge was definitely bigger than this morning. She'd just ease over it, get it behind her, and in another half mile she could get onto the freeway and—

BANG!

The noise of metal hitting metal made her hit the brakes and give a little scream. Good Lord, did that come from Raleigh's wrecking yard?

BANG! It was a huge noise of something slamming into a big rattly something else of metal.

There was a wide dirt turnout on the lumberyard side of the highway here, and Bea turned right off onto it. No way she would wait till something was actually coming at her. She made straight for a power pole near the lumberyard fence, pulled in between it and the fence, and killed her engine.

BANG! . . . BANG! . . . BANG!

Each time the noise of impact was crunchier. Something that sounded like a chain-link fence was buckling, groaning, giving.

"Stay right where you are!"

The voice almost gave Bea a heart attack. The workers in the lumberyard were at the fence right next to her car—a woman with a bushy ponytail was speaking. "Hey! You're Bea! From the Circle K?"

"Yes."

"I'm Marta Obregon! Remember me? I had that skateboard in high school you were always making me leave outside?"

"That was you? My God, you're grown up already?"

"Listen Bea, don't get out of the car. As soon as—"

WHAM-CRUNCH! Now there was a shriek to the impact and the snap of exhausted steel. The shadowed heaps in the wrecking yard, teetering bluffs and mesas of stacked car-corpses, were moving—shifting here and there, the stacks dropping, suddenly a notch shorter against the stars behind them.

WHAM-CRUNCH-CLATTER!

And out of Raleigh's turnoff rocketed a wide black convertible with a section of torn cyclone fence flapping from its front bumper. Its hood was crumpled, its windshield a fanged fringe of fragments, and its wheels gave off sparks as thick as a grindstone's. Framed in the windshield behind the wheel was a lolling skull-face with a rag of rotten black hair jutting down over empty eyeholes. It threw a turn south on Sequoia, launched up and off the bump, slammed down and swept flaring and blazing away like a comet into town. And then the rest began to follow, one after the other . . .

The unfaltering jet of blackness, with mountain-high pressure behind it, seemed to be built into the air, its hissing arc as stable as architecture. But under its footing on the lake, beneath the foam of its entry, glowing red roots were branching through the deeps. Frankie and Beiderbeck watched, jaws hanging.

"Why is it glowing?" asked the chemist, awed, almost whispering. "There's no pattern, no response to the currents. It's moving. It's moving . . . at *will*."

All around them, the lake's blackness was wormy with hot, scarlet light. In festoons and ribbons it draped the depths—it darted and coiled like pythons under them, till the gunwales were ruddy with the glow.

Frankie said nothing. His stillness was that of a steady flame. He understood that an ordained moment, a moment as all-containing as the night sky, was opening to him—him specifically, Frankie DaValli. An intended, a destined revelation. His scrotum bulged with lust, a lust like pregnancy, so big it must split him coming out, and coming out with it, a new self, a new soul would be born to him.

His senses brimmed. A seethe and mutter of inhuman voices filled his ears. The water of the lake, just to their right, began to bulge, and its water-swell shoved the boat aside and up it came: a floater—a drowned corpse, but huge!

Twice the size of the boat she was. Fat-ripe from the muddy bottom, grotesquely swollen, even her fingers and the black-purple jut of her tongue from her frozen jaws. She bobbed beside them, her huge breasts shedding moon-electric foam, a charnel-house stench gusted off of her.

And then the dead black wax of her staring eyes melted, thawed to consciousness. She *saw*. Her head turned towards them, and she smiled. Lazily, lustingly, her arm rose and she reached for the boat, as one might reach, upon waking, for a bedfellow.

All around them the water, veined with red, rose like tumbled blankets kicked into heaps and crooked pleats by furious fucking. Twelve feet high on every side, wrinkled muscles of water like clenching vulvae closed on them all, on the goddess and the men and the boat, and she was lifted, tilted, and turned on top of them.

Slick black skin as cold as an arctic whale's sealed Frankie's body. Water gripped him, silken, and he felt his clothes and the boat beneath him dissolve.

He hung in darkness, hugged by the goddess, and did not crave to breath; this cold placental grip *was* breath. Blindly they flexed and rolled, like mating killer whales, curving and coupling beneath the floor of time.

Frankie grew gigantic. His body was a cosmos festering in all its parts with residues of caustic richness. Corrosive still-bottoms crept from lymphatic labyrinths of his tissues, hot rad-waste clogged his bowels, monoxides bubbled from his pores, lubricating him within the water. He wore a sweat of blighting acids, and he stomached the entombed solid wastes of cities, nations.

And all this swelling cargo in him bulged towards the bliss of elimination. He housed in his hugeness the Mystery itself, the Miracle of Wealth and Power: shit into gold. Filth becoming wealth, and he the crucible it happened in.

Frankie knew his triumph then, a victory beyond the scope of other men. In the slow explosion of his climax all the wealth in him coalesced the intricate alembics of his loins and geysered out of him in one endless jet of the absolute black jism of greed.

Frankie awoke, nude, dripping, legs in the water, his face on the gravel. Beiderbeck, also nude, lay a short way down the beach. They struggled—slowly, slowly—to their hands and knees. Frankie's balls felt blown, like smoking bomb-craters, his brain reverberantly empty, like a sounded bell. Above them, a voice boomed.

"Stand up, boys, and come with me to my place."

It was Mamie Durtt, huge in the moonlight and naked as

themselves. She turned away towards her cove. They stirred like puppets, each fiber of them alive to her will. They rose and followed her.

With each shell Lazarian thumbed into the magazine of his riot gun, some of the pain and weariness thawed from his muscles. He left the door of the little apartment he had taken standing open behind him and all the lights on, when he stepped out to his van. It was his last habitation in this world. He was going up and over, stepping out.

When he fired up the van, the last soreness melted from his joints; his heart hammered majestically, with a rhythm like the beating of great wings. He moved through the lights of a downtown mall, through the mothswarm of people in bright California clothes, people whose faces seemed flat as cutouts. He found a wetsuit that would fit him, and a "micro-lung," faceplate, and ten-minute air bottle.

Just south of River Highway he saw a little tiara of arc-lights . . . the running lights of helicopters busy in the air above, during the refuse containment battle. The goddess had stepped openly out onto the plain to claim her empire. The night was alive with her energy. She was shaking the pillars of her mountain halls and booming now in the center of his mind: *Come face me if you dare.*

He dared.

He had been her acolyte, her trash man, all his life. He had served. He had earned the right to stand and demand his passage through the gate. She herself, was the gate, and she had told him that to enter he must tear his way through her. So be it.

The little crown of arc lights suddenly, and all at once, went out just before he turned up the hill . . . they were snuffed like candles. His nerves thrilled. She intended total war.

At the mouth of the shaft, Lazarian stripped and fought himself into the wetsuit. He donned the micro-lung, its demand valve dangling on his chest, and put on a respirator mask. With the pump riot in one hand he took up a lantern in the other.

As he raised the lantern, he turned to look at the shadow it made of him on the ground behind him: a sleek-bodied, bug-headed giant. It struck Sol as an abstracted, alien shape, that of a rare creature, evolved and streamlined to cross the hostile void. To travel between dimensions.

To confront a tarn of poisons with a gun, armored with an aqualung—it was ludicrous. But he knew that he must honor this moment with ceremony, that he must stand here in regalia that was in accord with his purpose. The paltriness of the arms did not matter. Their challenge, their declaration was the *Magic*. How she would oppose him was according only to her will. But he sensed that she would choose to meet him in a form that he could grapple with.

He started down. Time became something that he shed in his descent, an invisible viscosity that melted away from his movements, leaving him within each downward step, a part of one unaltered moment.

And then he reached the drenched zone and found that the pool was gone. The dragon had fled its lair.

The lantern's light fell hundreds of feet before him, showing him the empty throat of the shaft, glittering with the black gloss of poison. Its ceiling still dripped, threads of black syrup dangling, their fall making little, ticking echoes swallowed by the gulf below.

Frankie and Beiderbeck would have begun the drainage, of course, but only a few thousand gallons at first, to assure it worked. Thereafter they would drain just enough to match the intake of the sewage. But this million-gallon emptiness, as far as his light could reach!

Come up and see me, she had said. Where else but here? And was this a new mockery? A new challenge?

She had meant him to come here, to find this, to see if he would retreat. A crest of cold fire feathered along his spine.

Lazarian, choosing his footing carefully, carefully, continued down.

Thirty

Raleigh's Wrecking Yard was empty now. Nothing remained inside the fence but the shed and a litter of small parts. Bea grew aware of piercing pain in her hands. They gripped the wheel so hard it was agony to unclench them.

Marta said, "Listen, Bea. We all came to work in my car. I'm gonna let them drive mine back and I'll come with you—I'll drive if you want."

"Oh, yes, dear! Thank God! I feel so shaky! I'm up in Hopdale."

"Fine—I live just north of there. If we caravan, we have some back-up. We'll lead off and—"

"Mira!" shouted one of the workmen. His voice cracked as he pointed across the highway.

What first took their eyes was the big repair shed on Reed's lot. It was gradually rising into the air. Its husk of corrugated metal sheets, its spindly frame of two-by-fours, were shuddering, shimmying. The shed seemed to boogie with its boxy shoulders as it rose ten, twelve feet straight up into the darkness.

They realized that the shed wasn't just rising. The earth was lifting it. Making a vast, soft, crumply noise, the hillside was bulging towards them. Now the cyclone fence around both lots was folding, flattening, vanishing as the swelling earth rolled over it.

"Scoot over!" screeched Marta. "And put your belt on!"

She fired up the engine and floored it. The tires screamed, flinging up plumes of gravel as the rising hillside flopped like a vast paunch onto the edge of the highway, splitting as it swelled, gutlike blobs of blackness ballooning from the seams, and then the tire treads caught, and as Bea was still fumbling with her belt, the acceleration slammed her back.

Headlights leapt from the lumberyard gate behind them and both cars were launched. A thirty-foot wall of broken hillside and glittery filth rolled quivering across the highway just as they got asphalt under their wheels and rocketed north.

Behind them the ooze rolled crunching and slobbering, ever higher, fifty feet high when it swallowed the lumberyard, sixty feet when it engulfed the freeway and began to roll southward. Its first stop—which couldn't stop it: Gravenstein.

And at the same instant, fifteen miles farther behind the fleeing cars, thousands of revelers spread on the plain below the dyke paused and harkened. They paused in their beer-drinking, their boogying to their boomboxes, their happy conversations, and looked skyward to the crest of the dyke. They had heard something—a vast sucking sound—and felt something—a tremor in the earth. And then, beyond the line of lights that crowned their celebrations, a wall of blackness rose, and rose, and rose— three hundred feet into the air with the quickness of a darting hand, snatching helicopters from the air, and then, toppling over the dyke . . .

On his way out of town with his spinster sister and their three dogs, Candido, Aurora's second cousin, took her and Kim to his place of business, Candido's Can-Do Rentals on the south side of town, and dug a battered old canoe out of his storage garage for them.

They tied it upside down on the roof of the Dodge and Aurora drove them west from town, to take country roads through the plain up to Willy's. They passed about half a mile east of the containment dyke, and as its arc lamps dropped away behind them, Kim shouted, "Look!"—and they saw them go black, and heard a vast, ragged sound of human voices screaming that ended with a muffled boom and sudden silence.

"Dios mio," moaned Aurora. She pulled off onto the shoulder, leaning her forehead against the wheel. Her voice, when it came again, sounded thin and ancient. "It has started. You must drive, Kimberly. I am too weak . . . too old. You must hurry, there is no time to lose."

In the passenger's seat, the old woman slumped against the door. Her face shone with sweat. "The roads are very dangerous now," she said. Her voice trailed off, and her eyes closed.

Kim sped north. Her heart was hammering, though there was only moonlit asphalt ahead, and only the hiss of their tires, and the moan of the wind in the inverted canoe, clamped like a sounding board above them.

She remembered the monster in the field of fire, scornfully tossing Alex's life on the embers. Her guilt was equal to his—surely her life too was forfeited, and the monster only mocked her with this dismissal to embitter her death when it came—came soon now. She was doomed, entombed already in the Earth's curse. The canoe's hollow whisper above her seemed the sound of her own desolated womb, that absence in her where no child, no, would ever live. The lonely terror this caused her surprised her. It was the first time she realized she wanted children someday.

Now the two-lane wound through the foothills. The road poured towards her, poured into her eyes with a snakelike sway. She was driving too fast for these curves, but she couldn't slow down—her speed was a preparation, a limbering of her courage.

Because something was coming. She felt it now, coming straight for them, around this next curve here . . . or around this next one, then—something coming to take their lives.

There. Where the hillside bowed out into view past two lesser curves between, something big and dark swung into view, licking a wide tongue of sparks from the road.

"Oh, shit," Kim moaned.

"Be empty." Aurora's voice, frail as it was, touched her with hope. The old woman's eyes stayed closed, and her voice was little more than a whisper. "Do not hesitate."

The slick stone sucked at Lazarian's footing. Gripping his rifle by the barrels for a staff, he eased himself down, lantern high. With each step he worked his sole against the slime, seeking a bite on the rock beneath before putting his weight down. Yet with each step this got trickier, as if the rock itself were turning pliant, fleshy . . .

He slipped. His feet squirted out from under him, he came down hard, on his shoulder, and went squeegeeing down past several ties, their corners cruelly punishing him before he stopped himself. But he'd held fast to both rifle and lantern.

He rose, jaw clenched against the pain, and continued his descent. This was not a tunnel of stone—it was the goddess' throat, or anus, the rock her pliant tissue, teasing his balance.

Carefully, carefully, his rage a hot coal in his heart, he eased down, step by step.

And slipped again.

Feeling both rifle and lantern leaving his grip, he grabbed with both hands for the rifle, caught it, and slammed down upon the lantern, smashing it. In sudden, utter dark, the slick pitch sucked him down.

Bruised and battered he sledded blind, digging in with his heels, slowing at last, stopping.

He lay on his back, clutching the weapon, blinking his eyes to be sure they were open. His ribs were very badly cracked now, but still they had not pierced his lungs. His legs were still intact, and he was still armed.

All right then.

This deep in the earth, things slithered, they did not walk. He began to slide himself down the shaft on his back. A little ways, and then a stop. Then another little way . . .

After timeless work in the perfect dark, he developed a worm-like agility. He discovered that he could pour himself sinuously, heels finding projections to slow him but moving without pauses, an intimate bedfellow now of the blind mountain core, cozy and nimble as a maggot in a roadkilled cat.

He had dropped through a crack in the floor of time. His descent took forever. When he wriggled, slick and black from the mine's blown anus, it was a new universe he stood in. He stripped off his mask and let fall his unneeded micro-lung. He breathed the pure air of eternity.

A lake spread before him, looking like a galaxy, freckled with stars and moon-glints, and murkily red-lit within, as with the dust-cloaked energies of birthing stars. To him, this pocket galaxy brimmed with time. It digested billions of years in its slow wheel of evolution, while he himself stood high and clear above its little eons.

Weaving into his awareness came a low, mellow melody. It drifted in from down shore, somewhere in that cove of trees. It was a song that Lazarian knew. . . .

As Kim rounded the next curve, the black convertible came swinging broadside to them. It rode on its wide, cruel tongue of sparks.

For a long instant Kim was ice, rocketing straight for it, a long instant in which the dime-sized holes of the other driver's eyesockets grew to the size of half dollars, a long instant in

which she sat cold and empty, but not yet empty enough of herself, not yet empty enough of terror to—*NOW*—wrench the
wheel hard right and launch the Dodge straight off the road.

The earth dropped from under them, and their axles tremored as their wheels spun on air. Kim yanked the wheel hard left
and felt them veering and banking like a plane until their wheels
punched and got a purchase on the pavement. The highway
again poured under them, and the death car was miles behind.

She squalled through the next curve at fifty, outrunning
astonishment, outrunning any thought that might clutter this
fertile vacancy in her, its emptiness radiant-ripe with magic.

She shrilled through another curve, and there ahead, another
fireball bloomed—a van that had been sideswiped by a second
corpse-car. It rolled forward in flames beside its killer, a panel
truck with stove-in walls and a skull-less skeleton slumped at the
wheel.

Kim pulled back on the top of her steering wheel as on a joy-
stick.

The Dodge shuddered, its wheels beginning to pound the
pavement as if it were trying to gallop, and Kim had a moment
to wonder remotely how collision and fiery death were going to
feel, and then the Dodge lifted, like an old war-horse remembering, leapt with a stomach-flattening surge that cleared the on-
comers by inches, so that she felt the flames lick the frame
bottom under her footsoles.

They crashed back down on yelping shocks and roared on.
Kim no longer gripped the wheel. She held it loosely now,
gracefully, eyes absent, open to whatever came next.

When the nightmare caravan began roaring by on the highway,
the comet-tails of sparks told Willy, Reed, and Raleigh—packing
up with the women—all they needed to know. They drove their

three pickups out to the mouth of Willy's drive. Reed and Raleigh backed their tailgates up to the edge of the road as a barrier to anything that tried to drive through. Willy waited in his truck, aimed nose-out. They would pull aside and let him out if Kim and Aurora showed up needing help.

A late-model customized van, its front end completely caved in, roared past, a pair of decayed legs, jeans in tatters, dangling from a fissure in the impacted frame. It roared round a curve, all the way out in the oncoming lane.

"That ain't from my lot!" Raleigh shouted from his cab.

"Your lot's not the only—" Willy began.

"Christ, look out!" screeched Reed.

A living car—one, at least, with headlights blazing and no visible deformities, and with a canoe tied to its roof—roared out of the curve the van had just vanished into. Roared out a good six feet above the pavement.

It flew straight over Willy's fence and slammed down in the weeds on the edge of his property—*WHAM-CRUNCH!*—with a belly-flop that sounded as if it broke both the axles.

A hand reached out the passenger window with a small knife and cut one of the ropes that bound the canoe. The door opened and Aurora stepped out. Kim stepped out the other side. The two women looked at each other across the hood of the car. Kim's eyes looked a question. The old woman smiled and nodded once. Then she looked down and sadly touched the hood of the Dodge.

"I think, my dear old friend," she said, "that this was the end of you."

The men came awkwardly forward now. "I'm afraid so, ma'am," Raleigh said. "I think you broke both your axles. It's a miracle you weren't hurt, landing like that."

After a beat, this made both the women laugh.

Thirty-one

When Lazarian was younger, the extravagance of homicide, the boldness and abandon of it, had weighed equally for him with its spiritual importance.

During this period he had once killed five people to get at one.

First, hidden in trees near some trashcans in an expensive countryside neighborhood, he had surprised and killed the two men running the collector-compactor that stopped for the trash. Already dressed in overalls, he had gotten them both into the compactor just before some early commuter traffic trickled past, and stood there at the compactor's lever, presenting a routine appearance, listening to the complex crunching beneath the heavy iron blade.

Next he drove the truck to his target's house and left it idling in the drive until, one after the other, the target's two body-guards crept out to investigate. These he added to the pulped first two. Lastly the target himself and his wife.

And he had enjoyed a curious vision then, of the compound corpse he had just committed to a common tomb. What a creature he had sent across to witness the Beyond on his behalf! A being with twelve eyes and hands. A bright red undersea kind of creature of flesh finely ciliated with sixty fingers, all its mouths simultaneously open in the awe of death, murmuring revelations he could not—as always—quite hear. . . .

Now, as he moved along the path into the trees of the cove, he remembered this vision—because now he found it so vastly surpassed. All the people he had ever killed seemed gathered round him now.

He swam through shoals of them—whole coral reefs they peopled, jeweled with astonished eyes, pocketed with gaping mouths of wonder. All around him their countless limbs gestured urgently, cryptically, their gestures weaving messages in the undersea gloom of the moonlit trees. All the witnesses he had sent through that gate accosted him together, and they were telling him now he would see. Now he would see, they were telling him.

The treetrunks were flexing in the aqueous air, like luminous stalks of a kelp forest. Wetly they whispered around him. The path underfoot felt like flesh, sodden, but astir to his step, contracting like cold, sluggish muscle A glow ahead grew stronger.

He came to a clearing.

In it was a house, porched with big old beams that were luminous like swamp-rot. A wide yard before the house was filled with a glowing white tangle of spiderweb that radiated out from the porch, strands thick as cables like silvery laser beams shot in a thousand directions. Hanging nude in the webbing were Frankie DaValli and Bill Beiderbeck.

And up on the porch, where the webbing was covered in a tight silken funnel, crouched the goddess, her form now that of a gigantic spider-centaur. She had the head and shoulders of the woman in the tanker, but her great breasts now merged beneath with the glossy thorax—multiply socketed with legs—of the spider. Her abdomen's tapered, mottled sphere hung balanced amid the bristly, jointed arches of her legs.

Lazarian's body-hair squirmed in his wetsuit's tight grip, and his tongue cleaved to his throat.

But at the core of his horror, and beginning to spread in him already, like wings—was jubilation. For a monster such as this could only be set to guard the last of all gates. He had finally arrived at reality's frontier, and was about to step across.

He set the stock of the pump-riot to his shoulder. The spider's legs tautened in steeper arches, and the goddess' eyes were as like obsidian as any insect's. Lazarian knew he must speak—or better, shout, lest his voice crack with fear.

"Goddess!" It was pure joy, he found, throwing his voice at her—it was the thrill of priesthood. "Goddess! Open the gate to me now! Open to me whatever lies beyond this great trash-heap of a world! I have served you! I have striven to know your will, and you have demanded of me my defiance, my assault! Gladly I give it then, and you must give in return what I ask!"

And he *fired, fired, fired,* pumping double-ought into the hideous, tapered bulb of her abdomen. Her face never flickered. Her abdomen exploded in three different places, and a wave of smoking black fluid gushed from her wounds—it washed in a leaping, snaking tongue towards him, plenteous and impossibly quick.

Even as he leapt back the brew engulfed his feet to the ankles. Lazarian screamed as his flesh and bone melted.

He thrust down a hand to break his fall, and this too smoked and sizzled away where it plunged into the brew.

With the hand that remained he seized a strand of the webbing, which held him. He sank back groaning in the web's support, feeling the wetsuit now melting from him, dripping off in rags.

Now his nakedness mirrored Frankie's, and Beiderbeck's. His eyes sought DaValli's, which were glazed with despair. But Lazarian's shone through the tears of his body's agony, and he wore a twisted grin of victory.

"We're crossing over, Frankie," he groaned triumphantly. "She's taking us through to the other side, Brother Weasel!"

Thirty-two

Just after sunrise, Marjorie Hacker awoke on a couch in the main lobby of the Santa Marta Community Hospital.

She had sat reading to poor Morris for hours last night, helping the nurse with his frequent bedpan changes. He looked so shriveled and dehydrated despite all the IVs. And there seemed to be no end to his affliction! How could one man Morris's size have so much . . . affliction *in* him?

Reading for so long, trying to buoy her husband with her voice, left Marjorie feeling as if she had been physically lifting him all those hours. She desperately needed rest, but was afraid to leave the hospital. Poor Mr. Urbach and poor Mrs. Sawyer had already passed away earlier that morning, Mr. Shugg and Mr. Sawyer—all on the same floor—were losing weight alarmingly fast.

She found no one minded her stretching out on the couch in the lobby. Indeed, the hospital personnel scarcely noticed. Radios and portable TVs at every nurse's station furtively blended in the corridors with those heard from the patients' rooms. At the admissions desk Marjorie leaned with other visitors at the counter and watched, with the staff, the eleven o'clock report.

There were two "fronts" now. The awesome resurgence of the "southern front" had engulfed an estimated four thousand containment workers and onlookers in its first thirty seconds and had then moved at unprecedented speed due east, rolling across Highway 101 just south of Santa Marta in less than half an hour. Meanwhile there was the new "northern front," which had already swallowed half of Gravenstein and likewise engulfed 101.

The aerial footage was impressive. The airborne floodlights, trembling with the vibration of the helicopters that carried them, made shaky circles on a glittery black terrain where rooftops and treetops were islands in what looked like a slick sea of guts and bones. These rooftop and treetop islands were shrinking, shrinking, gone—even as you watched; even in these short clips you saw the speed of the monster mess.

Thank God they were in Community Hospital rather than another—it was perched on the crown of the hills behind Santa Marta. In any case, citizens were advised against taking to the roads. An epidemic of bizarre and fatal car crashes was being reported from all parts of the city and the surrounding plain. Spokespersons for the city and county officials now closeted in emergency session urged everyone whose homes were not directly in the path of one of the fronts to stay indoors and remain calm.

Calm was no problem. Marjorie lay back on the couch and was gone.

Waking sharply, she had the impression of being roused by the sound of passing feet and urgent voices, but the lobby was empty, the early light slanting in through the western windows. Then she saw the crowd of staff out in the parking lot.

They seemed to be arguing with a pair of uncomfortable-looking security persons in blue uniforms, one of whom, as Marjorie came out, surrendered some keys to a doctor, an angry Filipino woman who was leading the group of staff. With the keys, she marched to some elevators that served a helicopter landing platform on the hospital roof three stories up.

"Why's everyone going up?" Marjorie asked a young black woman in orderly's greens.

"You can *see* from up on the pad. Do you wanna count on the network news when you can see for yourself?"

The elevator was filled and Marjorie, with others, rushed up the stairs. Out on the breeze-swept roof, the gold light on their backs, they rushed to the western railing to look out over the plain. The bigness of the view stunned Marjorie. People cried aloud as they ran, awe and terror wringing it out of them.

"Dear Jesus!"

"It's not happening!"

"You can see it moving!"

"What the Christ is going *on?*"

"Oh dear Lord, we have sinned! We have sinned, dear Lord!"

Under the flawless sky the city spread out to a perimeter where it was . . . bitten off. There was a black wall to the west, to the south, to the north. Beyond the walls, a vast, unbroken black glacier glittered. The air swarmed with the stench, like a plague of invisible locusts that battered the brain to numbness. "Half the people in those houses are still asleep," someone said. A nurse, an older Latina woman with worn and kindly eyes, said, "We were *all* asleep." Her chin was thrust out with indignation, but there were tears in her eyes too. "And what good will being awake do us now?"

In the fields at the city's western edge were windrows of eucalyptus a hundred feet high. Marjorie watched them bow before the glacier, watched them swallowed, saw power poles snapping like matchsticks. Up into the sky's silence rose a wide, complex crumpling of buckling roofbeams, flattening cars and fractured trees, knit with a fainter music of human cries. You could just make them out here and there, the streams of people being corralled towards the city's center.

Sophie was nineteen. She was homeless because her stepfather molested her, because she had a drinking problem, because it was an adventure. Merril was seventy or so, and she was homeless because she was simple and because the sister who had always taken care of her had died five years before.

They were in the Courthouse Square of downtown Santa Marta. Merril was taking the triangular metal hats off the trash cans in the square and the two of them were sifting for aluminum cans, squashing them on the park walk and stowing them in a burlap bag Merril dragged. Merril was neat and industrious, solemnly teaching a survival skill to the girl. Sophie was sloppier, but having a good time.

No one was bothering them because downtown was a nuthouse this morning. The traffic was unbelievable, every street was jammed and no one was moving and horns were blaring and people on the sidewalks were stopping one another, shouting or talking a mile a minute and waving their arms. Sophie caught a sense of holiday from it all. She sneaked hits from a shooter of Thunderbird in the pocket of her grease-blackened Raiders jacket, and stomped the cans Merril dropped in front of her.

They approached a new trash can. Merril was reaching for the hinged lid to lift it off when the lid exploded straight up into the air, shoved upwards by a high-pressure column of wrappers, cans, and crumpled papers.

The debris clattered and smacked down all around them as—*pang-whoosh!*—another can shot its lid, and then another . . .

Trash was geysering everywhere in the square. Merril and Sophie stood there, jaws hanging, watching the trash forming great conical drifts around each can. It came amazingly fast and never faltered. In no time the drifts around the cans were twelve feet high, and spreading. With a flapping noise like wings the papers spewed over the grass, over the sidewalks, and out into the streets to snow upon the honking, frozen cars. The air was a blizzard of falling litter.

The two homeless women staggered, dazed, down the walk.

Absently brushing a crumpled, sticky burger-wrapper from her shoulder, Sophie nudged Merril and pointed across the street to the service alley next to the McDonald's. The lids of three big dumpsters there boomed open like cannons, and huge waves of refuse leapt out, tumbling into the street . . .

At precisely the same moment, twenty miles west, Tim is polishing the bar in the Pink Elephant. He likes this hour, the early light slanting in, polishing chairs and tables in peace and silence before the day's trade.

He hears a harsh, ragged voice shouting outside: *". . . eeee!"* Past his side window he sees a black, dripping figure run past from the direction of the river.

More screaming out on the main street now, feet running, other tradesmen coming out of their establishments. Tim does too, though he feels suddenly deeply reluctant to leave the bar, step into the unprotected outer world.

There is a small crowd around the figure standing in the middle of River Highway, a figure dripping with a reeking fluid blacker than tar. His eyes are oiled blind spheres as black as eight-balls, his hair is corroded away to show patches of nude, eight-ball scalp, and the cords of his neck pop out as he screams, again and again: "Fleee! Fleee!"

"Jesus Christ, that's Sonny Beasley!" someone shouts, and Tim too recognizes the guy, a local biker he hasn't seen around for a while. But the thing is, Sonny can't be alive—not with that black fluid squirting from the holes in his ribs as he wheezily screams one last time: *"FLEEEE!"* and then does so himself, suddenly sprinting towards a side street and back down towards the river, and leaping in.

Traffic is backed up in both directions but everyone just stands there, watching the black figure stroking madly, and dwindling out to the middle of the current, which snatches him away downstream. Then someone screams: "Oh my God, look!"

One of the sequoias flanking the highway near the Safeway at the south edge of town is moving. Twisting, shuddering, struggling against the windless air.

Its color is wrong. The fissured bark, normally a dull earthen red, is fever-bright, almost glossy. Its crown of scaly boughs slashes the air as it contorts—Tim and the others, a hundred yards away, can feel the tendony pull of its force through the pavement they stand on. A yellow smoke begins to rise from its base.

"It's on fire!"

"No! Look, it's melting!"

Now orange pus sweats from the trunk near its juncture with the earth, the wood there grows soft and cheesy and begins to distort under the trunk's twisting.

"Look out! It's falling!"

Its hundred-and-fifty-foot length, foliage fluttering, falls majestically, deliberately. A dozen vehicles, and those of their drivers who have ignored the wild gestures of the crowd, are slammed to scrap. Instantly, the giant begins to writhe on the asphalt, flexing, its branches suggesting the snout of some blind, bristly parasite probing for a host, the feverish red of its wood like live muscle. It sweeps left and pulverizes a real estate office, a bank, and a video store. It sweeps right and slams through the wide glass façade of the Safeway.

Now the street is a kicked anthill. There are big trees everywhere in River Nest, and everywhere, these trees are stirring.

A mighty crash is heard at the opposite edge of town, also across the highway. Drivers abandon their cars, dozens of people have already run to the bridge for shelter, out of reach of the trees on either riverbank. That looks like a good place to Tim. The roar of smashed buildings fills the air. He runs into the Pink

Elephant long enough to grab a suitcase and fill it with liquor bottles. He'll be outside on his own now, with the rest of the world . . .

Marjorie's first impulse had been to get Morris into their car and do as most of the hospital staff were doing, drive like hell out of the lot and head east, get the hills between them and this nightmare. And then the collisions began as the first cars out of the lot had been hit, and hit again by nightmare vehicles that seemed to come from nowhere, from everywhere.

The boom of impact after impact left her deafened, stunned. The whole street, the only way out, was a heap of automotive carnage, and slumped in the wreckage were the bleeding and, in equal numbers, those who were long past bleeding.

For a long moment she stood there, seeing that this was a universe she had never known, never guessed the size of. She could do something, anything, or she could go mad—like that man there, screaming and clawing at his eyes, or that woman on her knees with her arms wrapped around her head.

Get Morris on the roof. High ground. This was a flood— you did that in floods, so the rescuers could reach you.

In the hospital's corridors patients wandered, shouting questions, plucking at her sleeves, their slack cellulite buttocks pitiful in the open-backed gowns. Help was coming, she said, near tears, rushing on. As she neared Morris's door, Nick Sawyer scrabbled out the adjoining one on all fours, his gauntness and wild eyes terrifying her. He made a grab for her legs and, as she jumped back, Dave Shugg crawled out in pursuit. He pounced on Sawyer and got his hands round the county supervisor's throat. He looked even wilder and gaunter than Sawyer, drool hanging from his cracked lips as he rasped:

"Got you, you poisonous slime . . . maggot . . . you infected us all!"

Marjorie rushed into Morris's room. She got his robe on him, his IV bags into its pockets, and hooked one of his arms across her shoulders. He was so horribly light! His eyes white slits, and the smell of him . . . she dragged him out the door.

Sawyer lay, pop-tongued and dead in the corridor. Shugg, lying in convulsions beside him, pointed at Morris and rasped "He dies next!"—but then was shaken violently, passed a huge and reeking fecal flux, and died himself. Marjorie dragged her husband down the corridor.

She found some had stayed on the roof, detained by awe or resignation or despair. She laid Morris by the railing and hung his IV bags on the slight elevation it offered. She pillowed his head on her rolled up sweater.

"Look," the sad-eyed Latina nurse said. "It's speeding up. And it's climbing the hill there. It's coming for us."

Merril and Sophie were slogging through drifts of litter over their heads. Merril, being used to the incomprehensible, led the way and Sophie clutched her sleeve. They shouldered and elbowed their way, groping for clear ground, sticky papers clinging to them like starfish.

They stumbled stepping off a curb, found themselves in the street. A car lurched forward out of the gloom and immediately hit a van, also from nowhere. The paper-muffled noise of horns and collisions and helplessly revving engines was everywhere around them.

"Where *are* we?" Sophie wailed.

"Who knows?" Not knowing where she was didn't bother Merril as much as the look of terror on Sophie's face, Something struggled upward in her mind, a vague shape groping through obscuring litter. An idea. She emptied her burlap bag of cans. She tied one corner around her wrist. Sophie tied another corner around hers. They still had light, but it was getting dimmer, a polychromatic blur filtered through the wrappers, cups, cans, and newspapers deepening overhead. But now they would not get separated.

Merril jammed her ancient 49ers cap tighter down on her weedy white hair and they slogged forward again. Now they had red brick underfoot. The mall? Yes—there were windows with well-dressed dummies in them, they were at the mall and they had reached a wall.

They hugged the wall, and kept walking. No way was out, but they kept walking.

Marjorie thought that this must have been what you felt in a besieged city in the ancient world. The black wall was sixty feet high as it rolled to the farther edge of the hospital parking lot, and paused there.

There were many on the roof now, patients who could make up here but flee no farther. Others, she knew, were feeling what she did, a strange paralysis of the will, like a cast spell. She must stand here because she was going to be shown something. And she stood, swallowed in a terror so complete it was like calm. This branching of the filth-flood, the way this tongue of it darted upslope precisely towards the hospital, the way it waited now, the viscid wall quivering . . .

"What's that?" Marjorie asked Morris—for her husband was whispering something, all at once struggling to rise. As she knelt by him, the Latina nurse echoed her:

"What's that?"—pointing at something on the crest of the flood.

It was a big, boxy yellow shape, almost as big as a freight car.

A dumpster, poised on the lip of the towering slime like a boat.

And just where it paused, the front sent down a lesser tongue of ooze that rolled across the parking lot and flattened liquidly against the hospital's wall, rising almost level with the rooftop. The dumpster plunged down this tongue and coasted towards the railing they now recoiled from, and its occupants were revealed.

Foremost was the figure in the prow, who mounted up and stood, legs splayed, on the dumpster's rim: a huge naked woman. Behind her sprawled three naked men, half fettered with silvery webbing, and clinging to the dumpster's inner rim.

The woman was black—not racially, but with a liquid sheen. Her hugeness was all roundnesses, bunched moons glazed with ebony sweat. Her buttocks—fat, waxing crescents that clung to the awesome ellipsoids of her thighs—her buttocks swelled like planets of poisonous fecundity. Her breasts, stupendous melting domes, leaked from their rugged, volcanic nipples a black ichor that smoked and sizzled where it dripped to strike her belly, winding thence in steaming rivers through her pubic thatch like the black and brambled vegetation of a murdered rainforest. Her eyes, black relentless obsidian, mocked the thought of absolution.

Morris was struggling, his pithless arms and legs were flailing, and a rusty grunting came from his cracked lips. He reached blindly skyward—a seeking, or a warding gesture?—as the giantess reached out, her arm as flexible as dreamstuff, gripped his head, and plucked him up into the air.

His tubes fell from his arms and he hung kicking as she held him, her face an unconceding mask aimed down at Marjorie. The giantess tossed him back over her shoulder—Marjorie watched him sprawl into the webbing.

As suddenly as it had sprung out, the tongue of ooze retracted and swept the dumpster back up to the main front, which rolled laterally onward, crunching across the houses on the face of the hills, but advancing no higher.

Marjorie and the others stood, awed and empty. Below, the heart of Santa Marta was a shrinking circle within the great molluscoid closure of the ooze.

Thirty-three

In the first canoe, Maxie sat in the middle and Daddy sat in the rear, his thick legs against a big duffel bag stuffed under the strut he sat on, and up in the front sat 'Buelita Aurora. 'Buelita Aurora's face was astonishing, gullied and folded with wrinkles, and her eyes nested in nets of wrinkles. Her face fascinated Maxie, who remembered seeing her once or twice before, but not like this, with the slanting morning light all golden on her and every line so sharply shadowed.

But Daddy was very interesting to look at too, bald as a doorknob, his head a dome all tattooed with bright red scabs that oozed a brilliant amber pus. He was still Daddy, of course, but he looked so different! His ears were much bigger than Maxie had ever realized, and somehow being bald made his rather flat nose look bigger too, with bigger holes, so that he looked like certain drawings of trolls from fairy tale books that Maxie had read and that of course she knew weren't *real*, but still, looking at Daddy was a little scary until he said something and his voice confirmed that he definitely was Daddy beyond a doubt.

In the second canoe Mommy was in the rear and Reed up front and a lot of their gear heaped up between them. Reed kept saying over and over that a goddam *boat* should have a goddam *outboard* on it and it should be used on a goddam *lake* where the water didn't move *around*. An outboard was a boat motor, and you never used one on a canoe, really, and the reason Mommy was in the rear, the way Daddy was in the rear in this one, was because Mommy was good at handling canoes.

Both her mom and her dad were good at handling canoes, so that meant that Maxie herself would be good at handling them because it ran in both sides of her family and it was in her genes, spelled g-e-n-e-s instead of j-e-a-n-s, and Maxie had no doubts at all about how good she would be at it. She wasn't good at handling canoes *yet,* though. Her arms were too short, and that was all there was to it. So even though her life jacket felt boxy and uncomfortable, she was glad of it, and she was also very glad that Daddy was steering this canoe, since they had to ride in it.

In the third canoe Aunt Kim took the front and Raleigh took the back, with Granny Lucky in between them, and with Aunt Kim telling Raleigh that she was doing him a favor letting him take the rear because she could handle a canoe at least as well as he could. Aunt Kim could drive big trucks—Maxie had seen them—and so Maxie decided that Aunt Kim must be telling the truth, but Granny Lucky told Aunt Kim, "That's all right, sweetie, you want the blubber in the rear to keep your nose out of the water!" And it did look like their nose was higher than their rear with Raleigh in back, so that was probably OK.

When they first slid out onto the river it felt like being torn loose—like her body being ripped off of something that had glued her to the ground. It was a wonderful scary silvery ticklish feeling to be sliding, sliding like this, the current a snake whose braided back-muscles gripped the hollow bottom of their canoe and snatched them along. Up on the banks, stands of trees and acres of grapevines spun past them, the grapevines' rows reminding her somehow of bicycle spokes spinning, and all this scenery was more exciting than seeing it from the windows of their truck driving by it because here they were down on the *floor* of everything, and the trees looked much bigger and the grapevines with their branches stretched out on the wires and their big leaves all gold and red looked like fire, like flames blazing and flapping against the sky.

"Jesus Christ!" shouted Reed. "There's no wind blowing— none at all!"

There wasn't any wind blowing, that was true . . . and then it hit Maxie that all those grapevines and trees were acting like there *was* wind blowing, all flapping and twisting . . . 'Buelita Aurora looked back at her and smiled. Her pretty smile made tickly feelings, like ants, go up and down Maxie's back, but also her smile made Maxie feel less afraid, like Aurora's face, a Good Witch's face, was telling her that they were going into a place full of magic, like in a fairy tale, but that they would be OK if Maxie was careful and followed the magic rules, whatever they were. . . .

And then they came around a long curve, and there were no more grapevines, and there were hills on both sides of the river and trees coming right down to the banks on both sides, and all of a sudden Reed was shouting again, his voice high and crackly:

"It's alive! It's fuckin movin!"

—and Grammy Lucky braying, "Watch your goddamn mouth!" and then braying, "Jesus Christ almighty!" and up ahead was what they were shouting about, one of the big trees; all and straight like poles crowding the bank, which *was* moving, twisting and wiggling and twitching, its color different from all the others, kind of a shiny reddish-brown that you could sort of see through, reminding Maxie of those pupas Mommy sometimes dug up gardening and showed her that were shiny and brittle and you could almost see through them to the bug sleeping inside.

And the closer they swept the more it looked like that, like a giant pupa, veiny and brittle with something huge and shadowy struggling inside of it, and the whole tree bending now, bending, *falling,* yes! Down it went with a tremendous crunching sound, falling down in between all the trees around it and twitching and thrashing and breaking the trees around it so they toppled this way and that, and one, two of them slamming down into the water—*wham! wham-splash!*—but not far enough out to touch them, and now they had swept past it and were putting it behind them, and just as they did, Maxie saw the pupa-tree's brittle shiny trunk split open down a long crack, and saw that a big dark thing with a lot of legs was struggling inside it, and was putting out a long black bristly leg like a giant wasp's. . . .

"Daddy! Did you see that leg?"

"Don't worry, little pal," he said to her, and "Stroke it!" he bellowed to the others, making Maxie jump. But if Daddy said not to worry about it, then they were probably going to be all right. There were times, it was true, when Daddy was drinking a lot of beer, when he would say "Don't worry about it!" in a big happy voice, and then would turn around and trip over something or walk into something, but she hadn't seen him drinking any beer lately. But still Maxie felt very scared when she thought about that giant leg. Then Aurora looked back at her and said:

"A lot is going to happen, little daughter—just watch and let it happen." And Maxie nodded and decided that she was going to play a little game—was going to start pretending right now that they were all inside a story book, all inside a strange story where things were very scary, but they still couldn't hurt you, and that eventually the story would end and they would all come out of it perfectly OK.

Now here came two pedal-boats churning upstream towards them. There were trees moving, on both banks, twitching strangely, their trunks strange colors, but these pedal-boats held Maxie's attention because she knew them by their shapes and colors from a long way off—she'd pedaled in them last summer with Daddy—and they were moving *very* fast, very fast, even though they were coming upstream, which Maxie remembered was much harder to do than going downstream like their canoes were doing—they were coming upstream very fast, and she was just starting to worry that they were going to collide with their canoe, when Aurora shouted back at her:

"Close your eyes, little daughter!"

Which Maxie did, but first, of course, she had to take just a quick look at what she was closing her eyes *to*—and she saw quite clearly that it was *half-people* pedaling both these boats, that it was just the hips and legs of people in either boat—hairy legs in shorts, legs in jeans, legs in skirts—while above their waists they weren't people, but just big quivery *blobs* of what looked like the green, silky scum you saw in ponds, just big bubbly green knots, like muscular snot, pulsing and pumping the way she'd seen animal hearts do in science films.

They swept round the next bend and there was a big redwood down, its roots fifty feet up the bank but its crown sunk all the way over on their side, blocking them, with the only clearance a triangle of clear space over near the opposite bank, and Daddy bellowed "Pull for it!" and all three boats slanted out for the opposite bank and the tree as they got near it was twisting and pulsing and their boats shot one-two-three just under it, its bark just inches over their heads a hot, glowing red like Maxie's own face in the mirror when she had a fever. Up on the road on this bank other trees were down, down and twisting, worming, and Maxie could see the highway up there, and saw trucks and cars smashed and burning under giant trucks, saw people running down the asphalt, shouting, screaming . . .

"Don't worry about a thing, little pal," Daddy said behind her. He almost shouted it, actually, but Maxie held tight to the sides of the canoe, reminding herself that they were just moving through the pages of a scary story.

"Look at the bridge, Daddy!" she called. The bridge—it was the one near where they had gone in the pedal-boats last summer—had collapsed at one end. Cars were heaped in the water around its fallen end, and in the triangle of clearance under its still-supported end the water was choked with shapes that seemed to be moving furiously and churning up the water. The canoes angled over, Daddy bellowing "Pull! Pull! Hit it full speed!"—the canoe skating over, the shadow under the bridge sweeping towards them. And then they were under, amid the echoes of shouts and shrieks and torn, thrashed water, and among the shapes skimming past them Maxie saw the darting heads of white seals with blood-red eyes and blood-red gaping teeth, like hungry dog snouts among the wet-haired heads of struggling, screaming people. . . .

Sweeping through open water again, between walls of giant trees alive with giant motion, the water twisted everywhere with under-surface movement. Quick bulges appeared, sunken shapes struggling, slick arcs of strange flesh snaking up through the light and gone. And as their canoe gained speed going into the next great curve, its sweep felt to Maxie like they were in a giant swing, the river swinging them down, up, and out to the sky, as Daddy shouted behind her:

"Hang on, Maxie-pie! We're almost there!"

Merril and Sophie were shouldering, floundering, clambering upwards, like shabby dolphins bucking to escape a net. A windowed wall was at their backs and their arms were still linked by the burlap bag, as they clawed and climbed with hands and feet at the smothering debris, compacting it under them and ascending, bit by bit, one window sinking at their backs, the one above it inching down behind them. The copper tint of the window glass brought the building's identity to Merril's mind out of the debris of her memory—it was the bank building where, on the sidewalk somewhere below them, people took money out of slots in the wall—where she had gotten in trouble asking people for some of their money long ago, before she realized that only bums did that—she would rather die than do that now.

"It's moving!" Sophie shrieked in her ear. The debris was moving, stirring like an ocean, lifting them and shifting them sideways at the same time.

Wasn't this building the tallest one downtown? They could climb to the roof, couldn't they?

"Climb to the top!" Merril shouted. "Climb to the top!" Their fingers scrabbled at stone, at glass, the tide of papers, cups, and cans buoying them ever higher. But it also powerfully shifted them laterally, sweeping them past the building as their hands and soles clung desperately to stone, glass, stone. The mighty lift of the trash-sea dropped yet another window, another window, another window below them, and at last the surge was too strong. They lost their grip on the wall, their feet swung out from under them, and the tidal sweep lifted them spreadeagled on their backs towards the sky.

The roar of the trash, the oceanic rattle and crunch of it was deafening, and it rose to a crescendo as the ceiling of litter above them thinned, fragmented, and with a noise like birds taking flight, like a million papery wings hammering the air, the two trashwomen burst up into the whisky sky.

There was the crest of the bank building just behind them, and the sea of litter, wheeling, was about to carry them past it. Bucking and floundering, kicking up a spray of papers, they scrambled for it. A railed platform for window washers was bolted to the outer edge of its parapet. Merril reached, reached, joints popping, and caught the railing in one hand.

They dragged themselves onto the platform, which cleared the wheeling lake of debris by no more than a foot or so. On their knees, gasping for breath, they surveyed the scene.

"Oh my God," Sophie whimpered. Merril took off her 49ers cap and raked her weedy hair back with her fingers, a gesture she used to put her thoughts in order. It worked no better than it ever had, but for the first time in her life she felt that her confusion didn't matter because the whole world had completely changed. The courthouse square was gone—instead there was this great lake of trash moving slowly like a wheel, a little higher at the edges where it bulged over buried buildings, kind of sunken at the center. And beyond it, on all sides . . . beyond it was a black wall, a black glittery wall much higher than the building they were on. And this black wall, on all sides, was coming towards them. It was moving, yes! Towards them.

When they had dragged the canoes onto the gravel beach below the Sylvan Lodge they all looked nervously up into the trees. These were smaller than the huge ones upriver, being mostly pines, but they were moving. And there was still no wind blowing. The trees crowded close to the lodge, and you could hear the creak and bump of their branches against its big boxy walls, like clumsy inhuman hands on a drum, groping for some alien beat.

Up there, people were moving through the trees. It looked like an exodus of the Lodge's many tenants.

"If Gutley's here," Willy told the others, "he might know what it's like farther into the hills."

"We should unload the canoes," Aurora said. "We must get no nearer the sea by water."

They agreed with glances, to spare Maxie's young imagination further horrors, except for Reed, who said, "Why not? There's no trees at all a couple miles down." Signals from Raleigh failed to keep him from repeating, "Why not?"

"Because," Maxie told him, "there's a lot more things living in the sea than in the river. Bigger things."

They started unloading the canoes and making up backpacks, and Willy took his duffel bag up into the trees.

He didn't see Gutley at first in all the activity. The long-resident junk on the big porch—an old water heater, mattresses, bundles of newspaper, faded kids' toys—had been joined by the backpacks, bags, and bundles of people actively moving out. Panic hadn't erupted but it was just inches away. The ground felt alive under his feet with the tug of roots, and the Lodge was creaking and groaning—you could hear the big floorjoists moaning in there, and here and there on the walls you saw little tufts of splinters pop out on the stressed planks.

There was Gutley, up the gravel drive, sitting astride his bike and talking to a ponytailed couple in workshirts and a hefty woman in blue sweats with two small kids. Gutley signaled him with a wave, finished what he was saying with some gestures upslope, and coasted his bike down through the trees. They met a ways off in the trees where the trunks gave them cover, Willy not liking the wormy feeling of the ground and the creaking of the pines—you could see their bark faintly wrinkle like skin with their movement. Gutley's bike was a lean 650 with big knobby all-terrain tires.

He pulled a zippered plastic pouch from its saddlebag. "Count this while I check it out."

Willy gave him the duffel bag. He unzipped the pouch and thumbed through the worn fifties and hundreds in their little packets of five thousand each. Gutley thrust his hands into the duffel bag, pawing among the ziplocked packets, his bearded jaw jutting down as if he might climb into the bag, like a bear after honeycomb in a hollow log. Willy kept counting. The money's greenness was unreal here where the only sky was the green shift and slither of the contorting trees. In another world, its phony green was power; in this one, the only power lay in the earth, in the tree-whisper of the earth's anger. Willy jammed the money in the front of his pants snug behind his belt. Gutley tucked the plastic parcels into his saddlebags.

"I gotta be honest with you, Willy," he said. "If I can make it to Fresno with this shit, assumin nothing like this"—he gestured at the forest around them—"is happenin in Fresno *too*—then I'm gonna make out real well."

"I know it. But these are times it's risky to let go of cash in hand, so it's a fair trade. Another thing. This is the last stuff I'll ever grow, Gut."

"OK. Nuff said. You going downriver?"

"We'd rather go overland than meet what might be in the Pacific."

"That was my thought too. I came over on the fire-road, I was just tellin these people. You can pick it up just over that first hill above the road. It hits the crestline, an up there, there's no *movement,* least not when I came over."

They were both cringing just slightly, their bodies involuntarily shrinking from the unceasing whispery commotion of the trees. "I'd hurry though, man," Gutley added. "I feel somethin comin—don't you? Like a kind of a chill comin outta the ground?"

"Yeah. We're gone. Good luck, Gut."

"Right."

Returning to the beach—coming out of the trees—was such a relief it made Willy doubly aware of the terrible tension that was gathering there. "We gotta hurry!" he shouted to the others.

They had their packs on. He slipped on his. Maxie had a small daypack of trail food. He picked her up and set her on his shoulders. "You can hold onto my forehead," he told her, "but keep your fingers outta my eyes, sweetie, an try not to grab hold of any of my bigger scabs up there, OK?"

"OK, Daddy."

Up through the trees they went, up the Lodge's drive, across the road, and up the flank of the hill beyond it. Muscles and tendons twitched in the earth underfoot. They climbed faster, faster, an urgency goading not just them but the other people ahead of and behind them where now, as they neared the crest, they heard the Lodge break, a massive hollow wooden fracturing.

Barbara, toiling ahead, looked back at Willy. "Do you feel it?" she said, her eyes flashing, giving him an incongruously erotic pang of fear and imminence because he did feel it, something wanting to erupt, to hatch from the earth, everyone felt it, everyone starting to run now as they reached the fire road, Maxie wanting to run on her own feet now and Willy setting her down and all of them running along the road to reach the highest crest where the trees fell away and the sky opened out around them.
. . .

Down from the black wall that closed on the wheeling lake of litter—down from that dark, gelatinous dreadnought of millennial refuse a black tongue darted, a wedge that thrust into the papery whirlpool bearing a great yellow dumpster on its back.

Merril and Sophie beheld the figure standing in the dumpster's prow and understood. They looked on her hugeness, her black nakedness, her wild hair like spiky tar, the planes of her brow like shelves of brute granite, older than Life, beetling above her wild obdurate obsidian eyes, her mastodontic jaw locked in vengeance—the two derelicts, failed child and old madwoman, looked on her, and their tears spilled out, because they understood that a city that had discarded them was ending before their eyes.

As the black tongue thrust into the wheeling debris it sped up. The sides of the whirlpool steepened, and as the dumpster sailed past below they saw the giantess's naked captives in it, snarled in webbing: a big amputee who looked like a raving, rabid angel; two skinny ones, one of whom wept with rapture and cried in a broken, goatish voice, again and again—"We're coming, Cosmos! Oh yes we are!"; a dark wolfish one who fought his bonds to point a sinewy arm down the pit of the vortex they cycled towards. The black walls were draining into the vortex, quickening it, thickening it, and the pit, down in its center, got darker, darker.

"Frankie!" Lazarian shrieked, madly jubilant. "This is the Gate, Brer Weasel! We're breaking out! We're crossing over *alive!*"

DaValli's shriek was purest rage. "You fucking *freak!* Look at it! *Look* at it!"—pointing down to the pit they spun towards. The murky whirl had darkened, stilled. It was a patch of black space, studded with stars—an open manhole into the interstellar void.

"We're being popped out!" howled Beiderbeck. "Like zit-cheese! We're being popped out of the biosphere!" The chemist grabbed the sweat-slick shoulders of Morris Hacker, whose weakness could not fight the webbing, and bellowed in his ear: "We're goin down the *main drain,* baby!"

The searing cold of absolute-zero emptiness reached up and raked them with clawtips of eternity. The icy Null where countless stars hung eons distant opened to them.

"Open your eyes!" cried Lazarian. "Open your senses! Now we must attend! Now we will be shown!"

Frankie, in a duped rage—suckered into this!—unclenched

his jaw and flung his wrath out into the swallowing universe——
"SHI-

I-

I-

I-

I-

IT!"

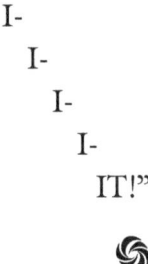

The hill lurched under them as they ran. Aurora almost fell but caught herself with a tricky step, like an aged dancer, and Maxie would have fallen, but Willy and Barbara, with the automatic expertise of parents, caught her from behind by either shoulder.

They all stopped running then. They had felt a great tension depart from the earth. The hills had sighed, it seemed. Finding one another's eyes, exchanging the first tentative looks of hope, they walked the last few yards to the crest where the trees fell away and the view opened out east and west.

They stood looking east. The far edge of the Santa Marta plain, where the city had stood, was a flat, glittery blackness from which rose a pillar of smoke—a single column of it like a colossal tree. They stood gazing for long minutes.

"Should we be looking?" Willy asked after a time. "I mean, maybe we should turn our eyes from it, like in the Bible . . ."

"We have been spared," Aurora said slowly, "in order that we *should* look, I think."

They rested on the grass, breaking out cheese, crackers, juice. Barbara got Willy aside from the others.

"So where do we stand?" she asked him.

Willy pulled a grave face. "That dickhead Gutley is a hard bargainer. So we only got . . . seventy-five thousand."

Barbara looked at him coolly. "You have to *know*," she told him, "that you will never do this kind of deal again. You know that, right?"

"I know that and agree with all my heart."

"Well, with that understood, I do have to say"—she grinned—"Halleluiah!"

Willy hugged her, also grinning. "Mmmm! My shapely little *chicana mamma!*"

"Mommy?" Maxie had ferreted them out. Barbara greeted her with a kiss.

Maxie regarded her with her clear grey eyes. "I'm imagining you without any hair on, Mom," she said.

"I must look pretty funny then, Maxie-pie."

"Yeah, but it's kind of scary too. I keep imagining all of us without any hair on."

Willy picked her up and gave her a consoling kiss. "That could be scary, but all you need to do is concentrate on how funny—"

"Hey, Dad!" she interrupted, her frank little fingers reaching up to rub one of the few unscabbed parts of Willy's scalp. "You've got hair starting to grow—tiny little scratchy hairs! Feel it, Mom!"

Barbara reached up and felt with the casual expertise of an authority on her husband's textures. "Stubble," she said.

"You're right, sweetie. Maybe it's gonna grow back. Boy, Willy—I sure hope it does!"

"Me too," Maxie said seriously.

Merril and Sophie stepped down from the railing onto a vast, glassy surface, still faintly fuming. Nothing protruded from its levelness but the peak of the building they had stood on. The surface crackled as it hardened, making a sound like miles of country crickets at midnight. Merril stood stupefied on this new world-floor. All the routes and refuges she had known, all the curbs and corners, the alleys and doorways and crannies under overpasses—all were gone, conjured away by this glittery desert. Sophie took her hand. "You see where it's green?" she asked Merril, pointing west to the hills. "There'll be water and shade there at least." Merril nodded, still numb. Sophie led her westward, over the black plain.

MOMMA DURTT

[novelette version]

It was a little past ten o'clock on a Friday night. Kimberly Haas, expert and easy, was riding the 580 rapids, steering a Titan northbound on that mighty freeway. Her half of the river was all ruby tail-lights, and the oncoming stream was all diamonds. *What a rush!* thought Kimberly, like riding a dinosaur—one that could do *seventy*.

She was hauling twenty-K gallons along the star-spangled rim of the San Francisco Bay, and the Bay was a *galaxy* in a space movie, this huge array of blazing lights. Black void at its center studded with islands and necklaced with bridges. Kim Haas, starship trooper . . .

"Hey Alex," she said to her partner, *"Starship Troopers!"*

They laughed.

This was their sixth run driving for Kleenco. Though the pickup-points varied, the kind of load they hauled never did. To-night: a pharmaceutical company in Hayward, a pesticide manu-facturer in Emeryville, and a plastics plant in Oakland: solvents, sludges, and still-bottoms. A witches' brew of industrial chemistry.

"Let's get a brewski," Kim said. "We're almost there."

"I dunno. We're almost late now, and Chip seemed *really* pissed."

"Yeah, but he's *always* pissed. And we're always gonna *be* late!" Kim, though in her early twenties, was already tired of men's pre-wired predictable hissy-fits. "We're always gonna be late, because he never gives us enough time, and because while we're pickin up there's always some holdup or other in loading this shit at three or four different places every night!"

Alex nodded, staring at the highway and feeling his own doubts about this easy money they'd been amazed to fall into these last few weeks. Brooding on the river of lights, he said, "True that. But he did make a reely big point of it tonight, comin straight back."

Kim looked at him with his new Zapata 'stache—still a bit thin as yet—and thought that she still liked him just as she had in high school. Basically a nice guy, a bit touchy sometimes. She was a white country kid whose dad had driven big rigs for the vineyards, Alex a brown country kid whose several uncles *still* drove truck back in Mexico. Since high school neither of them had done anything even close to as cool as driving this tanker. Kim had clerked at the Circle K and Alex had rented out scaffolding and weed-whackers for Action Rents.

And look at them right now: piloting this beautiful beast over the colossal crooked frame of the Richmond Bridge, cruising like a star-liner above the red-and-white river of traffic, the whole Bay encircling them with galactic scenery out of some sci-fi flick.

Kim didn't *want* to have any reservations about this totally cool job. But there was a side to it that nagged at her.

"Toxics," she said, as if trying the word out. Then a little more forcefully, "That's why he's always so uptight. All this is illegal." She waited uneasy, hanging that one out there. It had gone five nights unspoken, but now they'd said it, their unseen passenger, the truth.

He tossed it back: "Well *duuuhhh!* But look. Hey. Let's *get* a brewski. He sleeps up there, what's a few minutes? If he wants us on time, he's gotta *give* us more time."

They were just south of Petaluma, and Kim eased the rig down an off-ramp, steering the big tanker rocking and squeaking through dark streets to where a liquor store was the only thing alive for blocks around. They left the truck idling, and jumped down.

The store's neon shed a sick greenish light on the pavement. The sidewalks were eerily empty.

No. There was someone sitting on the dark curb just beyond the store. Someone *big* struggling to his feet . . . *her* feet? Yes. A bulky bag-lady in multi-layered shabby clothes.

Odd, how slowly she rose up, like a gradually inflating balloon of dirty rags. The two of them found themselves turning toward her, watching her rise. Then, just as they caught themselves and began to turn away from her, she moved with sudden energy, shambling crabwise, surprisingly quick for her great size, and intercepted them before they reached the store's entry.

Her face was swollen and crusted with dirt, and her breath gusted cold and vile from her wide, loose mouth. They shifted to steer around her, but her bigness seemed somehow to slow down their movements, as if she exerted a kind of gravitational pull.

"Drink up, kids!" she hissed, and thrust out a bottle at them. Kim received it and felt its cold in her palm. The huge derelict winked at them. A dizzying chemical whiff, like a still-bottom, came off of her.

Then she pulled her own bottle from her rags, winked again, hoisted it, and drank. She drank obscenely. Her flabby throat working up and down, her dirty jowls quivering, her scabby eyes squeezed shut in the bliss of guzzling.

Kim, flustered, stammered some thanks for the beer as they retreated and hustled away from the hulk. When she looked at the bottle in the light of the store's entry, she was surprised to it perfectly clean and new looking—*Great Old Ones Ale,* in gold Gothic lettering, arched across its label.

"What was that all about?" muttered Alex as they hustled into the store. At the counter, a wino was ahead of them puzzling out his pennies and dimes and when, at last, they came out with the sixer, the huge, eerie lurker was gone.

They got back in the cab . . . back on the freeway, both silent until Alex said "Man! She smelled like . . ." They both sat trying to put it precisely.

And groped for it until Kim said, "She smelled like the kinda shit we truck."

"That's it," said Alex. And they shared a moment of strange self-consciousness about this grand rig they were so jazzed about piloting. Here was their tanker, huge, towering above the traffic, rolling down the public highway, heavy with high-caliber toxins. High, wide and handsome their tanker cruised up 101.

Alex cracked a beer.

Kim looked doubtfully at the bottle of *Great Old Ones Ale.* "These micro-breweries and their weird-ass names. No way I'm drinkin it," and took one of theirs instead.

Kim swung them off 101, and now they rolled down a narrower highway through darker countryside. Sleeping orchards, a few vineyards, some country houses slid past them under the silver moon.

She geared their rig up through the switchbacks of the hills, the oaks gestured in the sweep of their lights. The big truck's headlights set all those crooked trees slow-dancing with their crooked shadows. Gaps here and there showed the young truckers fragments of the jeweled Santa Marta plain below and behind them.

"You gotta meet my auntie," Alex said, scanning that view. "She's like half Miwok or something. Anyway, she told me this mountain the mine's in was like a Spirit Place—like where you go to fast and have visions? Go to, like, face your demons and stuff."

"Spirits! Rad. I wish there *was* something cool like that about it, Alex, that would be something, but I think what these guys are doing up here is just plain old creepy and criminal."

"Yeah, but we don't really know that, not for sure. Anyway, we're definitely good and late now. Maybe he's just gonna fire us. When Chip said get back on time, he put a lot into it."

"I think he sounded scared," Kim said hauling on the wheel.

"He just doesn't wanna stay late."

284 ·

"Whaddya mean, *late*? He sleeps up there at the mine! What does he care?"

"He just doesn't like to wait up for us. He wants to go to *bed*." Alex turned his face away, irritated.

"Maybe, but *I* got the feeling he's got company coming that he doesn't want us to meet."

"Where the hell do you get that idea?"

She mimicked Chip's scoldings. "'I wancha here, download-ed, an *outta* here by eleven thirty! For once! Can ya manage it?' Why else would he be so pissed? He's scared."

Three quarters up the hill, the road mounted a broad shoul-der of the mountain, and halfway out across that shoulder was the gated compound of the Quicksilver Mine. Through gaps in the treeline, fragments of Santa Marta's jeweled plain glittered here and there below and behind them.

Chip was already rolling the cyclone gate back. Their head-lights latticed his scrawny little body in the chain-links' shadows as the gate slid aside from in front of him. He had his rubber boots and rubber apron on, and his respirator was hanging by its straps from his skinny old neck. They pulled in and he stomped over, mounted the step-up, and thrust his head in Kim's window.

"You goddamn kids think you signed on for a day at the beach?"

Very pissed. His back-sloped forehead suggested some brow-less animal, maybe a possum. "I can't believe you come a half hour late after what I told you! You two swing your ass up there, you *squirt,* an you *leave!*"

At the hill's crest was the mouth of the Quicksilver's shaft, breathing out the white light of arc-lamps at the stars. Down near the gate was the office trailer, and beyond that was a sizea-ble pyramid of disposal drums five tiers high, with just enough moonlight on them to sketch their rims and bulges. It had been explained to both young drivers that these were filled inside the shaft from the holding tank, and then conveyed down the tracks in the ore carts left over from the mercury mining days. Much farther below, the drums were stacked securely in storage adits carved from the shaft walls.

The only part of this process that Kim and Alex had ever seen was the offload hose snaking from their tanker up through the mouth of the shaft, as they sat idling and running their of-fload pump.

Initially they'd thought, "Great, an environmentally correct operation!" But somewhere in the course of delivering a hun-dred thousand gallons, they'd noted that the great pyramid of drums had never altered its outline. It suggested to Kim one of those old jungle ruins, moonlit and auraed with ancient evil, erected for strange gods and human sacrifice, left over from the Mayas or the Incas.

Chip, radiating anger and impatience, clung to the door of the cab as Kim backed the tanker up to within thirty yards of the shaft-mouth. There, he jumped down and hurried inside the shaft, pulling his mask on, to re-emerge a moment later dragging the fill-hose.

Was there any possibility this hose did fill a holding tank in-side . . . ? Naw. They were just squirting all this black poison straight into the shaft, to soak into the naked earth. Chip's gnomish fury, and his expression of disgust, proved that if noth-ing else did.

". . . just can't *believe* you kids! Unship your out-take!"

Chip helped them couple the fill-hose to the tanker's offload spout and switch the pump on. "I got *people* comin," he told them. "You squirt your goddam load, you uncouple, an you drive the fuck outta here. Can ya do that? Can ya manage it?"

He stomped back down to the office trailer.

They sat in the cab, a couple of scolded kids. "Just tell me straight," Kim said grimly. "Do you think Chip's just a really grouchy old man, or do you think he's afraid?"

"OK. How I heard about this job was my cousin Nolo, who was drivin for these guys. He left real sudden down to L.A., but I got him to give me their number before he went, couldn't believe he was dumping a gig like this. Now maybe I'm thinking Nolo got it right."

Over the sound of their offload pump they heard a vehicle coming up the highway. Headlights swung in through the gate. A big dark van stood idling there.

Chip hustled out of the office and stood by the van's driver's side. He was talking to the driver, a slight cringe in his posture. He made a gesture toward the tanker, seeming to dismiss it, to be explaining something.

The tanker's offload pump cut off. Kim and Alex got out right smartly, eager to be gone before they met whoever had just driven that van in. They uncoupled their offload spout, coiled it back onto its rack, and got back into the cab. They were hurrying to the max, while at the same time trying to seem casual.

But before Kim could slip the tanker into gear, the dark van rolled forward, climbing right up into their headlights. It seemed to intend coming bumper-to-bumper with them, but just a few yards away from them it swung right, showing them its glossy black flank, and idled there, its driver's head profiled in the tanker's lights.

The driver turned his head and faced them directly, deliberately giving them his face, faintly smiling. A startling face, its features finely chiseled. For several slow beats he blocked them there, staring. Then he slipped his brake and eased his van slowly up to the shaft-mouth.

Kim steered the tanker down the slope and into its slot beside the office. They jumped out and hustled down to Alex's old Chevy pickup. Usually Kim felt the contrast, felt diminished switching the big rig for her or Alex's four-wheeler. But tonight the pickup felt light and frisky, a godsend like an escape pod from a big spaceship that was blowing up.

Alex took the curves fast, and that was fine with Kim.

"What was that look?" he said. "Like he was showing us his face."

"No," Kim replied, her eyes fiercely fixed on the road. "He was looking through our headlights, trying to see our faces."

"How could he see anything?" Alex asked.

"You see his eyes? I almost think he could see us *through* our headlights. That was one spooky guy. You know what? Money or no money, maybe I don't think I wanna keep working here, much as I love driving this rig."

"Me either."

She glanced at him gratefully. "The thing is, I quit Circle-K and I'm seriously broke."

Alex gave her his hey-girl smile. "Check this out. I gotta friend I can move in with practically for free, an you could come too."

"Wow, thanks, but just friends, OK?"

"C'mon, gimme some credit. But hey, you wanna go out to-night? The Red Elvises are at the Phoenix."

"No shit?" They cracked two beers from the after-work sixer they kept in whichever ride had brought them up to work at the mine. The old pickup dove down toward the lamp-starred Santa Marta plain as they talked music.

Sol Lazarian parked his van well downslope of the shaft-mouth, so his soldiers would have to climb a bit with their burdens before carrying them down into the shaft. It was tricky footing down there, and he wanted them warmed up for the work.

Lazarian smilingly thought of tonight's task as "compounding the assets" of his employer, Lou Bonifacio of New Jersey: they were putting two of Bonifacio's dead enemies inside one of Bonifacio's toxic dumps in California.

Rather than seem to hide his face, Lazarian had given the drivers of that tanker a good look at it. A couple of kids—a girl and a young man. They'd brought, like him, their offering to this place. Had they felt its aura?

Sol thought that unlikely. He himself had frightened them, as he'd meant to do, but they, being young, had probably not sensed the terrible magic of this ground.

The driver before them, an older Latino, had perhaps sensed it and quit. The driver before *him* was still here down in the shaft, where Sol had put him. He hadn't sensed anything. He had just been running his mouth of an evening in the tavern he favored.

Sol shouldered the heavier of the two body-bags and led briskly upslope with it. His two helpers were slower off the mark. Big, bearded Junior Lee had the two satchels of weights. Sonny Beasley—almost as big as Junior Lee, but an edgier guy with acne-scarred cheeks—had the lighter body-bag.

"Look at 'im," muttered Junior, impressed. "That sumbitch musta gone two-forty at least," referring to the corpse Lazarian toted so lightly. Trudging up after, the pair watched the big man—so light of foot—leave them farther and farther behind.

Sonny grunted, low-voiced. "Don't it seem strange doin this? Fuckin *ocean's* just five miles west."

"Said we're goin way down in."

"So someone *else* could just walk way down in and *find* these stiffs there!"

"Maybe were gonna *bury* em down there."

"If we're gonna *bury* em, we could bury em just as deep up in these hills, without goin *down* in a fuckin mineshaft."

They saved their breath for the rest of the climb. Waiting above them, Lazarian stood back-lit by the shaft. His dreamy smile was invisible to them as he watched them come. Their faces were a quarter-turned to each other as they climbed, trading doubts perhaps, showing brief profiles of effort and unease.

Did these two simpletons feel the power here? Yes, rudimentary though their spirits were, Lazarian read in their eyes that they felt it as they came up and faced the shaft-mouth. Uneasily they registered the aura of that big, dark gullet.

Click. The image of them in this instant, strobed in his mind's eye, the way they looked right now in their moment of uneasy conference, repeating, repeating as if his visual cortex was a projector whose sprocket gear was slipping. When younger, these little epiphanies had unnerved him. Now he knew them to be a kind of signature radiation that his prey emitted as they neared death—like that given off by particles that were swallowed in a Black Hole.

"You need a breather?" Sol asked when they joined him up in the lip of the shaft-mouth.

"No! (*gasp*) Good to go!"

"No way, Sol!"

"OK. So let's pop on the masks, guys!" said genial Sol.

They all three set down their burdens and put on their masks, respirators with complex double filters that looked like the mouth-parts of insects. Even before entering, just standing here in the shaft's mouth the air was awesome. Sonny and Junior gaped at each other as they struggled with their straps. The vapors were a waft of pure uncanniness, moving through their brain-cells like the creepy fore-tremors of a major acid high.

Sol Lazarian was no less awed than they were. It was a reek so potent it became deafening, a pandemonium of stenches impacting the mind like a chorus of shrieking angels, a mob of divine sopranos gone mad.

His soldiers, watching Lazarian put his mask on, felt an identical little chill.

The big man's beauty was always a little unbelievable seen up close: the carven features, the rosebud mouth, the heavy-lidded eyes two pools of luminous candor. Shocking, though, when half that face was holstered in the mask, and you felt no mismatch between those lovely eyes and what looked like the jaws of a huge bug.

"Man, this air is messin me up, Sol," Sonny croaked through the crude amplifier. "You could sell it to junkies."

"Relax." Lazarian's voice came out mellow, almost unmangled by the mask. "Breathing through your filters, you'll be fine. And listen: count your steps going down. We think the guy running this place for us is ripping us off, taking other deliveries on the side. So count your steps down so we can check the fill-level."

He doubted his laborers could show the concentration for a count. His real aim was to create a pretext for leaving them down there while he went back up for the weights and bags he was going to use on them in their turn. They took up their burdens and lanterns again, and he led them down into the shaft of the old Quicksilver Mine.

Here in the well-lit shaft-mouth they were in a stage-set. There was a holding tank for delivered toxins, and a little stack of empty drums to be filled from that tank. There was a donkey engine mounted on the track, and some carts linked to it by cable—everything needful for lowering sealed drums of toxins carefully into the shaft for cleanly storage.

But sixty yards down the rails gave out, recycled long ago for their steel. Below that point, as they pushed their bubble of light down the steepening pitch, there was only the black, six-inch fill-hose running along down the shaft floor beside a crude staircase of rail-less cross-ties. And as they descended, their lanterns' light made the hose's shadow twitch and shift, like a giant house-snake, the resident genius of this place dancing down shaft beside them.

Ever deeper they sank down through a strange, ethereal inferno. Down here it wasn't the men who sweated out into the air, but the air that sweated itself into the men, air like dragon's breath, a micro-blizzard of molecular razors, and the brew that exhaled it was perhaps the perfect human solvent.

At this thought Lazarian's smile bloomed within his mask, a secret flower.

Even sooner than Lazarian had expected, they reached the black pool. It was always a shock encountering it. Its stillness seemed to mask a secret aggression, as if this slug of earth-socketed poison—more than a mile in depth—had stealthily been hastening up to meet them and had, just an instant ago, paused, pretending immobility, its flat black eye dazzling their lights back at them, its cold breath licking the skin of their faces like a demon's caustic tongue.

Oh, there was great power here. He had not been wrong to cross a continent with these corpses expressly to offer them here. This pool was Death's most absolute orifice, the threshold of a perfect annihilation.

He watched his soldiers awkwardly crouching, unlimbering wire, cutters, and weights from the satchels. Their dazed unease was understandable, entering this place for the first time. Even these morons sensed what was here.

"So what was your count, guys?" he asked them. Smiled again within his mask to see their eyes' identical looks of guilty alarm.

It made him wonder: were such crude life-forms as these an

insult if offered in sacrifice?

To the Power that he had from the first felt to be hidden in this shaft, were two such primitive souls worse than no sacrifice at all? Come to that, were even the slightly more intelligent, slightly more dangerous men inside the body bags also too crude, too worthless an offering?

How could he know? On the threshold of such a Mystery as Lazarian sensed down here, who *did* know the rules? In the end, his own instinctive sense of a presence, his Awe—that was the real offering. His soul's readiness was the incense he burnt on the altar. The sacrifices themselves must always be guesswork, mere gesture. They displayed his devotion, whether or not the god here valued them.

Granting all this, it was Lazarian's intuition that told him he did right. Every life, however simple, in passing through Death's membrane, forced open a seam between the space-time of this world and the unknowable Outside. Every death created a brief aperture through which something might be glimpsed.

"Never mind, guys," Lazarian said. "I kept count. They're overfilled." He pulled two fat packets of hundred-dollar bills from his pocket and waggled them. "I know how neat and tight your wiring's going to be, so I want you to take your bonuses now." Their eyes crinkled above their masks—so pleased, pocketing the cash!

And Lazarian *would* send them into the pool with their money still in pocket. Like grave-goods in the ancient world's funerals, it was a ceremonial responsibility. Death would reveal nothing to those who tried to get revelation for a bargain.

He told the men, "I'm going up to talk to the gate-man. Weight them heavy. I'll be back down before you get both of them wired."

Long minutes later, though they could no longer see Lazarian's ascending light, Sonny's voice was still cautiously low:

"You believe this stench?"

Junior—slightly dazed, his eyes goggled—shook his head. He was looping wire around the middle of the smaller of the two bodies and threading the wire through a ten-pound weight-disc. "Fuckin *smell* feels like it's leakin in through my skin!"

Their mask-muted voices rang strange to them, like buried men speaking from their graves. "Lift 'im a little higher," Junior said, as he threaded the wire through another weight.

The gaseous air lay like a lubricant mist on everything. The disc slipped from his grip. It rolled, bounced off a lower tie, and jumped into the pool. The pair recoiled to either side from the tongue of black slop thrown back from the splash.

"You dip-stick!"

"It slipped! Shoot me!"

"*Don't* slip!"

The booming of their angry voices suddenly subdued them. The after-splash of the weight into the pool made the pond gently vibrate and its rim kiss the walls of the shaft:

Slap-suck, *slap*-suck . . .

The echoes took forever to die down. It seemed to Sonny a long time that they crouched there, listening. He wondered if the air was stoning him, messing with his time sense. He was crouched there, meaning to get back to work, but not doing it.

It was Junior who got them moving.

"Tilt 'im up again."

They got back into it. Sonny manipulated the corpse while Junior paid off the wire. "They were so *stiff* when we loaded em," Junior said. "They're a bitch to handle all floppy like this!"

They'd crossed the country in a little under forty-eight hours. The corpses were stiff to start with, but now that rigor would have been useful, it was long gone. The slack stiff slumped, resisting their work.

Now that they had the third wire loop pinching into its bagged length, it had begun to look segmented, like a caterpillar.

Sonny remembered a book about Houdini he'd read in slam and thought of something funny. He weighed his words. You had to be careful, if you wanted Junior to understand something.

"Hey, Joon. You know that when you tie a guy in a buncha short lengths like this? Instead of tyin him in one long piece? You tie him in short lengths like this, and it's harder for him to get out of. You know—free himself, *escape*."

Bug-muzzled Junior sat goggle-eyed, staring at him. With just his eyes showing like this he looked . . . shocked at what Sonny had said. Wasn't getting the joke at all.

Sonny pulled down his mask a little to show Junior he was smiling, making a joke. "You know—get himself untied?"

Junior's brow corrugated. Really concentrating now and still not getting it. With his forehead corrugated like that, he looked almost terrified, as if these stiffs might suddenly try to untie themselves.

"You fuckin idiot," Sonny said, and then couldn't help laughing at that face of Junior's. "It's a *joke!* How're they gonna escape? They're fuckin *dead!*"

And then both of them looked for a moment at the bagged stiffs—as if they hadn't quite fully grasped that fact before.

They worked on. They said nothing more, but their least movements wove fine webs of echo around them.

The last weight was wired. Stiff Number One was now a black caterpillar of seven unequal segments, with the discs attached to it like the eggs of some parasitic wasp.

Sonny thumbed out the razor tip of a utility knife and cut the "window" Sol had prescribed—a big square flap out of the bag over the stiff's face—to let the solvents in to work on the nude corpse. As he cut, he felt the blade meet doughy resistance, and when he unmasked the face found a deep, unbleeding slice beside the nose.

"Sorry about that, wise guy."

"Who do ya think he was?" asked Junior.

"An East-Coast greaseball like the other one. Who cares?" He and Junior had staged a holdup in an Italian restaurant, which distraction had covered Lazarian's abduction of this guy from a back table.

Corpse Number Two had required the pair to enter the lobby of a plush high-rise and kick up a drunken fuss about being admitted to the elevators up to "Lulu's" condo. Four really big guys, armed, had poured from the elevator a moment later. Though the two bikers tried to prolong the distraction, they were thrown out on their ass PDQ, but Lazarian still had the big stiff in the van by the time they returned to it. Guy was wearing sweat-stained exercise togs, apparently had been having a workout in his home gym.

"You come a long way, Bo-seephus," Sonny told Stiff Number One. To Junior he said, "Why the hell did he take us all the way out *there* to get these guys, then bring them all the way back *here* to get rid of em?"

Junior shrugged mountainously. "Who knows? He's a goon, got his goon reasons. I mean, this is a pretty good hidin place."

"Yeah, but between here an *Jersey* there's three thousand miles of—"

"What's that?"

Slap-suck, *slap*-suck, *slap*-suck . . .

The pool was quaking again, still gently, but just a little stronger than before. Both men were lifelong Californians, but now they were discovering that a casual attitude about earthquakes decreased radically as the depth of your body under the earth increased.

"The stuff probably just keeps settling," said Sonny. "Down into cracks an holes down there."

"I don't see no bubbles." The cogency of this remark, coming from his slow-witted friend, irritated Sonny.

"OK, OK. So whaddya say we just quit fuckin the dog, Joon? You get that end, I'll get this end."

They stood up with the corpse hammocked between them.

"One . . . two . . ."—they had a fair swing going—"three!"

The dead goon was launched. He lay face up on the air for a moment. Framed in the "window" they'd cut, his eyes and mouth were pools of shadow in the oblique light from the lanterns. The shadows made the face live in that instant—it seemed to grimace as it fell.

It had to be this druggy air that made them both so late in jumping back—the splash was *big* and it wet their boots and spattered the lanterns.

Cursing, they wiped their boots on their jeans and set the lanterns higher up. Would the pond never settle? Jittering and splashing and slopping . . . They stood watching that turbulence and imagining the wise guy's journey down the steep shaft, a long slo-mo tumble down through the most perfect blackness there ever was. . . .

"How far down you think he'll go?" rumbled Junior.

Sonny understood exactly what Junior was picturing: the weighted mummy sinking, striking the shaft-floor a little farther down, jouncing up off the ties, tumbling slowly farther down, jouncing again.

They both looked up behind them at the tunnel's steep pitch. Sonny rumbled, "If the slope don't change he'll just keep bouncin down."

"So how far down's this tunnel go?"

"It's called a shaft, Joon. Tunnels you can come out the other end of."

"So how far down's this *shaft* go?"

"Well . . ." Sonny's mind kept jouncing down deeper and deeper with the corpse, and saw no end to it. "How should *I* know!?"

It was funny how they kept freezing up and *listening* down here. And now they'd done it again, just crouching there, the silence deepening around them.

"Know what I think, Sonny?" Junior's eyes had a look in them that Sonny had never seen before. It was like . . . *amazement*. "I think that this is some strange shit for us to be doin down here."

This declaration flashed Sonny on some of the other strange things they had done as "soldiers." He considered these, and then he nodded. "I think this *is* the strangest shit we've done yet."

"An' the hardest work too."

They roused themselves and started wiring Stiff Number Two. Heavier though it was, they were working more smoothly now—suddenly almost deft. Perhaps it was that they both felt a new tension in the shaft, felt the presence of something that seemed to applaud their work, to will it forward.

"Jesus!" Junior yelped, dropping a weight and his pliers. A roiling sound, a silken fizzing filled the shaft. The pool was foaming, bulging upwards at its center, mounting in a dome of turbulence, rising as if lifted by some powerful under-pressure.

Had the respirators melted from their faces? It felt as if the poisoned air had suddenly soaked through their skulls, and was licking the brain-meat out of them. The pressure-dome mushroomed to the ceiling and came surging at them.

They turned to launch themselves upshaft and tripped over the half-wired second body. Got up and scrambled past it, a voice in Sonny's skull saying: *One heartbeat too late.* They were just getting their stride on the ties, the lighter Sonny taking the lead, as the gust of the black wave's air-pressure touched their napes.

The wave punched Sonny's legs out from under him, gripped his waist like a cold, melting hand, and dragged him back down. He rammed desperate knees against the stone, felt bone crack and his fingernails torn off, but held on against the terrible back-drag of caustics draining off of him.

Looking back over his shoulder, he saw that Junior Lee had been dragged all the way down and now was up to his neck in the pool, his arms scrabbling for the shaft floor just out of reach. And there, just beyond Junior, Sonny saw what *stood up* from the pool, saw its hugeness and the wild night-black glare of its eyes. Awed, Sonny watched it seize Junior by the back of the neck and lift him up like a kitten and, with its free hand, hugely fisted, smite the pool, to send a second, mightier wave booming up the shaft straight at Sonny.

Again Sonny scrambled up-shaft, his knee broken but fighting himself up one tie higher, another tie, another . . . while a voice in his head was saying: *Just one heartbeat too late.*

A tongue of waste shot past him along the shaft wall, and as he reached the lanterns, the wave curved around just beyond them and came sweeping back down toward him like a gathering arm. For an instant the lanterns made a black mirror of the on-coming liquid wall, and in it Sonny saw himself: a bug-mouthed being on its belly and reaching for a lantern, its eyes bulging at its oncoming end.

The descending wave's satin mass wrapped him in blindness, flipped him on his back, and snatched him down, the stepped earth under him beating him, braining him, blotting him out. A perfect blackness was the aftermath. The echoes of uproar and choked-off shouts collided again and again with the stone walls, subsiding at long last to a faint liquid chuckle.

Shortly after, there came down the sound of a heavy tread descending the shaft from the far, faint circle of moonlit sky high above.

Sol Lazarian stopped at the limit of the drenched zone, which now extended fifteen yards upshaft of the pool itself. Not a sign of his soldiers remained, nor any sign of the two bagged dead they'd carried.

Fear, in Lazarian, was a darker shade of joy, it was the same radiation at a different frequency. When he broke a man's life in his arms, his prey's shock was his joy's fuel. And, when any horror laid its hand on him, he felt not crushed, but light, combustible, packed like dynamite with a savage sympathy for that larger joy, that joy more monstrous than his own, that might be about to consume him.

Already at thirty-eight, young for a real master, he had consumed a dozen other first-rate killers. Real samurai like himself, not moronic buttons—of those he kept no count. And all these gifted men had learned that to endanger Lazarian was to inspire and ignite him. His startling face got eerily prettier, his manner even more serene. You had him distracted. You watched him fail to spot your trap. You sprang it on him, and suddenly there was Sol Lazarian's forearm across your throat and Sol Lazarian's mellow baritone crooning unspeakabilities in your ear . . . and there was your neck breaking.

He stood thoughtful for a moment, ears straining.

Ta-da-dum

Ta-da

Ta-dum, *da* . . .

In the spectrum of things audible there is a doubtful zone

shared by that which is imagined and that which is faintly *heard*.

If real, this voice was beautiful and sad. A velvet-and-molasses gospel voice. It gave him a delicate attack of the creeps, a horripilation of the fine black lanugo that covered the back and shoulders of the pale giant, and that no living man had ever seen.

Ta-da-dum

Ta-da

Ta-dum, da . . .

Sol thrust his light further forward seeking some purchase on what he'd heard, and the movement of his light revealed that the blackness under his feet was a shape, not a blot. Something distinctly outlined in the stone and timber. His hair stirred. Its outline was precisely that of a huge, outreached hand.

Lazarian stood squarely in the palm of that hand.

You are mine, it said.

Give me more, it said . . .

Yes, it demanded more, as plain as printed speech. Demanded more.

Not many nights later Sol Lazarian had fetched another body from New Jersey, this one still living, though snugly bound: Lou Bonifacio.

Accomplishing this had been no slight feat.

Lazarian had had to kill no fewer than four buttons in swift succession—and quite good samurai they had been; two of them, anyway, so good Sol had for some moments considered bringing one—or even both of their bodies—back as additional offerings to the shaft.

But after all, the capture and sacrifice of his Capo must rightly claim his sole attention. To kill one whom he had served was an act of great spiritual weight.

Coming west, the securely bound Bonifacio had dozed for a

long stretch of hours—an aging body, perhaps subconsciously fleeing its dire predicament. But he came awake again as their van climbed the switchbacks toward the Quicksilver Mine.

He was gagged. Lazarian had been driven to gag him not long after their journey's outset. Lou's abusive raging had quickly exhausted Lazarian's intention to be courteous and sociable on the long drive west. Now, even after so long at the wheel, Lazarian had never felt more awake. His heart rose in him while his van, turn by turn, ascended the switchbacks.

He drove rapt, so clearly recalling it—the black hand perfectly articulated, telling him whose Hand he stood in.

But *whose?*

Who but the one he'd lived and worked to meet? It was the hand of Annihilation itself, standing up and reaching out. The whole world had altered in answer to his sacrifice of those two goons! The spirit in the shaft had seized both his kills and his hirelings, obliterated the four of them, and left for Lazarian an urgent sign, the extended hand that said *GIVE MORE*.

Very soon now he was going to learn what he would purchase with this more powerful offering. A full-fledged Capo plucked right from his fortress.

In that moment of his first offering's acceptance, his spirit had been enlarged, as if he had fed *himself* those lesser lives.

The odd thing was, that it was to Bonifacio himself that Lazarian wanted to talk about it, his Capo, a man who had himself offered human sacrifices. Who better able to provide a judgment of the eerie rightness of this shaft, the Dantean poetry of its deeps? It was to Lou he longed to confide that he found dread here too. For he did not know how much this black hand offered, and how much more it might *demand*.

If only they could toss it back and forth, as they had on other, no less homicidal excursions during their long shared past.

He smiled wistfully. *Honestly, whaddya think, Lou? I think you have to agree: apart from it being a really secure site, your life will unlock something big down here. Down here your life will buy me some kind of real power . . . doncha think?*

Lazarian steered through the last switchback and out onto the mountain's broad shoulder. A fragmentary moon showed them Chip sliding open the gate of the compound a moment before Lazarian's headlights splashed across him. Chip had been informed that his assistance tonight was required. He brought out a sturdy dolly. Lazarian stood the shackled Bonifacio in the dolly and bound him to it, and then hauled him up to the shaft. The shaft-mouth was wreathed in the mist of artificial light that it breathed out at the stars.

His tone gentle, Lazarian told the dollied Capo: "In plain, unvarnished English, Lou, I'm giving you to a god down in there. I don't exactly understand Her, and I don't know what She'll do with you. I sincerely hope it won't involve doing you any harm. I only want to say that in spite of my handing you over, *I* have never wished you anything but the best, Lou. And for all I really know, maybe She won't either."

As he spoke he was clipping lights to the dolly and to the bonds that bound Lou to it. Lazarian knew his little speech was disingenuous—was a false mercy of delayed revelation. Bonifacio was almost certainly going to end up in the pool.

He said, "Excuse me putting my mask on, Lou. The air down there's really intense. . . . There. Can you hear me OK? These things' speakers aren't so great."

Lazarian began to ease the dolly smoothly down the ties. So dance-like this kind of descent was. Very soon they were below the lighted zone and carrying their own bubble of light downshaft, utter darkness both behind and ahead of them. Softly they jolted deeper and deeper.

"I'm sorry about this dolly arrangement, Lou, but I think you'll agree it's the least painful way I can keep you both comfortable and secure."

Bonifacio was an older brute, beginning to melt down at the corners and angles of his great frame, but as Lazarian jolted him softly, steadily down the shaft, he lay rigid in his bonds, and his gagged glare never ceased to blaze at his captor. Lazarian had to smile.

"Lou, you're old-school in the best sense. If I hadn't gotten the drop on you, I'm sure you'd be grinding my bones to powder right now with your teeth! It's always a pleasure to be dealing with a professional."

Lazarian's great strength managed to ease down his massive cargo with a rolling smoothness, always iron-muscled in resistance to the earth's black yawn of gravity he stepped down into.

The steadiness of his descent gave a hypnotic regularity to the shaft's support beams, little timber stonehenges holding the earth apart, rising to swallow them at regular intervals as he stepped down, stepped down, stepped down . . .

> *Momma Durtt get you*
> *by degreees*
> *jus take hold*
> *an squeeze an squeeze . . .*

All doubt gone now, she was speaking to him.

Just to him, Lou didn't seem to hear it. Ever so faint it sounded, far down in that darkness beyond his bubble of light. Echoey now . . . *was* he hearing it? Or was it the low commotion of his own masked breathing?

> *Momma Durtt get you*
> *by degrees . . .*

To Lazarian's eyes, a faint aura was beginning to glow from Bonifacio's body. There was a kind of Egyptian pomp in Lou's big mummied mass as he floated half-recumbent down the shaft on his dolly, his eyes blazing above his mummied mouth . . .

And justly so, Lazarian thought, for in Lou he was sacrificing a kind of deity, one of those furious Elementals like Hades or the Midgard Serpent, brought to heel by gods in tales . . . he was auraed with infernal majesty. Then, far down below their light-bubble, from the perfect dark they descended to, something stirred . . .

A liquid sound? A soft, wet impact?

Lazarian stayed their descent and leaned near Bonifacio's ear to say, "We've conjured a god here, Lou, I'm sure of it. With my own eyes I've seen . . . unbelievable evidence. We've conjured a *goddess,* more precisely. I've heard her voice, heard her *sing.*"

The bound man's eyes flared with a new shade of fear—the fear of lunacy in his captor—which Sol Lazarian saw, and had to laugh. "No! I'm not crazy, old friend. I know how that sounds, but I *have* heard her sing!

"And I'm afraid I have to be honest with you, Lou. I've *procured* you, you might say, *for* the goddess here." He paused in their descent, resting briefly. "But the goddess, unfortunately, lives *in* the toxins, and that seems to be where her offerings must be placed."

Silence then between them, stepping down through the last long steepness, the burdened dolly's wheels groaning.

The ethereal reek swelled thicker, swallowing them like a cold reptile mouth.

And here was the pool . . .

Lazarian said, "I'm *offering* you, Lou—not *giving* you. Here I will stand you."

He propped the dolly upright on the lowest cross-tie above

the black tarn that breathed its sharp, glacial breath in their faces. "I'm not putting you in—just putting you where she can take you. If she is as real as I think, I suppose she . . . *consumes* you—I don't really know. But I hope that you know how truly I regret what's going to happen here."

Lazarian bent and locked the dolly's wheels. He gave Bonifacio's shoulder a pat and retreated four ties upshaft of him. Crouched there, uncramping his leg muscles.

Lou was standing very carefully balanced. He was snugly bound and bandaged to the dolly, but his rage and horror made the little lights he was decorated with tremble on the black pool, which seemed to be almost as still as stone.

But no, not absolutely still. The subtlest of tremors now and then, here and there, skimmed its blackness.

Here in this grotto, this *chapel* of annihilation, Lazarian groped for the proper gesture. What did the black gulf want of him? What gesture of his must call forth the thing that hid here? Should he show his awe? His gratitude? All he could think to do was to declare his reverence. He addressed the pool.

"I give you the one who conjured you. The one who fed you the poisons that your Nullity grew from. He is your food now, a token of my reverence. In return, grant me *vision!* Grant me power in your service!"

Bonifacio was an earthy man, of strong simple appetites. Teetering on this narrow footing at the rim of nothingness, he had as firm a grip on himself as a man thus situated can have. Hearing Lazarian imploring the pool of poison like a god, the Capo knew himself to be in the hands of Lunacy incarnate, and with a wordless prayer he commended his soul to the abyss.

At which instant a huge black hand rose dripping from the pool and seized him. Its mighty grip was more than half his height, but enough of the Capo's head and shoulders protruded to show that his features were as much convulsed with fury as with fear.

The great black knuckles liquesced as they gripped him, the huge fist melting as it lofted and seemed to heft him, as if assaying value. And then, in sudden shock, it seemed to Lazarian that he himself melted, that he hung unbodied in the lethal air, because what was happening? The pool behind the huge hand began to bulge and dome up as an immense face surfaced, her wet black eyeballs (big as human heads) glaring from a thorny thicket of hair, her jeering mouth a big whirlpool slowly spreading on her face.

The goddess thrust Bonifacio into the melting cavern of her mouth, wherein the Capo's wordless roar was echoed and then drowned out as he dove—dolly and all—from sight.

She faced Lazarian, this face of hers as big as his whole body, a melting face unendingly reborn, her eyes mockingly, merrily glaring in his.

And Lazarian's soul spoke within him: *I've done it! I've broken through! Into the world of miracles!*

"You will not die," her hissing lips of poison told him, each word a wet adhesion to his flesh. "You will serve me while this world lasts, and you will sow plague and poison upon it.

"I am the miracle you have lived and labored for. Of the Great Old Ones, I am the youngest, no older than this venomed globe itself, but until Dark claims us all again, you'll till my earth and feed my monsters up to strength to work this world's destruction."

Gleeful now, her seething face, she lofted her great melting fist and brandished it upshaft, and—far, far up the echoey tube—an engine growled to life, avalanching echoes down upon them.

Lazarian found his voice hoarse with grateful joy. "I will serve you, Great One! I will serve you to the end of our time!"

The black giant grinned from her tarn. "Then let us make

some *room* for your labor! Let us give scope to your service and give you the *power* to serve!"

A mighty din of fractured stone filled the shaft, as a huge convulsion shook the earth they stood in. Raining dust and gravel, the mine's walls and ceiling heaved shuddering away from Lazarian.

And when it stilled, the shaft's diameter had tripled, the crude-hewn stone ceiling was thrice his height above him, and the pool of poison was now a wide pond. The engine's noise, still high and far, came echoing down more hollowly now.

"In power and style you will serve me," the giantess leered at him. "Behold!"

Now, that distant engine's roar dove *in,* and its guttural howl came snarling down before it. Rapt, Lazarian gazed up at the lofty walls of stone that contained him—high and shrine-like they were now.

Here came the tanker's headlights blazing down from on high, its echoes a ghostly landslide that broke against him. The shaft tremored like a waking dragon around him.

He stood enraptured, unavoiding. The deep tarn was at his back, yet he stood serene as the headlights came down like comets.

Outside, far above him, under the silent sky, only a few deep dinosaur echoes welled up at the moon—some dim commotion far under the earth, but peace up here. Chip was gone—he'd taken off the moment the earth had shaken. A long and unmarred silence followed in the compound then, peace beneath the pale moon.

Until, at length, a growling began to *rise* from the Quicksilver's throat, rose quickly to crescendo, and out of the earth the Tanker erupted.

It launched its hugeness arcing through the air, surged airborne twenty yards or so, until it colossally *whumped* down, ponderously tap-danced on its heavy tires, then leveled off, and hit the highway.

You could tell she was full by the sway of her, but even so she ate up the switchbacks, tires smoking down the mountain, zig and zag. And impossibly soon, she hit the cross-country straightaway toward mighty 101—a linear glow past shadowy hills and groves.

Now as she rolled through the fields her looks improved. The moonlight seemed to wipe her bulky mass clean. Her tank turned a bright polished silver, and her cab grew glossy black with silver trim.

As she surged up onto 101, she was gorgeous, all scoured steel and glossy black enamel. She rode high in the river of southbound headlights, a star-cruiser cargoed with Death for the Cities of Light that rimmed the great Bay to the south. And high in her cab, commanding the wheel, sat Lazarian, his eyes rapt on the cities of light as he hurtled toward them. He drank with gusto from the bottle of ale which he gripped in one hand.

A week later, Alex and Kim had a window seat in a roadside diner. An on-ramp onto 101 climbed right past their window, up through a Friday night blaze of neon colors. As they gazed out the glass, a gorgeous tanker truck slid to the ramp and surged up it.

"Whoa," said Kim, "isn't that . . . ?"

"Damn. It is."

The pair watched with awe as the great machine roared onto the freeway and geared up for points south.

www.ingramcontent.com/pod-product-compliance
Lightning Source LLC
Chambersburg PA
CBHW060951030726
47503CB00003B/824